CHERRY SEASON

TRISH MOREY

The cleverest thing I did when I left Adelaide to work interstate many years ago, was to find and fall in love with the man who would become my husband and father to our four amazing daughters.

The cleverest thing we did when we ventured back to South Australia some years later with our young family in tow, was to settle in the beautiful Adelaide Hills.

It's a place of eucalyptus and orchards, of valleys and ridges, of people warm and real.
It's a place that feeds your soul.

For Gavin,
for taking me on all those years ago and staying the distance.

Thank you,

xxx

PROLOGUE

*S*an Antonio, Texas

THE TATTOO ARTIST on the corner of Geronimo and Vine preferred listening to Meatloaf's 'Bat out of Hell' to conversation, but Lucy didn't mind. She was in no mood for small talk.

Every few seconds he'd pull the buzzing gun from her shoulder and wipe over her skin with a cloth before the needle would find its place again and the buzzing and the pressure would resume. It didn't hurt so much as irritate, but still Lucy bit down on her lip when the press of the needle started to burn.

Finally it was done. He swiped her skin clean and held up a mirror so she could see how it looked in the mirror in front.

She stared at the reflection. Saw the design she'd drawn herself now etched forever into the skin of her shoulder and felt tears spring unbidden from her eyes.

It was perfect.

'Did it hurt?' the tattooist asked, frowning as he handed her the Kleenex.

'Yeah,' she said over the lump in her throat, knowing they were talking about different things. 'It did.'

CHAPTER 1

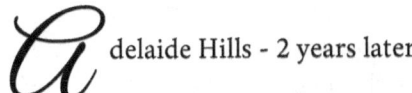delaide Hills - 2 years later

HIS SISTERS WERE UP to something.

Dan Faraday knew that for a fact. He'd known it ever since Hannah had suggested a birthday dinner. On a picking day, no less, when she would have known that any dinner couldn't possibly happen before nine.

The niggle at the base of his neck kept right on niggling as he stacked the last boxes of today's cherries in the cool-room. Oh, yeah, they were up to something all right. When you were an Adelaide Hills orchardist and your birthday fell slap bang in the middle of cherry season, there were much more important things to worry about than having a birthday party.

Like bringing in a crop for a start. The first decent looking cherry crop in three years, but the worry was that the birds would get to the fruit faster than it could be picked, or that the thunderclouds would roll in and the fruit would split and the most promising harvest in recent times would be ruined. Another bust year and the banks would stop circling like sharks and head in for the kill.

It was make or break time and Dan knew it.

The three sisters who'd grown up with him on the orchard should have known it too.

So what the hell were they up to?

He sighed and checked his reflection in the cracked mirror above the shed's washbasin, taking in the dust in his whiskers and the ring around his head where his hat had stuck his hair down all day. The dust was an easy fix. Hat head, not so much. He did the best he could to unflatten the ring of hair with his fingers but in the end there wasn't a hell of a lot he could do about it, and why worry anyway? It wasn't like he'd asked for this party. 'Occupational hazard,' he muttered as he flicked off the lights in the packing shed, calling for Molly out of habit, before realising with a thud that Molly was gone.

Bugger.

Outside, day was fast slipping away to night, the orchard sleeping under a blanket of wispy cloud. No possibility of rain and warm enough that there was no chance of frost according to the weather bureau. He slapped his dusty hat against his legs. Small mercies.

Laughter drifted up from the house where his family had gathered. Most of the time he was happy to have family show up – even more so when they helped him and Pop out. They'd all spent a couple of hours in the packing shed grading cherries earlier before Pop had taken off to collect Nan, and the girls had headed for the kitchen to get supper ready. But it had been a long day in a series of long days that had started two weeks ago and wouldn't let up until the season was over, one way or another.

Besides which, he just wasn't all that fussed with birthdays.

That was all.

THEY WERE all waiting for him inside, Nan and Pop together with his three sisters, twins Hannah and Beth, plus Sophie, their junior by a couple of years, along with Siena, Beth's eight-year-old daughter. All of them arranged around a table laden with platters of sandwiches and sausage rolls fresh from the oven, if his nose wasn't mistaken. In spite of his mood, his stomach rumbled.

'Finally!' squealed Siena, his niece's face lighting up as Dan shoved his battered hat onto a hook beside the door. She launched herself at him, wrapped her arms about his waist and looked up at him with big brown eyes. 'I'm starving, Uncle Dan!'

'You're always starving,' said Beth, as she reached for a bottle of sparkling wine to top up everyone's glasses. 'How about you wish your uncle a happy birthday instead of thinking about your stomach for a while?'

'I already did!' Siena protested. 'And I can't help it if I'm hungry.'

'She did too,' Dan agreed, as he patted his niece on the back, because Siena had burst into the packing shed ahead of Beth when they'd arrived, brimming with the news that they had a big secret for his birthday, which was kind of the same thing, surely? And despite the uneasy feeling in his gut about whatever this surprise might be, he was still clinging to the hope that the big secret comprised a bag of mixed nuts and a bottle of port, like it usually did.

'Of course the girl's hungry,' said silver-haired Nan, greeting her grandson with a hug, a surprisingly strong one for a woman in her late seventies who barely came up to his shoulders. 'Siena's growing and she's got hollow legs. You were all the same at that age.' She planted a kiss on Dan's cheek and he caught a whiff of the Estée Lauder perfume he'd bought her for Mother's Day, the same perfume he bought her every year, and if he didn't know that she loved it so much, he'd think she was drinking the stuff. 'Happy birthday, Daniel.'

'Nan brought a cake,' said Hannah.

'A sponge cake,' Sophie said with a wink. 'Your favourite.'

'Yeah? Thanks Nan,' he said, giving her another squeeze and starting to relax. Maybe he'd been overreacting, maybe he was just cranky after a long day in the orchard, because Nan made the best sponge cakes and whatever else was happening, if there was sponge cake involved, it couldn't be all bad.

He snatched up a sausage roll, still warm from the oven, then dipped it in a bowl of tomato sauce and almost swallowed it down whole because he was so hungry. And suddenly he found himself thinking that maybe getting together for dinner tonight hadn't been such a bad idea after all, and it wasn't just because for once he didn't have to rummage around in the freezer for something to heat up.

They hardly ever got together as a family these days. Sophie sometimes dropped by when she'd finished work at the local school, but between the cherry season, Beth's shifts with the ambos, and Hannah being on call more often than not at the vet clinic, it would probably be Christmas before they were all together again. The way Siena was shooting up, she'd be a good couple of inches taller by then.

Best of all, it was an excuse for his Nan's sponge cake . . .

'Bubbles for you, Dan?' asked Beth, offering him a glass filled to the brim.

He shook his head. 'Not that kind. I'll grab a beer. How

about you, Pop?' he said, as he headed for the fridge. 'Can I get you a beer?'

'Pop?' he said, standing there a few moments later with the fridge door open, because if his Pop had answered, he hadn't heard it. But Pop was sitting to one side, staring down at his untouched plate. Dan frowned and pulled a couple of stubbies from the door.

'You right, Pop?' he asked, when he pulled up a chair alongside.

'Wha –?' Pop said in his gravelly voice, blinking as he looked up. And then he saw the beer and smiled. 'Oh, yeah. I'd better have a beer to celebrate my favourite grandson's birthday.'

Dan snorted. 'Only grandson, more like it,' he said as he unscrewed the lids on a couple of Coopers and handed one over before taking a long, satisfying swig of the other. 'Long day,' he said at last, figuring that Pop must have been dog tired before he'd gone home to pick up Nan and heading back again. He might be as strong as an ox and look a good deal younger than he was, but the old fellow was pushing eighty. Dan ought to remember that.

Pop grunted as he put his untouched plate back up on the table. 'They're all long this time of year.'

'You're not hungry?'

'Indigestion. Need a good burp, that's all.' He grinned and raised his beer in Dan's direction. 'This'll fix it. Happy birthday, lad.'

They clinked bottles and both drank deeply. Suddenly Pop gave a good, long burp.

'Clarence Faraday!' chided his wife, while Siena giggled and Clarry simply sighed as he patted his belly.

'Ah, that feels better.'

Even Dan found a smile, because Pop was right. After a long hot day in the orchard, nothing beat an ice cold beer.

Unless it was a supper he hadn't had to prepare. He loaded up his plate and tucked in, happy to let his three sisters drive the conversation. Not that he had much of a chance of getting a word in edgewise anyway with them eager to pick up the discussion they'd left off when he'd come inside. Something about how much they all had to get done before Christmas, but which was rapidly escalating into a dispute over which one of them deserved a holiday the most.

Which was a laugh, he thought, reaching for another sausage roll, because as far as he was concerned, there was no contest. He couldn't remember the last holiday he'd had.

'People don't appreciate how hard it is,' said Sophie, 'chasing after other people's kids all day. Not to mention, dealing with some of the parents.'

'I hope you're not referring to Siena and me,' said Beth, quick to take umbrage.

'Of course not! If all the kids were like Siena, it'd be a cake walk. Trouble is, they're not.'

'You're not going to get much sympathy from me,' Hannah said, clearly unimpressed. 'I'm on call, two weekends out of three at the vet surgery, and you work normal hours and get ten weeks paid holidays a year.'

Sophie shrugged. 'We need those holidays. There's got to be some kind of compensation for educating other people's kids.'

'So what compensation do I get,' Beth intervened, 'for having patients throw up and worse over me?'

'You get the satisfaction of knowing you're saving lives,' nodded Sophie, as if that was compensation enough.

Dan sipped on his beer and left his sisters to it, content that at least they weren't ganging up on him for a change.

Three sisters. What were the chances? And while their Dad had hankered for another son, and Dan wouldn't have said no to a brother to share this orchard caper with, given that none of his sisters seemed keen, he wouldn't trade any of these three for quids.

'Oh, hey, while I think of it,' Sophie interrupted, 'I meant to tell you all about the quiz night coming up at the primary school in a few weeks.'

'You've got to be kidding me?' Beth said. 'At this time of year? There's plenty enough going on in November and December without squeezing another event into the calendar.'

'Not to mention a cherry crop to bring in,' growled Dan. Was nobody else worried about the cherries?

Sophie held up both hands. 'I know, I know. But this is a fundraiser for Jamie Hanson. You know, that little year two boy who's been diagnosed with that rare cancer. His family has to raise one hundred thousand dollars for his treatment in Germany and they can't wait until February. We have to do it before school breaks up.'

'Oh, that poor child,' said Nan. 'Of course we'll go, won't we Clarry. We've never said no to a quiz night yet, and we're not going to start now just because it's a busy time of year – not when there's a little boy's health at stake.'

'Well, don't count on me being there,' said Dan. 'I'm flat out enough this time of year without finding other stuff to do.'

'It's to help Jamie,' protested Siena.

'A very good cause,' Beth conceded. 'I'll be there. So long as I'm not working late shift .'

'We'll all be there,' Nan said, nodding sagely. 'It wouldn't be a quiz night if the Faraday table didn't show up.'

'Excuse me, am I the only one who's actually worried about this year's crop?'

'Hey, the cherries look great,' Hannah said.

'We still have to get them in,' he grumbled, and went back to nursing his beer.

Pop moved out of his seat for a minute and Sophie sat herself down beside him, clinking her wine glass against the beer bottle in his hands. 'Meant to tell you, Mum dropped me an email today. She said she'd popped a card in the post but to wish you a happy birthday in case you hadn't had a chance to clear the mail lately.'

He smiled. Now there was a woman who understood the demands of cherry season. 'Good of her to think of me.' Although to be fair, he knew there was more to it than just being nice. Wendy had married his dad when Dan had been nine years old and while she'd always been a great mum to him, she'd never tried to pretend he hadn't had another before her, or made him feel like he didn't belong when the girls had come along. In fact, three years after John had died, it had been Wendy who'd moved out of the family home.

'You're thirty now,' she'd said to him, explaining her decision to move with Sophie to a small unit down in the suburbs now that the two older girls were settled in a flat close to uni. 'You don't need your step-mum cramping your style.' He'd missed her, but he couldn't blame her for wanting her own space given that Dad was gone.

'How is Wendy?' he asked.

'Good. She wanted me to warn you though, there's an invitation in with the card. She and Dirk are getting hitched. She would have called herself only she knew we were coming around tonight and you'd be busy. But she wanted you to hear it from us before someone else blabbed the news.'

'They're getting married?'

Sophie put a hand on his arm. 'You don't mind do you? It's ten years now since Dad passed away.'

'Oh no,' he said, snapping himself out of it, 'not at all.' After all, Wendy deserved to be happy and Dirk seemed like a nice guy and he'd been on the scene a while. 'It's . . . kind of nice. I'm happy for her. For both of them.'

She squeezed his arm and smiled. 'I told her you would be.'

'Thing is,' Dan said, 'how do you feel about it? You're the one who's going to be impacted the most, aren't you?'

Sophie shook her head, setting the ends of her short dark bob swaying. 'Mum's moving in with Dirk - she's practically living with him as it is - and leaving me the unit for now.' She grinned. 'Just in case, she said. Not that there's any chance of it not working out, I reckon.'

'That's cool,' Dan said, liking the idea more and more. 'Tell her I'll be there with bells on.'

Sophie grinned. 'I'd like to see that.'

'Who's been sitting in my chair?' growled Pop, and Sophie jumped up.

'Just keeping it warm for you, Papa Bear,' she said, heading back to her sisters.

'Well that's all right then,' he said, handing his grandson another beer before he sat stiffly down. 'Cherry auction's coming up this week. I reckon those Bings are going to be hard to beat.'

'Yeah,' agreed Dan, knowing the cherries had never looked better. 'That's what I'm hoping.' To get the cherries noticed and a swag of orders to follow. It wasn't too much to hope for, was it? 'So long as Des next door keeps his bloody cherry slug to himself and the weather holds out, the season might actually turn out all right for a change.'

'Hey you guys, no talking shop!' Beth interrupted, offering around a plate of cheese and crackers. 'Besides, Dan, I need to ask you if you're still okay to pick up Siena after Cassie's party on Sunday?'

Dan helped himself to some crackers and a few wedges of cheese. 'Sure. Balhannah wasn't it?'

'Yeah, the Duncan place, you know the one, the big double storey on Mugga Road. Four o'clock pick up, okay? I should be back pretty close to five, so just drop her off home.'

He nodded. 'Sure you don't need me to take her as well?'

'No, she's having a sleepover with Cassie the night before. Gotta warn you though, it might take a bit to prise her away.' She glanced over her shoulder at her daughter, who was sitting on Nan's lap and telling her a longwinded story about something, before turning back and whispering apologetically, 'It's a pony party.'

Oh. 'Thanks for the warning,' he said. The last time he'd had to pick up his niece from a pony party, it had taken forty-five minutes and a whole lot of wailing before he'd managed to lure her away from the horses and her friends and into the car. Siena had cried all the way home. Lucky this time he had a plan B.

Across the table, Hannah clapped her hands. 'Eat up, everyone, or we'll never get to cake.'

'And Uncle Dan's surprise,' added Siena, sliding off Nan's lap.

If he hadn't already been looking forward to his Nan's sponge cake, he might have been suspicious right about then. He might have read something into Hannah's eagerness or the glare Beth shot her daughter. But his stomach was full and he was halfway through a rare second beer and despite the casual way his family made light of his concerns, he was feeling mellow.

Until Sophie stood and moved the plates out the way for Hannah to swing the cake into pride of place on the table, and he saw the candles on top.

Bloody hell!

The birthday cake was practically groaning under the weight of tall curly candles in every colour of the rainbow. The last time he'd had more than one candle on a cake, he'd been about Siena's age, and that was more than a quarter of a century ago. What the hell were they playing at?

He turned to his niece, trying to keep the grump from his voice, because if someone younger than ten years of age had thought of it, he could just about forgive them for it. 'Is this your idea, Siena?'

'It was mum's idea,' she said gleefully, the reflected flames dancing in the chocolate brown of his niece's eyes while she watched the twins working quickly to light all the candles, even as the first ones started to drip wax onto the cake before the last had been lit. 'Mum's and Hannah's.'

'Is that so,' he said, because with a sick feeling, he realised he'd been right. His sisters had been up to something and here was the proof.

'Thirty-seven years years old,' Hannah said, working a lighted match around her end of the candles. 'How does it feel to be so old?'

'Three years till the big four oh,' said her twin, gleefully joining in the harassment as she worked her side of the cake. 'That's almost middle-aged, bro!'

'You'll be on a pension soon,' predicted Sophie. 'Do you have any last requests?'

'Yeah,' he said. 'Mostly for my sisters to stop banging on about my age.' There was a good reason he wasn't fussed with birthdays. A damned good reason. 'You do realise age is just a number.'

'And now for the finishing touch,' said Hannah, oblivious to his deepening scowl. She held four sparklers to the match flame and then stuck them at the four points of the cake, the lighted sparklers showering the table in silver sparks. 'Ta da!' she said triumphantly.

Dan couldn't prevent the roll of his eyes. With sparks flying every which way, it looked like the fireworks going off at the Royal Adelaide Show.

Siena clapped her hands, and squealed her delight. 'Yay, Uncle Dan!'

His sisters, he noticed, couldn't stop grinning.

Even Nan put her hands over her smiling mouth and said, 'Oh my. Have you ever seen anything like it, Clarry?'

He never heard his Pop's reply, over Hannah's, 'Siena, quick, turn off the lights. Okay, everyone all together, one two three,

Happy birthday to you . . . '

They all joined in. His three sisters and his niece, his Nan doing soprano and his Pop bringing in a quaky baritone. If Molly had been here, she would have been howling along with the lot of them.

Oh no.

Please God, tell me they haven't got me a new puppy.

'Happy birthday to you.'

The sparks flew and the curly tapers melted and sagged against each other and the flames merged and shot higher still.

'Happy birthday, dear Da-an.

'Happy birthday to you.'

He looked at the growing blaze on top of the cake, felt the heat from the flame and followed the smoky heat trail to the smoke detector screwed on tight to the ceiling above and hard-wired to the monitoring service, and thought, uh-oh . . .

'Han,' he said, trying to get her attention.

'Hip hip – hooray!'

'Han!' But Hannah, his biggest little sister who'd bossed him around unmercifully since she was two years old, wasn't letting go of the reins just yet.

'Hip hip – hooray!'

'Hannah!' he said, pointing up to the ceiling. 'The bloody smoke detector!'

She looked up and managed a slight frown, but she was

on a mission and there was no stopping her now.

'Hip hip –'

The alarm in the corner started screaming. Siena shrieked in an even higher pitch, and everyone ducked their heads and covered their ears, even Dan. 'I told you!' he yelled across the table.

She shook her head. 'What?'

'The smoke detector!'

'So blow them out!'

He craned his head over the table. 'What?'

'Blow the candles out!'

He snorted. Fat chance of that, – already they had a blaze that would do the Olympic flame justice – and lunged instead for the fire blanket hanging near the hotplates. The siren inside was joined now by the whoop of the alarm outside, and he had the silver blanket pulled from the package and unfolded and ready to throw when Hannah grabbed hold of his arm. 'Don't you dare!'

'But –' He glanced over at his Nan who looked close to tears, her hands over her mouth as she turned her face into Pop's chest, though whether from the cacophony going on around them or the thought that her precious sponge cake might be flattened, he couldn't tell.

Aw, hell. He threw the blanket aside and grabbed Siena's arm instead. 'Siena,' he shouted, 'help me out here.' He wasn't sure if his niece had heard him but he started blowing, and Siena joined in on his right flank, because there was no turning off the alarm until this bloody bushfire on a plate was out. Between the two of them, they somehow managed to get it under control, leaving a stunted forest of deformed candles and twisted sparkler wires sending tendrils of acrid smoke coiling into the air.

He turned on the exhaust fan in the kitchen on his march to the alarm panel and was punching in the code when the phone rang. 'It's the security agency,' said Beth, with her hand over the receiver. 'They want to know if there's a problem.'

Like she had to ask? Yes, there's a bloody problem all right, thought Dan, but he didn't say that. Instead he sucked in air and took the phone, gave them the password and assured them that yes, everything was under control and no, there was no need for an appliance.

No thanks to the three musketeers here.

'That was exciting,' said Hannah, clearing off the remaining savoury food when Dan got back to the table, still shaking his head. Yeah, normally he wouldn't swap his sisters for quids, but if someone was offering right now, he'd be sorely tempted .

'My ears are ringing,' said Nan, who'd recovered and was busy pulling out candles and picking out the worst of the wax from the top of the cake. She began cutting it into thick wedges, while Beth was boiling the kettle and organising coffee and tea. Dan picked up what was left of his beer and looked at it and put it down again, wondering what had happened to feeling mellow.

'Well,' said Pop, sounding almost breathless, 'that was a real heart-starter. I must be getting too old for all this palaver.'

Dan frowned, because now that he looked at him, Pop didn't just look tired, he looked grey, and every bit of his eighty years old. It struck him that his Pop hadn't moved at all during the excitement, let alone tried to put the fire out or deal with the alarm. He'd assumed he had been holding onto Nan, but now he wondered if it wasn't the other way around. 'Are you sure you're okay?'

'Course I'm okay,' he said, puffing out his chest. 'Fit as a mallee bull, if you must know. A piece of Joanie's cake and I'll be right as rain, won't I love?'

'If you say so, Clarry, it's never failed to work before. Now, who else for cake? Birthday boy first. Siena, you can hand them out.'

'Can we do presents now?' asked Siena, as she passed plates of cake to her uncle and then her pop.

Oh, God, Dan thought. So the birthday cake from hell hadn't been the surprise. Please just let it be mixed nuts and port.

'Of course, we can,' said her mum. 'Uncle Dan can't wait, and besides, we can't stay much longer. You've got to get up early for school tomorrow.'

'Aww, do I have to go to school?'

'Yes you do,' said Beth, nodding.

'But it's almost holidays.'

'And when it's holidays, you can stay home. Until then, you go to school.'

The girl tossed her head up to the ceiling, looking pained. 'But Mu-um.'

'No.'

'I know,' said Siena, her brown eyes already alive with an alternate plan. 'I could come help Uncle Dan pick cherries.'

'No.'

'Sure, you can,' said Dan, only to earn himself a what-the-fuck frown from his sister. He grinned at that, happy to have scored a point against one of his sisters, when he was down so many. 'But you have to be here ready to start work at six.'

The girl pouted. 'I don't have to get up that early for school.'

'Ah, in that case you're better off going to school.'

For a moment, she looked like she wanted to argue the case.

'I thought you wanted to do presents,' said Beth, and the girl huffed off to forage in a basket, back a scant twenty seconds later with two familiar shaped packages hugged to her chest. And judging by the grin on her face, her disappointment was all but forgotten.. 'Happy birthday, Uncle Dan.' She handed them over one at a time and he took them in each hand and then wrapped his arms around her in a big hug to say thanks.

And never before had he meant it so much.

He'd have recognised those packages anywhere. Still, he took his time unwrapping each present carefully, expressing surprise and delight when sure enough, first nuts and then port were revealed.

'Fantastic,' he said, and meant it. 'My favourites.' Siena's grin widened.

'Something simple from us both,' said his Nan, handing him an unmistakably shaped box that also contained no secrets. And still he could be excited when he opened a box of chocolates.

'That's great guys, he said. It's really good of you all to be here tonight. I appreciate it.'

'Hey,' piped up Beth, 'not so fast. There's one more present.'

Sophie handed him the small flat package. 'Happy birthday, bro. This is from us all.' He smiled and kissed her cheek and weighed it up in his hands; too thin for chocolates, not near enough legs for a puppy, but there was something inside – maybe some DVDs? That'd be all right too.

He ripped off the gift wrap and stopped and stared at the plain black box inside, a box embossed with the golden letters of a website.

'What's this?' he said, turning it over in his hands. 'What's hea dot com?'

'Not hea. H-E-A dot com,' spelled out Beth.

He shrugged. 'So?' It still meant nothing to him.

Hannah licked her lips, looking sideways at her sisters. 'We thought you could use a helping hand – so we bought you a profile on Happy Ever After.' She waited a few seconds while she let that sink it. 'It's an online dating service, Dan.'

And Siena clapped her hands. 'Surprise!

'You bought me a what?'

'It's a subscription, Dan,' said Hannah, softly.

'Just for three months,' Beth added.

'To a dating agency,' Sophie offered, smiling hopefully but sounding decidedly tentative. 'A really good one. Maybe you even might find someone to take with you to Wendy's wedding.'

'And the quiz night,' said Siena.

He growled and slung the black box skidding across the table as if it were poison, and looked at his sisters. 'Is this some kind of joke?'

But not one of their faces cracked a smile, so he turned to his Nan and Pop, expecting them to be just as offended and horrified as he was. Because, of course, anyone in their right mind would be. He snorted. 'Can you believe this?'

His nan looked nervously away and he watched her put her hand across her chest and cough. 'We're all just worried about you, Dan,' she said, as she rose and started stacking cake plates. 'It's not as if you're getting any younger.'

Well, sure. Of course they were worried about him. 'But a dating agency? Really?'

He looked searchingly to his pop, who apparently felt a similar sudden need to clear his throat and still looked none the better for doing it. 'None of us is getting any younger and nobody lives forever. Your sisters would just like to see you settled. We all would. What's wrong with giving it a try?'

It was the longest speech he'd ever heard his pop give that didn't concern the weather or the cherries, but right now that wasn't something to celebrate. He turned back to his sisters. 'You really think I need signing up to a dating agency like some loser who can't find himself a girlfriend?'

If he'd expected them to look sorry, he was wrong. Hannah wasn't about to make any excuses. 'Nobody said you were a loser, Dan. We just thought it might offer you a few more options.'

'Options.' He nodded slowly. Exaggeratedly. 'For finding a girlfriend.'

'Exactly!' she said. 'Because isn't that what you ultimately want? Someone to share your life with and have a family and maybe even a child or two to pass the orchard down to – given none of us are lining up for the task? You can hardly find a wife if you don't find a girlfriend first.'

'Give me a break! Don't you think I'm perfectly capable of going out and finding myself someone to share my life with?'

His sisters exchanged looks, and it was what they didn't say that was more telling.

'What?' he demanded, his hands spread wide. 'What does that look mean? That I've got no chance otherwise?'

Beth shrugged. 'Well, face it Dan. It's not like you've dated anyone for a long time. What is it - ten years - since Margot?'

No way it could be ten years, but right now he wasn't about to argue that point. He held his arms out. 'And did it occur to anyone here that it's cherry season and I might be just a bit busy to go out socialising?'

'We know that!' said Beth. 'But if you don't mind me asking, what have you done in between cherry seasons?'

'Well,' he said, 'there's apple and pear season right on its heels and then there's winter and stuff to do in the orchard, and then it's spring again. What do you think, I've been sitting on my hands here?'

'Nobody thinks that,' said Hannah. 'We know how hard you work, which is why we thought it might be easier to meet someone online, and work out whether you're compatible before you meet them in person.'

'But I don't need to meet women online before I figure I

want to date them!'

'Because?'

'Because there's heaps of women around here that I could date if I just asked.'

'Like who?'

He shrugged. 'Like that woman from the school library. Helen, or whatever her name is. Her!'

'You mean Ellen Coburn?'

'Yeah, that's the one. She seemed nice enough when I saw her at Siena's school music concert that time.'

Sophie slowly shook her head. 'Ellen got married a year ago.'

'Oh. Well, what about that woman who works in the pub sometimes? The redhead. Or is she married too?'

'If you mean Heather Adams, then no,' said Beth. 'She's not married, not last I heard.'

'You see? So I don't need this kind of – help – if that's what you call it. I'll look her up at the cherry auction next week.'

The girls exchanged glances. 'Exactly how long is it since you've been to the pub, big bro?'

He blinked and rubbed his stubbled jaw. 'I dunno. Couple of months, I guess. Why do you ask?'

'Heather left for South America more than six months ago. She took one of those volunteer jobs teaching kids English.'

Dan cut the air with his hands. Whatever their point was, he didn't want to hear it. 'So maybe I just don't have time to go to the pub!'

'That's just it, Dan,' cooed Hannah, stroking his shoulder and looking all too understanding, and Dan got the distinct impression this is exactly the way she'd be in the surgery, soothing a frightened labrador before sticking a dirty great needle in its leg to send him to sleep before she lopped something off. 'We know you don't have the time, so why don't you give it a try? What have you got to lose?'

He shook off her hand. He didn't need to be soothed. He didn't want to go to sleep and wake up and find his sisters had lopped anything off – even if it was just his right to decide how and when he'd meet women.

'I haven't got time for any of this.'

'Ah, but that's the best thing,' said Beth. 'It won't take a minute of your time because we've already set up your profile for you.'

He coughed. 'Excuse me. My *what?*'

'Your profile. So women can see what a fabulous catch you are.'

He snorted.

'But you are, Dan. Thirty-seven years old and never been hitched. Clean living and fit and if you weren't a cherry farmer, you could just about be a male model for one of those RM Williams catalogues.'

'Bullshit!'

'Dan,' scolded Nan, 'there's a child present.'

'Bugger. Sorry,' Dan said, and cursed himself again, even as Siena looked up and said, 'I've heard worse than that at school, Nan. You should hear what some of the kids say at recess when they know Mrs Innstairs isn't listening. They say –'

Beth clapped a hand over her daughter's mumbling mouth. 'We don't want to hear it, young lady,' she warned. And then she turned to her brother, wearing a smile that he didn't trust one bit. 'It's perfect, Dan. You don't have to leave home, you don't have to do a thing,' said Beth. 'Except wait for all the matches to roll in.'

'There's probably half a dozen lined up panting already,' said Sophie. 'Hey, so why don't we log in now, and show you how it works?'

'Great idea,' said Hannah, picking up the black box and brushing off a few stray crumbs before she held it out to Dan. 'All the details are inside. We can check out your potential matches right now.'

'Yeah, do it!' said Beth. 'See how good this is. You're gonna love it, bro.'

'I want to see!' said Siena, squirming out from under her mother's silencing hold, and the fact that an eight-year-old was interested in his love life – or lack of it – was the last straw as far as Dan was concerned.

'No! Nobody is going to see anything.' This was rubbish and he had to put a stop to it. 'I don't know why you're all so worried about my love life. I don't see any of you guys lining up to get married.'

'Hey,' said Beth, looping her arms over her daughter's shoulders and pulling her in tight. 'I would have been.'

'Aw, Beth . . .' Dan put a hand to his head. What a stupid, dumb arse thing to say. Beth had beem the only one of them that ever looked like getting married. 'I'm sorry. I didn't think.'

'Nobody's given you a chance to think tonight,' clucked his Nan, doing what she did best and mending bridges. She got up and gathered various bits of Tupperware together, finding a moment to give Beth's shoulder a squeeze. 'I think we should all let Dan explore his present in private and at his leisure, don't you, girls? Come on, Clarry. It's getting late.'

'Yeah, we have to go too,' said Beth, propelling Siena into action. There were murmurs of agreement from his other sisters and in a few moments the kitchen was filled with activity as everyone began collecting their bits and divvying up the leftovers, with the lion's share being left for Dan.

Outside by their car, Dan leaned down to give his Nan a kiss and a hug. 'Thanks for the cake, Nan. And the chocolates.'

'My pleasure. And Dan?'

'Yeah?'

'Have a think about what your sisters are trying to doing for you. This thing doesn't have to be all bad. You know we'd all like to see you happy.'

'Who says I'm not happy?'

'You're the grumpiest orchardist in the district,' his Nan said bluntly. 'At least, that's what I've heard.'

'So I'm busy!'

'But you don't have to be grumpy. Do us all a favour and check this thing out. Before it's too late and nobody wants you.'

He rolled his eyes but still managed to summon a smile. 'Yeah,' he lied, 'I'll think about it.'

They were all gone, the last of the dishes were in the dishwasher, and the house was silent except for the ticking of the old grandfather clock – the sound louder than it had ever been, it seemed to Dan, as it counted down the minutes and hours of his remaining life.

Bloody hell, he wasn't that old. But neither was he stupid. He hadn't appreciated being presented with a done deal, but he was a pragmatist. He'd always planned on getting married and having kids one day. God, he might already have been married if Margot hadn't taken one look at Wendy and Nan still tending the raspberry canes, and got cold feet. But then it's just as well she had, because the orchard life was no place for a woman who didn't contribute and who wanted to be looked after.

But Margot was years ago – more than ten, he suddenly realised – and he'd always expected the marriage thing to happen naturally without too much effort, kind of organically, by osmosis or something.

He picked up the little black box from where it lay unopened on the table, and tapped it against the fingers of his other hand. If his sisters were right and there were single women already lined up waiting, it couldn't be too hard to find a wife. It wasn't like he had nothing going for him, even if his sisters were laying it on a bit thick when they made it sound like he was God's gift to single women.

And after his experience with Margot, it wasn't like he didn't know what kind of woman the orchard needed. In fact, if he thought about it, it wasn't that hard to hammer out a list of requirements.

Someone sensible and mature.

Someone responsible and not afraid of long days and hard work.

Someone ready to start a family, probably around thirty to thirty-five years old who'd be a good mum.

Looks desirable but not compulsory. He wasn't a fool; he wasn't expecting too much in that department. She didn't need to be drop-dead gorgeous by any means – but if she had good teeth (because he'd heard from some of his mates that orthodontic bills for their kids were a killer) that'd be a bonus.

He thought of the leftovers in the fridge. Oh yeah, and someone who could cook.

It wasn't like he was asking for the world, he rationalised. He just needed someone who could fit in to a primary producer's life and who understood the responsibility and commitment that went with it.

That was about the size of it.

He looked at the box in his hand and tossed it back on the table. No, his sisters were underestimating him as usual. He'd check it out later if it came to that.

Now that they'd flagged the issue and he'd nutted out exactly what he was looking for, the hard work was just about done.

A woman like that shouldn't be hard to find.

CHAPTER 2

M elbourne

LUCY MARINO STOPPED STUFFING gear in her pack for a moment and scanned the bedroom of the small Carlton share house where she'd been staying this last month while its occupant was touring the beer halls of Germany. Something was missing. Something important. And then she remembered and headed for the kitchen.

Someone had made an attempt at renovating the little terrace house many decades ago, knocking out a wall to combine the kitchen and living rooms, and her flatmate was slouched with his back to her in one of the armchairs, his feet up on the coffee table and clearly absorbed in whatever game he was playing. She didn't interrupt him. She knew better than to interrupt a man vying for world domination on his Nintendo. Besides, she just wanted her wok.

'So you're still going then?'

She looked up, surprised that Dylan had even noticed she

was here. Even more surprised given he hadn't turned, hadn't moved a muscle apart from the ones attached to his thumbs still firmly engaged on the controls. 'Going? As in packing?' After two months in Australia, she was getting used to some Aussieisms, but there were still times when she couldn't be sure exactly what something meant.

'Going. As in leaving.' And suddenly the Nintendo was flung to the other armchair and he was up on his feet and facing her, his long fringe flopping over his eyes in the way that usually made her smile because it made her geeky engineering student flatmate look adorable. It didn't make her smile today. There was something way too unsettling in his troubled eyes. 'You're still planning on leaving then?'

She cradled the cookbooks and her wok that she'd retrieved over her chest and smiled, aiming at keeping it light. 'Well, yeah. That was the deal. I rent Mike's room while he's away and he arrives home tonight.' She shrugged, hoping that was the end of it.

'You don't have to go.'

'But Mike's –'

'I've been thinking. You could stay. You could share my room.'

Oh. So that's what he was stewing about.

So much for thinking he'd forgotten, or that he'd put that night behind him, put it down to grief and sympathy.

'I mean, if you wanted to, that is.'

She lowered her eyes, grieving for him again, as she remembered that night she'd come home late from work and found him curled up and sobbing on the sofa. She'd knelt down next to him and stroked his head and asked him what was wrong, and through his tears he'd chokingly told her about the call from his father, the call to say his mother had been involved in a head on collision with a semi, and both his mother and kid sister had been killed.

And so he'd booked the first flight out of Melbourne in the morning and he was packed and ready to fly back to his mid-west NSW home, but now he couldn't sleep, couldn't stop thinking, couldn't do anything but shake and cry. So she'd hugged him tight and held him while he'd trembled and sobbed against her, and much later, when his tears had subsided and he'd reached for her in a different kind of way and comforting him had moved to a different level, they'd made slow, sweet, life-affirming love. He'd slept afterwards, in the circle of her arms, and she'd let him rest until it was time to wake him with coffee before the taxi arrived to whisk him to the airport.

A week later he'd returned. At first he'd seemed awkward and avoided making eye contact, but things had slowly returned to normal and in the two weeks since then, neither of them had mentioned that night. It was like it had never happened – or so she'd thought.

Until now.

And he was such a sweet guy. Sometimes funny, sometimes intense; at just twenty years old he was like an almost grown puppy that was all long lean limbs just waiting to fill out. And she liked him, but despite what had happened that night, there was none of that spark between them that happened on those rare occasions, that magical spark between a man and a woman that might last a week or a month until it fizzled out.

Because it always fizzled out.

And when there was no spark to begin with . . .

'Dylan –'

He pushed that flop of hair back with his fingers. 'I mean, it's not like you have any plans. You don't even know where you're going.'

'I never have plans. You know enough about me by now to know that's not how I operate.'

'So why not stay then?' He swallowed and she saw the kick of his Adam's apple and the tight press of his lips and she knew what it must be costing him to expose himself this way.

She shook her head softly, because he'd already suffered so much loss and it was awful to add to it, even though that had never been her wish. 'I'm sorry, Dylan. I have to move on. That's what I do. That's what I always do.'

He nodded then, his lips pressed tightly together.

'That's cool,' he said, 'I just thought I'd ask. I'll miss y –' He stopped himself, his eyes wide, as if he'd said too much, before they fell on the wok and her books in her arms, and he took a deep breath. 'I'll miss your cooking.'

And she smiled and wrapped one arm around his shoulders and kissed his cheek – a brief, no-more-than-friends kiss. 'I'll miss you too. I'll send you a postcard when I get settled somewhere.'

'Yeah,' he said, and gave an awkward kind of shrug before flopping back in the armchair and reaching for the controller to resume his game. 'That'd be cool.'

An hour later Lucy hitched her pack higher on her shoulders and stuck out her thumb on Sydney Road. That sounded promising. 'Bondi Beach, here I come,' she said, as the traffic whizzed by, the people who had to be somewhere in a hurry before they had to hurry somewhere else – the shopping, running the kids to school, a job that sucked out your brain.

That life was not for her.

Staying in one place was not for her.

This time tomorrow she'd probably be dipping a toe into the surf of that famous beach. A bit of sun and surf would suit this southern Californian girl. She needed a fix of the white foamy stuff every now and then. Hell, she needed a fix of some decent sunshine, and while this November day was warming up, Melbourne's ability to turn on four seasons in one day had caught her out more than once.

A horn blared as a removals truck passed by, pulling up a little way ahead of her, the passenger door swinging open as a sideways head peered out, round-faced and shaggy with a red beard.

'Wanna lift?' he yelled, as she jogged up to catch up to him. 'Gonna get too hot later today for luggin' that thing,' the driver said, one hand resting on the wheel, the other on the seat as he leaned down to talk to her, and Lucy got an impression of a bear in a blue singlet and tatts. A friendly bear, she decided in an instant, as he asked, 'Where're you headed?'

'How far are you going?'

'Adelaide.'

And Lucy blinked, the answer so unexpected. 'I hate to be the one to tell you this, but this is actually Sydney Road.'

The truck driver snorted and smacked the heel of his hand against the wheel. 'Bloody hell, I've done it again! I always get them two mixed up.' And then he grinned. 'Nah, it's all good, love, I turn off and head west soon. I should have figured you'd be headed for Sydney.'

Was she? She'd assumed she was, but that was the beauty of not planning. You never knew where life was going to take you next and it didn't matter a bit if you veered off course.

She grinned up at the driver. 'Adelaide sounds pretty cool to me.'

The tattooed bear at the wheel grinned right back. 'Then climb on board, little lady. The name's Mick, what's yours?'

'Lucy,' she said, as she slid the pack from her back and passed it to him before clambering up into the high cab and pulling the big door shut behind her.

'Good to meet you Lucy,' he said, extending a paw to shake her hand. 'Where are you from?'

Nowhere.

Everywhere.

'I was born in California,' she said, reeling out her usual short version response. 'How about you?'

'Shep,' he said, as he fiddled with an iPod while she got herself settled, big bear paws surprisingly nimble on the controls. 'Shepparton. It's about an hour and a half north of here. But Adelaide's home for me now. That's where the family is.' He put the iPod down and jammed the truck into gear. 'Hope you like country music.'

'Is there any other kind?'

He chuckled as he checked his rear-vision mirror for a break in the trams and the traffic before pulling back onto the road. 'I can see we're going to get along just fine.'

The cabin filled with the strains of country music. Australian country music, she figured, and a bit different from the Blake Shelton she was used to. And it was surprisingly okay.

'Been in Melbourne long?' Mick asked, as the suburbs fell away behind them and the highway snaked through paddocks either side of them.

'Two months.'

'Time to move on?'

'Yeah.' She bit her lip, remembering Dylan's offer to stay. They'd hugged at the front gate before she'd headed off, and any spark between them had been conspicuous by its absence. She closed her eyes on a sigh. 'Time to move on,' she said, repeating the same words she'd told Dylan. 'That's what I always do.'

The man beside her nodded. 'I get that. I'd go stir crazy in a regular job. Got to keep moving, that's me, even if now I've got the wife and kids at the end of it. But that's what you gotta do, eh, if you wanna settle down sometime – find the happy medium, right? The best of both worlds?'

'I guess,' she said, though if there was anything her life had taught her, it was that it was better to keep right on moving.

'Hey,' Mick said, turning up the sound as the chorus kicked in, 'this one's a real goody,' and he started singing along.

The truck rumbled to a stop for a coffee at Horsham where the jagged purple outline of the Grampians hovered on their left, and then again at Keith, where the horizon over stubbled golden fields shimmered with the heat haze and the flies stuck like glue when they climbed down from the cab to stop for lunch. By the time the truck was wending its way down the freeway and through the hills towards Adelaide, Lucy knew the lyrics to just about every song Lee Kernaghan had ever written and was belting out 'Boys from the Bush' along with Mick.

And then, like someone had flicked a switch, the cleft in the hills widened and the bush suddenly gave way to traffic lights and the city of Adelaide sprawled out before her. 'Wow,' she said. 'We're here?'

Mick reached for the controls in between changing down gears and turned the volume down. 'Yup. Li'l old Adelaide. City of Churches, they call it. Makes it sound a bit boring if you ask me, but that's okay. All those folk over on the east coast, they don't know what they're missing. So, where do you want to be dropped off?'

She had no idea. 'I don't know much about Adelaide,' she admitted, 'but if there are beaches, I could always get a job in a cafe or something.'

'The beaches are that way,' said Mick, using his thumb to point left as he negotiated the truck around to the right. 'Adelaide spreads for miles along the coast and between the hills.'

'Okay,' she said, nodding. 'Maybe you could drop me somewhere I can hitch a ride that way?'

He held up one hand. 'Yeah, I could do that, but if you want my advice, you'll head for the hills.'

She laughed. 'That's a joke, right?'

'No joke. A bit further along and up over that way –' he gestured with his right hand to the hills that stretched along their right '– is where the seasonal fruit picking work is. Cherries now. Apples and pears and even grapes later. I reckon you'll find work there. Good money too. I can drop you somewhere you can pick up a ride if you like, otherwise it's an easy trip into the city and on to the beach from there.' He shrugged. 'Up to you.'

Cherries? That would make a change from waiting tables in a cafe. She could always head for the beach on her day off. 'I'm kind of liking the sound of that fruit picking idea,' she said.

'All right,' he said, fiddling with his iPod control. 'We've got time for one more round of "Boys from the Bush" before I drop you off, if you want.'

'Oh yeah,' she said, preparing to sing her lungs out. 'I want.'

CHAPTER 3

'You brought Spitty!' Siena squealed as she came belting out of her friend's house, a yellow balloon bearing a big smiley face in one hand, a party bag in the other, and mere seconds after he'd burbled into the driveway. He hadn't even had to knock on the door, let alone drag her out. 'I love it when you've got the top down!'

'I thought you might,' Dan said knowingly as he opened the passenger door so she could climb in, smiling as he tied the balloon down in the back parcel shelf, remembering his sister's warning. After the disaster of the last party pick up, he'd figured there was no better way to get his kid niece away from a birthday party than to dust off his dad's old Triumph Spitfire and take it for a spin. Seems he knew something about kids. But then it was pretty rare to find anyone who wasn't taken with the tiny red sports car. Even now Siena's friends and half a dozen parents had come out to wave her goodbye. 'So how was the party?' he asked, as he adjusted the seatbelt over her checked shirt and jeans that smelt suitably equine and told him all he really needed to know right there.

'So cool!' she said, waving to her friends as they pulled away. 'Cassie got a pony called Star for her birthday. Her own pony! And there were three more called Misty, Chuckles and Pumpkin, for the rest of us to ride. Why can't I have a pony, Uncle Dan?'

'Well,' he said, waving as they passed a couple of cars heading in the long driveway for pick up as they headed out, 'it's not really me you should be asking that question.'

'But Mum always says no. Can't you talk her into it?'

'Me talk Beth into something?' He cocked a questioning eyebrow at his passenger. 'You reckon?'

She crossed her arms over her chest and slid down in her seat until the top of her head barely came up to the window.

'Hey, Siena,' he said. 'Be reasonable here. Ponies cost an arm and a leg and your mum is working flat out looking after you as it is.'

'But it's not fair!'

'Life's not fair. It's tough, I know, but that's the way it is.'

'I wish it wasn't. I wish we could be rich. I wish I could have my own pony.'

'Well, you can wish all you want, but wishing alone isn't going to get you anywhere.'

'Why not?'

'Because there's no magic about wishes. You've got to work at it if you want your wishes to come true. You've got to make them come true.'

Beside him the girl harrumphed into a sulk. Okay, so he didn't particularly like it either, but that was life. You dreamed and worked and hoped for the best and sometimes . . . He felt his gut clench as he navigated the low sports car along the windy hills road. Yeah, sometimes it might even come off. Please God let it come off this year. He hoped the cherries would make a big splash at the auction and that sales were strong and that the weather held out . . .

'So did you get a girlfriend yet, Uncle Dan?'

'Huh?'

'A girlfriend. Mum and Hannah and Sophie, they said there'd be lots of girlfriends on that website. Have you looked yet?'

'Um. No. I've been a bit busy.'

'Wouldn't you like to get married and have kids one day?'

'I guess, one day.'

'Would you get your kids a pony – if they asked for one, I mean?'

'Probably not.'

'Why not?'

'What do you reckon?'

His passenger sniffed at that and turned her attention out her side of the car as he drove between vineyards and orchards. He hoped it was an end to the matter. The little car zipped along the roads, sticking to the curves like glue, the air deliciously warm, the November sunlight filtered by the overhanging trees, all of it tugging at the stray ends of his tension. It was good to get out for a while. At home in the orchard he was surrounded by problems. Out here, on the open road, it felt like he could breathe again.

'Do you ever wish you had a girlfriend?'

He sighed. At least Siena wasn't banging on about ponies any more. 'Sometimes, I guess.' He shrugged.

'Wishing for it won't make it happen, Uncle Dan. You have to work at it. You'll have to open that program.'

And too late he realised the trap she'd sprung. He snorted. 'You're a chip off the old block, Siena, do you know that?'

She frowned. 'What?'

He ruffled her dark hair, already wild with the wind. 'Nothing.'

'If you do get married, Uncle Dan . . .'

'What?' he said, looking at her when she left her sentence hanging.

'Can you marry someone who has horses?'

He smiled. 'I'll try my best,' he said, as they pulled into the driveway of Beth's little cottage on a hill overlooking the Piccadilly Valley with its fields green with spring vegetables.

'Hey, Mum's home already,' she said, spotting Beth's small Toyota down the side of the house as she unclicked her seat belt and reached for her party bag on the floor. 'Do you want to come in?'

'Better not,' he said, because he knew his sister wouldn't ask any fewer questions than her daughter, and Beth wouldn't be distracted by the talk of ponies. 'I have to go get . . . petrol,' he said, seizing on the quarter tank of juice as his excuse to escape.

It was as good an excuse as any. Even if he'd just about used that quarter tank up driving around the hills by himself by the time he eventually headed down towards the servo. It was too long since he'd taken Spitty out and he didn't know when he'd get the chance again.

He was filling up the tank when horns started blaring across the road, and straight away he could see why. A truck had pulled over and a line of traffic was caught queued across the intersection behind it. Stupid place to stop, he thought, and went back to watching the numbers spinning around on the bowser until the truck's engines revved and he turned back to see the bearded driver waving to the traffic behind, his beefy arm covered in ink, as the big beast lurched into motion and rolled away, leaving a figure standing there.

A blonde girl in jeans and a singlet top was juggling a pack that looked almost as big as her. She lifted a hand in the direction of the disappearing truck before turning back towards the intersection.

A hitchhiker. Well, that explained a lot.

The bowser clicked off and he pulled out the nozzle before screwing the cap shut, wincing when he saw how much was about to be added to his account. There were all kinds of reasons this cherry season had better be the bumper crop it was shaping up to be. At least a dozen creditors were banking on it. Still, the Spitfire didn't get out of the shed much these days, so he might as well go for broke. He popped her bonnet to check the oil and water. At least the water was free.

STRAIGHT UP MAGILL ROAD, Mick had said, and up into the hills at the end, and Lucy would soon come upon the orchards where she was sure to find work. That was fine, but it was getting on for seven o'clock now so maybe the hunt for work could start tomorrow. Assuming there was somewhere cheap and close at hand where she could find a backpacker's or youth hostel.

She pushed the walk button on the pedestrian crossing. Someone at the gas station on the other side of the road would probably know.

The road was hot beneath her sandals when the signal changed to walk, the late afternoon sun warm on her shoulders, and already it felt different to Melbourne, the air drier. It reminded her of the desert air of California and the summer coastline of Italy, or the air of a sunny village market in Crete.

She liked it. She liked the view too. A few miles still up the road, the Adelaide Hills rose from the plains, a band of sun-browned land dotted with the dull grey-green of gum trees.

She didn't mind the view as she crossed the gas station's forecourt either. There was a cute little red convertible with shiny chrome bumpers with its top down and its hood up, the owner leaning down low over his engine the way guys do so that women might notice them. And then he straightened, pulling out a dipstick to examine it. So okay, maybe this guy had another reason to lean over the engine, but it was hard not to take notice of denim pulled tight over a butt like his did. There was something about long legs, lean hips and well-fitting denim that never got old. Such a shame it was rude to stare. She peeled her eyes away and waited while a car slipped out of a filling bay before her, and then headed towards the shop.

A sign in red on the sliding door read *No helmets, No bags,* so she let her pack slide to the floor and propped it up just inside the door before heading to the fridge for a soda.

DAN LOWERED the bonnet and clipped down each side before wiping his hands and heading in to pay. He glanced back over his shoulder to check the number of the bowser and sighed when he saw Siena's bloody balloon still grinning in the back parcel shelf, and almost tripped over a bag someone had left just inside the door. 'Stupid damned place to leave a bag,' he muttered, before checking out the freezer section for something to have for dinner and finding a likely looking box before he joined the queue. The queue that wasn't moving. Which is when he looked around the people in front of him to see what the hold-up was and realised hitchhiker girl must have crossed the road, because that sure looked like her, three places ahead of him and right at the front of the queue. He nodded to himself. That would explain the bag near the doorway too.

Figured. She had a can of Coke up on the counter and was chatting to the young kid who was serving, as if she had all the time in the world.

And given he was smiling and completely oblivious to the growing queue behind her, she clearly did.

The kid looked smitten. Maybe it was the blonde hair she wore tied up in some kind of messy knot that had ends going every which way, or maybe it was her accent. From what he could hear, she sounded American or Canadian – he always got those two mixed up – but then the attendant wasn't the only one interested.

The guy behind her was chipping in and suddenly there was a three-way conversation going and she turned her head over her shoulder to him and Dan caught a look at her profile closer up and thought – okay, not just blonde then, but blonde and seriously pretty. With those blue eyes and that killer smile, no wonder the attendant was in no hurry to see the back of her. A pity about the stud glinting in the crease of her nose and the ink on her shoulder. The guy in front of him shuffled impatiently as he looked at his watch and Dan got a better look at her shoulder. A bird in flight. Okay, so it wasn't a skull, but that didn't make him like it any more. He turned his attention back to the box of curry and studied the directions. He'd never seen the point of tattoos. Thank God his sisters had never done anything dumb like that.

And he remembered his wifely wish list and added two more things to his list.

No random piercings.

And definitely no tattoos.

Given the kind of woman he was looking for, there was

probably little chance of either, but he figured it wouldn't hurt to be clear on the details upfront.

'Hey Dan! I didn't see you back there,' he heard the attendant say. Dan looked up, resisting the temptation to say he wasn't surprised in the least he hadn't seen him. He was so focused on his pretty customer, he would have been hard pressed noticing an elephant in the room. 'This girl's looking for work cherry picking. You know of any jobs going up your way?'

He looked at the girl with the stud in her nose and the ink on her back and who knew what else where else, and who was looking at him, her eyes bright and hopeful, before they widened, her lips curving into a half smile, almost like she recognised him.

His eyes narrowed. What was that about? He'd sure as hell remember if he'd ever met someone like her before. In snug faded jeans and a cotton singlet that hugged her breasts and waist, she had the kind of all over good looks you only ever saw on the big screen, or on the front of women's magazines. 'You ever pick cherries before?'

'No.'

He needed pickers. He'd prefer experienced pickers, given how much he was relying on this crop, and he hardly needed a blonde bombshell who'd probably distract all the other male workers, but right now, beggars couldn't be choosers. After all, it wasn't like he was going to marry her. When it came down to getting the fruit in, the colour of her hair or the fact she had tatts or piercings mattered for nothing.

And she sure looked young and fit enough to cope with the work.

Real fit.

'Yeah,' he said, needing to cough a bit to clear the frog in his throat. 'Matter of fact, I do.'

IT WAS HIM.

The guy with the cute car. The guy with the even cuter butt. And he didn't look too bad from the front either. A bit like a serious Bradley Cooper, high brow under darkish hair swept straight back, long straight nose and lips set in a straight line between a day or two's growth of stubble. She wondered what he'd look like when he smiled.

While he paid for his gas, Lucy retrieved her pack and dusted off the bit where it looked like someone had kicked it, and then waited outside for him, thinking about the chances of a road called Sydney taking her to Adelaide and to a job picking cherries of all things. She liked the twists and turns of life, the discoveries she made and the adventures that she happened upon simply by being open to whatever the journey offered.

She wouldn't change her life for anything.

The glass door slid open and he emerged, slipping a receipt into his wallet before pocketing it. 'So,' he said. 'You're looking for work.'

'Yeah. You're from up that way? You know somewhere I can find work?'

'I do, as it happens. I'm looking for cherry pickers right now. I pay the going rate. You won't find better.'

She looked at the unlikely car and then back at the unlikely him. He was wearing a checked shirt with those jeans, the shirt open at the neck to reveal a tantalising vee of chest and a glimpse of dark hair. A man with broad shoulders and slim hips that looked good in denim and drove a cute car. 'You're a cherry farmer, seriously?'

He frowned. 'Orchardist, we call it. I've got cherries, apples and pears. Some raspberries. A bit of rhubarb. But cherries is what we're picking now.'

'Wow,' she said. 'Sounds like you've got a veritable fruit salad going on there.'

It was meant to be a joke but his scowl only deepened, and she realised she wasn't going to find out what his smile looked like that way. She schooled her face to look responsible and nodded. It was, she figured, a kind of job interview. 'Cherry picking sounds good.'

He grunted. 'But you've never picked before.'

She blinked. 'No, but I'm sure keen to learn.'

'And you're a backpacker,' he said.

She glanced over her shoulder. 'Apparently.'

But that only earned her another scowl as he planted his hands on his hips. 'So how long you planning on sticking around?'

'How long does cherry season go?'

He looked up at the sky. 'We could finish up by Christmas, but it depends on the weather. We may go into New Year.'

'Sounds good to me.'

'Only I don't want to employ someone who's going to decide they've had enough before we're through. Things get pretty hectic in the run up to Christmas. I can't afford to waste time chasing up extra pickers then.'

'Like I said, it sounds good.' She held out a hand to him. 'Lucy Marino reporting for duty. So what time tomorrow do I show up and where?'

'Dan Faraday,' he said, regarding her hand like it was a loaded weapon, before taking it in his. She felt his big hand surround hers, felt his strength and the warm rasp of the pads of his fingers and palm against hers and thought how different a man's hands were when he worked out of doors.

The strangest thing was, she kinda liked it. Not that she had much time to enjoy it, the way he whipped it out of hers so quick and landed it back on his hip.

'I'm heading up there now if you want a lift.'

'Thanks, but I've still got to sort out somewhere to stay. The guy inside said there were some backpacker places in the city. I thought that might do, at least until I can figure out something closer.'

'He told me he'd said that. If you're interested, there's a van on the property. Save you having to travel – especially since you don't appear to have any wheels, and seeing the buses stop at the bottom of the hill about five k's shy. But the van's vacant at the moment. It's yours while the job lasts if you want it.'

'A van?'

'A caravan. One of those things you pull behind a car. It's old and it's nothing flash but it's got a bed and its own little kitchen.'

'Oh, you mean a trailer.'

His frown lines deepened. 'Well, I mean a caravan but you can call it whatever you like. Interested?'

'I sure am.'

He stood there a second, hands firmly back on hips, and she got the distinct impression he was having second thoughts about offering her the job when clearly she didn't even speak the same language. Until a car horn blared and they both turned around and saw that whoever was queued behind his tiny car was getting impatient. 'Ah, hell,' he said. 'We better get going.'

'All right, buddy,' he said to the guy glaring at the wheel of the car behind, as he lifted the trunk on the little car so she could drop her pack in. And it was lucky her pack wasn't any bigger, because there wasn't a whole lot of space left over.

'Cute car,' she said, as she opened the door to climb into the low convertible. Lower than she realised when she fell the last few inches into the seat. ' Whoa,' she said, laughing, 'that's way low.'

He said nothing, still didn't crack a hint of a smile, just passed the strap of her seat belt and turned the key in the ignition. The little car growled into life and settled into a rumble as he eased it out of the bay toward the exit, waiting for a break in the traffic.

She found the other end of the belt and clicked herself in for the ride, still smiling. If the car had been cute from the outside, it was adorable on the inside. It had a wooden panel in front with big round dials and black knobs like she hadn't seen in a car forever.

'What kind of car is this?' she asked, as he accelerated out onto the main road, the little car's engine roaring as it picked up speed, louder still with the top down, the wind whipping at the ends of her hair.

'A 1969 Triumph Spitfire.'

'It's fun. Very James Bond.' She reached her hand toward one of the little round black buttons on the dash. 'What does this do?'

'Don't touch that!'

'Why, is it the ejector seat or something?'

'Hmm, I'm beginning to wish.'

'Hey, I like your car. Wouldn't have thought it was a car for a farmer though.' Or for someone who didn't look like he knew how to have fun.

'Orchardist,' he said.

'What?'

'Orchardist. Not farmer.'

'Oh. So what's an orchardist doing in a car like this?'

'My dad won it in a raffle. It was his pride and joy.'

'Was?'

'He died about ten years back. I like to take the car out for a spin every now and then to keep it running okay.'

She nodded, letting the reference to his father slide by. He didn't seem the kind of guy who needed to hear empty platitudes and she wasn't about to give them. Besides, how did you say sorry when you didn't even know what it was like to grow up with a father, let alone lose one?

She glanced over her shoulder. 'And you like to take your friend out for a spin too?'

'What?' And then he glanced the way she was looking and said, 'It's not actually my balloon.'

'Yeah?' She smiled. 'Go figure.'

'Where are you from?' he countered, and she got the distinct impression he was changing the subject.

'I was born in California.'

'Uh-huh.'

'Although I do believe I was conceived on a beach in Hawaii.'

He shot her a glare. Damn, she really was going to have to work better on finding a way to this guy's smile.

'Too much information?' she asked innocently.

'That's one way to put it,' he answered through tight lips, changing gears as he dodged around a bus pulling up on the left.

WHAT WAS HE THINKING? He never acted rashly. And yet all of a sudden he was offering some blow-in a job. An untested blow-in, for that matter, with a tatt on her shoulder and a stud in her nose and a propensity to talk about stuff he wanted to know nothing about.

And just because he needed a few pickers.

He glanced at the girl beside him, She was probably expecting the next few weeks to be some kind of all-you-can-eat picnic.

She'd probably turn out to be a rubbish picker too. He

wasn't sure how he was so sure of that, only that after two terrible years he was getting used to things going pear-shaped and he didn't expect her to be the one to change anything. Especially not looking the way she did. New blood amongst the team. Pretty new blood at that. Drop-dead gorgeous blood, if he was totally honest. She'd probably have all the male pickers vying for her attention and the parrots would get to the cherries while the blokes were all fighting over her.

Might as well put up a neon sign telling the birds to come on down.

'You know,' he said, looking for an out, because he'd missed the chance to spell it out back there in the servo, 'you'll be working with an experienced crew. If you can't keep up after a few days, I'll have to let you go.'

'Oh, okay. I understand.'

'Because the orchard can't carry anyone. Especially not this time of year.'

'I get that.'

'So you'll have to pull your weight otherwise you'll be looking for another job, real fast.'

'Hey, boss, I get it.'

'And you're okay with that?'

He glanced over at her and found her already looking his way, and found it all the more disconcerting because she was smiling at him. And his dark mood took a dive into even darker territory, because for the life of him, he couldn't remember saying anything even remotely funny.

'Um, boss, I think you've made it pretty clear. If I don't perform, I'll be moving on.'

'Yeah,' he said. 'Right.' He harrumphed into silence. He sure hoped she understood, because that'd make it easier when he had to let her go. Which he'd inevitably have to do, nothing surer.

And meanwhile, he better put some feelers out for a few extra pickers.

LUCY SAT BACK in her seat, still smiling. It was hard not to smile. She had the sun overhead, the wind in her hair, and Mr Grumpy alongside her looking grumpier by the minute.

What was eating him? She'd cope with the work. She always had. She'd never picked cherries before, but she'd picked oranges in California and she'd have fun proving that she could pick cherries too. Meanwhile she would sit back in her little black leather seat and enjoy the ride. The little car hugged the road, low and tight, zipping in between the other traffic while the four-wheel drives towered over them. After being so high up in the truck's cab, it was disconcerting. Especially when they zipped past a bus and the heads craning down to watch them were all so high up.

'We sure are low down.'

His eyes flicked her way for a moment.

'You're more used to hitching rides with truckies, I gather.'

She looked at him. 'Who says I am?'

'I saw you getting dropped off at the intersection back there.'

She shrugged. 'Trucks. Cars. Whatever's on offer. I don't mind hitching.'

'Bit of a risk, though.'

'Do I look that dangerous to you?'

He snorted. He wasn't touching that one with a barge-pole. 'Come on Lucy, I'm serious. You could get picked up by anyone, surely you know that. I saw the guy who dropped you off across from the servo. He looked pretty rough. He had tatts all up and down his arm for a start.'

'Hey, I've got ink.'

His jaw might have been set in concrete. 'I saw.'

'Is that a problem for you?'

'I just don't see why anyone in their right mind would want to go messing with their skin that way.'

'It's actually just a form of expression, like singing or dancing, you know.'

'A permanent form of expression.'

'What's wrong with permanent?'

'Nothing. If it's been well thought out and planned. Not some spur of the moment decision that you're going to regret for the rest of your life.'

'I don't regret getting mine.'

'Maybe not now.'

She saw the design in her mind's eye. Felt the kick of pain as she remembered. 'I'm never going to regret getting it.' And then she sniffed and looked away. 'Anyway, I'll have you know Mick Jasper was an absolute gentleman.'

'Who?'

'The truck driver.'

He guffawed.

'So he's a six foot two, three hundred pound giant with a few tatts and a big beard. He's got a heart of gold.'

'You could tell that, I guess, from sitting next to him.'

'I sat next to him for about nine hours. He picked me up in Melbourne.'

'You drove all that way with a complete stranger?'

'He was hardly a stranger by the time we got here. He's got a two year old daughter and a baby son expected within the month, and he couldn't wait to get home to the wife he just happens to be madly in love with.'

Dan grunted. 'So maybe you got lucky. It's still a foolhardy thing to do though.'

She swivelled as far sideways as her tiny seat allowed. 'Are you always this uptight?'

'What?'

'Uptight. You know, straitlaced. Conservative.'

'I know what it means. Who says I'm conservative?'

'Are you kidding me?' She started counting on her fingers. 'It's risky to hitchhike. You don't like tattoos. What else are you opposed to? Saving dolphins and whales?'

He turned his head and she saw his eyes zero in on her nose before snapping his attention back to the road.

'Ah, of course. You wouldn't be much of a piercing fan either, I take it.'

Alongside her he sniffed, changing gears as he scooted around a car waiting to turn right. 'Ears are fine.'

'As in, pierced ears, you mean?'

'Yeah. Nothing wrong with pierced ears.'

She made a point of checking his ears. 'But yours aren't.'

'Well, hell no, of course they're not.'

She sat back in her seat. 'Ha, like I said, conservative.'

'Hey, so I'm not a fan of doing anything foolhardy. Is that some sort of crime?'

'Foolhardy?' She laughed. 'That's the second time you've used that word. How old are you exactly?'

Dan bristled. Normally a reference to his age wouldn't faze him, but he was still stinging from the birthday party from hell. He didn't need a reminder. 'What's my age got to do with anything?'

'Because you sound like you're ninety.'

'Do you want this job?'

'Of course I do.'

'Then you might actually try not to piss me off before we even get there.'

O-kay, so maybe he had a point. He was going to be her boss, after all. Just a pity he had no sense of humour.

She crossed her arms and sat back in her seat, content to watch the passing parade of businesses and shops and gum trees that lined the road, as the range of hills before them loomed ever closer. Until all of a sudden, the hills weren't in front of them anymore, and the road led into a valley that disappeared into the range.

They could have been in another world. Gone were the suburbs and the crisscrossing streets while all around was green and calm as the road followed a snaking waterway deeper and deeper into the cleft between the hills, trees towering high over the road on either side, their canopies tangling overhead in places so it felt they were traveling through a tunnel lit with dappled sunlight. The air was cooler here. Sweeter.

Deeper into the valley, the walls opened up and she could see orchards marching up the steep hillsides. They passed a couple of places that had signs out advertising cherry sales, and she half wondered if he was going to pull into one of the driveways, but he didn't stop. The Spitfire clung tightly around a hairpin bend, before the road rose steeply up the side of the hill, leaving the valley floor. Soon the whole valley spread below them, the slopes glowing red as the sun slipped lower in the sky.

Lucy was blown away. For all her travels, for all the wondrous places and sights she'd been and seen, never had she expected so much beauty here so close to a city, a city that hadn't even been on her radar a scant twelve hours ago.

'Wow. It's gorgeous!'

'If you look back over your shoulder at this next bend, you'll get an even better view over the city to the sea.'

She looked at him, surprised because she hadn't realised she'd spoken out loud – even more surprised because he didn't sound grumpy anymore. He almost sounded like a tour guide, like he was proud of where he lived.

But she couldn't let her gaze linger on his profile for long. She was keen to see a view that extended from the hills to the ocean, and instantly she was rewarded by the sight of the setting sun, molten at the edges and dipping into a now rose coloured sea. All that was missing was the sound of steam hissing from the union of water and fire.

'Magic' she murmured, the sun and the sea and the orchards clinging to the steep hillsides all painted in a gold and red wash.

And then they were at the top of the hill, marked by a hotel aptly called, The Scenic, before he steered the little car down a road heading down into another green valley with another tree-lined ridge beyond. It was a world away from Melbourne's cosmopolitan cafe society, and a world she'd never expected to find here.

'How long have you lived up here?' she asked.

'All my life.'

'What, all of it?'

'Yep.'

You've never lived anywhere else?'

'Nope.'

'Doesn't that get boring?'

'Did that sunset look boring?'

Well, okay, maybe he had a point. But still. 'I couldn't do that. Hang around in one place forever.'

'Why not?'

She shrugged. 'I'm not built that way. I get bored and I have to move on. It's what I've always done.'

He glanced over at her. 'Must be nice not to have responsibilities.'

'Yeah,' she said, deciding that the censure in his voice was totally envy-based and feeling not the least bit apologetic for it. 'It is.'

She was still looking at him when he braked suddenly, the

tyres squealing a protest. 'What's wrong?' she said, bracing herself with a hand on the dash, and then looking back at the road as she caught her breath.

He nodded. 'That.'

In the fading light she noticed something waddling down the middle of the road, something furry and grey with a big butt. She peered closer. 'What is that?'

Just then it stopped and plonked itself down on that big butt and turned a brown and grey fluffy eared face to look at them. 'Oh my god,' she said, reaching for her phone. 'It's a koala bear! It's adorable.'

'It's not a bear and it's a bloody nuisance, that's what it is.' He checked his rear-vision mirror and put on his hazard lights on before climbing out. 'Go on fella,' he said, leaning down and scooping his arms through the air to shoo it away. 'Get off the road, you silly bugger, before you get yourself cleaned up.'

The koala looked up at Dan as if to say he'd sit wherever he liked. Lucy shoved her phone at him.

'Can you take a picture of me with it?'

Dan looked around, exasperated. 'For God's sake, what are you doing out of the car? We're in the middle of the road here.'

'*You're* out of the car.'

'Only because that daft koala is almost as big as the car.' The daft koala that was holding its ground and refusing to budge. 'What did you expect me to do – hit the damned thing?'

'Of course not. How could you do that? It's so cute. Can I pet it?'

'No! Have you seen those claws?'

'But it's so cute.' She made a move towards it and the koala did the sensible thing and was up on all four paws and loping for the scrub on the side of the road. With a bit of effort, he scrabbled up the hill and disappeared into the bush.

'Wow, that's so cool. Did you see its fluffy ears? And that big black nose!'

'Get in the car Lucy.'

'Did you see?'

'Yes, I saw it, and if you hang around here any length of time, you'll see it enough times that you'll soon get over it.'

'Never,' she said, shaking her head. 'I'd never get over that. That's so cool!'

'What happened to the easily bored girl?' he asked, back to grumpy as he climbed back into the car.

'So she makes exceptions for cute,' she said as she climbed in beside him.

He grunted as he checked his mirrors before turning off his hazard lights and moving again. 'Now there's a life plan if ever I heard one.'

She laughed. Curse her.

'What's so funny?' he said, jamming the car into first.

'You are. What's your other car – the one you drive when you're doing orchard type business?'

'What?'

'Just answer the question.'

'A Subaru ute. You know, with the tray at the back,' he added, when he saw her frown.

'Really? A pick-up. Oh, okay.'

He knew he shouldn't ask. He damned well knew it. But still, he had to. 'Why the really?'

'I just figured you'd drive something sensible. Y'know, like a Volvo.'

He sighed. No need to ask her why she'd figured that. The

next time he got the urge to ask her something, he bloody well wouldn't. And no way was he about to admit that he actually liked Volvos. 'Yeah, well, maybe you shouldn't judge a book by its cover.'

She tossed her head and cocked an eyebrow at him as she smiled, all white teeth and sun-kissed good looks and he felt the impact of it all the way down to his toes and back up to a throat that suddenly felt like it needed clearing.

'Yeah,' she said, 'maybe you shouldn't.'

And Dan wasn't entirely sure he'd won that skirmish.

CHAPTER 4

They pulled into a driveway lined with enormous camellia and rhododendron trees in full bloom over a sub storey of leafy agapanthus putting up flower spears, stopping outside a rambling stone bungalow, and there, on the ridge behind, Lucy saw them – a line of pencil pines pointing into the fading sky. She felt a sudden sizzle down her spine. There was nothing unusual about the trees – surely nothing more than a little taste of Italy in the Adelaide Hills – but the stone house and the pines, they just reminded her of . . . something.

'Here we are.'

Lucy said nothing. She was too busy chasing a blurred memory around her head, a feeling of warmth coursing through her heart. The memory was fuzzy and indistinct at the edges, but there was a kernel inside, a glimpse of an old woman, white-haired and dressed all in black, and a line of pointed trees from some place, a long, long time ago.

She tried to hang on to the memory, to fix it in her mind so that she could pin it down, build upon it and explore further, but the image flitted and faded, leaving only a tantalising feeling of something warm and comforting – and then only emptiness.

'Do you need a hand with the pack?'

Lucy came to with a start. 'N– no.' But Dan already had the trunk open and was hauling out her bag.

'Jeezus, you don't believe in traveling light. What the hell have you got in here?'

'Everything I possess.'

Something clanged as he dropped it down on the concrete driveway. 'Including the kitchen sink, I presume.'

'My wok.'

'Your what?'

'My wok. You know, one of those things that you cook with.' She knocked low down on the pack with her knuckles, making a metallic sound. 'Stir-fry, noodles, curries, you name it – it does them all.'

'You can cook?'

'Don't sound so surprised, boss. I may not be into planning for my long-term future but I'm pretty good at organising the odd meal or two.' She looked back the way they had come. 'And probably just as well too, seeing as I haven't seen a take out joint since we left the suburbs behind.'

'You don't have to call me boss.'

She grinned, her blue eyes glinting. 'You want me to call you Mr Faraday?'

'I am not that old,' he growled. 'Dan'll be fine. Come on, I'll show you the van. It hasn't been used for a while though, so it might need a bit of a tidy up.'

TALK ABOUT AN UNDERSTATEMENT, thought Lucy, when he showed her the trailer on the edge of the orchard. She took a peek inside and out of the ageing relic. 'So where do you attach the horse?' For one fraction of a moment, she almost thought she saw Mr Grumpy's lips twitch, before he disappeared to fetch fresh sheets and towels.

An hour later, after she'd cleared out most of the spider webs and accumulated dust from the ancient caravan and brightened it up with a few mementoes of her travels, she stood in the open doorway and took a moment to admire her surroundings. In the light of the moon, the cherry trees stood in their regimented rows, their dark leaves rippling in the warm night air, their branches heavy with the plump ripening fruit. And there, on that back ridge, stood that beguiling row of pines that reminded her of – *something*. She stared at their silhouettes a while, before she gave up wondering, and flopped onto the narrow bed instead. She'd have to do something about the ceiling, she figured, as she surveyed the yellowing strips of nylon lining dangling from it and swaying in the gentle breeze. But later. For now, the door and all the windows were open and the musty smell was finally starting to clear. She'd soon have the place looking and feeling like home. . .

Home.

There was a concept. She couldn't remember ever having anything resembling a proper home. Her mom had always been on the move, and Lucy with her, until she'd grown old enough to decide for herself where she was next going. She'd lost count of the number of schools she'd attended; of how many sofas she'd bunked down on. Lost count of how many friends she'd made, only to lose them in the churn of new locations and new beginnings.

She was a drifter, just like her mom. Like a gypsy, it was in her blood. Part of her DNA.

And now, here she was, a drifter in her trailer - or caravan. What could be more fitting?

A loud rap on the side of the trailer broke into her thoughts.

Dan poked his head in the open door and leaned his arm up against the doorjamb. 'Fancy something to eat?'

Lucy raised herself onto her elbows.

'You mean not only do you do five-star accommodation, you do room service too?'

He grimaced. But only, she noticed, once he'd managed to drag his eyes away from the region of her breasts. 'Hardly,' he said, his voice going down an octave and his eyes now fixed firmly on a spot on the wall behind her. 'But there's some paperwork you need to fill out and there's curry – you mentioned you like curry. Interested?'

Lucy's stomach chose that precise moment to rumble. Loudly.

He nodded and shuffled his feet, like he was anxious to get out of there. 'I'll take that as a yes. See you up at the house in a couple of minutes, then.'

'Sure,' she said, although he beat such a hasty retreat, she wasn't sure he'd even heard her. She lay there a few seconds, confused about what to make of her new employer. He'd made it pretty clear that he didn't think much of her or her life choices, and he still hadn't smiled, but he was kind to furry animals and he drove a cute car and he sure looked good in faded denim. And the way he'd been looking at her and the way her skin had prickled – well, he was a man, no two ways about it.

And now, to top it all off, he'd offered to share his dinner with her.

Maybe Mrs Faraday had suggested it. That would make more sense. Because there was bound to be a Mrs Faraday, and no doubt a clutch of little Faradays into the deal – one of whom was no doubt happy to be reunited with his balloon. Lucy probably shouldn't be thinking about her boss's assets when he was most likely a happily married man. No wonder he'd looked guilty.

She pushed herself to her feet, smiling as she dusted off her jeans and changed into a fresh tank top.

She could just about picture those little Faradays. There'd be at least four of them, all mini-Dans, aged around eight going on forty, and dressed in matching jeans and checked shirts with not a piercing or tattoo between them.

Oh yeah, she though with a grin. That could explain why he never smiled.

DAN GOT BACK to the house and all but hurled the packet of curry in the microwave, hitting the buttons to send it spinning. He wasn't exactly sure why he felt the need to slam the microwave door so hard or punch the buttons quite so deliberately, but it sure felt therapeutic all the same.

No, he bloody well did know. It was Lucy. It was bad enough that he'd turned up and found her lying on her bed, but then she'd done that thing where she'd raised herself up on her elbows and thrust those damned breasts northwards, and then her singlet had pulled east west and it was a wonder he'd been able to remember why he was there, let alone unglue his tongue from the roof of his mouth long enough to invite her over to share dinner.

And what had that even been about?

On the odd occasion when pickers had stayed in the van, he'd never felt the need to invite them over for dinner on the pretext of filling in a few forms. What was it about her?

Well, aside from those breasts.

And that waist.

And that California girl smile.

Yeah, aside from all that.

He sighed and walked over to the black box that he'd done his best to ignore up till now. So he'd worked out a list of requirements – what was he actually doing about finding himself someone to share his life with?

Absolutely nothing.

And if he was starting to lust after the hired help, maybe it was time to be a bit more proactive. Maybe it was time he checked this dating website out.

But that would be like admitting he was a failure, surely? If he checked it out, he'd be saying his sisters were right, that he'd never find a woman on his own. And did he want them being right about that?

No.

He put the box down. Lucy was cute, sure, but the novelty would soon wear off and he'd get used to having her around.

He wasn't that desperate, was he?

THERE WAS NO MRS FARADAY, as it turned out. No clutch of mini-Dans in jeans and checked shirts. Instead there was just Dan and her and the smiley helium balloon tied to a chair at the big table in a large open plan kitchen-dining area made of glass and timber, with slate on the floor and a serve of – well, a serve of something distinctly nondescript in front of her.

'Um – what do you call this, boss?' She prodded at the soft grey bits with her fork, pushing them around her plate and testing the consistency of the pale sauce in which they were submerged.

'What's wrong?' he asked between mouthfuls as he stood and swivelled over to the sink for the empty packaging, giving her another eyeful of faded well-fitting jeans. Even if the food wasn't exactly to her taste, she could hardly complain about the views. And given there was no Mrs Faraday, she didn't have to feel guilty about enjoying them . . .

He swivelled back and she almost got her eyes back to his in time. He scowled. 'I thought you'd like it, seeing how you said you're into Asian food and all that.'

She took the box from him. 'Mild Thai Style Chicken Curry,' she read unconvincingly, surveying the professionally photographed and attractively presented 'serving suggestion'. She looked from the picture on the box to her plate then back at the box before looking up at him.

'Are you sure this came out of that box?'

He put his fork down. 'You don't like it.'

'Gosh no!' she said, before adding a big fat lie. 'It's great, really it is.' And it was great that he'd offered to share his food, even if it was just about inedible.

She toyed with the lumps on her plate, watching the trail they left as she pushed them through the sauce. It was hardly his fault if this was his idea of curry. At least she could eat the rice. That didn't look too challenging. And maybe she'd change the subject into the deal.

'So tell me what I need to know about your cherries.' She deposited a forkful of rice into her mouth. Apparently satisfied that she was going to eat at least something, he took a deep breath and picked up his own fork again.

'All right. So the season runs for the next six to eight weeks so we could be done by Christmas or the new year, depending on the weather. We pick from six in the morning and when it gets too hot in the afternoon, we move into the shed and help with the grading. I've got a couple of locals who won't climb ladders but they're great cherry graders, so they'll start sorting and packing as soon as the first buckets of cherries come in, but they'll need help in the afternoon.'

'It sounds pretty intense.'

'It is. I've got a few different cherry varieties in the orchard and each one ripens at a different time. The Violas are picking now, then there'll be the Merchants, with the Stellas and then the

Lapins coming on in the lead up to Christmas. They're big black glossy ones and are our best sellers.'

'And you have to pick them fast before they burn in the sun?'

'Well, we want to get them in and to market as soon as they ripen. The weather's more of a problem if there are storms and heavy rain or hail. It's complicated this year because I bought an

adjoining property a couple of years back and after the trees there had been neglected for so long, they're still a bit of an unknown quantity. They're Bings, a bit of an old fashioned variety now, at least in these parts, but they're big and sweet and more susceptible to splitting if the weather turns.'

'And split fruit is no good, I take it.'

'Nope, other than for cattle feed.'

'Okay,' she said, finished with her rice and putting down her fork. 'Well, I for one can't wait to get started.'

Dan scooped the last of his curry and rice into his mouth.

'Do you want some more?' he offered, reaching for the leftovers.

Lucy held up her hand. She was already contemplating a certain block of chocolate she knew she had hidden away in her pack.

'Couldn't fit another thing in,' she lied. By sheer force of will she managed to keep a straight face.

He didn't try to argue with her, just loaded up his plate and launched into it with gusto. He was obviously a man with a healthy appetite. How he could be satisfied with TV dinners was anyone's guess.

'Coffee?' he asked a few moments later when he'd emptied his plate.

Lucy nodded. It would save her fiddling with the little gas stove in the trailer tonight. 'Sure.'

He rose to put on the kettle, inadvertently giving Lucy another chance to check out the great view from the rear. It wasn't like she was perving, but he sure made it hard not to notice.

She shook her head. It was the weirdest thing. He was so uptight and conservative and so completely not her type, and yet there was something about him that made all that seem irrelevant.

Well-fitting denim and great buns clearly had a lot to answer for.

Though to be fair, the checked shirt hugging his torso was doing its fair share of the work. There was nothing wrong with broad shoulders and a tightly packed waist. Nothing wrong at all.

'Maybe you should taste -' He looked over his shoulder and stopped mid-sentence as he caught her checking out his assets. His eyes narrowed. His words dried up.

She cocked one eyebrow and grinned, because she figured she'd only look guilty if she looked away – and she wasn't a bit guilty, not when she was pretty sure he'd been checking her out in the van.

He looked flummoxed, and she'd swear there was colour creeping into up his neck and into his cheeks. It was kind of cute.

'Do I want to taste - what?' she prompted, unable to keep the tease from her voice.

'Oh, just – ah . . . Stay there a moment. Be right back.'

And then he rubbed his hands on the back of his jeans and was gone, the screen door slamming behind him, leaving her wondering if she'd scared him off. Surely he wasn't that shy. The phone started ringing in the hallway a couple of seconds later. She glanced at the receiver, then looked at the screen door and figured that if he'd been neighbourly enough to offer her dinner, the least she could do was return the favour and answer it.

She picked up the handset. 'Hey.'

There was silence at the end of the line. And then, 'Hello?' and the long wait had Lucy rethinking Dan's relationship status. If he didn't have a wife, maybe there was a girlfriend.

Awkward.

'Hey, sorry. Were you after Dan? Only he had to pop out a minute. He'll be right back.'

'Um, yeah. But –'

The screen door squeaked open and closed again. 'Lucy?'

She waved him over, covering the receiver with her hand. 'It's for you.'

He put the bucket he was carrying on the table before heading her way. 'You don't say,' said as he took the phone. 'Hello?'

'DAN?' Damn. He could hear Beth's need-to-know gene kicking in right there. Without a doubt, there would be questions. 'Who's the woman?'

Yep, right on cue.

He turned sent a scowl in Lucy's direction. She grinned back and he felt his scowl deepen. What was this thing she had with smiling? Surely it wasn't normal to be so cheerful. He turned his back to her, then remembered that strange look on Lucy's face when he'd turned and caught her looking at him while he'd been standing at the sink, and decided it was better to swivel back around and keep an eye on her.

'Is there something I can do for you, Beth?'

'Yeah, you can answer my question. Who's the woman?'

'I've got Siena's balloon, yeah. I forgot to give it to her when I dropped her home.' He looked over to the chair where he'd tied it and frowned. It was still smiling but it had lost a good ten inches of height since he'd brought it inside. The helium must be leaking out already.

'Are you mad? What balloon? Don't change the subject. Who's the woman?'

'She's not a woman,' he said, looking at her now, all blonde, blue eyed innocence. If she had wings, she wouldn't have looked out of place on top of a Christmas tree. 'She's a picker.'

Across the room Lucy raised her eyebrows, her grin widening.

'She sure sounds like a woman. And she answered your phone. What's going on up there?'

'Nothing's going on. Actually Beth, I'm kind of busy right now but I'll call you back later.'

'Dan!' He heard her call as he put the phone down. He felt a bit guilty about it but he wasn't interested in playing twenty questions with one of his sisters right now, especially with Lucy in earshot.

'Sorry if I got you into trouble with your girlfriend.'

'What? Oh, she's not my girlfriend,' he said, rubbing the back of his neck as he headed back to the table. 'She's my sister. Or one of them.'

'Well that's lucky, I guess.'

He grunted. He wasn't sure a girlfriend or even a wife could give him any more grief than his sisters were capable of dishing out. Then again, he was hardly in a position to know.

'How many sisters have you got?'

'Three.'

'Older or younger?'

'Younger, not that that stops them thinking they can boss me around.'

She laughed. 'Sounds like fun. I don't have family. Well, there's my mom, but she was somewhere in Spain last time I caught up with her.'

'So there's just you?'

'Yep. Footloose and fancy free, that's me.'

'Half your luck,' he said, though he didn't really mean it. They drove him mad at times, but he couldn't imagine life without his family. 'Check these out,' he said, pushing the bucket in her direction. 'This is what you'll be picking tomorrow.'

'Wow.' Lucy picked up a cluster of three fat dark cherries. 'Are these yours?'

'Yep. Straight off the tree today. Go ahead – try one.'

LUCY POPPED one into her mouth and bit down on the firm fruit, sending a burst of sweet cherry juice over her tongue. She closed her eyes, in heaven as she chewed, savouring the luscious fruit.

'Good?' he asked.

She opened her eyes, spitting the pip into her hand.

'They are the best cherries!' she admitted, and blow her down, she'd almost swear he was smiling. Not that she was distracted enough to stop herself from trying a second cherry. Again she closed her eyes to savour that burst of flavour.

'That's what I reckon, too. I'm donating a couple of boxes to charity at the cherry auction they're running at the pub this week. All going well, we'll come away with a fistful of orders.'

The second pip joined the first in the palm of her hand.

'Well, you've convinced me.' She plucked the third cherry from its stem and put it to his lips. 'Here, you have one, I hate to eat alone.'

He blinked, and for a moment she thought he was going to push her hand away, but then he parted his lips and took the fruit, his brown eyes intent on her lips, his lips grazing her fingers. It was only the briefest of touches, but she felt the tingle all the way down her arm until it found a home in her breasts, making them tight.

Interesting.

Because she hadn't meant anything by the action. She hadn't been trying to flirt. She was just being herself. Lucy.

But there it was. Spark, pure and simple. And coming from the most unlikely of men.

So yeah, interesting.

THERE WAS cherry juice on her bottom lip. She either didn't realise or didn't care because she was too busy looking up at him, but the red juice was like a flag, an imperfection on an otherwise flawless face – an invitation – and his fingers itched to reach out and wipe it away.

Weird. Never before had he thought of eating cherries as erotically charged, but this woman made it so. She'd popped that cherry in her mouth and her face had lit up like a Christmas tree and he'd felt a surge to the groin as all his blood headed south.

It stirred there now while he watched her mouth and that juice was still there and he knew it would taste sweet and he was just about to reach out and wipe it away when the tight focus of his gaze panned out and the stud in her nose glinted at him and he blinked and thought, no, not the only imperfection.

He spun away, berating himself for coming so close to doing something so utterly foolish as touching her. She was an employee. A picker who'd blow out of here at the end of cherry season just as easily as she'd blown in – if she even lasted that long. He must be mad.

What he needed was a wife.

Not a blonde haired, blue-eyed distraction.

He spat the cherry pip down into his hand, opened a cupboard door under the sink and slung it into the bin drawer inside before turning, leaning back against the benchtop with his arms folded on his chest.

Nonchalant, he told himself, aim for nonchalant. Like you weren't just looking at her parted cherry stained lips with anything more than a passing interest. 'So yeah,' he said, coughing a little to clear the frog from his throat. 'That's our cherries. They're good. So, you've got your paperwork. Is there anything else you need before we say goodnight.'

Her head tilted over to one side, her lips curved into a smile. 'Well, there was that cup of coffee you offered me.'

Damn. 'Sorry,' he said, mentally kicking himself as he headed for the kettle. 'I forgot.'

'That's okay. It's funny how your mind plays tricks on you when you get older.'

He scoffed. 'I'm not that old.'

She nodded. 'Sure, you're not.'

'I'm not!'

'Hey, I was agreeing with you.'

'No you bloody well weren't,' he said, snapping on the kettle again. He could do coffee. She wouldn't be off the premises quite as quickly as he'd like, but it was only coffee.

'So how do you take it?'

'White,' she said, 'with one.'

The same as him. For some reason he didn't like it that

she took her coffee that way. He wasn't comfortable with the idea of having anything in common with this woman.

'Grab the milk, will you?' he said, barking orders as he spooned coffee and sugar into mugs.

'Sure.' She opened the fridge door. 'Wow, you have cake.' She brought it out and popped a fingertip covered in icing into her mouth – that mouth with the cherry stain – only now her lips were wrapped around her finger as she sucked it clean.

He looked at the ceiling. *Lord give me strength.*

'Was it someone's birthday?'

'Yeah,' he said, willing his blood to go anywhere but there. 'Mine. Couple of days ago. I'd forgotten about it. Help yourself.'

'Really? Wow,' she said, her lips still wrapped around her finger. 'Happy birthday. How many candles?'

' Eighty,' he said gruffly, handing her a mug of coffee, not wanting to be reminded of the candle debacle. 'But who's counting?'

CHAPTER 5

For someone who'd claimed to be full, she'd sure managed to put away an indecent amount of cake. Not that he minded any, there was plenty to spare, but he was relieved when she'd finally gone and the house was his again. Being in her proximity was like having a one hundred watt globe on in every socket in the house, lighting up his neglected libido with it. Only there was no off switch.

Maddening.

But all that light had served to illuminate one fact.

He was *that* desperate.

Lucy hadn't been gone five minutes and he had the computer on, the machine humming and beeping into life. Lust was fine, in its place, but he had no use for it now. Lucy might be drop-dead gorgeous, but she wasn't what he wanted. He needed someone much more grounded. He needed to find himself a sensible, hardworking, practical wife who'd be an asset to the orchard, and the sooner he started doing that, the sooner he'd stop being distracted.

It had been too long, that was all, but if he was going to break the drought, it wasn't going to be with some blow-in.

It would be with someone there was a decent chance of building a relationship with.

He clicked on his email program and waited for his dodgy internet connection to kick in. Mind you, he still had his doubts about this online dating business. It still didn't seem possible – or even right – that it could be that easy to find someone you were going to spend the rest of your life with, but if he was thinking about swiping the cherry juice from a picker's lips, it was probably high time he gave it a try.

His inbox started pinging with messages. Cherry orders from local greengrocers by the looks. He clicked on the first to make a note of the details, and by the time he got to the second, there were a dozen more emails, none of them looking anything remotely like cherry orders.

His eyes bugged at the subject headers:

Welcome Dan Faraday, to HEA.com!

Dan, we've found ten matches for you.

Eight new matches waiting to meet you.

Log in to meet Meredith – today's match of the day!

Whoa, he thought, as he counted up at least two dozen potential matches already according to the subject headers. So many women in Adelaide looking for a partner? This was going to be a piece of cake. One of them was bound to be exactly what he needed. Why had he waited so long to check it out?

He clicked on the welcome email, was asked to log in, and scrabbled for the box, opened it up, found the identity and password his sisters had created.

Username: Dan Faraday
Password: Cherry

. . .

VERY FUNNY, he thought drily, as he plugged in the details and hit enter and the site took him to a page loaded with what looked like the dating equivalent of a smorgasbord. More than a dozen photos of women, from blondes to black-haired and they all looked pretty reasonable, he supposed. There was Donna, aged 32; Carly, 34; Simone, 30; and Debbie, 32. And that was just the first line of page one.

And there in the top left corner was a photo of him. It must have been taken last Christmas at Nan and Pop's because there were decorations and a tree. Someone had taken a snap of him opening his present from the girls, a fancy radio-controlled gyrocopter that he remembered had bounced off the walls and terrified the cat. It was probably the only picture they could find of him where he was washed and clean-shaven. Crikeys. He was almost smiling.

He looked . . . all right, he guessed. Not too shabby if there were all these women waiting to meet him.

He clicked on Donna's picture and learned that she was a librarian who liked going to the movies and line-dancing. Carly was a public servant who liked cats and Debbie was a dental technician who kept fit with Zumba. He blinked – he didn't even know what that was – and went back to Donna to read more. After all, he figured he should start at the beginning and line-dancing sounded half country.

Donna had been burned by love, according to her profile, and she was looking for a lasting relationship with a man who was genuine and affectionate and who had a good sense of humour.

He nodded at the screen. Yup, that sure sounded like him.

There was a big blue button to one side. Message Donna, it said, promising she'd get no more details than his name. He took a deep breath, cracked his knuckles and hit the button.

Hi Donna, he typed with two fingers. Your profile came up in my matches. I thought I'd say hi.

He looked at it. Short, sweet and to the point. He signed his name and hit send. Whoosh.

That was easy.

He stretched his arms up high over his head. Nope, nobody could accuse him of not trying now.

The phone rang again. He regarded it suspiciously. What were the chances that it was Beth again, looking to pump him for information? He really ought to get caller ID. Then again it might be a buyer too, so . . .

Tentatively he picked up the receiver.

'You didn't call me back.'

He picked up a pen and scrawled *Get caller ID!* on the pad under the order he'd noted down.

'Oh sorry, Beth. I forgot,' he lied.

'Like hell. You were avoiding me.'

Imagine that.

'So, about this woman,' his sister said, not beating about the bush.

'What woman?'

'The one who answered the phone last time I called!'

'Oh, you mean the picker.'

'Maybe, but she sure as hell sounded like a woman first and foremost. What's going on over there anyway?'

'Nothing's going on.'

'But you have this woman –'

'This picker.'

'Whatever . . . Where'd you find her?

He sighed. 'If you really must know, I met her at the servo on the way home from dropping off Siena.'

'What do you mean, you met her at the servo? Don't tell me you picked up a hitchhiker? You?'

'Jeez, it wasn't like that. She was looking for work when I went in to pay and so I offered her a job.'

'Just like that? How did you know she was looking for

work? Did she tell you? Was she carrying a placard or something?'

'Look, what do you want – a blow-by-blow description or something?'

'It would help, Dan. It would save me having to use a hammer and chisel to extract the facts.'

'There are no facts worth knowing, that's why you're having trouble. There's nothing to know other than she was looking for a job and I offered her one.'

'Are you kidding me? Just wait till the others hear this.'

'Jeezus, Beth. Why do you need to tell anyone? I found a picker. End of story.'

'Is she as cute as she sounds?'

'Does it matter?'

'Ha! So she is. And you said there's nothing to tell.'

'Beth!'

'It's okay Dan, I'm actually kind of impressed. We tell you to go find a woman and you take matters into your own hands and pick one up on the way home. Gotta say, I like your style. Which room did you give her?'

'I didn't. She's in the van.'

'What? That old wreck?'

'What's wrong with the van?'

'It's a firetrap for starters. Besides, you've got three spare bedrooms in the house, bro, and you stick her out in that fleapit without even a bathroom?'

'She's a backpacker, Beth, she's hardly expecting the Ritz. And she can use the back

bathroom. I don't want anyone in the house.'

'But it's so old, it's an accident waiting to happen. Does the door even lock these days?'

He sighed. 'So I'll make sure she keeps anything valuable in the house safe.'

There was silence on the other end of the line. Dan knew better than to think it was the end of the interrogation.

'So – when do we meet her?'

'Jeezus, Beth, what part of *she's a picker* don't you understand? This isn't a social event, it's a business arrangement.'

'I get that, but if she's a long way from home, it'd be nice to meet her and make her feel welcome, that's all.'

'Lovely. Beth, you stick out the welcome mat if you like. I've got a cherry crop to bring in.' His computer pinged and he glared at the interruption until he read, *Donna messaged you.*

Hello.

His fingers hovered over the mouse, but he wasn't about to click on anything while Beth was on the phone. She'd be wanting to know what that was all about next. 'Anyway sis, it's getting late. What was it you actually called about?'

'I wanted to thank you for picking up Siena.'

'Not a worry. It was good to take Spitty out for a spin.'

'No trouble prising her away?'

'Not with Spitty. You should have seen her come running.'

'Masterful stroke, bro.'

He grinned. 'I do have my moments. I'll catch you later. Tell Siena I'll drop off that balloon some time –' Aw hell, now it was flying at half-mast, its sideways grin more like a leer. '– but it might not be quite as perky as it was.'

'No worries, I don't think she's that bothered. Give my love to your new picker. Hey, what's her name?'

'Why?'

'Just curious.'

'It's Lucy.'

'As in *I Love Lucy*? Cute.'

'Bye, Beth,' he said, rolling his eyes, and hung up, looking at the message notification. With a decisive click of his mouse, he opened it.

. . .

HI DAN. *Nice to hear from you. Your profile looks interesting and you sound like someone I'd like to meet. Sounds like you're up in the hills. I'm in the foothills. Close, LOL!*

HE FROWNED AT THE LOL. She was either very forward or she'd misspelled something. Yeah, much more likely. He got his index fingers busy.

SMALL WORLD.

YEAH, that sounded pretty cool.

I KNOW! Let me know if you'd like to go for a drink sometime. (Easier than typing out a conversation, LOL). Cheers, Donna.

THERE WAS that LOL thing again. But a drink? That was quick. This dating thing sure was a lot easier these days than he remembered. He looked at her profile picture again. She had a dark bob, her hair was almost black, and she was smiling, but with her mouth shut, so he couldn't check her teeth. But her nose was straightish and wasn't brandishing a stud. She was wearing a bright pink blouse over black jeans and boots. A little overweight maybe, but he wasn't that fickle. He had much more important considerations, and she sure looked nice. Homely. And he hit the keyboard again.

. . .

Hi Donna. Just wondering, do you have any tattoos?

No. I'm not really a fan, at least not for me. Why do you ask?

He huffed out a breath and rubbed his hand together. It just got better and better.

No reason. Would love to catch up for that drink.

CHAPTER 6

The next morning, Lucy was up with the birds, literally. There was no way she could have slept in, what with the new day's light streaming into the windows and the chorus of birdcalls coming from the trees outside. How different to hear birds and not the sounds of a city roaring into life.

She stepped outside and stretched her arms up high into air that held the promise of heat, but for now was deliciously cool and sweet. A fine mist lingered in the floor of the valley below, where a willow lined creek appeared as if through a soft focus lens.

Magic, she thought, pausing to enjoy the moment and imprint it on her memory – another slide to add to the picture show of her life – before she headed for the bathroom.

The first of the other pickers arrived at the packing shed around the same time she did, four guys whose eyes bugged when they saw her, their conversation suddenly choked, before one, the tallest and leanest of the group, with dark hair and sharp features, stepped forward and introduced himself as Rod, and the others as Evan, Steve and Sandy.

They collected around her, asking the usual questions: 'Where are you from?' 'How long have you been here?' 'Do you like Australia?'

She answered them all with a smile until the one called Rod worked up to, 'Do you have a boyfriend?' and she laughed, because boys were the same everywhere.

'No,' she said, shaking her head. 'Not at the moment.'

DAN HEADED for the packing shed feeling pretty chipper, which was a bit unusual during cherry season – at least in recent years. But then, he had good reason to feel chipper.

He'd chatted with Donna online for a while last night, though to be fair, she'd done most of the messaging, and his answers were mostly the one liners, but then she could type faster.

In the end they'd agreed to meet for a drink at The Scenic Hotel. Somewhere halfway between them. Neutral territory.

The only fly in the ointment was that she was taking off to Melbourne tomorrow for a three day conference, which meant that they couldn't meet before Thursday night.

Three whole nights from now.

He rubbed the back of his neck. He'd expressed his disappointment, but cautiously. He hadn't wanted to look too keen, but he had a good feeling about Donna. He had a list of questions he'd been working on, and he was confident he was going to get the right answers. She was only the first possibility, of course, but the signs were positive.

And in the unlikely event she didn't work out, there were plenty more like her. Another two emails with even more matches had turned up in his inbox this morning. It shouldn't take too long. He'd soon prove his sisters wrong. Of course, he could find himself a wife.

He heard voices coming from inside the packing shed. Male voices and female laughter.

Lucy.

He reached the door and took one look at his new picker and the posse of boys circling, heard Rod ask if she had a boyfriend, and felt his grump return. He'd known that she'd be a distraction. Oh yeah, they'd all love a girl with a tatt on her shoulder and a stud in her nose who had a vacancy in the boyfriend department.

'Morning all,' he said gruffly, and the boys peeled away from Lucy like the petals of a flower.

No, not a flower, Dan thought a moment later, realising that petals might open up to reveal its stunning centre. This was more like the jaws of a shark opening to reveal its needle sharp teeth. Because he figured a girl like Lucy, who lived her life footloose and fancy free and who thought nothing of accepting rides from any Tom, Dick or Harry, would know how to tear a man limb from limb. These boys would be toast.

'I see you've met Lucy.'

The boys nodded, their eyes unusually bright for this time in the morning. No need to waste time wondering why. Apparently she did that one hundred watt thing wherever she showed up. Today she was wearing some light coloured hiking pants and another of those little singlets that stretched across her chest and made her waist look tiny. It was no wonder they were all tripping over their tongues.

'Right,' he said, looking around. 'Where's Kate?' As if on cue the freckle faced redhead stepped into the shed.

'About time, Carrot Head,' said Rod. The other boys sniggered.

The girl screwed up her nose and glared at him. 'I love you too, Ratface.'

'Settle down, you two,' said Dan, holding up his hands. 'Kate, we've got a new picker on board. This is Lucy.'

'Hey,' said Lucy, with a wave.

'Hi,' said Kate, smiling. 'Nice to have another woman on the team.'

'Who's the other one?' ribbed Rod, looking around.

'Enough!' Kate and Rod were his two most experienced pickers. They were good workers – when they weren't at each other's throats – otherwise he might have asked one or other of them to find work elsewhere by now. 'Grab a bucket, everyone, and let's get going.'

'You want me to show Lucy how to pick cherries?' asked Rod.

And Dan almost said yes, because he had more important things to think about than teaching some newbie how to pick, but then he saw the look in the young man's eyes and thought, Dammit no, discounting Kate as Plan B in the next instant. He needed his best workers to pick. Rod could flirt on his own time. If only Pop was here today he'd put him onto the job, but he was off with Nan getting his eyes checked for his driver's licence.

'No,' he said, half snarling because it was the last thing he needed or wanted to do. 'I'll do it.'

THE PICKERS SPREAD out across a line of trees. 'Did you sleep okay?' Lucy asked, as Dan led her towards a heavily-laden cherry tree.

Don't ask, he reminded himself, just don't go there. 'Yeah.' He looked back over his shoulder, and sure enough, she was doing that smiling thing again. Nope, don't ask.

'I did,' she volunteered anyway, sounding as chirpy as if she'd just enjoyed five-star luxury bedding complete with pillow-soft mattress and comforter, rather than the van's narrow cot. 'I mean, it felt a bit hard at first, but wow, I haven't slept that well for ages.'

'Good,' he said, thinking he could head Beth off at the pass with that little gem next time she suggested the van was somehow inferior accommodation.

'Although it got a bit cold at one stage,' Lucy added. 'I had to pull on a T-shirt.'

Dear God. He closed his eyes, glad she was behind him and couldn't see his reaction. So she slept naked. Or nearly naked. Either way, he did not need that visual stuck in his head.

'I'll dig out a couple of spare blankets,' he said without turning around, his mouth bone-dry, needing to change the subject. He looked around and figured this tree was as good as any. He held down a branch, laden with ripe red fruit. 'Okay, now this is the way to pick cherries.'

'Hey Dan,' someone called and Dan looked around to one of the guys working a few trees away.

'What is it?' he yelled over his shoulder.

'You might want to take a look at this. Not sure if it's cherry slug.'

Dan cursed. 'Stay here,' he said gruffly to Lucy, before he strode away.

LUCY WATCHED HIM GO, all hard wired testosterone on legs. He sure didn't sound like a man who'd slept well. He was growling like a bear with a sore head and Lucy was pretty sure she was a big part of the reason why. It was obvious he felt uncomfortable in her presence. So why was he torturing himself when he clearly didn't want to be in her company? Last night in the kitchen he'd jumped away from her like he'd been struck by lightning.

They'd both felt it – that strange electrical zap that had crackled into life between them. She'd seen it in his eyes as they'd focused on her lips. She'd felt his heat, and his need, and that weird, unexpected magnetic pull between them.

Okay, so it had taken her by surprise too, but in her experience sparks were all too rare. She liked to give them a little oxygen and see if they flared into life.

Whereas he'd done his best to stamp it out.

So he was attracted to her and he didn't like it? Well, that was his problem.

But then why didn't he let Rod or one of the others show her how to pick the precious cherries and save himself the grief? She snorted, remembering his scowls and the fact he seemed incapable of smiling, he seemed to be a man who liked to have something to grumble about.

She looked up into the branches, where the cherries clustered under the deep green leaves like red baubles on a Christmas tree, and pulled out her phone to take some snapshots of the morning light filtering through.

And then, because Dan wasn't back and the cherries were right there and it couldn't be that hard, she figured she might as well start picking. She reached her hand up for a cluster of cherries, had them in the palm of her hand ready to tug, only to have her wrist snared by an iron grip above her head.

'What do you think you're doing?'

She blinked over her shoulder, waiting for her heart to stop racing at the shock. She'd been so absorbed in her thoughts, she hadn't heard him returning. 'I thought I might as well start picking.'

'I told you to wait,' he growled, his voice rumbling deep into her bones. 'Don't you listen?'

His hand still held her wrist, but not so firmly now, and the thunder in his voice had lost its edge. But with him standing so close behind her and with the clean scent of lemon soap over man in close range, her heart was having a hard time slowing down. She liked the roughness of his hand against her skin and the friction that sent tingles down her arm with every tiny movement. She liked the heat of him close to her back and the soft morning breeze that wrapped his scent around her.

'No you didn't,' she argued, her voice sounding breathless, even to her own ears. 'You told me to stay. I stayed.'

'Jeez, Lucy,' he said, scowling as he let go of her wrist and stepped away. 'Do you have to argue the point? I meant wait. Why do you think I need to show you how to pick cherries if you can just be let loose on the orchard?'

She kicked up her chin. 'I've picked fruit before. It's not exactly rocket science.'

He pulled off his hat while he took a deep breath and raked a hand through his hair.

The man had a genetic disposition not to smile. That must be it. He could scowl and he could frown – he had those down pat – but smiling was clearly foreign to him.

But it wasn't his scowl she registered right now, so much as the look of him. Today he wore stone-coloured work pants and a work shirt that had been washed so many times the fabric had lost any stiffness it once had, so that with every movement it shifted and draped softly against his body. The hat, battered and worn, only added to the appeal.

It was rugged and country and she liked it.

She smiled, even though he was still scowling at her, because it was impossible not to smile at him. 'So show me how to pick your cherries, boss.'

He pushed his hat further back on his head and took a deep breath, as if he was priming himself for the task. 'All right.' He lifted a heavily laden branch and pointed out a cluster of cherries under its canopy of leaves. 'The trick is not to damage the tree, and here's why.' He pointed out the nub from which the cherries hung on their stalks. 'This is what we call the fruit spur and its from where the cherries grow. And this bit here – right on the tip here – can you see these tiny buds?'

She peered hard. The buds were no more than tiny bumps, so tiny she wouldn't have noticed them otherwise. 'Oh, yeah. There are what, three – no, four of them.'

'That's them. They're the buds for next year's crop. One of those will be a leaf bud, the other three, fruit. So the trick with picking is to make sure you don't just rip off the cherries because you could snap off that fruit spur, and that would compromise next year's crop.'

'I never knew that.'

'Most people don't. That's why, when you're picking, you need to get your thumb and forefinger right to the top of the stem, and twist, so the cherries come cleanly away without damaging the fragile spur. Like this.'

He had big hands and long fingers topped with neat nails. She'd known that when she'd watched his hands on the steering wheel. She'd been reminded of it when he'd held her wrist and his fingers had wrapped right around. His hands looked too big for such a delicate task, but his fingertips closed around the top of the stems and he deftly twisted off a pair of cherries. 'You see?'

'I think I get it.' Now she could appreciate why he'd stopped her. Now she was glad he had.

'One more time,' he said. His fingers found the top of the stems and she watched and thought about those large, long fingered hands with their rough skin and delicate touch, and she couldn't help it. She tingled all the way from her scalp down her spine.

With a twist, a triplet of cherries came free. He dropped them softly in the bucket. 'Now, your turn.'

'Okay.' Now that she'd had a lesson, she was good with it. She reached her hand up, two cherries cupped in the palm of her hand as she slid her thumb and forefinger up the stem, feeling the point where it met the fruit spur.

She felt his hand surround hers then and she shuddered at his touch. Unexpected again, but not unwelcome. 'A little higher,' he said.

She swallowed, knowing damn well her fingers could go no higher. 'Got it.'

'Okay, now twist. ' And his hand shifted sideways with hers until the cherry stems came clear of the spur.

'Wow,' she said, not necessarily talking about the cherries as these joined the others in the bucket. Because for someone who didn't want to have anything to do with her, he was sure doing a good impression of exactly the opposite. And then, because she was supposed to be thinking about the cherries and not about the boss, she said, 'Thanks for the lesson. Sorry for jumping the gun before.'

'It takes a little time to get up to speed when you've got to get it right. But it's definitely not rocket science.'

She looked over her shoulder at him. Was he laughing at her? He sure didn't look like he was laughing – there was maybe the merest trace of a smirk – but who could tell with this man? And who could tell why he stayed there, watching her pick more, standing so close she could feel his breath fanning the hair above her ear.

'Got it now?'

'Yeah, I think so.'

'Bucket's full, Dan!' Rod called from a nearby tree.

'And mine!' called Kate.

'Slowing up in your old age, Carrot Head.'

'Shut your mouth, Ratface.'

'Give it a rest you two,' yelled Dan, and then said to Lucy, 'I have to get these cherries back to the coolroom. Will you be okay?'

'Sure. I've got it. I'll be fine.'

'I hope so. And you better not get sick of cherries, because you're going to be seeing an awful lot of them.'

'You know me, boss,' she said with a smile, remembering the scene in the kitchen the night before. 'I love cherries.'

DAN DIDN'T WANT to think too much about Lucy loving cherries because it reminded him of last night and Lucy with that damned cherry juice on her lip. But it didn't matter what he wanted, because there was something about her, he mused as he wandered back to the equipment shed to get the quad bike.

Something indefinable.

Something bothersome.

She was maddening and exasperating.

She acted impetuously and challenged his authority.

The way she'd argued with him about whether he'd told her to wait or stay, like she was intent on making him look like he was in the wrong.

Definitely maddening.

Why else would he have held on to her wrist for so long? Because he'd been distracted. He'd forgotten. That was all.

But why couldn't he stay mad with her like he should? Like he wanted to? Instead he found himself wavering between frustration and fascination, trying to forget the smoothness of her skin and the feel of her slim wrist in his hand, and the ever so slightly discombobulating fact that she smelt of sunshine and vanilla.

Definitely exasperating.

Because he didn't want to be fascinated. Thursday night he was having his first date with Donna, and that's what he should be focused on.

That and the orchard and the future.

That's what he should be thinking about, right now.

He started up the quad bike and trailer and headed back to the orchard to start collecting the fruit. Once upon a time they used to leave the cherries in bins under the shade of the trees until they'd finished picking for the day before getting them back for sorting. Nowadays he liked to get the freshly picked fruit through sorting and into the cool room as soon as possible.

Yes, the crop, he thought, making a side note to check how Lucy was going, he should be thinking about the crop.

DAN WAS JUST COMING in from the packing shed and thinking about what there was in the freezer to heat up for dinner when the phone rang. 'How's it going at the orchard?'

'Pop! So how did the eye test go?'

'What? Oh yeah. As well as can be expected for a man my age, I s'pose. But now the doc wants me to have more bloody tests and he's lined them up for tomorrow.' He heard Pop sniff. 'I told him I had a crop to get in – '

'Hey, you are supposed to be retired, you know. Let me worry about the orchard and you concentrate on taking care of you and Nan.'

This time the old man snorted. 'Beth said you've got a new picker. An American lass.'

Of course Beth would have spilled that bit of news. 'Well, yeah.'

'Any good?'

Dan didn't have to think about that too long. He'd kept an

eye on her today, checking out the fruit in her bucket and watching her as she'd graded her first cherries, sorting them for size and imperfections, and he had to admit, she'd done a pretty decent job for someone who'd never worked in the industry before.

He was glad he hadn't made the mistake of touching her again though. He wasn't going there after that first time when he'd forgotten he was even holding her. Thankfully there'd been no need for further instruction, seeing she'd been doing okay.

'Oi, Dan. You still there?'

Dan jerked back to the present. 'She did okay.'

'Pretty girl, according to Beth.'

'Well, I don't know how she knows that, seeing she's never met her.'

'Is she?'

'She's okay, I guess, if you like that sort of thing. I hadn't given it a lot of thought.' *Liar.* 'Pop, I gotta run,' he lied, heading off any more questions. 'Good luck with those tests. Let me know how you get on.'

'OH. MY. GOD. I HATE CHERRIES!'

Lucy collapsed onto her narrow bunk and it felt like paradise. Every part of her hurt like hell. By the end of the day just holding herself upright had been a lesson in endurance.

'I never want to see another cherry in my life.'

Laughter followed her into the van. 'The first two or three days are the worst,' Kate said. 'Then you'll be right into it like the rest of us.' She stuck her head in the door. 'Hey, 'I love what you've done to cheer the place up.'

Lucy had hung a woven shawl on the end wall. There was a scarf she'd found in a market in Paris hanging from a hook, a sequinned cushion she'd found in an Asian street market on the bench seat, and over her bed was an embroidered bedcover she'd bought in Istanbul, turning a bland interior into a splash of bright colours. 'They say home is where you hang your hat,' she said, pushing herself to sitting, her tired muscles protesting all the way. 'I hang my scarves. They help me remember the places I've been'

'They're gorgeous,' Kate said, fingering the scarf. 'It must be so cool to travel all round the world like you do.'

'You don't travel much?'

'I've been to the Gold Coast once. Haven't made it overseas yet.' She pulled a face. 'I'm a bit of a coward. I'd never be brave enough to travel by myself like you do.'

Lucy smiled. 'You'd be fine. It's just what you're used to.' She liked Kate. She had an old-fashioned face with a little snub nose and cupid bow lips, and with her curly red hair, pale skin and curvy body, she reminded Lucy of the women she'd seen in renaissance paintings in the galleries of Europe. The two of them had spent lunch break together, chatting while sitting in the shade of a willow tree by the creek, while the guys had taken off in one of their cars and come back with a feed of steak sandwiches and chips.

She'd even invited Lucy home for dinner.

Which reminded her . . . She jumped up when she remembered the reason Kate had stopped by. She opened a small cupboard where she'd stashed some of her stuff and pulled the old dog-eared and stained books out. 'Here,' she said, passing them to Kate. 'See if these are any use.'

'*Moosewood Cookbook*,' said Kate, flicking through the pages of the first with their handwritten recipes and quirky illustrations. 'Ha, *The Enchanted Broccoli Forest*. Wow, how old are these?'

'Years. They were my mom's – she was a wannabe hippie

until she decided she liked meat too much and passed them on to me.'

'They're fabulous.'

'You can borrow them if you like. Have a look through and copy anything you'd like to try.'

'Seriously? You don't need them?'

'I know most of the recipes I make by heart. Besides, I cook a lot of stir-fries these days – so if you know a good Asian market, I need to get a few supplies. The cupboard is seriously bare.'

'Hey, I'll take you into the Central Market sometime after work if you like. It's right next to Chinatown. It'll be the best place for anything you need.'

'After work? Will there be time?'

'Sure. How about Friday? The market closes late that day so we'll have more time. But you'll owe me a meal – all right?'

Lucy nodded. 'You got it.' She flexed her arms. 'God, I hope you're right about getting used to this,' she said. 'Dan would be so happy to have an excuse to get rid of me.'

'No way.'

'Oh yeah. He warned me plenty that if I couldn't pull my weight, I'd be out of a job.'

'Really? That doesn't sound like Dan.'

Lucy cocked an eyebrow. 'Are we talking about the same Dan? The scowling, grumpy Dan? I mean, does the man ever smile?'

'Well, surely he must.'

'Have you ever seen him?'

Kate chewed her lip as she thought about it. 'Actually, now that you mention it . . . But then I usually only see him around picking time, and the last couple of seasons were a bit grim. I guess he's got a lot riding on this season.'

'I guess.'

'Besides, even if he does have a good year, he's probably a bit worried about what's going to happen with the orchard.'

'Why? What's going to happen?'

'Well, the Faradays were some of the earliest settlers around here and the orchard's been in the family for four generations, but Dan's the end of the line. None of his sisters are keen on following him into the orchard business and if he doesn't hurry up and have kids to pass the orchard down to, he'll eventually end up having to sell it. It'd be the end of an era.'

'He's not that old, surely?'

'He's thirty-seven!' Kate said, as if that was way over the hill. 'That's nearly twice my age. Not that he's bad looking for it exactly.'

Lucy laughed, but Kate was right about one thing; Dan didn't look bad for his age. The weathering of his features and the lines around his eyes just added to the appeal. Why should she be the only one to notice?

'Anyway, Dan's sisters gave him a subscription to an online dating agency for his birthday because they're worried he'll never get married and have kids if they don't help out.'

'Seriously?' Lucy gave a very unladylike snort. 'How do you even know all this?'

'Mum got it from Sophie, Dan's sister. Mum works in the local post office a couple of days a week and Sophie dropped in to pick the school stuff and they got chatting. Mum knows everything that goes on around here.'

'Handy,' Lucy said, though she was only half listening. She was too busy thinking about that spark she'd felt last night, the rasp of the pads of his fingers against her skin and how her scalp had tingled where his breath had fanned her hair today in the orchard. Pity, she thought, because here was a man in search of a wife. This was one spark going nowhere fast. Then again, it had been the most unlikely of sparks.

'You ever use a dating agency?' she asked Kate.

'Nope, though I've thought about giving it a try.'

'Yeah? You haven't got a boyfriend?'

'Nah. But I don't want to wait till I'm thirty-seven to start looking. I want at least four kids.'

'Four!'

'Sure. I'm one of six. I like big families. You going to have a family one day? Do the whole husband-kid thing?'

Lucy shook her head as an old familiar pain stuck her like a knife and twisted hard. Once upon a time she'd almost thought it possible, but . . . 'No,' she said, forcing a smile. 'Not for me, I'm afraid. I'm the love 'em and leave 'em kind. Anyway, what's this thing between you and Rod, then?'

Kate screwed up her face. 'Me and Ratface? Nothing. He's just a dickhead.'

'That's all?'

Kate shrugged and picked up the cushion off the bench, sliding the palm of her hand over the sequins. 'We went to school together and he was always a pain in the arse then. He's still a pain now. Anyway,' she said, putting the cushion back on the seat as she stood, 'thanks for the cookbooks but I better get home and freshen up before tea. I'll come pick you up around six.'

A SHOWER HAD NEVER FELT SO good. Lucy stood under the hot stream, luxuriating in the pounding massage on her aching shoulders and neck. Despite her stiffness, she liked the return to more physical work. It was good to work outside, and she'd done okay too, if the comments from the other pickers were any indication. Although Dan had just grunted each time she'd filled a bucket.

Dan, whose fingers had lingered over hers far too long to be accidental.

Dan, who was apparently looking for a wife.

She snapped off the taps. That thought was like a bucket of cold water right there. There was no point dwelling on Dan. He was her boss. He might be cute and he might think the same about her, but if he was looking for a wife, all the spark in the world was going to get them nowhere. Because she was definitely not in the market for a husband.

KATE'S FAMILY lived less than ten minutes away in a cute little log cabin overlooking the next valley. The cottage featured flower pots hanging by the front door and a driveway that circled a colourful rose garden, but it was to the view to which Lucy's eyes were drawn as she stepped from the car. Like the valley they'd just left, the hillsides here were a patchwork of eucalypts and orchards, but this time interspersed with grapevines marching in straight rows up the hill, the bright green of their leaves a contrast against the grey-green of the native foliage. The late after-noon air in the valley was warm and dry, the sky above an expanse of clear blue, and everything was crystal clear with not a hint of smog. Lucy drank it all in, marveling at the fates that had brought her to a place that had never before been on her radar but was now delighting her with every turn.

'You coming in?'

Lucy looked over her shoulder to see her new friend waiting, a quizzical expression on her face.

'You know, you're real lucky, living in a place like this.'

Kate frowned and looked around as if seeking to find whatever secret Lucy had stumbled upon, before shrugging.

'It's okay, I guess,' she said, 'if you don't mind living a million miles from civilisation.

That was the thing, thought Lucy, as she followed Kate into the house. You could be a million miles away here, and yet the city was just down the hill. 'Mum?' called Kate, leading the way into the pretty cottage style kitchen where a woman in an apron was sticking a skewer into something in a pot on the stove. 'This is Lucy. Lucy, Mum.'

There was no question the woman was Kate's mother. A couple of decades on and with a few more curves maybe, but the resemblance was unmistakable. Like Kate, Lucy liked her at first sight.

'Pleased to meet you, ma'am,' Lucy, raising one hand in greeting. 'Thanks for having me over tonight.'

'No trouble. Always room for one more. And please, call me Heather.' She looked at the books in Kate's arms. 'What's that you've got there?'

'Cookbooks,' said Kate, holding them up. 'Vegetarian ones. Lucy lent them to me. I thought I'd try out a few recipes without meat for a change.'

'Vegetarian?' She squinted closer at the covers, looking sceptical. 'Well, I don't know how your brothers are going to react to that.'

'They can like it or lump it,' declared Kate, peering over her mum's shoulder. 'What are we having anyway?' Kate asked, peeking over her mum's shoulder.

'Sausages and mash.'

'Seriously? Is that it?'

'Of course not. There's carrots and peas too.'

'Oh, sorry Lucy. You see why I need these books?'

'Hey, don't be sorry. I'm easy.'

'Why should you be sorry?' said Heather, draining a pot, sounding aggrieved.

'Because Lucy's a really good cook - she's got a wok and

makes her own curries and everything - and I was hoping maybe tonight we might be having something a bit more special.'

'Honestly, it's not a problem, I love mashed potato with anything. Frankly, any meal I don't have to prepare myself is special.' *Especially if it didn't come out of a box.*

'You see?' said Heather with a grateful smile in Lucy's direction, 'Now stop making such a fuss and set the table while I mash the spuds. Lucy, how about you butter some bread. The boys will be in soon.'

The boys were in soon. Five strapping boys aged from ten to nineteen who took one look at Lucy and turned collectively mute if you didn't count the ten-year-old who giggled every time Lucy opened her mouth. Kate's dad arrived hot on their heels and greeted Lucy like a long-lost friend and reminded the boys to wash up.

A few minutes later they were all sitting around the big table, the boys diving for buttered bread to wrap up their sausages. 'So how are you finding the orchard work so far?' asked Heather.

'I like it' said Lucy. 'I was waiting tables in Melbourne, so it's a nice change to work outdoors. I'm a bit sore after my first day, but I'll get used to it.' She looked around. 'Excuse me, can someone please pass the ketchup?'

The ten-year-old giggled and his closest brother gave him a clip around the ear while another brother passed the tomato sauce down the table.

'So Dan's looking after you?'

'Everyone's really nice,' she said, not wanting to single Dan out as she squeezed ketchup onto her hotdog. 'The team he's got is really good.'

'And the boys aren't giving you any grief? Kate always complaining about that Rod Grainger.'

'I dunno why, he's kind of funny.'

'He's a pain, more like it,' said Kate.

'Yeah? I just think he likes you.'

'What?' Kate went bright red and snorted that possibility away. 'No way!'

The ten-year-old dissolved into fits of giggles at that and his dad told him to stick a sock in it.

Lucy smiled on a shrug. 'Okay. So maybe I read that wrong.'

'You sure did,' agreed Kate who glared her little brother into submission.

Heather shook her head as she squeezed sauce onto her mashed potatoes. 'You have to feel for Dan. He's got Clarry, his Pop, of course, but Dan hasn't had an easy road, what with his mum dying when he was just a toddler.'

'Oh?'

She shook her head. 'So sad it was. And then his dad remarried and what are the chances, three sisters. Lovely girls and all clever in their own way, of course, but I bet his dad was just hankering for another son or two who might want to help carry on the orchard.'

'What happened to his father? asked Lucy, both fascinated and saddened to learn more about this man who was her boss.

'His quad bike rolled,' Kate said, and adding when she saw Lucy's frown. 'His four wheeler.'

Lucy thought back to the day she'd spent today in the orchard, where Dan had collected the buckets of cherries with the four wheeler. 'They're dangerous?'

'They can be, if they roll.'

'That's rough,' said Lucy.

'It was,' agreed Heather. 'It hit everyone in the valley hard. And it wasn't long after that Beth lost her fiance, just a few months before Siena was born.' She signed. 'Such a lovely young man too. Such a tragedy. If the Faraday family hasn't had its share of bad luck by now, I don't know who has. It's about time they had a change of fortunes.'

And then Heather looked down at her empty plate and said, 'Who's for fruit salad and ice cream?'

It was another half hour before the men and boys disappeared and the women were left to their own devices. Lucy and Kate helped with the washing up before they took coffee out on the vine covered pergola. Far away and below lay the twinkling lights of the south eastern suburbs of Adelaide, like a twinkling ever shifting tapestry.

'This is gorgeous,' said Lucy. 'So pretty. Thanks for having me.'

'It's a pleasure,' said Heather. 'Tell us, what's it like where you come from?'

Lucy smiled. 'That's a hard one to answer. I don't exactly have a home.'

'But your parents . . .?

'Well, there's just my Mom. She's in Spain now but who knows for how long. She moves around a lot. Always has. That's where I get it from, I guess.' And the one time she had thought about settling down had been a complete disaster. She huffed in a breath. No, better to keep moving.

Heather shook her head. 'I can't imagine what that would be like, not with this lot to run after. But what does she do for money?'

'Anything. She cleans. Waitresses. There's always some kind of work going.'

'Like cherry picking,' offered Kate.

'Exactly.'

Kate yawned and stretched. 'And we've got an early start, so I better run you back.'

'Good thinking,' Lucy said. 'Don't want to annoy the boss.' Any more than she already had.

Heather put together a small survival package with a few

supplies for Lucy to last her until Kate took her to the market and Lucy hugged her as she said her thanks.

'Anytime,' she said. 'You're always welcome here. It's nice to bolster the numbers.'

DAN FINISHED up in the packing shed and switched off the lights, pausing a moment as he thought about his new picker and wondered if she'd managed to find something for dinner. She might have gone to The Scenic of course, there was always that option. But just in case she was at a loose end and needed some milk or something, maybe he should ask.

There were no lights on as he approached, but then, it was still light enough she probably wouldn't need them yet.

What if she was asleep?

He turned around. She worked hard today, for a rookie, he'd been watching her. She might be tuckered out. She'd hardly want him banging on the door.

But she had no transport and what if she needed milk or something?

He turned around again. It wouldn't hurt to knock. He stopped at the van, lightly rapped his knuckles on the door and held his breath.

Nobody home. Well, good.

TUESDAY SAW Lucy's muscles protesting when she climbed out of bed, but that wasn't going to stop her giving the job one hundred per cent. Besides, she'd slept so well, she was ready for anything.

'Morning boss,' she said, at the sink filling her water

bottle when Dan arrived and found she'd beaten him to the shed again.

His eyes narrowed. 'You sound chirpy.'

'It's a beautiful day. There's a lot to be chirpy about.'

But Dan just grunted and shoved his hat on his head as he walked back out.

Kate turned up a moment later. 'What did you say to Dan? He's like a bear with a sore head this morning.'

Lucy shrugged. 'I just said it was a beautiful day.'

Kate nodded. 'Yeah, that'd do it. Come on, let's get to work before those bozos turn up.'

THE NEXT COUPLE of days flew for Lucy. Apart from picking cherries, Dan had Kate take her to the patch of raspberry canes to pick the fresh berries, plump and sweet from the canes. They were weighed into little punnets and whisked off to a local greengrocer before they'd even had time to realise they'd been picked.

The next morning, he had the team pulling rhubarb and she learned that, like the cherries, there was a knack to harvesting rhubarb too. Kate showed her how to grab the stalk and give it a gentle twist as she pulled it from the plant. It wasn't half as interesting as when Dan gave her a lesson on where to place her hands, Lucy reflected, but then he seemed to prefer to keep his distance. Not that he didn't keep an eye on her.

Waiting for me to muck up, she figured.

Well, she'd show him.

'You know, I don't think I've ever eaten rhubarb,' Lucy said to Kate during lunch break afterwards. They were munching on some apples Dan had found at the back of the cool room. They were last season's, but they still tasted pretty good. Lucy finished up and wiped her hands, pulling her small notebook and pen from her pants pocket.

'You should try it. Mum makes a mean apple and rhubarb crumble for special occasions but it's nice stewed just with ice cream too.'

'Yeah? That sounds okay.'

Kate kept crunching on her apple when she said, 'Oh, I've found a recipe in those books I want to try. Well, there's heaps, but I'm going to make this one on Sunday for dinner. Mum says the kitchen's mine.'

'Yeah? Which one?' said Lucy, who was busy doodling the funny red rhubarb stalks with the big leafy green ends. They'd looked pretty funky just picked. They hadn't looked half as interesting once they'd been trimmed and bagged.

'Cauliflower-cheese pie.'

'The one with the grated potato base? I've made that one. It's great.'

'I'm hoping. Mum reckons she'll have some rissoles on hand, just in case there's a rebellion. I'm going to get the ingredients when we I take you to the market.' She paused. 'What are you doing?'

'Just drawing.'

Kate looked over. 'Wow, you're pretty good.'

Lucy looked at the picture she'd drawn with a critical eye. She'd never be an artist as such, but she enjoyed playing with lines on the page. 'It's okay.'

They were heading back to the packing shed when the car pulled up outside.

'G'DAY SOPHIE,' said Dan, pulling off his hat to scratch his head. 'What brings you here.'

His sister greeted him with a smile as she got out of the

car before pulling something from the back seat. 'I brought back the plates I borrowed after the party. Thought I may as well drop them over in my lunch break. How's things?'

'Good,' he said, leaning over to give his sister a kiss on the cheek and take the plates. 'Thanks for bringing these back. You didn't have to make a special trip, though.'

'Ah, is that your new picker?' she said, looking around him, and Dan got the impression that maybe his sister wasn't being as altruistic as she made out. 'Wow, she's pretty.'

He sighed when he turned and saw Kate and Lucy heading towards the shed.

'Hey Kate,' Sophie called. 'I had your little brother in library this morning.' She turned to the other woman. 'And I'm guessing you must be Lucy.'

There was no way around it but to make the introductions. 'Sophie's the librarian at the local primary school up the road,' he explained.

'Hey,' Lucy said, 'nice to meet you.'

Sophie looked like the cat that got the cream. 'Likewise.'

'Anyway,' Dan said, knowing Sophie would be on the phone to her sisters two minutes from now giving them a full report. 'Thanks for that Sophie. We better get back to work.'

'SOPHIE'S NICE,' said Lucy, as they headed back to the cherry trees where they were working. 'Pretty too.' She was petite with a wide mouth and dark shoulder length hair tucked behind her ears and didn't look much like Dan at all. Lucy figured she must take after her mom.

'Her sisters are stunners too,' Kate said, 'only they're blonde.'

'Good looking family,' she mused, thinking about Dan. All of them. Some of them even knew how to smile.

'Hey,' Kate said, 'let's go to the pub tomorrow for dinner. I've got a discount voucher we can use.'

'Sure,' Lucy agreed, knowing her meagre supplies had dwindled and after another day working in the orchard, she could do with a good meal. 'You're on!'

By the time Thursday rolled around Lucy was feeling like a regular part of the team. She was loving the orchard work, the summer heat and the cherries. She was having fun. And she was looking forward to tonight's dinner at The Scenic.

Lucy showered quickly after work, before pulling on clean jeans and a floral blouse. Kate had offered to pick her up, but today Lucy wanted to walk and stretch her legs. And if she happened to spot another koala in the trees along the way, she wouldn't mind that either.

She swept a comb through her wet hair, knowing it would air dry in no time on the way, before swiping on some mascara. Then she headed back to her van to put her things away.

She was halfway there when the shot rang out.

CHAPTER 7

*L*ucy ducked. It was pure instinct. She'd been a visitor to too many troubled countries to ignore that sound.

Then came the second blast. It was close.

Too close.

A deafening racket of bird cries pulled her attention upwards as the sky was filled with what looked like a hundred panicking parrots in flight. Flashes of screeching colour filled her vision before another loud blast.

This time, though still keeping low, she saw a bird suddenly flail, its flight arrested by the shot, until it clutched desperately at a passing branch.

'No!' she screamed, watching the bird wavering, beating its wings helplessly in an attempt to remain upright. Its struggle fruitless, it toppled from the tree, its colourful wings askew, landing unceremoniously on its back. Even then, it struggled to right itself, desperate to escape.

Further shots rang out, punctuated by the screeching of dying and panicking birds as she ran to where the parrot had fallen. Panic in its eyes, it surveyed her approach. It fought to get up, to get away from her, but all it could do was flap and strain, beating the ground with useless wings. She tried to talk soothingly as she approached, then reached down and scooped up the injured bird in her hands. It stretched out its wings and tried to flap some more, desperate to flee. She stroked its tiny head, the warmth and the softness of the feathers strangely at odds with its bright slashes of colour.

'I'm sorry,' she whispered, a tear squeezing from her eye. 'I'm so sorry, you beautiful creature. I don't know why anyone would want to hurt you.'

The bird's tiny heart beat a frantic tattoo against her cradling palm. Now she could see that a pellet had entered its fragile body through the chest, the tiny hole in its feathers ringed with blood. As she crooned words of comfort she hoped the bird might somehow understand, wondering what she could do to save it, its heartbeat became fainter and slower until its head suddenly lolled backwards, rolling off her hand to hang limply, its struggle over.

Tears squeezed from her eyes.

Boom!

Lucy screamed, ignoring the hot stream of tears burning down her face. The thought of other birds suffering a similar fate spurred her on.

'No!'

She rose, her hands still cradling the bird. There was someone not far away through the trees, a big bear of a man just on the other side of the fence line. He was lining up for another shot skywards. She ran over.

'Stop!'

The bear hesitated for a moment, then disregarded her presence as he readjusted his sights, took aim and fired his shotgun into the pine trees where the birds were seeking sanctuary. As the flock wheeled upwards and away, pine needles and feathers rained down to the ground.

'Gotcha, ya buggers,' he yelled, punching one arm triumphantly up into the air.

'Stop it,' she cried, frantic. 'You're shooting the birds.'

He looked across at her as if she was an idiot before casually breaking the firearm open and inserting two new cartridges.

'That's the general idea, yeah.'

He purposefully clicked the barrel shut and rested the weapon across his expansive stomach.

'But you're killing them.' She thrust out her hand with its colourful, limp carcass. 'Look what you've done.' She choked back a sob. 'This one died in my hands.'

The man flicked his eyes over the body.

'Bloody good thing it's dead. Otherwise I'd have to wring its neck.'

Lucy saw red. 'How could you kill such beautiful birds? What sort of monster are you?'

'They're a pest.'

'But they're only harmless birds.'

'They're eating my fruit. I've lost tons to the blighters and I don't intend to lose any more.'

He went to move away, eyes already searching for the next prey.

'I'll call the police. You can't go shooting harmless birds.'

He turned and gave a leery grin. 'You do that, sweetheart, and see how far you get. And while you're at it, you tell Dan Faraday that he might lend a hand to control the birds on his side of the fence.'

'What do you mean?'

'I mean if he's serious about cherry farming, he's going to have to pitch in like the rest of us in controlling these pests.'

She raised herself up and glared at him. 'Dan would never do such a cowardly thing. He would never stoop so low.'

The fact Lucy had known Dan for barely a week didn't

figure in the equation. He'd never resort to such tactics. At least, he'd better not while she was around.

The rumble of a quad bike powering through the orchard made her turn. It was Dan at the wheel, brining the bike to a stop, and scowling as he took in the scene.

'Dan,' she screamed, pushing aside her confusion as she ran over to where he was climbing off the bike. 'Look what this maniac's been doing.' She thrust out her hands with the dead bird.

He looked at her, taking in her tear-stained face and her dead cargo, and then strode over to the fence.

'Des,' he stated flatly. The man acknowledged Dan with a brief nod, and Lucy noted with satisfaction that the exchange took place with a total absence of warmth.

'What's been going on?'

She ran over to his side, her arms still outstretched as if he hadn't already seen.

'He's murdering the parrots.'

'Lucy, I'll handle this'

'But he's killing them.'

'All right, Lucy!' He turned to his neighbour. 'Des, what the hell's going on?'

'Just what I warned you would happen. Those parrots are trouble. Ain't going to leave us a thing. Didn't I tell you this was on the cards? I told you we'd have to deal with them, one way or another.'

'Yeah, well, it would help if you actually tried to get the fruit in. Are you even picking this year? Because if you're not – again – maybe you should try netting your trees if you're so bothered by the birds.'

'This is the only way to deal with these buggers. I'm telling you, I know how to handle these birds.'

'You don't have to murder them, you coward,' interjected Lucy. 'Why don't you pick on something your own size?'

'Lucy!' The word exploded from Dan as he seized her shoulders. Lucy almost dropped the bird in her hands with the shock, as his face came within inches of her own. And his skin was drawn so tight over his features , his brown eyes so wild, that she knew she should be afraid, but when she eventually breathed in again, all she could think about was how good he smelled. Warm. Masculine. So good that she wanted to gulp down great breaths of it.

He squeezed her shoulders gently, the gesture belying the look of war on his face. The warmth his touch generated washed through her, turning her anger into an emotion much less

tangible and infinitely more disturbing.

'I told you I'd handle this,' he assured her, speaking more softly. 'Go back to the house. I'll talk to you in a few minutes.'

'What about . . . the birds?' she asked, her voice cracking.

'Go! Now!' he ordered, pointing in the direction of the homestead.

Lucy turned and fled, but not before she heard the neighbour protesting to Dan to keep his loopy girlfriend out of his way.

'She's not my girlfriend,' she heard Dan say. 'She's a picker. Nothing more.'

Whether it was the words themselves, or the way Dan had said them, or simply the aftermath of the confrontation, but Lucy was suddenly aware that she was shaking. She felt drained,

physically and emotionally.

Her route to the house became more and more circuitous as she found and collected three other tragic parrot corpses, their bright plumage making them unmistakeable against the barren

summertime earth. By the time she got to the house with her arms full, she was crying again at the sheer waste of it.

At a loss to know what to do with them, she eventually wandered around to the packing shed and laid the four birds down in a row. Still sobbing, she took a couple of prepared cherry boxes and scrunched up some soft tissue paper to line them. Into each box she gently laid two parrots, side by side. They were bigger than they looked in the sky, and heavier than she'd imagined and they just fit. It wasn't much but it seemed important that she should make their final resting place comfortable – in some small way to make up for their final turbulent living moments.

She looked at them one final time, apologising for the injustice of it all, and smoothed their feathers as she prepared to close the carton lids.

'I was looking for you up at the van. What are you doing in here?'

Dan's sudden appearance startled her. She turned, still kneeling.

'I had to take care of these.' She gestured to the birds in their improvised coffins. 'And these are just the ones I could find. Who knows how many more there are out there.'

She looked up at him, unable to conceal the anguish she was feeling. 'Why does he have to shoot them? Is he sick or something?'

Dan took a deep breath. 'He's my neighbour, and I'm finding it hard enough to get along with him without all this going on.'

'It's not my fault. He's the one shooting. What's he planning to do – shoot every bird in the district? It doesn't make sense. Can't we call the police or something?'

'He has a licence to shoot the birds if they're threatening his crops.'

She was about to interject when he continued over her.

'You have to understand, people around here make their living out of producing the best fruit in the state. And after the two worst years on record, they don't want to see it go in bird food.'

'But they're so beautiful. And how can you blame them for eating the food you grow under their noses?'

She looked back at the parrots, reaching out a hand to smooth a twisted feather. 'When I was in a street market in Asia, I saw a pair of birds like these for sale.' She turned her tear-filled eyes to his. 'Do you have any idea how much they were asking for a pair?' She waited a second for any response.

'Thousands of dollars! I thought it was cruel that they had been ripped from their homes to live caged and helpless so far away. But how much crueler is to be shot, simply for eating the food that is right under your nose?'

'Lucy, look –'

'No. How is it that birds like these can fetch such a high a price overseas, yet here people are content to blast them to kingdom come? There must be something we can do to prevent it?'

He looked skyward for a moment, as if for inspiration, before taking a deep breath and turning back to her.

'Lucy, they can be a pest. They can and do destroy entire crops. It's people's livelihoods that are at stake.'

'But you wouldn't shoot them – would you?'

He sighed again. 'It hasn't come to that yet – thankfully. But Des is right, the birds are bad this year because the cherries are so good and we're going to suffer losses for sure.'

'You mentioned nets, but you don't use them.'

'I did. A few years back I gave them a try, but they weren't perfect. It was a hassle putting them on and taking them off, and they snagged and wore and I'm not sure they're the silver bullet we thought they'd be.' He shrugged. 'So this year I've gone back to basics – trying to get the cherries in as soon as they're ripe.'

He looked over at the boxes. 'What do you propose doing with those?'

'I'll bury them somewhere – if that's okay? It might seem a bit silly but I thought they deserved a decent send-off at least.' She bit her lip. 'I hope you don't mind about me using the boxes . . .?'

He looked across at her for a moment, then his lips curled up ever so slightly at the corners. It was the closest he'd come to smiling and the unexpected sight warmed her heart.

'That's okay. I might be able to help if you'd like a hand with the digging. Just leave them there and we can take care of them tomorrow if you like. I've got a . . . um, a meeting I'm already late for.'

Lucy suddenly remembered her own dinner arrangement. 'Oh no, what's the time? I was supposed to meet Kate at the hotel.'

'The Scenic?' he asked, and she nodded. 'That's where I'm going. Give me five minutes and I'll give you a lift.'

'Thanks, boss.' She watched him go. Dan wasn't too bad when it came down to it. At least he wasn't shooting up the wildlife. And as long as he wasn't shooting, the birds could seek some sort of sanctuary here.

Then she caught sight of her once fresh top, now smeared with grime and blood, and realised that she needed to get changed herself. She folded in the lids of the boxes and was about to go get changed when she figured that dead birds and a forecast hot day tomorrow probably didn't mix. It would be a much better idea to put them in the coolroom overnight and retrieve them in the morning for burial.

There was plenty of space inside. Lucy chose a handy spot just close to the door and mentally applauded herself for her forethought. It would make tomorrow's burial a lot less unpleasant.

THEY WERE HALFWAY up the hill towards the pub when they went over a pothole and the clipboard Dan had stuck in between the seats bumped out onto her feet. Lucy picked it up before he could stop her. 'What's with the questionnaire?'

'Um, that's confidential,' he said, tugging it from her hands and turning it face down on his lap. 'If you don't mind.'

'Are you interviewing someone for a job?'

He cleared his throat and made a show of checking his mirrors as he slowed for the corner. 'What? Oh yeah, kind of.'

'On the orchard?'

He pulled into the hotel car park. 'You could say that.'

THE DOOR of the pub had a big poster advertising Saturday night's cherry auction and Dan felt his gut clench. He didn't want to be reminded of how much he had riding on the auction. He pushed the door open, giving Lucy her first glimpse of the interior of The Scenic with its scattering of tables and chairs and a big stone fireplace opposite the bar where half a dozen local council workers in fluoro vests were lined up nursing schooners of beer.

They all turned to look over the newcomers. A couple nodded in Dan's direction, but it was Lucy they were more interested in. The man on the closest end dipped his head and tried his hand with a, 'G'day.'

'Hey,' she said with that smile thing she did, and the crusty road worker looked like he'd just about melted on his stool.

Bloody hell, thought Dan. It wasn't just pickers she reduced to dumb animals then. 'Dining room's through this way,' he said, guiding her past the line of men holding up the bar.

'There's Kate,' he said a little nervously, indicating a table and clutching the clipboard under his arm a little tighter as Lucy thanked him and peeled away. Because he was more nervous than he'd been all week, in spite of being as prepared for meeting Donna as he could be. He had his list of questions all ready and from their brief online chat, he was pretty confident that her answers were going to be the ones he was looking for. Hell, he needed them to be the right answers so he could put this wife-search thing behind him and get on with what he was supposed to be doing.

But thinking about actually meeting someone he'd connected with on-line, well, that was a whole other ball game. What if she didn't like him?

He took a deep breath as he scanned the room. He knew what Donna looked like from her profile picture of course, and she'd told him she'd be wearing pink, so where was she? For one heart sickening moment, he thought he'd been stood up. After she'd sounded so keen too.

'Excuse me,' came a little girl's voice behind him, and he moved aside, thinking he must be blocking the walkway. 'Are you Dan Faraday?'

He spun around and there, sitting at a table tucked so neatly behind the wall that he'd walked straight past on his way in, was Donna, larger than life. Larger than her profile picture at any rate.

Whoa.

'Donna?'

She giggled, this little lilting giggle that made her sound all of about ten years old, and completely at odds with how she looked. Completely at odds with all that pink. She wasn't so much wearing it, as housed in it. She had on some kind of twin-set thing like his Nan wore, with the little T-shirt thing underneath and the jacket over, except this was in bright pink and there had to be metres of fabric there. On the table in front of her was a pink purse and if he wasn't mistaken, she was wearing pink eyeshadow to match her lipstick. If she'd had a tiny dog nestled under her arm, she could have been Barbara Cartland on steroids.

'Pleased to meet you, Dan.' She looked like she was pleased too. She looked like the cat that got the cream. 'You look just like your profile picture.'

Really? He'd assumed that was the whole point. But then, he was new at this. He smiled, or tried to, only he wasn't feeling like smiling. Truth be told, he was feeling a tad peeved.

Except surely he wasn't that superficial? This wasn't about hooking up with Miss Universe – this was about finding a wife. And seeing she'd seemed like a good match and he was here . . . He put his clipboard face down on a chair. 'I might get us some drinks. Can I get you something?'

She smiled up at him. Straight teeth. There you go, it wasn't all bad.

'A glass of moscato would be nice, thank you.'

'Moscato?'

'I know, I should be sweet enough, LOL.'

He blinked. There it was again, only this time it was in audio. 'I'll be right back.' He found a spot at the bar where he could lean in and give his order, all the while the LOL thing niggling at him.

'Excuse me,' he said quietly to the young woman who brought his drinks, 'but can you tell me what LOL means?'

'LOL?'

'Yeah. Is it supposed to stand for something? Other than "lots of love"? I mean, it can't mean that.'

'Oh, do you mean, laugh out loud?'

'I don't know. Could that be it?'

She shrugged, and started pouring the neighbouring bloke's beer. 'People write it in texts and stuff. Shorthand.'

Dan thought back to Donna's messaging that night. That could have been what she'd meant. 'But people don't actually say it, do they? I mean, it's not actually a word?'

She screwed up her mouth. 'Not unless they're a bit weird.'

Dan looked back in the direction of their table, where Donna in pink was waiting for her drink. 'Excellent,' he said, without meaning it.

'Hey Dan,' a familiar voice said from behind him. 'A bit unusual to see you in here. You got time for a drink?'

Dan turned, his beer and Donna's moscato in his hands, and wishing he'd seen the obvious flaw in choosing to meet someone here in his own stamping ground. 'G'day, Nick,' he said, greeting one of his apple producing neighbours. Nick had grown cherries too until a few years back when he'd got sick of the uncertainty of it and pulled out all his cherry trees to concentrate on apples and pears. 'I'm a bit busy right now. I'm er, just interviewing someone.'

Nick looked at the glasses in Dan's hands and across at the table he'd just left. He smiled. 'Very civilised way to do it. Will we see you at the auction tomorrow?'

'You bet,' said Dan, on more confident ground. 'My cherries are going to blow everyone's socks off.'

'Can't wait. Good luck with your -' Nick paused to give him a wink. '- interview.'

'Yeah, thanks,' said Dan, rolling his eyes before he headed back to the table. Something told him it was going to be a long night.

'So I hear you're into line-dancing,' he said, as he put Donna' glass of moscato on the table in front of her. He'd memorised question number one and it seemed a good place to start. 'Why don't you tell me about that?'

'Oh, I don't do that anymore. The doctors told me I have a dicky knee and not to exercise until it gets better.'

'Right.' Dan swallowed as he reached for his clipboard, wondering if she'd stopped doing that about the time her profile picture was taken. Not that he was game enough to ask that question. It was going to be a very long night.

'Wow, check out the view!' said Lucy, looking out the French doors next to their table. Before her the hills peeled away to reveal a wedge of the city that was starting to light up and a silvering sea beyond. Then she saw what was in the tree right in front. 'Oh my God, there's a koala sitting right there! Look!' She pulled her phone from her jeans and started clicking.

Kate looked over at the view and the koala, but seemed distracted by something. 'Yeah, it's not bad. I thought you said you were walking.'

'Dan offered me a lift. He said he had to meet someone. You won't believe what happened just now.'

Kate shifted a bit to the right and peered at something over Lucy's shoulder. 'Did he say who he was meeting?'

'No,' she said, putting her phone down, distracted from telling Kate the story of the parrots. 'Just someone for a job on the orchard. Why?'

Kate straightened and looked her in the eye. 'A job in the orchard. Doing what?'

'I don't know. Isn't he looking for more pickers?'

Kate looked at that place over her shoulder again. 'I'm pretty confident that one won't be climbing ladders to pick cherries any time soon.'

Lucy looked behind her and saw Dan head for the bar after putting his clipboard down on a chair – a chair opposite a largish woman with black hair and a penchant for pink. Lots of pink. Although she'd only spent the one week in the orchard so far, she guessed what Kate said was right.

'Maybe he's looking for a housekeeper?' Lucy said, sipping on the cider Kate had ordered and had waiting for her. 'Someone to cook and clean the house while he's out in the orchard. Or maybe a bookkeeper, to keep track of sales or something.'

And Kate's brown eyes opened wide. 'Oh my god, not a housekeeper. Not a bookkeeper. I'll bet Dan's on a date!'

Lucy's head swung around again. She blinked. Kate could not be serious. 'A date?'

'You know, this matchmaking thing his sisters signed him up for – I'll bet he met her online.'

Lucy took another look. ' Surely he could do better.'

'Hey, she's probably really nice.'

'Yeah.' Lucy pretended to study the menu. 'What are you ordering?'

'Are you trying to change the subject? Anyone would think you cared.'

'Get real, Kate, why would I care? I just think he might be aiming a bit low.' She shook her head. 'Anyhow, since when does a guy take a clipboard along on a date, huh?'

'This is Dan we're talking about.' Kate raised an eyebrow.

And Lucy had to concede that maybe she had a point. 'Anyhow, I'm starving. I'm going to order the Scenic Burger with the lot.' She put the menu down. 'Now, let me tell you about the lunatic next door . . .'

Six LOLs, two OMGs and three fits of giggles later, Dan put down his clipboard and conceded defeat. He was barely halfway through his questions, but what was the point? He wasn't a man prone to headaches, but he sure as hell felt one coming on right now. A headache and an overwhelming desire to throttle his sisters.

Not that he could blame them entirely. He'd picked this particular 'match'. More fool him. He was going to have to do a bit more than blindly pick the next one on the list. Maybe he might even ask how old their profile picture was first up next time.

Clearly he had a bit to learn about this online dating game. He looked at his watch and brushed imaginary bread-crumbs from his clipboard. Imaginary because they'd never actually got to ordering anything to eat. That would mean lingering and there was no point postponing the inevitable. 'Well, thanks Donna. It's been great meeting you. I really should be heading home. Early start and all that.'

'Oh,' Donna said, and gave a nervous little giggle. 'Maybe we could go out for coffee or a movie sometime?'

'I'm busy that day.'

Her face fell. Hell. Now he felt really lousy. 'Sorry, Donna. I just don't think this is going to work.' He stood and turned and almost collided with the person walking past.

'Lucy,' he said, thinking this day could not get any worse. 'Sorry.'

'No problem,' she said, and right on cue, there was that damned smile. Blow me down if Kate wasn't right behind her and grinning too. What was that about?

He nodded one last time to a disappointed looking Donna and paid his tab at the bar before heading for the exit.

Lucy and Kate were in the car park and Kate was rummaging in her bag for her keys when he got outside. 'Hey, Dan,' Kate said, 'if you're going home, how about you give Lucy a lift and save me the trouble.'

Dan wasn't in the mood for bright company right now. The extractor from the pub's kitchen was pumping out the smell of chips and his stomach was rumbling up a storm, but it would have been churlish to refuse. 'Fine,' he said on a sigh, and headed for the ute.

'So how did your interview go?' Lucy asked as she climbed into the cabin.

'Not as well as it could have.'

'That's too bad.'

Wasn't it just?

'I gotta say,' Lucy continued alongside him, clearly not picking up on his need for silent brooding, 'Your hotel does amazing food. That Scenic Burger is the best burger I've ever had. And those fries – oh my God, they were amazing. I am so stuffed full.'

'Excellent,' he said, not meaning it for the second time tonight, wondering if he had a can of soup in the pantry. And, given how easy he'd thought this on line dating thing would be, maybe a nice slice of humble pie to go with it.

CHAPTER 8

'Did you ask Dan how his date went last night?' Kate asked, as she plonked herself down next to where Lucy was sitting in the shade during smoko. They'd started work this morning at different ends of a line of trees and it was the first chance they'd had to catch up

Lucy swiped at an ant that was weaving a determined path up her pants. It was thirty-five degrees in the shade today - ninety-five where she was from - but the air was clear and dry, with barely a breeze to disturb the leaves, the only sounds the occasional blow fly buzzing by and laughter drifting over from where the boys clustered around one of their cars, checking out someone's new speakers. 'Why would I do that?'

'Aren't you curious? God, I am.'

Lucy shrugged. 'All he said was it didn't work out as well as it could have.' Which was kind of obvious given the way he'd made such an awkward escape. He sure hadn't looked like someone who'd wanted to prolong the meeting.

Not that she cared, exactly.

He was her boss. It wasn't like he was her love interest or

anything. Hell, when it all came down to it, it was none of her business. Even if she did think anyone who looked that good in denim could do better.

'Hey,' Kate said, 'Meant to tell you, I can't do the Central Market tonight, I have to pick up Mum from the hospital.'

'She okay?'

'It's just a day procedure, but they won't let her drive after the anaesthetic, and Dad's got a work thing he can't get out of. We can go tomorrow, though, if that's okay. We knock off at lunch time so we'll have more time then.'

'Sure,' Lucy said, tossing out the dregs of her coffee as she saw Dan emerge from the packing shed, signalling the end of the break. Her eyes narrowed. Yep, the man might be grumpy as all get out, sure looked good in denim. He'd appeared in the tangle of her dreams last night, and she'd woken confused and with her skin on fire as if from the touch of a work roughened hand. She blamed the wool blankets he'd dug out of a cupboard for her, but the experience had still left her a little shaken. When did she ever dream about any man, let alone one so eminently unsuitable, and who was entering the marriage market with a vengeance?

Never.

It was that damned spark's fault. Even though she knew he wasn't her type – even though she knew he was looking for wife material – it didn't matter. Every time she saw him that spark spat and flared. Every time she caught his eyes on her she felt the sizzle crank up to a slow burn.

Pointless.

She shook her head as both girls got to their feet, dusting off their pants. 'Tomorrow suits me better anyway. I've still got to bury those parrots.'

Kate turned to her. 'Oh, sorry. Now, I won't be able to help you.'

'No problem, I can manage. They're only birds.'

Lucy took Kate's cup, while Kate drifted back to where she'd been picking. Rod had peeled away from the guys and just happened to be drifting back the same way, she noticed.

'What's up Carrot Head?' she heard him say.

'Piss off, Ratface,' snapped Kate back at him, but Rod just laughed and Lucy smiled because Rod was right. Kate hadn't sounded very convincing. She rinsed out the cups in the sink and head out of the shed into the bright, clear day.

'So how's it going?

She jumped, her eyes yet to adjust to the bright outdoor light, her senses buzzing at being taken by surprise. 'Dan,' she said, a little breathlessly. 'Good. I'm going okay.'

'Yeah,' he said, his face all shadowed under the brim of his hat. It didn't help any that the sun was almost directly above his head. 'That's what I reckon too.'

Despite the flutter of nerves still going on in her stomach, it was impossible not to smile. 'Really?'

'Yep.' He took off his hat and raked a hand through his hair before jamming it back on again. 'You're doing okay. You've come up to speed really quickly.'

'Wow. So I'm keeping up okay, then.'

He dipped his head. 'Yeah.'

'And the orchard doesn't have to carry me?' she added mischievously. 'I'm pulling my weight?'

Even with the sun behind him, she saw his mouth pull tight and knew he was remembering it too, the list of warnings he'd given her in the car on that first day that she'd have to perform or she'd be out of a job. And she'd always known she could handle the work, but it was so good to hear it.

He cleared his throat. 'Yeah, well, maybe I should take my own advice, and not go around judging a book by its cover.'

She grinned. It wasn't exactly an apology, but given the man it was coming from, it was as good as. 'Yeah, maybe I shouldn't either.'

. . .

DAN REALLY WISHED she wouldn't smile at him. When she smiled, her face lit up and he felt the zing all the way down to his groin. It didn't help any that he'd been responsible for making her smile. It made it worse.

He checked and rechecked the boxes of cherries that would be collected first thing in the morning, shuffling things around a bit on the cool-room shelves so they couldn't be missed, and then did a run to the post office to clear the mail. Sure enough the box was stuffed so full, the mail was jammed in tight. He really ought to clear it more often. Back in the car, he flicked through the pile.

Window envelopes mostly. Bills. Council rates, electricity, the usual suspects. And one big square flashy envelope that could only be the promised wedding invitation. He pulled it from the envelope and a birthday card fell out onto his lap with it. He smiled as he read them both, nodding at the date of the wedding. January twentieth. He had to hand it to Wendy, cherry season would be well and truly put to bed. At least his step-mum was looking out for his interests.

DAN WASN'T around when Lucy went looking for him after work, but Lucy figured he'd have no objections to her burying the parrots without him. In fact he'd probably be impressed she'd shown a bit of initiative and taken care of it herself. She grinned to herself as she pulled open the big cool-room door. She'd shown him she was a good worker, now he'd see what she was really capable of.

Carrying the two boxes whilst dragging an old shovel just about finished her after a week's picking. By the time she found a spot down near the creek, the boxes were feeling as heavy as lead and she was no longer grinning. The thought of digging just about did her head in, but the ground was softer than she expected and soon she was able to slide the boxes alongside each other into the shallow hole. Then, after a few murmured apologies and promises to try to prevent any more senseless killings, Lucy covered them over, stamping down the soil with the back of the spade.

She returned to the shed and found a few bits and pieces from which she fashioned a cross, and then decorated it with the slightly rubbery contents of an old paint tin, before she picked a few camellia flowers from the trees lining the driveway to place on top. When she was done, she stood back to survey her handiwork. It wasn't much of a ceremony, but at least she'd been able to do something for the birds.

She rubbed the dirt from her hands and looked up at a sky painted red by the westering sun and drank in the view, her gaze stopping at that line of pencil pines on the ridge above, as once again she pictured the old woman in her mind and felt that strange zinging feeling down her spine.

Tuscany, she told herself, shaking her head as she headed back to the van. She'd been there herself. She was remembering a valley somewhere in Tuscany where there were villages full of little old ladies wearing black. That was all.

'Coming to the cherry auction at the pub tonight then?' Kate asked. They were piling bags into the trunk of Kate's car. After two hours weaving around the Central Market stalls and Asian grocery shops hunting for ingredients, Kate had ingredients for cooking up the recipes she wanted to try from the Moosewood Cookbooks, and Lucy reckoned she had enough supplies to make curry paste to last her till the end of the season. And with fresh vegetables from the local produce market Kate had told her was held every Sunday, there would be little other need to shop. Or hardly any reason to eat out. Her meal at The Scenic had been fabulous, but she could hardly afford to eat out every night. And given she'd be whipping up a batch of curry paste as soon as she got this lot home . . .

'I don't think so, Kate. I might pass on that.'

'But it's the cherry auction! You have to go.'

'Says who?'

'Everyone! It's practically compulsory. It'll be the biggest thing to happen in Norton Summit since . . . well, forever, really. There'll be TV cameras there and everything. Dan's pinning all his hopes for the orchard on doing well.'

'Are things that grim? His cherries are great.'

'This year they are, but it's going to take a bumper year to make up for the last couple. If he can get his cherries noticed at the auction, he'll be in with a good chance. You have to be there to cheer him on.'

Lucy wavered. She liked hanging with Kate. She liked what little she'd seen of the locals so far too, who could have been a different species to the customers she'd served in Melbourne's cafes. They seemed less preened, more laid back and somehow more real.

And then there was Dan.

She'd spent more time than she probably should analysing the conversation they'd had yesterday. He'd taken her by surprise with his declaration that she was doing okay when he'd made it clear at the start that he didn't think she'd cope. Not that she should take it personally of course — he was just interested in getting the cherries in as fast and as economically as possible — but his admission that she was doing okay and that maybe he'd misjudged her had warmed her bone deep anyway.

And if doing well at the cherry auction meant so much to him, maybe the least she could do was go support him?

. . .

'COME IN, number four, your time is up!' joked Kate as her eyes demanded an answer. 'So are you coming, or not?'

Hell, why not? It was a chance to be part of something that she'd never seen, to celebrate the season.

'Okay,' she said, 'So long as I get this lot taken care of, I'm in.'

'Great,' announced Kate, purposefully snatching up carrier bags and parcels. 'Let's get going then.'

NAN LOOKED surprised to see him when she opened the door, but then Dan hadn't called to say he was coming. He hadn't known it himself until ten minutes ago, when he'd been washing up the week's dishes and decided he had to get out of the place. The pickers had all knocked off and the place was suddenly too quiet - all except for the rattle of doubts and fears in his mind. Tonight, he'd thought. It all hinged on the cherry auction tonight. And his nervous gut had clenched tighter before he'd spotted Siena's balloon lying limply on the floor underneath the chair where he'd tied it.

'You and me both,' he'd said to the balloon, and figured that even though Siena wasn't that worried, like Beth had claimed, he really should have dropped it off to her by now.

And given it was on the way, he'd figured he could maybe kill two birds with one stone and drop in to see Nan and Pop – and check out what was happening with Pop's tests while he was there. Because the more he'd thought about it, the more he'd wondered if there had been a reason Pop had looked a bit dodgy the night of his party last week. It was high time he paid him a visit, given Pop sure hadn't bothered to volunteer any information.

'How's it going?' he said, leaning down to give Nan a kiss on the cheek.

'What a nice surprise,' she said. 'Come in, come in. What brings you over this way?'

'I had to drop off something for Siena. Figured I might say hello on the way.'

'I'm glad you did. Are you hungry? I made a pasty slice for lunch and there's leftovers.'

'Thanks Nan.'

'Look who's come to see us, Clarry,' she said, as she pulled a tray from the oven. She sliced him a piece of pasty and handed him the bottle of sauce. 'It's Dan.'

Clarry was sitting in his armchair watching the telly. Or he would have been if the telly had actually been on. 'You right, Pop?' Dan asked, holding his plate and a fork and more worried now than ever that his grandfather didn't even seem to notice. 'We've missed you at the orchard. How'd you go with all those tests?'

'Bloody doctor's an idiot,' he said. 'Reckons I have to slow down.'

'Get out of here,' he said, trying to keep it light. 'Why would he say something like that?'

'Because he's a drongo, that's why! They're all drongos, the lot of them.

'But that's it? Seriously? He just wants you to slow down?'

'Isn't that enough!' Clarry snapped. 'I go in for a simple eye test and the doc thinks it's his excuse to stick me in hospital and plug me up to every bloody machine he can find - bloody money making scheme if ever I saw one.'

'But you're going to do like they say and slow down though?'

'Pig's arse.'

'But Pop —'

'But Pop nothing! I told them it was indigestion, but would they listen to me? Drongos I tell you,'

'He's been stewing about it all afternoon,' said Nan, nodding. 'Like a bear with a sore head and nothing I say or do gets through to him. Maybe you can talk make him see sense.'

Fat chance of that. But maybe he could try to brighten him up a bit. 'So, er, Pop, I've had a bit of a think about it, and we really ought to get this team together for that quiz night. Can't afford to let the Faraday name down, can we?'

'Damn right, we can't! What took you so long to see the light?'

The screen door slammed shut. 'What took who so long?' said Hannah suddenly arriving, still wearing her work overalls, her hair pulled back in a ponytail. She put her bag and a litre carton of milk down on the bench. 'Hello Nan, I got your milk. Hey Pop,' she said, sidling alongside the chair to kiss Pop's brow before looking up at Dan. 'Big brother. Fancy seeing you here. What's up?'

'Dan reckons he'll be coming along to that quiz night after all.'

'Yeah?' said Hannah, sending her brother an evil look. 'Gonna bring your new girlfriend with you?'

'What?' said Nan and Pop and Dan all together.

Hannah didn't disappoint. Her eyes opened wide and she grinned. 'You sly dog, Dan. You mean you haven't told Nan and Pop about the date you took to The Scenic the other night?'

'He did what?' said his Nan and Pop together again.

'Who told you that?'

'Nick Pasquale. I ran into him at the supermarket after work just now. He mentioned he'd seen you there with some woman.'

Bloody hell. Dan liked Nick. He liked to think he was his best mate. Or he had until now. 'So I had a drink at the pub? So what?'

'No, it's great. You took a date to the pub, that's awesome. Did you meet her through HEA.com?'

'I did not take her to the pub. We had a drink there, that's all.'

'But you met online?'

'Maybe.'

'Woohoo! So you checked it out, hey?'

'Maybe.' He winced. He was starting to sound like a broken record.

'Are you going to see her again?'

'No.' That one was much easier.

'Very emphatic. You want to think about it?'

'No.'

'Why not?'

'Jeezus Han!'

'Dan . . .'

'Okay, all right, because she giggles, her every second word is LOL, and in real life, she was at least double the size she was in her profile picture. Very possibly three times. So no, I'm not seeing her again, if that's okay with you, that is.'

'She actually said LOL?' Han laughed. 'Oh, you poor thing.'

'Good of you not to be hanging out for the engagement.'

'I'm sure you'll find someone nice,' said Nan.

'I better go,' said Dan, seeing it as a chance to escape, but making a mental note to call Han later to see if she knew anything more about these mysterious tests Pop had been having. 'Will I see you at the cherry auction later on, Pop?'

'Wouldn't miss this one for quids, lad. We got a lot riding on it.'

They sure did. Dan had made his goodbyes and was halfway down the front steps when he heard Nan say behind him, 'Hannah, what's this LOL thing?'

BACK IN THE trailer Lucy attacked her shopping, chopping and roasting herbs and spices, filling the air with such a heady tang of herbs and spices that she had to open the door of the van to let out the fumes. At one point she heard Dan's car coming up the driveway, and she toyed with the idea of going over to the house and letting him know that she'd taken care of the parrots yesterday, but he'd known about her plans to bury the birds, so there was really no point.

It was better that she kept her distance. Deprive this inconvenient spark of oxygen and let it die a natural death.

Besides, she had work to do. So instead she hummed her way through batches of red and green curry paste and a fiery combination of garlic, chilli and lemongrass whose pungency pierced the air with needles that threatened to lance her sinuses. Oh yeah, this was the kind of heat she should be concentrating on.

OUTSIDE THE PACKING SHED, Dan was finding it hard to concentrate on what he was supposed to be doing – fixing the fuel line on his four-wheel motorbike. It had started playing up a bit yesterday and he really should have repaired it before he'd headed over to Nan and Pop's today.

Dan reached for a spanner, frustrated that he couldn't find one the right size. What the hell was happening to him? Suddenly all sorts of things were happening that had no place in his plans.

And it wasn't just that he was getting increasingly nervous about the reception of his fruit at the auction tonight, although that was cause enough for the odd ulcer or two. After the last two years, he was counting on this year's crop to pull the orchard out of the financial mess he'd made when he'd bought the neighbouring property.

But what could go wrong?

The boxes he'd overseen yesterday in preparation were perfect - the cherries plump and perfect- the best of this year's harvest, with better to come.

He threw down the spanner in disgust, watching it skip into the dirt and kicking up a puff of dust before – not for the first time – his nose forced his head up and around.

It was simply impossible to concentrate on anything with that damned smell drifting over from the van.

What was she up to in there? He was almost tempted to go take a look but that would be foolhardy.

No, not foolhardy. The word was nowhere near strong enough and besides, she'd only laugh at him. But going over to take a look would be insane. It was clear she wasn't his type. Every time they talked it wasn't two minutes before the verbal sparks were flying. Even when he'd told her yesterday that she'd done okay this week, she'd used it as an opportunity to score points. No, far better to keep right away.

Especially when he was supposed to be finding himself a serious girlfriend .

It didn't help though, that he remembered the feel of Lucy's hand wrapped in his, her body scant inches from his, her hand reaching high into that tree. It didn't help that he'd looked at him that way, like she was half interested. It didn't help at all that the first time he'd been tempted by a woman in as long as he could remember was when he was supposed to be looking for someone else. Someone permanent.

And so what if she had soft skin and a million dollar smile and a little singlet that stretched tight . . .

Dan shifted position, moving to a kneel.

'Hell!' If he was going to get all hot under the collar over a picker, he needed to find a wife quick smart.

He reached for another spanner.

The gentle spring breeze brought another waft of the spicy concoction his way, and with it an intoxicating promise of heat His gut clenched involuntarily and the spanner slipped off the nut he was wrenching, sending his fist slamming into the machine.

He jumped up swearing and aimed a firm kick at the bike's tyre. It didn't make him feel any better but at least the pain in his toes balanced the throbbing in his hand.

What the hell was wrong with him lately?

CHAPTER 9

*D*an had a knot the size of Texas in his stomach as he squeezed himself into the overflowing pub. This was it. Make or break time. Sure, he'd have his regulars ring up with orders, whatever happened tonight, but if he wanted his cherries to be noticed – really noticed so he could charge the big bucks – this was the big one.

A few blokes said g'day or wished him luck as he carved a way through the noisy throng – other orchardists and a few locals – and though most of the crowd were strangers, he knew there would be buyers from the major supermarket chains here too, scouting for the best cherries to buy for their Christmas customers.

They'd be impressed all right. His cherries were the best they'd ever been, but would the sale be enough to drag the orchard out of the financial hole it was in? God, it had better be.

His eyes scanned the crowd. He nodded to Nick Pasquale across the room and remembered to smile even if he was still annoyed with him telling Hannah about his appointment with Donna, but where was Pop? He pulled out his phone and checked reception – one bar – and put the useless device back in his pocket again. Probably just running late. No point trying to call him if he was driving, even if he could get a decent signal. He jammed his hands in his pockets and leaned up against the wall as the auction got under way, and the knot in his stomach pulled tight. Bloody hell!

'GOTTA GO PEE,' said Kate, in a break between offerings. 'Mind my seat.'

Easier said than done, thought Lucy. Kate was right about everyone being here. The hotel was packed, the French doors flung open so the crowd spilled out onto the balcony, but somehow Kate had wangled two seats near the bar. Lucy tried to peer through the crush, looking for a familiar face without admitting that there was only one face she was particularly interested in seeing. Dan had to be here somewhere.

He'd been so tense today he'd barely said a word to anyone in the orchard, just had this faraway look in his eyes. Maybe if his cherries did really well tonight, and the orders flooded in, he might be a little less strung out. She hoped they sold well.

It wasn't that she cared, exactly, but it would be good if he had a good year after a couple of bad ones.

By the cheers coming from the crowd as each box was auctioned, it looked like being a very good year for the local orchardists. People were happy. She looked around – what was taking Kate so long? – and when someone moved she saw Dan squeeze into the space, looking around as if he was searching for someone. His eyes fell on her and faltered, darted away and came back. Her stomach did a little flip-flop thing. She smiled and gave him a thumbs up signal, and after another scan of the room, he made his way over.

'Lucy.' His words were clipped and to the point and she could just about feel the tension emanating from him. 'You're here.'

'Kate said it was part of my job description.' There was so much noise in the room, they just about had to shout at each other.

He looked around. 'Kate . . .?'

'Bathroom,' she said, indicating left, 'but she's been gone for ages. You want to sit down or you looking for someone?'

'Yeah,' he said, with another check of the room. 'My Pop. He said he'd be here, but I haven't seen him.'

'Have her seat, if you like. It'll make it easier to hang on to.'

He nodded. 'Might as well grab a drink while I'm here.' He gestured towards her glass. 'You?'

'Cider, thanks.'

'Nervous?' she asked him, as they waited for their drinks. 'Your cherries must be coming up soon.'

He exhaled a long sigh.

'The cherries are perfect. There's no point worrying now, but –'

'I know,' she said, feeling his tension and seeing an unusual vulnerability in a man who needed to be in control. 'But it looks like it's going well. You'll be fine.'

'Here's hoping,' he said, as he handed her the drink and raised his own schooner of beer to hers. 'Cheers.'

Dan took a mouthful, the white foam sticking to his upper lip before he swiped it away with his other. 'Ah. I needed that. Bloody quad bike.' He leaned over so she could hear without him having to shout. 'Seems like you've been pretty industrious yourself. Gotta say, I like your work.'

Lucy nearly fell off her stool. He'd seen where she'd

buried the parrots? And she hadn't screwed it up? Wow. 'I'm glad you don't mind. It's just something I felt I had to do.'

He raised his eyebrows. 'Why should I mind? You can do what you like while you're staying on the property.'

She blinked at him. Double wow. She'd never expected him to be so accommodating. It seemed she really had underestimated him.

'Mind you, the doctor's going to hate you when he doesn't have any patients Monday. I suspect you single-handedly cleared every sinus in the district.'

What?

She opened her mouth to ask him what he meant, confusion spawning anxiety in her stomach, just as the Master of Ceremonies resumed his place at the microphone, tapping on it several times to ensure it was on.

'Thank you everyone,' he said, attempting to yell over the hullabaloo. 'Now that you've all had a chance to wet your whistles, how about a bit of hush.'

Dan looked around. 'Kate's still not back. Mind if I stay?'

Not the birds, she realised with a thunderclap. He meant the curry paste!

Dan must have interpreted her silence for a dismissal, because the next thing she knew, he was standing up. 'No!' She lunged for his arm, but she must have startled him in the process as his hand let go the beer glass, spilling its foaming contents down his jeans before it thudded onto the carpet.

Dan glared down at himself disbelievingly before raising his eyes back to Lucy.

'Uh oh,' she murmured, unwilling to meet his gaze as she reached for the cloth the barman was passing to her. She made a move towards Dan's jeans but he recoiled.

'Don't touch me!' he barked, snatching it from her hands, and began furiously wiping down his drenched legs.

'Settle down now back there, ladies and gentlemen,' continued the MC, noticing the fracas near the bar. '

There's only a dozen or so more boxes to go. There'll be time enough for fun and games later on. Let's see if we can keep the action going.'

Dan resumed his seat, but his body language said unmistakably he didn't want to be anywhere near her. She could hardly blame him. Here he was, approaching what could be the crowning moment of his year and he was wet, uncomfortable and no doubt smelled like a brewery. The next boxes were auctioned successfully, with active bidding for all of them. The cheers continued and everyone looked happy and Lucy crossed her fingers and toes that it went well for Dan.

Finally, it was Faraday Orchard's turn.

'And now,' announced the MC, 'we have what we like to think is the pick of the crop. These two boxes are from cherry trees that just three years ago were earmarked for ripping out.

But then Dan Faraday took them under his wing and by all accounts, he's turning the old orchard around. I was out there a few days ago and actually got to tasting a few of his cherries myself, and let me tell you, ladies and gentlemen – and without casting aspersions on any of the other fine fruit we've seen here tonight – these cherries are the biggest, fattest and tastiest of any of our early varieties, and that's why we've saved them for last.'

'Wow!' Lucy glanced at Dan. 'How cool is that?' They'd saved his cherries till last. But Dan refused to look at her, his attention one hundred per cent on the auctioneer.

'Now here's your opportunity to show him how much we appreciate his efforts by bidding well for these very special fruits of his labours. Where are you, Dan? Show yourself.'

Muttering something under his breath, Dan raised one arm, giving a brief wave.

'Come on, Dan. Stand up and come out here where we can all see you.'

Lucy caught the expletive as Dan stayed resolutely where he was.

'He needs some encouragement, everybody. Let's give him a hand.'

Immediately the crowd started clapping, cheers interspersed with cries of 'Come on, Dan' and 'On ya, Dan'.

He gave her a fierce glare that said, Now look what you've done, and made his way to where the MC was waiting.

'Ho ho,' the man chortled, taking in the wet patch on the front of Dan's jeans. 'It seems that we've got one very nervous cherry grower here!'

Amid the laughter, Dan looked like he was about to turn around and head right back to his seat but the MC grabbed his arm and pulled him to the microphone.

'It was my beer,' yelled Dan to the MC over the crowd noise.

'Well, I'm not sure about you,' laughed the MC into the microphone, clearly enjoying his role in the entertainment, 'but most of us prefer to drink our beer, not wear it!'

Lucy could see that if Dan had been holding a beer right then, it would have been the MC wearing it. She bit her lip, knowing that this little episode would result in yet another black mark against her name. And just when she'd been doing so well.

'Anyway,' continued the MC, 'we're not here to talk about Dan's drinking problems . . .'

Another laugh. Dan shifted uncomfortably and threw an accusatory glance in her direction.

'We're here to auction these fine cherries.'

He gestured toward his assistant who was positioning two cherry boxes on the display table next to the auctioneer's lectern.

Dan was so strung out, Lucy could almost taste his anxiety as he stood near the boxes, hands clenched at his sides. He seemed to be barely breathing. This was the moment he'd been waiting for and it wasn't enough that he had to endure the suspense, but he also had to put up with the antics of a would-be stand up comic.

'Now, ladies and gentlemen, before we lift the lid on these, our last offerings of the night, let's hear from the man himself.' He turned to Dan. 'Is there anything you'd like to add?'

Dan turned on a scowl that even Bradley Cooper would be envious of. 'I think you've said more than enough, thanks all the same.'

'Quite right. Now, how about a round of applause for Dan Faraday for being such a good sport. We'll let him resume his seat so he can watch the action. Someone get the man a beer – his pants are starting to dry out a *wee* bit.'

Dan didn't need to be invited twice to sit down, but in reclaiming his seat amidst the laughter and applause, he didn't look once at Lucy. She felt she should say something to him, just to break the ice.

Leaning across, she whispered, 'I think that went very well, considering.'

His head snapped around to face hers, his eyes blazing. Lucy felt her bravado diminish as she inched back from his dangerous gaze.

'I don't appreciate being made to look an idiot.'

'I know. That man was very rude.'

He looked at her as if she were mad. 'I was talking about the beer!'

'It was an accident. What can I say? I'm sorry.'

He crossed his arms and looked away.

'Now ladies and gentlemen,' the MC continued, 'after hearing so much about these here cherries, you'll be wanting to take a look at the pick of the crop. Let's open those boxes, please.'

All eyes were on the auctioneer's assistant, who started to pull off the lids.

'Let's not forget, all the proceeds from this auction go to charity, so dig deep – it's all for a good cause. Now, who'd like to start off the bidding? What am I bid for these fine . . .'

The assistant pulled back the tissue paper lining. 'Wha . . .?'

'No!' The sound tore from Dan like the cry of an animal in distress.

Lucy looked at him as his head fell into his hands. 'What's wrong?' she asked, before she turned her eyes back to the stage and registered the problem. Something wasn't quite right. There were too many colours for cherries; too much green, too much blue . . .

Too many feathers!

'Oh my God!' she cried, as the full horror sank in.

'Bloody big cherries,' yelled one bloke in the front row. 'What kind of fertilizer are you using, Dan?'

The deathly silence that had fallen over the crowd at the sight of the dead parrots erupted into a riotous cacophony of laughter and shouts as Dan surged back to the podium, now strobe lit with popping flashlights, and snatched up the box, searching to find the grower's name stencilled on the side. Similarly he checked the second before ripping off the lid.

More parrots!

Kate suddenly appeared at the hotel's door, and threw Lucy a what-the-hell-is-going-on look before Rod followed her in.

Rod with Kate?

But there was no time to think about that. She was too busy shrinking down against the bar, trying to work out how this could have happened. She'd buried the dead parrots yesterday – hadn't she?

A chill descended her spine as she realised. She'd buried two boxes but she'd never checked to see they actually contained parrots. She hadn't had the courage to look at their poor bodies one more time. And the boxes had been so heavy. She swallowed.

Uh-oh.

But right now it didn't matter how it had happened. What mattered was that Dan would blame her for sure. And he'd be right.

The MC, meanwhile, was beside himself. He pounded with his gavel for order.

'I call open this meeting,' he managed between fits of laughter, 'of the dead parrots society.'

'They're not dead,' yelled out one wag. 'They're just resting!'

'They're late parrots!'

'They're pining for the fjords!'

She didn't understand what was so funny as she slid off her stool, wondering what she could do to make up for this. But whatever it was, it was going to have to be good.

THE CROWD and the media were loving it, of course. Lapping up every Monty Python dead parrot sketch reference they could get. And it would have been hysterical, he supposed, if it had been anyone else's orchard going down the toilet.

'Mr Faraday,' called a reporter. 'Can we have a comment?'

Dan growled as he pushed up his sleeves. He didn't want to talk to the media. His heart wasn't in it. Right now he had something a whole lot more important on his mind.

Just how he was going to kill Lucy.

CHAPTER 10

'What have you done with my cherries!'

Lucy spun around as Dan burst out of the hotel door. He stood there with his feet apart, his stance reminiscent of a gunslinger in a shootout, and she had no doubts who he was gunning for. She gulped, relieved the reporter and cameraman she had just spoken to were already stashing away their gear in the van.

Dan still only took a second to work out that something had been going on. His dark eyes narrowed suspiciously.

'What the hell are you doing now?'

Lucy took a deep breath. It was time for damage control. She took a couple of steps towards him, trying to bridge the distance – if not the worlds – between them, but he bore himself upright, making himself even more unreachable.

'It's all good', she said, trying to soothe. 'I was just explaining to the reporter about what happened –'

'You what?' he blustered. 'Don't you think you've done enough? Do me a favour – don't talk to anyone, ever again, about what happened here tonight.'

'But it's all good! I was just telling them –'

The reporter appeared from the side of the van holding a pen and pad. 'One last thing, Lucy, how do you spell your last name?'

She was just about to open her mouth when Dan cut across her.

'Try F-I-R-E-D!'

The reporter jotted down half of the letters before looking up, frowning, but by then Dan was already tugging at Lucy's arm, dragging her away.

'Come on. You've got some explaining to do – in private.'

'Hang on!' she protested, fruitlessly attempting to resist while gesturing desperately towards the pub. 'I need to tell Kate –'

'No you don't.' He pulled her to a halt next to his car. 'What you need to do is explain how come your dead parrots ended up here at the auction instead of my cherries?'

He was facing her now as she stood with her back pressed against the hard metal of the ute door, his face looming just inches from her own and the cool night air turning his breath to vapour – or maybe that was steam.

'You said I could use the boxes.' She waited a second, giving him time to remember. 'All I can think is they must have got mixed up in the coolroom.'

'What?' He threw his hands up in the air. 'What the hell were your boxes doing in the coolroom?'

'The parrots were dead. How could I leave them outside all night?'

'Jeezus, Lucy. Of all the stupid –' But then he stopped, and she saw a distinct glimmer of hope in those dark eyes. 'You mean – my cherries – they're still actually in the coolroom?' He plunged his hand into his jeans pocket and pulled out his car keys. 'Maybe there's still time . . .'

'Maybe not,' she muttered, peeling herself off the car, not wanting to shatter his illusions but suspecting that any moment they would come crashing down around him anyway.

'They must still be in the coolroom. Fool must have picked up the wrong boxes this morning. Lucy, you go inside – tell the auctioneer to hold on. I'll be back with the cherries in a couple of minutes.'

Lucy edged around the car, pausing alongside his window. He looked up, annoyed to see her still there. His window slid down.

'Didn't you hear me? Tell them I'll be right back.'

'I heard you, Dan. It's just not that simple.'

'What's not simple? They picked up the wrong boxes. I'll get them now.' He fired up the ignition, gunning the engine.

'Well, it's just that . . . I have this sneaking suspicion . . .'

'What suspicion?'

'That the cherries . . . They may not be in the coolroom.'

'Why the hell not?'

There was nothing left but to spit it out. 'Because I think maybe I buried them.'

WHETHER IT WAS the ignition choking or a desperate groan from Dan, Lucy couldn't be sure, but she knew enough that she needed to go into damage control.

'But it's not all bad,' she said. 'What do they say – no publicity is bad publicity? This will be huge. You just wait. I'll fix it.'

He sighed and pushed his hair back over his head. 'It's already huge,' he said. 'Tonight's humiliation is going to be all over the radio and the TV. I don't believe it. My one chance of making this orchard succeed has been hijacked by a woman who puts dead birds before people's livelihoods. Four generations of work down the toilet in one fell swoop, and the only thing I can be grateful for is that Pop wasn't here to witness it.'

He turned to look at her and Lucy felt the weight of those four generations right there in his eyes. 'I got to hand it to you, Lucy. You fixed it, all right.'

'Dan, I –'

'Don't say a word. Just get in the car, Lucy, and don't say a bloody word.'

Neither of them spoke on the short trip back to the orchard, and it was only when Dan had pulled on the hand brake that he found his voice. 'Show me.'

'Excuse me?'

'Show me,' he said again, 'where you buried my cherries.'

She looked across at him uncertainly. It was dark and what was the point? 'Now?'

'Now!' Dan pulled a flashlight from the glove box of the Subaru and flicked it on. Lucy led the way down through the orchard to the small clearing. Her roughly constructed and brightly painted marker caught squarely in the bright beam, the camellias wilting on top of the grave.

'Your handiwork, I presume?' he asked in barely more than a whisper.

She swallowed and nodded.

He sighed. It wasn't just his cherries buried there, she could see. It was his life, his future, his plans.

He looked so defeated her heart went out to him. It had been easier when he shouted at her, when he had raged his accusations. This quiet acceptance of her failure was unbearable.

'I had no idea I buried the wrong boxes. You have to believe me. I never planned for this to happen. But –'

He didn't let her finish, suddenly regaining some of his old fight. 'That's just it! You don't plan anything, do you? That's your problem. Maybe if you had some idea of what you were doing and of the repercussions of your actions, maybe then you could avoid turning everything you do into some sort of major disaster.'

His words bit deep into her conscience and Lucy fought back the sudden prickle of tears. Because she could plan. And yes, she knew about repercussions. Especially when plans went wrong.

'I'll give you one day to get yourself sorted, but I want you packed up and gone by Monday. I'll pay you what I owe plus another week if you're gone by then. It'll be worth it just to be rid of you.'

'But . . .' Lucy began to protest but one look at Dan and she knew it was pointless. 'Fine. I'll go then.'

He took one more look at the burial site and it's crazy not-quite-a-cross before shaking his head as he stalked off toward the house.

CHAPTER 11

The cemetery was quiet late the next afternoon, and empty of the living – that is, if you ignored the cockatoos busily shredding pine cones in the surrounding trees and the baby magpies squawking for food as they chased after their mothers for a feed. Clumps of white Mount Lofty daisies flowered beneath the gums that lined one side and the warm breeze carried the sweet scent of the flowering shrubs.

Dan clutched a bottle of water and the rough bunch of pink and red camellias he'd lopped from along the driveway and headed down the hill to the plot that had been his mother's final resting place for thirty-four years and his father's for the last ten. It wasn't either of the anniversaries of their deaths.

It wasn't either of their birthdays.

Dan just wanted to come and say sorry.

Because he'd blown it.

Ten years ago he'd said goodbye to his father and promised he'd look after the orchard. And he thought he'd been doing okay too, until after a few good seasons he'd thought it a good idea to buy up the neighbouring property when Gracie Burrows had decided to sell. He'd paid top dollar for the acreage on the backs of a couple of good seasons – even though he'd known the trees would have to be nurtured and coaxed into productivity again – only to be caught carrying debt as the industry lurched into its two worst years on record.

He didn't begrudge the sum he'd paid Gracie. That had been the market and it was her own good luck that saw her selling then. It had been his own crappy timing that had got him into this mess. His own crappy risk-taking. And now it was his own crappy judgement – over a picker, of all things – that was threatening to ruin him.

He hunkered down beside the grave and pulled out the dried remnants of the flowers he'd left last time he'd come, shocked when he realised exactly how long it had been.

Mother's Day.

More than six months ago.

And guilt piled upon guilt.

He filled up the water in the flower holder and stuck stem after stem into the holes until there was a bright pink and red pompom at the foot of the grave of a mother he barely remembered and a father whose trust he'd betrayed.

The cherry auction wasn't the be all and end all, his Pop had reminded him last night when he'd called to tell him it had all gone pear-shaped. And maybe Pop was right, but they'd been counting on it to kickstart the season. Now, after the humiliation of the auction, he was going to have to work doubly hard to get probably a fraction of the result. He'd be a laughing stock - even more than he already was - and the only bright side was that Pop had scored a nail in a tyre and the spare was flat and he hadn't wanted to bother Dan for a lift, and so he'd missed the whole sorry debacle.

The downside was a whole lot bleaker. If they scored a

thunderstorm or two and the fruit split before they could bring it all in, it would be hard to fend the banks off for another year. Hard to convince them that he knew what he was doing when they'd never wanted to extend credit in the first place and had been on his back for the last two years running. They wouldn't be on his back anymore, if it came to that. They'd be circling for the kill.

God, maybe he was better out of it. Being a primary producer was a mug's game.

He shook his head as he plucked some gum leaves and twigs from the gravel that topped the grave, then smoothed the gravel nearest him with a sweep of the palm of his hand, a lump in his throat threatening to cut off his breathing as he felt the sun-warmed stones under his skin. It took a while before he could speak.

'I'm sorry, Mum. Dad,' he said, his voice as rough as the stones under his palm. 'I've blown it.'

HE GLANCED in the direction of the van as he drove back up the driveway to home. He'd got rid of her just like he'd always known he'd have to. He should be at least pleased with himself for that – after all, she'd cost him a fortune in lost sales. The idea of the cherry auction had been to give growers a head start with orders for this season. He'd come home with zip orders and a healthy dose of humiliation to boot.

No doubt about it, Lucy had only got what was coming to her. Right now she would be packing her things and tomorrow morning she'd be gone.

And yet still he felt lousy.

Dan pulled a container from the freezer, slammed it into the microwave and stabbed at the controls. Having taken care of dinner, he reached into the fridge for a beer.

Tonight he was going to spend a quiet evening in front of the telly, eating his 'authentic' Mexican chilli beef with refried beans and rice then maybe watching the late night movie. By tomorrow morning the biggest mistake of his life would be behind him and he could start to plan how to make up for some of his lost sales. He still had a crop – he was just going to have to work harder to get those big sales he was needing.

He popped the cap and took a swig of beer, wiping his bottom lip with the back of his hand.

He'd sacked a few employees in his time. It wasn't something he enjoyed doing, but normally once he'd done the deed, he felt better. Lucy had proved to be a disaster area of an employee. He should be celebrating.

Though that wasn't entirely true. For the few days he'd seen of Lucy's actual work, she'd done fine. He'd even thought she'd had the makings of a good picker.

And a darned good looking one at that. He still had to battle to keep his eyes off her every time she was around. The way she moved, the swish of her hair around that dynamite smile of hers, and a body . . . Well, a body that no cherry picker in his employ had a right to have. Not when it reminded him of how long it had been . . .

That only plunged him into an even deeper gloom. Disconsolate, he carried his microwave meal and beer into the lounge room and sank into an armchair, flicking on the telly with the remote control.

The news greeted him. It was the usual stuff; a severe cold snap in Europe, a puppy stuck down a drain somewhere else. It was just about time for the sport segment when he saw it – the familiar exterior of The Scenic Hotel. And standing centre screen, her honey blonde hair bleached white in the bright wash of the cameraman's lighting, was none other than Lucy.

'Shit!' He jumped up, his plate spinning off his lap, tipping the remnants of his dinner across the floor.

He growled as he grabbed for the remote, turning up the volume and ignoring the detritus of his meal lying scattered on the rug.

'Only one person has been brave enough to stand up against this senseless slaughter,' she was saying. 'Dan Faraday has risked his entire future in the industry to bring home the truth about what is happening up here.'

The screen was suddenly filled with a still shot of the dead parrots lying in their boxes. Lucy's voice came over the top.

'Dan believes that there are better ways to control the birds – we don't have to kill these beautiful and defenceless creatures.'

Oh. My. God!

Was there no end to this nightmare?

'Some people might suggest,' prompted the reporter, 'that this is nothing more than a publicity stunt and that Dan Faraday is just looking for a bit of free advertising to promote his cherries after a couple of bad years.'

'Everyone knows Dan grows the best cherries in the region. He doesn't need free advertising.'

'Huh! At least you got something right', conceded Dan, momentarily siding with Lucy as the reporter's cynical suggestion left him incensed.

'And Dan doesn't care if no-one buys his cherries –'

'Yes I bloody well do!' Dan shouted at the screen.

'– so long as the killing stops.'

The remote control bounced off the frame of the television just as the reporter was signing off.

A loud guttural roar filled the room, a potent combination of frustration, helplessness and rage, as any remaining regrets about his earlier decision to sack Lucy were quickly dispelled.

Enough was enough! She was going to be leaving now – right this minute – if he had any say in the matter.

He'd just made it to the back door when the phone rang. He hesitated, looked out in the direction of the van and back at the phone. Lucy could wait a couple more minutes for what he had to say.

It was no surprise that the phone was ringing. No doubt someone who'd seen the news report. He growled. Better not be another bloody reporter or they'd get an earful. He'd switch on the answerphone after this call. Better still, he might even take the phone off the hook.

THIRTY SECONDS later he was standing with the receiver in his hand, totally stunned. 'You want to buy how many kilos?'

The buyer repeated his offer and Dan looked around for a chair, feeling a sudden need to sit down. 'My wife loves the parrots,' the buyer explained. 'She insists I buy only cherries from an orchard that doesn't harm the birds. She won't let me buy any other.'

Bloody hell. He put the phone back in the cradle, and his hand was still on it when it rang again. Another order. Then another right on its heels.

It was a full twenty minutes before he managed to snap on the answering machine during a brief respite. He took a few calming breaths, battling back the intoxication of a sudden adrenaline rush brought on by the knowledge that things were suddenly looking very, very good for the orchard.

Not even if his cherries had sold to rapturous acclaim at the cherry auction last night, would he have expected this amount of attention. Now he had all the orders he could handle and more for the next few weeks. His disaster of a season had turned into a boomer.

Totting up the figures in his head, Dan calculated that if he could satisfy all these orders, by season end he'd have wiped out the last two years of debt.

He couldn't wait to tell Pop.

He frowned, distracted by another incoming order as he assessed his immediate needs for the orchard. He was going to need a couple more pickers on the team, just to be sure the crop could be brought in at peak condition. It would cost a bit more in labour, but at the prices his new buyers seemed willing to pay, it would be worth the expense this year to ensure quality control – especially if it meant retaining them as long term customers.

He'd stick up an ad at the post office tomorrow. Meanwhile the rest of the team, himself included, were going to be working their butts off to fill these orders. Might even see if some could put in six and a half days a week. Most of the pickers wouldn't mind. They came to make as much money in the picking season as they could. The offer of a few more shifts wouldn't faze them at all.

A gentle spring breeze puffed through the screen door, caressing him with its cargo of fresh herb scent. His head lifted involuntarily, nostrils flaring to drink in the aroma. And given he'd lost most of his television dinner to the floor, his stomach rumbled. She was cooking again.

Lucy!

He'd forgotten all about her in the excitement.

Right now she would be just about all packed up, ready to leave in the morning, just as he'd demanded. And he'd been about to insist on her leaving tonight.

God! What was he going to say? What could he say?

A cold mist of anxiety drizzled down his spine.

She'd done this!

It was her actions that had resulted in these fantastic orders. It was her ridiculous television appearance that had turned around the fortunes of the orchard.

While he'd been mentally applauding himself on exceeding his own long-term plans, he'd forgotten how this newfound success had come about.

He could hardly sack her now. He almost choked on his next thought.

He might even have to thank her!

LUCY SPREAD out the blanket on the grass outside the van and breathed deeply. It was too balmy a night to spend cooped up in van when she could be outside, savouring her last sunset views of this orchard. It was so peaceful when the lunatic next door wasn't blasting away at the bird life.

Once more she wanted to see the trees glow gold in the dipping sun. Once more she would watch the parrots wheel in the fading light as they descended into the trees to feast on the ripe fruit.

Not that she would be so far away tomorrow. Kate's mum had offered to squeeze her in, and she could have moved her gear there today, but Lucy wanted just one more night in the orchard she'd grown to love. Silly of her, she knew, but she did feel a connection with the homestead she still could not explain.

Back in the van she piled some steamed rice into one bowl and some red curry into another. Then she grabbed a fork and a light beer, and headed outside.

She cocked her head as the sound of a ringing phone filtered over from the homestead, before sitting down, cross-legged, on the rug. Boy, Dan sure was popular tonight! His phone had been going non-stop for the last half-hour. No doubt all his mates wanting to commiserate with him.

A pair of parrots landed in a nearby tree. Lucy watched them, fascinated by their behaviour. They followed each other from bough to bough, never more than a wingspan apart, before they launched themselves into the next tree. They were the parrot equivalent of married, she decided.

Not for the first time she noticed the way they nibbled at the fruit, taking only a peck from some cherries before moving on to the next cluster. That could be a bit annoying for the orchardist, she conceded with a slight frown, if they wasted so much fruit. But then, there were so many cherries and not that many parrots.

'Lucy, I . . .'

Her head snapped around as she dropped her fork. She'd been so engrossed in the birds that she didn't hear the approaching footfall and now Dan was standing near the van looking confused. What was that about?

'You said I could stay until tomorrow,' she challenged, jumping to her feet, tugging down the brief, frayed sides of her denim cut-offs.

He took a hesitant step forward. 'About that . . .'

HE'D ALWAYS THOUGHT she was a stunner but he'd never seen those legs before. They were unbelievably long for someone of her height and they were tanned gold, their gentle muscle structure clearly delineated below her smooth skin. Normally they were hidden under jeans or long pants and now he wondered how he was ever going to look at her covered legs again without wanting to peel them off. But then, he wouldn't be seeing her again, not if she left tomorrow . . .

He forced his eyes back to her face, wondering just when it was that the mild mannered orchardist he'd always thought himself had turned into a dirty old man.

'You're having dinner,' he said, stating the obvious because he was rapidly losing track of what he was doing here. 'I didn't mean to interrupt.'

'That's okay.' She looked at her bowl. 'Hey, have you eaten? I made way too much – trying to use up a few things before I have to leave . . .' Her words trailed off.

'Um, well, it sure smells good.'

'Of course it's good,' she admitted without false modesty, smiling at last as she disappeared into the van. 'I made it myself.'

She returned moments later with more curry, rice and beer.

'Here. Have a seat.' She placed his bowls opposite her on the rug, patting the spot where he should sit. He gave a small shrug and wandered over, hitching up his jeans legs as he squatted down and she continued talking.

'I'm just enjoying this view one last time.'

He liked it better from where he was sitting. Smooth legs. Sexy thighs. He blinked and forced his eyes away before he could notice any more. 'Thanks,' he said instead, realising he was already sweating and he hadn't even touched the curry.

He stabbed his dish with his fork and took a taste and quickly followed it with another, and a couple of minutes later and his temperature had everything to do with the food.

'Wow!' He wiped his forehead with the back of his hand. 'That's hot stuff.'

'You like?' she asked. 'There's more.'

'I like.'

She took his bowl and when their fingers brushed he felt a sizzle that had nothing to do with the curry. He watched her go, enjoying the swivel of her hips and the glimpse of round bottom beneath her short shorts every time she took a step.

She was something all right. He couldn't remember ever lusting after a woman like this one. Life would be a hell of a lot easier if she did go. Which reminded him . . .

'I have to talk to you about something.'

SHE'D JUST HANDED him his seconds and she picked up on his change in mood. He wasn't angry but something was definitely up. She nodded, signalling that she was ready to hear it, whatever it was.

'Have you got plans for tomorrow.'

She bit back on the urge to say she didn't make plans.

'Kind of. Kate's family has offered to put me up. They don't think I'll be long without work, not this time of year.'

He nodded but it was impossible to tell whether that meant he was satisfied with her response or not.

'What about if I said you could stay on here?'

She raised her eyebrows. 'Excuse me? I didn't realise it was an option.'

'If it was an option – do you think you'd consider it?'

She shrugged. Just then the external phone bell rang and she looked across to him expectantly. 'Do you need to go answer that?'

'The machine will take a message.'

'It's been going all evening.'

'Yeah, I know. It's been practically non-stop ever since a certain blonde appeared on television tonight . . .'

Lucy frowned, not understanding.

'. . . alleging I don't care if no-one buys my cherries . . .'

Her eyes widened.

'. . . so long as no-one harms the precious parrots.'

She put her hand to her mouth. 'I did say that, didn't I?'

'You sure did.'

'And you saw it?'

He smiled. 'Yup.'

She blinked. 'Hang on. You just smiled.'

'You got a problem with that?'

No. It was great to see him smile. It was just that it didn't make any kind of sense.

'Course not,' she said, covering her confusion by collecting up their dishes.

HE WATCHED her go with a growing sense of wonderment. She was one out of the box, that was for sure.

He looked out over the orchard, watching the golden rays of sunset fading under a grey blanket of dusk. His brow creased as he studied the activity of the birds. There were more than ever.

Now that he had all these orders he was going to have to do something to keep them out of his cherries. He couldn't afford the losses now.

Moments later Lucy reappeared in the doorway, arms crossed, a frown creasing the bridge of her perfect nose. There was clearly something on her mind.

'I'm confused.'

'Why's that?' he asked, getting to his feet and moving towards her.

'Because you're not mad at me. I can't work it out. You should be mad at me.'

He stopped right in front of her and placed an arm up against the same side of the van she was leaning against.

He saw her eyes widen with surprise at his proximity, saw that surprise turn into something more like appreciation as they slid all the way down to his boots and all the way back up again, and felt his blood pump a little bit faster.

They were the same height now, and he could see right into her blue eyes. They were confused, sure, but their big black centres told him there was something else going on in there too. Something that just might explain that tiny tweak of her posture that pushed her breasts an inch closer to his chest.

'Why should I be mad at you?'

'Are you kidding me? Every time I do something it's like I've ruined your plans. Every time I speak it's tantamount to creating disaster in your neat, well-ordered life. You were born mad at me - and that was before last night.'

He frowned, even though he knew she was right. He'd pegged her for trouble the moment he'd set eyes on her and she'd well and truly proved him right. He'd never for a moment imagined that she'd somehow manage to turn last night's disaster around.

Just for once, though, it was Lucy on the back foot and not him. She was the one confused and he was enjoying the change in fortunes.

'Not that I can't appreciate where you're coming from,' she continued, 'being a control freak and everything. You can't help yourself.'

'Is that right?' he managed to insert, not sure whether to be amused or annoyed that this woman was now making out that he was the one with the problem.

'And yet,' she added, 'You don't seem mad about me being on television. I don't get that.'

At that moment those blue eyes looked so perplexed as they gazed intently into his, her lips, moist and pink, slightly parted as they awaited his response – lips he could still see with his eyes shut, still wearing that tempting drop of cherry juice – and he didn't know if it was heat from the curry that was making his head spin, but he was almost overcome with the crazy desire to curl a hand around her neck and draw her close and kiss those waiting lips senseless.

'Maybe,' he murmured edging closer as he wondered if it was worthwhile fighting off that particular impulse, 'you've been underestimating me.'

'Maybe,' she murmured so softly and so close Dan was sure he had felt the word rather than heard it.

Now only a hair's breadth separated them and Dan decided he was through fighting one particular impulse any more. He wanted to kiss her. He could tell she wasn't about to stop him. Why the hell shouldn't he?

She tilted her chin up right at that moment, offering her lips, as her eyelashes fluttered closed and he was lost.

His lips tilted and dipped, brushing hers in the faintest of passes which left him near breathless, as her taste, touch and smell combined in him into one overwhelming sense of need.

He moved to answer that need and the world suddenly exploded. Cannons went off in time with the thunderous pulse in his head and just as he dropped his hand to gather her even closer, he realised she was already gone.

By the time he'd turned to look for her she was already halfway to the boundary.

'Come on,' she was yelling back to him. 'We have to stop him!'

Comprehension kicked in as the next shot rang out. Raising his eyes to heaven, Dan breathed a long, frustrated sigh as much for the benefit of putting his libido to bed as anything else.

'Damn!' he cursed, before racing after her.

CHAPTER 12

'Who's going to stop me?' demanded Des, his chubby trigger finger perceptibly twitching. His son, similarly armed and already on his way to matching jowls, sniggered nearby.

Without hesitation, Lucy pointed at Dan.

'He is.'

Thank you very much, thought Dan.

'And just how do you intend to do that?' bellowed his neighbour.

Dan cleared his throat and pasted a thin smile to his face. 'Maybe it's time we had a talk about what's going on here, Des.'

'Ha,' guffawed Des. 'I'd rather talk about that debacle at the pub with your "giant cherries".'

Dan flashed a fiery look over to Lucy and cursed under his breath.

'There was a mix up.'

'Mix up? More like a cock up.' Des dissolved into fits of laughter, mimicked by his young clone. Both men wobbled dangerously in the half-light.

'I didn't notice any cherries from your orchard up for auction,' said Lucy. 'Is the fruit you produce so bad that you can't offer it publicly? Are you afraid no-one would make a bid or that you'd have to pay someone to take them?'

Des stopped laughing. His son, obviously not too quick on the uptake, took longer, only stopping with the assistance of a sharp rifle butt dig to his well-padded ribs.

Dan mentally applauded. As much as he wished to avoid confrontation, he was getting sick of trying to be neighbourly to someone who was such a lousy neighbour. Des had bought the property ten years back and the longer he'd been there, the more convinced Dan was that he'd bought it for some kind of tax dodge. He sure wasn't interested in his trees. Perhaps he'd bought it for the sport.

'There's nothing wrong with my cherries,' Des insisted, puffing his chest and his red cheeks up like a toad. 'Or there wouldn't be, if the bloody parrots would leave them alone.'

'Don't blame the parrots,' Dan retorted. 'You don't look after your trees. They haven't been cared for in years. They're full of cherry slug and I have to work twice as hard to make sure it doesn't cross into my orchard. If your yields are down, it's because of your neglect – not because of the birds. Face it, Des, your orchard is a mess.'

Dan saw Lucy's head wheel around, her mouth open, and he almost smiled. He hadn't felt so good in ages. All the concerns he'd had for months about his neighbour's orchard, but been afraid to mention, had finally been broached. Des would have a few things to think about tonight.

Des was so stunned, it looked like he was about to have a stroke.

'Da-ad?' ventured his son uncertainly, obviously not comfortable with the turn of events. 'Mum said tea was nearly ready. Maybe we should get back to the house before she gets mad at us.'

Des snorted a couple more times before the voice of reason and the fear of she-who-must-be-obeyed finally got through.

'Yeah, well,' he offered, making a show of checking out the gloom now surrounding him, 'It's too dark now anyway. Might as well go inside.' He turned on his heel and huffed off, his son in tow.

They watched the departing neighbours until they had disappeared into the orchard. Then Dan turned to Lucy and dusted off his hands. 'Mission accomplished?'

SHE NODDED as she rubbed her shoulders with her hands. Now that the heat of the confrontation had dissipated, she felt chilled in the increasing dusk.

'I have to say it; that was some speech. I don't know who was more surprised, Des or me.'

He smiled and dropped an arm around her shoulders, giving it a squeeze as they turned and headed back across the orchard.

'Someone had to take the heat off you,' he offered, 'after that jibe about his cherries not being too special.'

Lucy chuckled but her thoughts were not of the words she'd spoken earlier. As she fell into rhythm with Dan's stride, safely ensconced between his arm and his chest, all she could think of was what they had been doing prior to the shots being fired. What they'd been about to do . . .

What would have happened if Des hadn't interrupted that kiss? Where would it have led?

Nowhere, that's where.

While Dan had been more relaxed in her presence tonight, their dealings to date had for the most part been marked with frustration and friction. And that damned spark.

She was leaving tomorrow. Maybe that's why he'd let the kiss happen – his guard was down and he knew she'd be off his hands by morning. Maybe that was why he'd allowed himself to kiss someone who obviously fell so far outside his idea of a perfect match.

After all, he'd been checking her out all week. She'd seen him watching her. She'd felt the heat of his gaze. Was he just hoping to satisfy his lust with a quick roll in the hay before he booted her out?

He dropped his arm from her shoulders when they got back to the van and straightaway she felt colder. There was a gap of one or two breaths, then he said, 'How about you come up to the house for a coffee? Pay you back for the curry?'

She smiled and her stomach did a little dance. And she was so tempted to say yes. So tempted to go up to the house with him and see where it led. So tempted . . .

She took a deep breath and looked up at him, his features barely distinguishable but for the glint in his dark eyes in the pooling dark. Yet still she knew that he was watching her intently.

'Thanks. But let's face it, what would be the point? I'm moving out tomorrow morning and I've still got some stuff to organise.'

'I want you to stay.'

'You what?'

'I was wrong to ask you to leave. I was wrong to fire you. Please stay, if you want.'

'But you said –'

'I know what I said. I was wrong.'

Lucy felt her insides flutter, a tangle of confusion mixed with a drop of hope.

'Why, after all that's happened, do you want me to stay?'

She held her breath as his hands went to her shoulders, held her breath as he brought her closer and tingled all the way down to her toes as his lips brushed the top of her head, before he put her away from him.

'Because, my clever Lucy, your starring role on television tonight has just turned the fortunes of this orchard around.'

It was the right answer, Lucy told herself as she washed the dishes. It was the only answer. Any other answer would have made no sense at all.

So why wasn't it the answer she'd wanted to hear?

CHAPTER 13

*L*ucy was staying. That was a good thing, wasn't it?
Dan cleaned up the floor in the lounge where he'd
scattered his beans and rice and he was almost sure
that was a good thing. Asking her to stay was the right thing
to do. After all, her television appearance had turned the
debacle of the cherry auction into a coup for the orchard. It
would be churlish to insist she leave after that.

But he never should have kissed her. Oh no. Kissing her
had been a big mistake. Thank God one of them had the
sense to say no to coffee.

What the hell had he been thinking? Huh, that was easy.
He didn't think with his brain when he was around her. Now
that she was staying, he better get himself right back on that
internet dating horse.

The phone rang again and the machine cut in, but this call
he wanted to pick up. 'Hey Han, how's it going?'

'Hey yourself! The orchard is famous, and you've got
yourself a real star picker there!'

'You saw it, huh?'

'Beth called me when the news came on. Sophie was right, Lucy's gorgeous.'

'Yeah,' he said, chewing his lip. She was that. But her sister calling reminded him of something else that had been playing on his mind. 'Han, do you know what's going on with Pop? All these tests he's been having must be for something.'

'He told me it was indigestion. No, heartburn. One or the other. Anyway, he said it was nothing a bit of Nexium or antacid couldn't fix.'

'Yeah,' Dan said, 'he told me something similar. But then he's been acting a bit weird'

'What do you mean, weird?'

'Well, he hasn't been near the orchard all week, which is pretty unusual for a start. And he didn't make it to the cherry auction last night. Said he had car trouble – a flat tyre.'

'And you think he's hiding something?'

'I dunno. But normally he'd walk over hot coals to get himself involved in anything to do with the orchard. Has he said anything to you? Or has Nan?'

'No. Nothing. You think it's something more than indigestion?'

'He'd hardly miss the cherry auction for a bit of indigestion, surely.'

'Yeah, you're right. It doesn't sound like him, at all. Maybe he really did have a flat.'

'Maybe.' But Dan wasn't sure he believed it.

AFTER HE HUNG UP, Dan fired up the computer and logged in to HEA.com. He looked at the page of matches, saw Donna still there at the top, smiling out at him with her ten-year-old grin. He sighed. Carly and Simone and Debbie were still there, along with a host of others. Then he noticed Marie in the bottom row. 34 years old, slim and with a nice smile. Straight teeth. A bookkeeper. That'd be sure be handy for the business and a bookkeeper was bound to be sensible. He flicked her a message to say hello.

And then, because there was no time to waste, he clicked on Carly's profile too; Carly, the public servant who liked cats. Well, he liked cats too. He liked dogs better, but after Molly he wasn't having another one. Not when they ripped your heart out when they died and not even having a vet for a sister was enough to save them.

He checked his email for orders and printed off another bunch. It was turning into a very good season. By the time he'd done that, both women had responded. Oh yeah, a very good season indeed.

Coffee and cake tomorrow evening with Marie? Sure thing.

Drinks with Carly the night after? No problem.

But forewarned was forearmed. After the Donna disaster he'd worked out a plan – first of all he'd check to make sure the profile photo was recent, and then;

a) agree to meet somewhere a little further afield than the Scenic, and

b) eat first (just in case).

AN OLD MAN in battered work clothes and dusty boots wandered into the shed the next day as Lucy filled up her water bottle before heading out to start picking. 'Pop!' Dan said, 'You're here.'

'Of course, I'm here. What kind of a welcome is that?'

'So you're okay?'

'Of course, I'm okay,' he growled. 'Why else would I bloody well be here?'

And Lucy couldn't help but laugh. Maybe Dan's grumpiness was genetic after all. The old man spotted Lucy at the sink and his eyes lit up. 'So this is our TV star? You must be this Lucy I keep hearing about.'

'Hey,' she said with a smile, joining the pair and offering her hand, 'Not really a star' He wrapped her hand in his large knobbly fingers, a surprisingly strong grip for someone she'd heard was in his eighties. And Lucy could see his grandson in his weathered features, and in the shape of his eyes and the line of his jaw. He would have been a good looking man in his prime. He was still handsome, in a rugged leathery-skinned way.

'Lucy,' Dan said, 'this is Clarry.'

'But you can call me Pop.'

That earned a frown from Dan and Lucy smiled. 'A pleasure to meet you, Pop.' And the old man beamed.

'My dad fought alongside the Yanks in the Pacific. Always reckoned you Septic Tanks were the real deal.'

'Pop!'

Lucy must have looked confused, because the old man went on, 'You know, rhyming slang. Septic Tank — Yank.'

'Pop? Really?'

'Oh,' Lucy said with a laugh. 'I get it.'

'Good girl,' said Pop, peeling the paper from a roll of something called QuickEze and tossing it into his mouth. 'But what are we doing in here? We've got a crop to get in.'

There was almost a party mood in the orchard that day, in part due to the return of Clarry to the fold, but Lucy was the main reason. Dan even threw an impromptu morning tea, buying a massive cheesecake from the hotel to celebrate the orders, which made him boss of the week right there. Everyone was excited about the prospects for the orchard, cheering when he told them there'd be two bucks an hour more in their pay packets if they picked their hearts out.

Kate tossed her paper plate and napkin into the rubbish bin as she said to Lucy. 'Didn't I tell you that you wouldn't want to miss the cherry auction?'

'Hey, I've been meaning to ask, what happened to you anyway? Where did you disappear to all of a sudden?'

'I had to go to the loo.'

'They've got an outside can?'

She shrugged. 'I needed some fresh air, that's all.'

'Uh huh, and Rod needed some fresh air too, I guess?'

This time she snorted. 'Me with Ratface? Are you kidding me? Nah, he was just having a smoke or something. He probably just came inside at the same time because he wanted to know what all the fuss was about.'

'Hey, why would I care if you were seeing him?'

'Seeing him? Are you kidding me?' She jerked her head over to where Rod was sitting with the guys. 'That's a laugh. Hey, we better get back to work.'

'Sure,' Lucy said, eating the last bite of her cheesecake, not entirely convinced but figuring what Kate did was her business. Everyone was drifting back outside when she walked up to Dan. She wanted to run a few ideas by him.

'Hey boss,' she said, as he packed away the leftovers in the box. 'I was thinking.'

'Yeah?'

She picked up one of the cherry boxes, all folded together and stamped with the Faraday Orchard name and prepped for two kilos of cherries to come off the grading belt. 'Maybe you should put a logo or something on the boxes. You know, something that says "bird friendly" rather than just your name.'

Dan's brows drew together, one eyebrow cocked. 'What did you have in mind?'

'I don't know. Maybe a circle around a stylised parrot or a picture of a couple of birds in flight or something.'

'You reckon there's any point?'

'Well, the colours would really make the boxes stand out and there'd be no mistaking which cherries come from a bird-friendly orchard, even if they forgot the name.'

Dan thought about it. It wasn't a bad idea. 'We'd need to engage some kind of designer though, and we'd be hard pressed to get something organised before cherry season is over.'

'I could do it.'

'You?'

'Sure. How about I come up with a few designs and see what you think?'

He scratched his head. 'It wouldn't hurt, I guess, if you want to give it a shot.'

'Yay,' she said, punching the air with her fist. 'I'm onto it!' And headed back to pick.

DAN WAS STILL SCRATCHING his head. He'd have to see what she came up with of course, but maybe there was more to her than met the eye. Maybe she had hidden talents. Other than an uncanny ability to short-circuit his brain whenever she was anywhere nearby.

Don't go there.

He put what was left of the cake in the fridge. Someone would polish it off at lunchtime for sure. As for dinner, he was meeting Marie tonight and this time he was determined to eat something for his troubles. He heard voices drifting in from the orchard. Pop's gravelly tones followed by Lucy's bright and breezy twang. Yeah, that'd be right, she'd charmed the socks off the old man already.

At least Pop seemed to be coping. He'd started off a bit

slow, like he was stiff or something from his days off, but he was catching up fast.

And then he heard Lucy laugh and the sound has his head turning to follow it, like turning his face to sunshine.

He sighed. He hoped Marie worked out. It was about time he had a change of luck.

LUCY WAS JUST MAKING coffee that night when there was a knock on the side of the van door.

'Hey,' she said, putting down her sketch book where' she'd been doodling some designs for the orchard, before opening the screen door. Two women were standing there with a girl in between.

'You must be Lucy. Hi, I'm Hannah.'

'And I'm Beth, and this is Siena.'

The girl looked up at her with big brown eyes, studying her nose.

'Hey Siena.'

'Hi,' she said back, clearly fascinated.

'What can I do for you?'

'We're Dan's sisters. '

'Two of them anyway.'

'Oh, were you looking for Dan? I think I heard him go out a little while ago.'

'Er, no,' said the one called Beth.

'Actually, we came to say hello to you,' said the other.

'You came to see me?'

They could be bookends, these two, thought Lucy, looking from one to the other. Both blondes, unlike Sophie she'd already met, one had her hair pulled back in a ponytail and was wearing overalls with a T-shirt underneath, and the other had her cut shorter in a pixie style around her face and was wearing a denim mini, but their features were almost identical. They even sounded alike, and though she searched for a trace of Dan in their features, it was hard to find. Then again, maybe that's because these women know how to smile.

'We wanted to meet you. We heard what happened at the cherry auction.'

'Oh.'

'And what you did afterwards. Dan said he's got sales coming out of his ears.'

Lucy let go a breath she hadn't realised she'd been holding. 'I kind of put him in an awkward spot.'

'Did that hurt,' asked Siena between them.

Lucy looked down. 'What? The awkward spot?'

'No, that,' she said. 'In your nose. Did it hurt to get a piercing there?'

'Siena,' the girl's mother warned.

'I was just wondering.'

'No, it's okay. You can ask. It hurt a bit a bit more than when I got my ears done, but it didn't take long to heal.'

'I want to get pierced ears, but mum says I have to wait until I'm ten.'

'That can't be too far off.'

The girl crossed her arms and huffed theatrically. 'It's two whole years, but then I have to wait until the end of netball season.'

Beth smiled apologetically. 'Life's just full of injustices when you're eight.'

'I guess.' She smiled down at the girl. 'What's netball? Is that like basketball?'

Siena smiled. 'Kind of, but it's seven-a-side and it's mostly girls. I could teach you how to play if you like?'

'Yeah, why not. Hey,' she said, happy to have visitors, 'Do you guys want a drink? A coffee or a Pepsi or something?'

'A Pepsi would be cool, thanks,' said Siena and the three

women looked at Siena and laughed, before Lucy pulled open the fridge door.

'One Pepsi coming right up. Anyone else?'

'STRIKE TWO,' said Dan to himself, as he climbed in his car and headed up the hill to home. He tried to tell himself that it was okay, that there were plenty more fish in the sea and that he was meeting another of the fish tomorrow night, but he couldn't help but feel a bit disappointed. Marie the book-keeper had sounded perfect. What the hell was he doing wrong? He must be missing something.

But where was the hint on the profile to tell him that Marie would be sidling up next to him and trying to sit in his lap a minute after saying hello, or that she'd start stabbing her fork into his cake for a taste as if they were already married? He wasn't sure he'd want to share, even if he was married.

So he'd eaten his cake – what he could get of it – and he'd downed his coffee and he hadn't even got to his questions. But then, there didn't seem to be any point.

Straight teeth and bookkeeping skills notwithstanding, she was as bad as the parrots who pecked at his cherries.

And there were already enough of the bloody parrots.

Damn.

Tomorrow night had to go better or he'd be starting to wonder about this online dating thing.

It was supposed to be saving him time, not wasting it in the busiest part of the year.

He drove up the driveway, preparing himself for a last check of his emails for orders and then bed, when he saw Hannah's car.

What was she doing here?

But there were no lights on inside the house and when he opened the door and called her name, there was no reply. And then he heard it – the sound of laughter. Women's laughter. He turned his head. It was coming from the somewhere in the orchard, in the direction of the van.

Oh, yeah, he thought, as he climbed out. That'd be right.

'And then,' he heard Hannah's words drift through the orchard, 'the fire alarm went off and all hell broke loose. You should have seen Dan's face – he looked like he wanted to shoot the lot of us.'

They were laughing. Yeah, it had been hysterical. Absolutely hilarious.

And then he came upon them, the girls sitting outside the van, Hannah and Beth in a couple of deck chairs, with Siena on the ground between them and Lucy on the step of the van nursing a cup between her hands.

Siena heard him coming first. 'Uncle Dan!'

The others looked around. He looked at them. 'Well, this sure looks cosy.'

Lucy grinned, and damn it to hell and back, she looked more gorgeous every time he saw her. 'I've got visitors,' she said.

'So I can see.' In spite of his grump, he smiled. 'Hannah. Beth. Did you guys want to see me?'

'Not particularly,' said Hannah.

'Though it's always good to,' chimed in her twin.

'We came to meet Lucy,' volunteered Siena, and Dan thought, Oh right, it just gets better and better.

'In that case –' he started, ready to turn and go.

'Would you like a coffee or a beer or something?'

Would he? He could sure do with something to wash away the taste of disappointment in his mouth. Lucy was looking at him, that sweet smile playing around her lips, but it wasn't just Lucy. His sisters and his niece were watching him too. All of them were watching and waiting like they were now on Team Lucy or something.

If he left, they'd probably make something of it. They'd talk about him for sure. He could hear the laughter behind his back already. He'd be sitting at home listening to it drifting over on the balmy night breeze and he'd be gritting his teeth wondering.

Nope. Much better to play it cool.

'Coffee'd be great, thanks.'

'White and one, right?'

He caught the glance his sisters shared, as if there was something special about Lucy knowing how he took his coffee, because there wasn't, but he wouldn't have minded one bit if she'd forgotten either.

'Yeah.'

Lucy stood and turned and stepped up into the van, and for a moment before she disappeared, he was mesmerised by the sway of her hips as she climbed the steps. He shook his head and dragged his eyes away. 'How's tricks?' he asked.

'Busy,' said Hannah. 'Getting a lot of pets with snakebite this time of year. Even managing to save a few.'

'Had one of those the other day myself,' said Beth. 'A guy had been bushwalking in thongs, can you believe it?'

'Moron.' Dan sniffed. 'Hey, did you hear Pop's back at work? Turned up bold as brass this morning like last week never happened.'

Han shook her head. 'So maybe it was just indigestion.'

Dan turned to his other sister. 'You're the paramedic Beth, what do you reckon?'

Beth shrugged. 'Pop told me it was just routine tests, so I'm as much in the dark as you guys. I'll drop in this week and see what I can find out from Nan, but if he's back at work, surely it can't be too serious.'

'I'll keep an eye on him in the orchard. The doctor did tell him to slow down.'

Han snorted. 'What else would a doctor tell someone Pop's age who's still working?

'You don't think it's his prostate?' said Beth. 'And he's too embarrassed to tell anyone.'

'God, at his age it could be anything.'

'What's prostate?' asked Siena between sips on her Pepsi.

'Never mind,' said Beth.

'Anyway,' said Han, a knowing glint in her eyes, 'what I want to know is where've you been all spruced up? Another date?'

'Have you got a girlfriend yet, Uncle Dan?' asked Siena.

'Out, maybe and no,' he answered. 'In that order.'

'Oh, no good then?'

'Nope.'

'Ooh, why?'

'Care to go into details?'

'Not really.'

'Didn't she like you, Uncle Dan?'

He crouched down, his elbows planted on his legs, and looked at his niece levelly. 'She wanted to eat my cake.'

Siena screwed up her nose. 'I don't like her either.'

There was a clatter of kettle on stove from inside the van and the clink of a spoon in a cup and then Lucy was back, cup of coffee in hand. 'Here you go,' she said, as she handed him the cup.

'Thanks,' he said, and watched that bottom sway right back to its seat on the step of the van.

'A bit of a shame though,' said Hannah. 'Sophie's quiz night is coming up soon and I thought you might find a date to take along.'

'There's still time, surely,' said Beth.

Of course there was still time. If he wanted to take

someone along and subject them to the early and no doubt intense scrutiny of his family, that was.

Anyhow, he already had Carly lined up for drinks tomorrow night, not that he was about to share that detail with this particular audience. Especially in front of Lucy.

THERE WAS something about a man kneeling down on his haunches, Lucy mused. Something country that transcended borders and accents. A man in boots and jeans and a shirt unbuttoned at the neck so you got a sneak peek of that curl of chest hair – well, it was hard not to like it really.

Likewise it was hard not to enjoy the interplay between these women and their brother. They were like a tag team act, the way they played him, like they knew what the other was thinking and could build on the teasing.

'Something'll turn up,' Dan said, sipping on his coffee.

'Why don't you take Lucy?'

He spluttered, as everyone looked at Siena.

'Excuse me?' Lucy said.

The girl shrugged. 'Well, it's just that if you don't have a girlfriend by then, wouldn't it be nice to take Lucy, Uncle Dan?'

'Hey,' Lucy said, meeting Dan's eyes and seeing the panic flare in them. 'I might decide to go along to this – quiz thing – all by myself.'

'Done,' said Beth with a big smile. 'We'll put your name down for a ticket then.' She turned her eyes onto her big brother. 'And if Dan wants to bring someone else as well, that's good too.'

'Excellent,' Dan said, with a total lack of conviction, tossing the dregs of his coffee onto the ground. 'Thanks for the coffee, I better get going.'

Lucy took the cup and got a hint of his aftershave, spicy and earthy but all masculine, as he moved. It suited him. The aftershave he'd worn to meet another woman, given the conversation she'd just overheard.

It was just as well she wasn't interested.

It was just as well that almost kiss hadn't led anywhere. Because clearly, it had nowhere to go.

'Yeah, we better get going too,' said Beth. 'I'm on earlies and you, missy, have school.'

Siena rolled her eyes. 'Bor-ing.'

'Which means I'm leaving too,' said Hannah. 'See you again, Lucy. Thanks for the coffee. I look forward to seeing you at that quiz night.'

CHAPTER 14

*D*an arrived ten minutes early at the restaurant where he'd agreed to meet Carly the next night. He wanted to give himself time to find a seat that faced the door, so he could scope out whoever came in. Two strikes so far, so he reckoned he was due for a change of luck but he wasn't counting his chickens just yet.

He was going to be prepared for anything.

Except that when he gave his name, the waiter pointed to a table where a woman was already sitting. He blinked. That was unexpected. He wandered over. She looked nice, just like her photo. She had shoulder length brown hair and a nice face and she was wearing a floaty kind of top that had cut outs over her slim shoulders. Tattoo-free shoulders. She smiled as he came closer, showing her teeth.

Straight teeth.

A stud free nose.

'Hi,' he said, trying not to sound too excited. She might yet turn out to be a another cake-stealing parrot in disguise. 'You must be Carly. I'm Dan.'

She held out a hand to him. 'Nice to meet you, Dan. You're early too. It drives me mad when people are late.'

'Yeah,' he said, sitting down, his mood picking up by the minute. 'Me too.'

Two hours later he was feeling even better. Carly, the public servant who liked cats, had worked in the same department since she'd finished school. She'd studied for her university degree part-time because she'd wanted to better herself and now she was a manager in the human resources section. And one day she'd realised that she wasn't going to meet anyone at work and if she wanted to have children one day like she'd always expected, she'd better do something about it. Three children, she thought, and she wouldn't mind a bit if they were all boys – she had three brothers growing up.

A drink had turned into dinner and they'd both ordered pasta. She'd said no to a second glass of wine because she was driving, and Dan didn't need to refer to his list of questions because he was so busy ticking off boxes.

She got to appointments early.

She was responsible and hardworking.

She was sensible.

Even better, she hadn't stuck her fork in his pasta once.

Oh yes, Dan thought as he drove home, she was just about perfect.

Talk about third time lucky.

CHAPTER 15

'These are really good!' It was the next morning before work and Lucy had knocked on the back door to show him her designs before they hit the orchard. Dan held one sketch in each hand, seriously blown away. They were done in coloured pencils on sketch paper and each was little more than a few strokes on the page, but her simple sketches had somehow captured the beauty and vitality of the birds. 'I mean, really good.'

'Thank you,' she said. 'I think the colour really makes the designs pop. So which one do you like best?'

He couldn't decide. One was a circle featuring the words 'Bird Friendly Orchard' around a stylised parrot with its wings outstretched. The other was a pair of parrots sitting on a cherry bough complete with cherries, with the words written beneath.

'I like them both.' He thought for a bit. 'They remind me of something.' Then he looked at her. 'They're a bit like that bird on your shoulder.'

She dropped her eyes. 'I designed that too.'

'Really? So what's that thing in its beak? It looks like string.'

Her lips pressed tight together before she said. 'Just a ribbon. So –' she gestured to the sketches '– which one?'

He shook his head. 'I reckon they're both great. How about we put it to the team for a vote at smoko.'

'For real? Great! Oh, and I was thinking that's now's maybe a good time to do a new sign for the orchard too – the one on the gate is looking a bit tired. I could do that too.' She smiled. 'I kind of know where you keep the paint, after all.'

He looked at her, at this woman who he'd thought he had pegged at day one and who was surprising him at every turn, and he smiled back. 'Thank you, Lucy.'

'All part of the service,' she said. 'See you in the orchard.' She breezed out of the house, and he'd almost swear the temperature dropped a couple of degrees when she'd gone.

Sunshine indeed.

Carly shouted Dan to the movies on their second date the next weekend. She had one of those books filled with discounts for anything from movies to car tyres, which he thought was a pretty sensible idea when she explained how it worked. Dan stumped up for the popcorn. It was a sci-fi flick, which wasn't exactly his cup of tea, but there was plenty of action and besides, it was so long since he'd been to the movies, he would have sat through anything for the sheer novelty of it.

And it was such a nice night that afterwards they wandered down The Parade in Norwood and had coffee and cake at a little Italian restaurant. and talked about the movie before moving onto their respective work.

Dan was just telling her about how things were going in the orchard when Carly asked, 'So who's Lucy?'

Uh-oh.

He swallowed. 'Lucy?'

And Carly smiled her very pleasant straight-teeth smile and said, 'It's just that you've mentioned her three times already.'

'Really?' He thought back. That couldn't be right. 'Oh, she's just a picker. Though she did design our new logo. And she makes a mean curry.'

'Wow. She sounds like a woman of many talents.' And Carly was still smiling, but her eyes narrowed, and he got the weird impression Carly saw Lucy as some kind of threat.

Ridiculous!

'I guess,' he said, tugging at the collar of his polo shirt. And because he didn't want Carly getting the wrong idea about Lucy, he added. 'She'll be leaving soon.'

'Oh?'

'Yeah, she's a backpacker. Just here for the picking season, you know, before she moves on.' He shrugged for good measure. 'To who knows where?'

Carly shook her head and picked up her latte, and when her eyes met his again they were bright once again. 'You now, I could never live that way, always moving on. I'm a real home-body.'

'Yeah,' he said, relaxing again. 'Me too.'

So sure, there'd been that little hiccup, but he must have put her mind at rest, because when he walked her back to where she'd left her car, she said good night and then surprised him by leaning up and giving him a quick parting kiss on the lips.

Wow.

LUCY CLIMBED into the highest reaches of a cherry tree, straining the last few inches to gather as many cherries as she could, but it wasn't really the cherries she had on her mind

Dan was avoiding her.

When you lived and worked in the same orchard together, you wouldn't think it possible, but she always seemed to be working where Dan wasn't. Crazy really. If she was picking, he was in the packing shed. If she were asked to sort and pack, Dan would start tinkering outside with the farm bike. And she heard him go out in the evenings too. He could have been visiting his family of course, but then again, he could be just as easily over at the hotel, interviewing more candidates to find himself a wife.

Maybe he'd found one.

Her heartbeat froze, her fingers poised over a group of cherries.

When her heart resumed beating again, so did logic. One thing was certain: he wasn't pursuing her. If she was wondering where that almost kiss outside her van that night might have led, she could forget it. If Dan had wanted to pursue her, he'd had plenty of opportunity since. Clearly, he'd moved on.

Lucy surveyed the handful of cherries she'd collected. Frowning, she discarded at least half of them for having obvious pecking scars. The birds were getting to be a big problem. The other pickers had been talking about it too. She'd overheard them talking at smoko and saying that Dan was going have to do something now to control them or risk not being able to fill some of his orders.

At least he wouldn't shoot them – not when the bulk of his order list was predicated on the basis Faraday's was a bird-friendly orchard.

The crew had voted for the circular logo and Dan had organised for express stickers to be made and now every box of cherries that went out bore Lucy's logo. A new sign also hung proudly on the fence.

She grasped another cluster of cherries. From below they

looked perfect, fat with a blackish-red lustre. It was only when she was about to drop them into her bucket that she noticed the tops had been eaten away, ruining the lot.

'Damn parrots,' she cursed, as she slung the offending fruit away.

WHEN SHE WASN'T with Kate, Lucy spent her free time exploring the district. She enjoyed her long walks around the valley, mapping every detail in her head. More than two weeks had already passed in a blur and in a few weeks more the cherry season would be over and she would move on. But she wanted to be able to look back and remember the valley with clarity.

She often took a stroll in the late afternoon. From the tops of the ridges she could see the patchwork of orchards on the hillsides and how the fruit trees differed in appearance. Now she could tell from a distance which were the cherry trees and which were the apples and pears, their crops still a few months short of ripening. Interspersed among the orchards were stands of eucalyptus and towering pine trees, many of which had been planted more than a century before.

There was an old school along the way that dated back more than a hundred and fifty years. It was carved of stone and had a bronze bell near the front door that used to ring out the school day. And there were fields with sheep and cows and an old grey horse covered with a green blanket that watched her curiously from the cover of its rustic lean-to shelter, before losing interest, flicking its tail and turning back to its oats.

But always, the highlight of her walks was spotting the koalas sitting up above, their big furry bottoms settled into a fork of the tree, their fluffy faces watching her as she wandered by. Seeing them would never get old, and when they had a baby koala on their back, that was the best.

She'd return to the trailer - though half the time she found herself referring to it as a van too - and sketch what she'd seen. Other times she'd just sit for a while, outside the van if it was balmy, and drink up the atmosphere and sense of peace about the place and wonder about a line of trees that made no sense but that drew her eye every time. She committed all of it to memory, hers and her phone's, and to her sketchbook, for she knew that one day soon she'd be moving on.

Tonight though, she was feeling unsettled as she took in the tranquility of the valley. It was all so beautiful. And she was just seeing the orchard during the late spring, early summer period. Kate had already told her of the magic of seeing the valley change with the seasons. She'd been enjoying it all her life and still didn't tire of the wonder of it all.

And for once in her life, Lucy knew something akin to envy. She wouldn't be here after the cherries. Once the fruit was picked, her job would be gone. She would never get to see the valley in the autumn, which Kate thought the best time of year, as the leaves turned to russet and gold before catching and floating off in the breeze, leaving the trees bare and exposed to the winter cold. She'd never get to see the first buds of spring, the orchards bursting into life with the pink and white of the cherry and apple blossom.

She would miss all of it.

Unsettled was right. She didn't stay in one place. She'd tried that once before and look how that had turned out. No, it was better to keep moving. Keep it light. Keep it temporary.

Keep it painless.

Needing a distraction, she grabbed one of the postcards

she'd bought the first time she'd gone shopping in the city with Kate. It had a picture of a koala sitting in a gum tree with a baby on its back, and she smiled at it now before turning it over and penning a few lines to Dylan, like she'd promised to.

She'd keep it simple, just a few words about where she was and the work she was doing and how much she loved working in the orchard and how beautiful it was and how she loved working with Kate and the team and even grumpy Dan and how she wished cherry season could go longer. . .

So much for keeping it simple. So much for snapping out of it. Now it sounded like she was trying to sell the Adelaide Hills as a destination. What did it even matter? Dylan had probably already finished his exams and headed home to be with his family. She sighed deeply as she signed off and put the orchard's post box number on the off chance, before trooping into the van to think about cooking up a meal.

Feeling sorry for herself was unfamiliar territory. Feeling sad because in a few weeks she'd be moving on was not the way she operated. She loved her life precisely because she did move around so much – didn't she?

And who knew what amazing places lay there waiting for her to discover them? She wasn't born a drifter to stay in one place. Maybe she should call her mom. Hearing about Spain might reawaken her travel bug. She hadn't touched base with her since she'd left Melbourne, so it was time she gave her a call.

She went inside and lit the gas burner, then splashed some oil into the wok and reached for some potatoes and a peeler. She knew she shouldn't, but every now and then a girl just needed a feed of fries.

The boom made her cry out, despair and anger coming to the fore, and barely a moment later she was out of the van and running towards where the sound had come from. She rounded the side of the packing shed and collided slap-bang into Dan. She bounced off him breathless, as if she'd just run fifteen hundred metres, rather than barely ten.

And she couldn't understand why he looked so unconcerned.

'Hey,' he said, holding onto her shoulders to steady her. 'I was looking for you.'

'Didn't you hear it?' she demanded.

'Sure I heard it.'

'Then come on,' she said, tugging on his arm. 'We have to do something.'

'Why?'

'He's shooting. We have to stop him!'

He hauled her back.

'Lucy, it was me. I came to tell you –'

For a moment everything she thought she knew about Dan seemed to spin and lurch. She was too stunned to speak. She took a step back and surveyed him like he was a stranger. 'You? How could you – after everything that's happened? After you promised to look after the birds? What about your customers? How could you shoot those beautiful birds?' She took a gulp of air, swallowing a sob that was forming in the back of her throat.

'Lucy, listen –'

'I don't know how you could do such a thing. You're just as bad as he is!' she spat, tossing her head in the direction of the Neanderthal next door.

'Lucy!' Dan's brow creased with frustration as he fought to get her attention. 'Will you listen for just one minute?'

She planted her hands on her hips and her eyes blazed.

'Give me one good reason why I should listen to anything a bird killer would have to say!'

'That's it! I've had enough!'

Before she even had time to close her gaping mouth, let

alone register a protest, Dan picked her up and threw her bodily over his shoulder. Her world turned upside-down as she bumped against his back and suddenly her senses were filled with the smell of him and the touch of his firm, strong torso. She panicked. She pummelled his back with her fists and she wriggled but his grip only tightened, his heat of his hands feeling like a branding iron through her jeans.

And her anger was suddenly not the only source of heat. His long strides bounced her, creating friction, stirring heat wherever their bodies touched, and it took all of her concentration to focus on being outraged when her flesh was celebrating the close contact.

'What do you think you're doing?' she demanded.

'Making you listen.'

'I don't listen well upside-down.'

'Lady, from what I've seen you don't listen well any way round.'

'Cave man,' she muttered under her breath. 'Put me down.' But her heart wasn't entirely in it. Somewhere along the line the hand at her thighs had shifted higher and now lay perilously close to her butt, and her muscles tightened instinctively at his proximity. Each long stride of Dan's felt like a caress as she jostled between his shoulder and his warm hand, but it was deep inside her that the heat was playing the greatest havoc. His touch set off a flame at her core, which coiled and snaked, making her more aware than ever of her femininity and the blatant masculinity of the man carrying her.

'I'll put you down when I'm good and ready and not before.'

HIS WORDS SOUNDED FORCED, he knew. Carrying her like

this did all sorts of things to him and no wonder. Her bottom felt great, so round and firm, and it was with mixed emotions he considered how it would be if she was wearing those oh-so-tight shorts she'd had on the other night.

Yeah, that's right, he thought. Torture yourself even more.

He wasn't supposed to be thinking about her like this.

He looked to heaven for inspiration. He tried to think about Carly, to imagine what it would be like to throw her over his shoulder, but he couldn't. After their two dates he knew enough about her by now to know that Carly would never do anything that necessitated him going all caveman.

She was too rational.

Far too sensible.

Totally predictable.

In short, she suited him perfectly, whereas Lucy was a mistake from start to finish.

Throwing her over his shoulder was an even bigger one, but how else would he have got her to listen?

Carly, he told himself. Think about Carly.

But it was hard when his hands were full of Lucy.

He sighed with relief when he finally plonked her down on her feet, his hands lingering longer than strictly necessary around her waist to steady her, giving him an eyeful of her breasts and the bullet points of her nipples. He raised his eyes to hers, now a vivid blue, her lips parted like she was breathless, and he could see that she was as flustered as he was.

Oh boy. He let her go quick smart.

'AT LAST,' Lucy said, doing her best to sound convincing despite her breathlessness, never more relieved to spot the contraption next to her, even though she had not a clue what it was.

It was metal and stood on a pole set into a base of four metal legs. Set on a platform were several cylindrical shapes, some wires and a long blue and red barrel about four foot long, rising at an angle of about thirty degrees. A gas bottle stood alongside.

'What is that?' she asked, circling the device cautiously. 'Some sort of bazooka?'

'It's a gas gun.' He caught her startled eyes and shook his head. 'No, it doesn't shoot pellets. It just sounds like it. That was the noise you heard.'

'But that was a shotgun, surely?'

'No, but that's exactly what the birds are supposed to think. It's designed to frighten them off harmlessly. I had it in the shed for a few years – put it away while I tried netting the trees – and thought, now that there's finally a crop to protect, maybe I should dust it off and give it another try.'

She looked up at him, still uncertain. 'And you think this will keep the birds out of the cherries.'

He shrugged. 'Everyone used to use them, before netting got popular. But I reckon the birds got used to them back then. Now there's so many netting and hardly any gas guns, the birds will think they're the real thing. That's what I'm hoping, anyway.'

'So how does it work?'

He moved to the control panel and flicked a switch. Something hissed inside the device.

'Hear that?'

She nodded.

'A valve lets the gas come into this chamber here,' he pointed, 'and then shuts off automatically once it's full.'

As if in response to his words, there was another discernible click.

'Better cover your ears,' he warned. 'It's about to blow.'

DESPITE THE WARNING, Lucy wasn't quick enough and the blast almost knocked her off her feet.

'Wow! That's amazing. You'd swear it was a real shotgun.'

Her eyes were large and bright and had a luminous quality about them as the layered edges of her honey blonde hair swayed seductively with her movement. She flicked them away from her face while he tried to remember what he was talking about.

'That's the idea. I'll set it up in the orchard and give it a try.'

'Now?'

He looked up at the early night sky and the falling dusk.

'No. It's getting too late now. Legally gas guns can only be fired between the hours of dawn and dusk and then only ten shots an hour. I'll do it tomorrow morning.'

He should set it up tonight. He knew it. He'd only gone to get Lucy to show her the gas gun but right now he'd lost interest in his new toy. Right now he was more interested in Lucy and the way her face looked softly rapturous as the sun cast its rays sideways and turned the world and everything in it a rosy red.

Every time he saw her she looked more beautiful. But now he knew she wasn't just beautiful. She was clever. She'd turned a disaster of a cherry auction into a resounding success. She'd designed a logo that was making people who hadn't even heard of what had happened that day sit up and take notice. She'd turned the orchard into a brand.

Why had he ever thought she was a flake? How could he have got it so wrong? She was beautiful and spontaneous and passionate and clever, and how could that be so bad?

And maybe she had a stud in her nose and a tatt on her shoulder and she didn't plan her life to the nth degree, but was that such a crime?

He watched her now as she circled the gas gun, enjoying the neat curves of her body and the way her jeans fitted in all the right places.

His breath stuck in his throat as Lucy absentmindedly ran one hand along the hard, steely length of the barrel, and immediately he found himself wishing that gas guns came fluffy and pink and not in the least bit phallic.

He adjusted his jeans, which suddenly seemed too snug for comfort.

Lucy turned to him with something like admiration in her face. Her blue eyes were sparkling, and her lips curled into a smile, moist and inviting. 'Thank you.'

'Well . . .' He searched for something neutral to say . 'We're kind of in this be-nice-to-birds thing together now, aren't we?'

' I can't believe you did this because of me. I mean, you got it out for the birds, but –' She didn't finish whatever she was going to say, just launched herself into his arms, locking her own around his neck.

'You're wonderful!' she cried, before she buried her face in his shoulder. 'I mean, it's wonderful. Thank you.'

Oh God, he thought as she crushed her breasts to his chest, convinced he could feel the twin peaks of her protruding nipples.

This is it. This time she's not getting away.

Strategically he placed one hand behind her head, fingers splaying into her thick, layered hair. The other hand moved around her slim back, just in case she was thinking of pulling away.

He ran his chin over the soft hair at his shoulder and breathed in the fresh, spicy smell of her.

'I really mean it,' she said, raising her face to his. 'Thank you.'

And as he gazed into those blue eyes, the sparkling depths of which opened up now to swallow him whole, he knew he was past the point of no return.

A sound came from deep in his throat, a sound full of longing and desperation, but as his lips meshed with hers there was no more need for talk. Not with the sweet taste of her in his mouth, her soft breath intermingling with his and the feel of her supple body pressed against the hardness of his own.

He wouldn't have heard it anyway, with the thrum of surging blood loud in his ears. No question where all that blood was headed, he reflected, as he shifted slightly, centring the growing bulge against her belly.

God, he needed this. He loved the way their mouths fitted so well, the way her tongue simultaneously sparred yet caressed as it darted teasingly with his, the way her body pressed so absolutely, so convincingly against his, as if to say that touching wasn't close enough, that her body wanted to be joined with his as much as he wanted to fill hers.

His tongue left the tender depths of her mouth long enough to taste the light salt of the skin of her throat and feel the throb of her own racing pulse beating in time to his before he was drawn back to the beckoning insistence of her lips.

His hands scorched a trail down her back, found what they were looking for in a cleft between top and jeans, and pressed hungrily into the gap, sweeping up and across the flesh of her back, noting with satisfaction and another rush of blood that there wasn't a bra strap within cooee.

Pressed on by her own hands, now scrabbling under his shirt, and burning a trail with her fingertips, he levered up the back of her top, sliding the fine, knitted fabric upwards until at last, without taking his mouth away, he released her breasts only long enough to entrap them within his hands.

Her breath caught in her throat and in the same instant he noticed her eyelids flutter as she arched into his hands.

God, he was hot!

He dipped his head, crouching onto one knee and was momentarily transfixed by the sight of her swollen breasts, now at eye level. He gently rolled her hard pink nipples between his thumbs and forefingers, teasing her until he could stand it no longer and then took each of them in turn with his lips, lapping at her nipples before drawing them, deeper and deeper into his hungry mouth.

Her fingers wove through his hair, across his shoulders and pressed him tight against her breasts as she simultaneously tugged his shirt upwards, finally raking her nails across the skin of his back.

It was his turn to press into her. He raised himself to drown once more in her mouth and sighed as the delicious sensation of skin against skin assailed his senses.

It couldn't be happening – it shouldn't be happening – but it felt so right. Her skin belonged here, next to his. Her lips belonged here, locked with his own. She fitted against him so perfectly that he wanted to test exactly how far this unexpected compatability went.

God, he was so hot.

Nothing was going to stop him this time.

SHE WAS BURNING UP. Lucy felt tiny beads of perspiration breaking out on her skin, collecting between her breasts and forming a single droplet that trickled down until his pressing body impeded its progress.

Her hands felt the sweat slickened skin of his back, his flesh burning with heat and want and combusting into need.

And one clear thought appeared first and foremost.

She wanted him.

His touch, his hot mouth; both were giving her indescribable pleasure. How easy it would be to let herself go, to slide along with the passion and the ride. Was it worth worrying about the aftermath, the regrets they'd have afterwards?

Her body said no. Her body told her that this was right.

His hands moved down and cupped her butt as he lifted her slightly, bringing her sex into line with his. The feel of his erection so close to where she wanted it was as intoxicating as it was frustrating. She wanted him inside her now. She threw back her head and gasped.

It was so hot. It was so hot she couldn't wait to get out of her clothes. It was so hot she could just about smell the smoke.

His mouth closed on a nipple. She arched into his mouth and wove one leg around his body, trying to reduce the gap between them. She cared nothing for balance and staying upright. All she cared about was that she was here and his heated lips were wrapped around her breast.

Her nostrils twitched. It was smoke, her mind registered, immediately filing away the irrelevancy. Right now there were more important things to think about.

His tongue circling her nipple was all that mattered right now. His teeth gently grasped the swollen bud and released it suddenly. Then a cool stream of air hit the moistened nipple and a wave of invigoratingly chill pleasure ran down her spine.

She looked down and caught him just as he finished the breath and turned his attention to the other side. Again he rolled the nipple in his mouth, sucking gently with a firm pressure over and over before releasing the bud and blowing evenly. Again the thrilling chill of pleasure went through her and immediately she responded, pushing her breasts towards him, harder and more swollen, as if reaching out to his lips for more.

But instead, he lowered her gently to the ground and his lips grazed her ear.

'Should we go somewhere more comfortable?' he suggested, his breath ragged and blurred. His eyes sought hers, asking a different question, and she didn't need to say a word. Her eyes told him everything he needed to know. His mouth turned up slightly at the ends and straight away he swept her into his arms and set off toward the house.

He'd gone only a couple of steps when she noticed a black plume of smoke coiling skywards beyond the packing shed.

'What the hell?'

'What is it?' she asked as she felt his hold slacken.

He took a step to the side, and then another.

'It seems to be coming from somewhere near the van,' he murmured, before yelling, 'It is the van!'

He dropped her to the ground and Lucy watched him race away, shock turning to fear as a sick wave of nausea crash over her.

'Oh, my God!' she cried as the horrible realisation sunk in. 'The gas!'

CHAPTER 16

The van blew a moment later, sending bits and pieces flying in all directions. Luckily neither of them were close enough to be hit by the debris.

Somebody in the valley must have called the CFS because soon the unmistakable wail of a Country Fire Service siren was echoing through the hills, and before long there were men in yellow overalls and helmets everywhere and Dan was busy helping them clear away nearby branches as others hosed down what was left of the caravan.

It didn't take long. Though intense, the fire was short-lived and within a few minutes the van and all it contained had been reduced to a charred chassis and a sodden patch of black earth.

Lucy watched on from the sidelines as the firies mopped up before stowing their gear back in the truck and heading back to base. She and Dan had barely straightened their clothes before the fire truck had arrived, and only then she'd realised her top was inside out, but that hardly mattered now.

Because everything she'd owned was in that van. Everything. She'd lost all her clothes, the bedcover she'd bought in Turkey, the scarf she'd bought in Paris, and her purse. Even her sketchbook was gone. If not for the fact that Dan had offered to keep her passport in his safe, she would have lost that too. As she made an inventory of all that she had lost, and what she'd have to replace, her mind felt stretched to breaking point.

But now when she looked at Dan, bending down to check out a piece of debris, all that meant nothing. First of all she was going to have to work out a way how to tell him it was her fault.

Maybe he wouldn't be mad. Maybe he would accept it was an accident.

Maybe.

He looked up then, as if tuned in to her thoughts, and a frown creased his brow. He wandered over to where she was sitting in the gloom with her hands wrapped around her knees.

'You're shaking,' he said from his standing position above her.

He was right, she realised. Even her teeth were chattering. She took a shuddering breath before she whispered, 'I'm sorry.'

He crouched down on his knees in front of her and put his hand on her shoulder, rubbing it. 'Hey, you've just lost all your gear. Why the hell should you be sorry? I should have listened to Beth. I didn't realise what a firetrap that old van was. It was lucky you weren't inside it at the time.'

It hurt so much to look at his eyes that she dropped her gaze to the ground.

'It was my fault.'

'Come on, Lucy, I know that I've blamed you for a few things in the past, but that doesn't mean you have to take the rap for every single thing that happens around here.'

She looked up at him. 'No. You don't understand. When the gas gun went off – I think might have left the ring burning in the trailer.'

Dan's eyes opened wide. 'You what?'

'I was just about to cook dinner. I thought it was a gun. I'd just put the wok on –' she looked up at him '– and I raced out so quickly. I thought Des was shooting.'

Dan swivelled and rose in one movement, giving a loud groaning sigh. Then he turned suddenly and looked down at her, one hand on his hip, the other raking through his hair as if looking for answers.

It was as if everything that had happened before had all been a dream. Just a few minutes ago, it had felt like he couldn't get close enough to her. Now he felt a million miles away. Even his eyes were veiled and distant. And Lucy knew that it wasn't just the trailer flames that had been extinguished.

'Don't you ever think about anything more than two seconds into the future?'

'Well, maybe not like you do, but —'

'But nothing! I can't believe you are incapable of thinking about the consequences of your actions. What were you thinking? That the gas would miraculously turn itself off? Or is it just that because you don't own anything and it's not yours, you don't care?'

She felt her insides constrict as all her 'maybes' evaporated into thin air. There it was again.

As far as Dan was concerned, the greatest crime in the world was not planning for the future. Of not thinking about the consequences of her actions. She'd been found guilty as charged by a jury of one – again – and it was really starting to get her back up.

So okay, she'd left the gas on, but he wasn't entirely innocent here. Her anger at the injustice gave her strength and she got to her feet, mirroring his stance with her hands on hips.

'You hang on one goddam minute, mister,' she insisted. 'Just who was responsible for setting that thing off? You knew it sounded like a shotgun. You knew, more than anyone, that I'd be upset and angry. So why didn't you warn me? How the hell was I to know that it wasn't real?'

'And if it had been real? You were still going to go out and take on Des next door without turning off the gas? Great!'

'So if you hadn't fired the gas gun in the first place, none of this would have happened!'

Their faces were inches apart, their eyes wild as they glared hotly at each other. His breath came in short sharp bursts and Lucy could almost swear she felt steam. Dan grunted, dropping his head.

He grunted. 'Well, okay. Maybe I did take you by surprise. I guess I was so excited about showing you the gas gun, I didn't think about whether you might get a shock.'

'Are you kidding me? You mean you the world's foremost planner didn't think ahead for once?'

Immediately the words were out, she wished she could get them back, but it was too late. They were out there hanging between them, the sarcasm dripping thickly like sap from a tree.

He looked her in the eye again and she flinched at the intensity of his gaze and the aggravation she saw there. 'I don't think it's possible to plan a thing with you around.'

In days gone by, she might have snapped something back, something glib and cutting, aimed to keep the battle going. But for now she was weary of the war. She didn't want to fight. Not with Dan. 'I'm sorry,' she said again. 'I shouldn't have said that.'

But she couldn't admit to him why. An hour ago she'd thought there might be common ground somewhere between his land of life-plans and her land of take-it-as-it-comes. They'd come together to work a way around the birds. Surely they could find a way to coexist? But she'd been wrong – the only place it looked like they would ever find any sort of common ground was between the sheets. That's if they ever got there.

That's where they would have ended up if she'd only turned off the gas. They would have made love – God, and how much she'd wanted to make love with him – but nothing would have changed about the way he felt about her. He would still find fault with her every chance he got.

He would still resent the very person she was.

And she was no better. The first thing she'd done was to ram her objections to the way he lived his life down his throat again. They were both hopeless. Maybe it was just as well she'd left the gas on and blown any chance of her and Dan getting together sky high.

'Jeezus Lucy,' he said at last. 'I'm the one who should be apologising. I should have warned you. You're right, I didn't think about what you might be doing. I wanted to surprise you.' He sighed. 'And now you've lost almost everything. I'm so sorry. I should have listened to Beth and put you up in the house to begin with.'

She blinked up at him, blindsided by his change of heart. He'd listened to her. He'd thought about it, and now he was actually acknowledging he might have made a mistake?

'Come on,' he said, gesturing toward the house. He gave a weak smile. 'Let's go find you a room. Looks like I've got myself a lodger.'

DAN CHEWED his lip as he snapped the kettle on, waiting for Lucy to reappear, because he there was another apology he owed her. Strange how one minute you could be convinced you were doing the right thing and then the next, you knew you were better out of it. But that's how she affected him. He'd known he shouldn't touch, but once he had, he couldn't stop himself.

Maybe it was just that he'd been too long without a woman. — and God, he didn't want to think about how many years it was since Margot, because that made him really sound like an old man — that any woman would have felt good. But then why hadn't he wanted to sleep with Donna or Marie or even Carly, for that matter?

Or maybe it was this online dating thing that was making him think about women more than he had in a long time.

But how could it be that Lucy had felt so right in his arms when it was obvious they weren't suited to each other? How did that work?

In a way, the fire might even have been a good thing. If the van hadn't blown, they'd be in bed now and what a bloody mess that would be. The fire had given him time to think, to clear the fog in his mind – and boy did she fog his mind.

Living under the same roof as Lucy wasn't going to be easy. Not unless they established a few ground rules. Because he could hardly kick her out now, not after all she'd done to put Faraday Orchards on the map. Even if she had nearly wiped it out in the process.

He grimaced. He had to stop thinking like that. He had to remember she'd lost just about everything she'd owned. He shared an obligation there. No, he could hardly ask her to find somewhere else to live. It would be cruel to make her leave. But ground rules. They definitely needed ground rules.

Lucy re-emerged and plonked herself down at the table, still looking shell-shocked. He spooned coffee and sugar into cups, and he felt bad all over again, but it had to be said. They had to clear the air.

'Lucy, I'm sorry about what happened out there.'

'Yeah, you said.'

'No. About before the fire. About what we were doing. It was a mistake and I'm sorry and I want you to know it won't happen again.'

'Oh.'

The kettle boiled and he filled the cups and added milk and stirred their coffee, all the while watching her face. Waiting for any kind of reaction. He put the cup on the table before her and then leaned back 'So you'll be safe – in the house I mean. Because it won't happen again.'

She cradled the coffee in her hands and stared blindly at it. 'A mistake, you say. So which bit was the mistake?'

'What?'

She turned her eyes up to his. 'Was the mistake wanting to make love to me? Or almost giving in?'

'What?' He shook his head. 'It's all a mistake. It shouldn't have happened, that's all.'

'Oh. I thought maybe you were telling me I wasn't good enough for you, or something.'

He held out one hand, his coffee in the other. 'Come on, Lucy, it's not like that. It's just that we're not suited to each other and you'll be leaving in a few weeks anyway, and there's no point starting something that's bound to end.'

'Wow, I hadn't thought about it like that. That's three great reasons right there.'

'And that's before even considering the age difference. I've got at least ten years on you. I mean, you're practically the same age as my little sister.'

Her eyebrows shot up, 'Well, when you put it like that . . .'

'Yeah,' he said, frowning down into his coffee because he had the distinct impression she was laughing at him. But someone had to think this thing through logically and come up with all the reasons this wouldn't work.

Now all he had to do was remember them.

LUCY SPENT a good portion of the next morning on the phone to her bank to replace her bank cards, a task complicated by the fact there were no local branches closer than Melbourne, and then went to the city in the afternoon to replace her clothes. Dan had offered her compensation, which was good of him under the circumstances, and given her the time off. In reality, she suspected he was relieved she'd be out of sight and out of mind for most of the day. The distance might give things a chance to settle down, he'd even suggested.

Lucy stared at the change room mirror, trying to focus on what she was supposed to be doing, choosing some new clothes.

A chance to settle down. That was a laugh. There was little chance of things settling down while they were sharing the same house.

Especially if Dan paced the floors every night like the way he had last night. For someone who was so sure he had all the answers and a rulebook to follow, he sure hadn't enjoyed the uninterrupted sleep of the trouble-free.

But why was she wasting her time thinking about him and about what could have been?

Of course there was no future for them. He was hell-bent on finding himself a wife. A suitable wife for a sensible orchardist with a propensity to scowl.

She should leave him to it.

Lucy tried to focus on the mirror, but all she saw staring back were her eyes, marked red with the telltale traces of her own sleep deprivation. She gave up trying to decide and just shoved the couple of tops and shorts in her basket. They would do. With a few more basics to join them, she headed for the checkout.

It didn't take long to replace material possessions. If only it was as easy to replace her own battered psyche.

THE NOISE of the gas gun going off greeted her when the taxi dropped her back. So Dan had got it going again. Good for him.

She dropped the bags on the bed and lifted her arms skyward, stretching as high as she could go, trying to ease the tension in her back and shoulders.

The screen door squeaked open and closed and there was a knock at her door.

'You're back,' Dan said behind her, stating the obvious. 'Did you get everything you needed?'

She turned in the stretch, her arms still high, and caught Dan's eyes fixed on her midriff. Well, what do you know? It looked like his hands-off policy didn't extend to his eyes.

She dropped her hand to the top of her head and his eyes lifted. 'Yeah, right on both counts.'

'You have a piercing. Another one.'

'I do.' She lowered her other hand to her belly button. He obviously hadn't noticed it yesterday – but then he had been kind of busy with her breasts. No need to ask what he thought of it. 'I thought I'd head out soon and get in some picking, if you like.'

'Great. We could do with a hand in the packing shed actually. I'm just – heading out for a bit myself.'

He stepped away from the door for a moment. 'Oh, meant

to say, so far the gas gun seems to be working. It could be just the thing we needed.'

She smiled at his use of the word 'we', sure he didn't even realise he was doing it.

'I'm glad,' she said.

A moment later she heard the screen door swing shut behind him.

CHAPTER 17

*S*iena pulled open the front door when he arrived at Nan and Pop's small cottage in Summertown. 'Hi Uncle Dan.'

'Hey, Siena,' he said, ruffling her hair as he stepped inside. 'You're here too? Beth working today?'

She rolled her eyes and smoothed her hair down with her fingers. 'She's at home in the studio. Creating.' She emphasised the word with air quotes. 'Han brought me over to help Nan and Pop with the dishes and stuff.'

'Creating, huh?' He nodded. He knew the code word and thought about the date because it had to be something significant if Beth had taken to her studio, but still he drew a blank. 'Where's Nan and Pop?'

'Sitting out back with Han.' She looked around him 'Did you bring Lucy?'

'Why?'

The girl shrugged. 'She's cool, I like her. And I'm just getting bored of old people.'

'With old people.'

'What?'

'Never mind. Good to know you don't consider me an old person.'

She blinked up at him, and then pushed open the back door to the verandah. 'Uncle Dan's here,' she announced, and three heads swivelled before Siena flopped into the nearest chair and picked up a biscuit from the plate sitting on a coffee table.

'G'day everyone,' he said, frowning when he saw his Pop dressed in fleecy trackie daks and Ugg boots – in the middle of summer. His swing chair overlooked a neat lawn edged with rose bushes flowering in every colour of the rainbow 'You all right, Pop?'

'Why wouldn't I be?' snapped Pop.

'Just asking,' said Dan, bending down to kiss Nan on the cheek. 'I brought you some cherries,' he said, setting the bowl on the table.

'Oh, lovely, let me get you a coffee,' Nan said, making a move to get up.

'Siena can do that,' Hannah said. 'Can't you Siena? Nan, you were going to show me your new David Austin roses.' The girl rolled her eyes but got out of her chair and sloped inside, still munching on her Delta Cream.

'Thanks Siena,' he called after her, as he pulled up a chair alongside his grandfather with a sigh. He was going to enjoy this cup of coffee a hell of a lot more than the one he'd had an hour ago with Carly in the cafe. 'So how are you feeling after a few days back at work?'

'I'm fine. Why does everyone keep asking?'

'Because we were all worried about you, that's all. It's not like you to miss a whole week at the orchard.'

'I had to have all those bloody tests.'

'Okay, but now you're back at work, I just want to make sure you're not wearing yourself out. You know the doctors told you to slow down.'

He snorted. 'Bloody drongos. What would they know?
Anyway, forget that, what's this I hear about a fire?'

'You heard about that, huh?' Not that he was surprised.
Just because it had happened on a weekend, wouldn't mean
he wouldn't have an ear to the ground.

'Nothing happens around here without everyone
knowing about it, you know that. I would have called but
Joanie said you'd have it under control.'

'Well yeah. It was nothing really, just a small fire.'

'You had a fire?' said Han, who was done with looking at
Nan's roses and was apparently moving on to what she loved
best, which was sticking her nose into his business. 'I didn't
hear that.'

'I thought you were checking out roses.'

'Nan thought she heard the phone.' She plucked a cherry
from the bowl and pulled out the stem. 'So, this fire,' she said,
before the cherry disappeared into her mouth.

'It was nothing really,' Dan insisted.

Pop nodded. 'Burnt the van to the ground though.'

'What?' Hannah spat the pip into her hand. 'Is Lucy okay?'

'She's fine,' he said. 'She wasn't in it at the time.' He wasn't
about to spill the beans on exactly why.

'Well, well, well,' said Hannah, and it irked him that she
looked almost delighted. 'So what have you done with Lucy
now?'

He cleared his throat. 'She's moved into the house, of
course. Into one of the spare bedrooms.'

His sister turned hazel eyes on him that he'd swear came
with a laser sharp edge. 'As opposed to yours, of course.'

'Han!'

'I like Lucy,' declared Siena, emerging with his coffee and
Dan had never been happier for an interruption. 'She's really
pretty and she's got a stud in her nose and a tattoo of a bird
on her shoulder.

And that's not all, thought Dan, recalling the gem in her navel that sparkled like an invitation.

'Do you think mum would let me get a bird tattoo for my birthday?'

'No,' everyone said together.

Siena pouted and reached for another chocolate biscuit.

'So how's Lucy getting on, anyway?'

'Why?'

Hannah looked at her half-brother curiously. 'Is there a problem?'

'Of course not.' He shrugged. 'I just wondered what it was to you.'

'I'm just wondering how she's getting on with the picking and everything, given her new celebrity status. Hasn't gone to her head, or anything?'

He made a show of rubbing the back of his neck as if he was having trouble sorting out which one of his team was Lucy. 'Seems to be managing okay. Pulling her weight. I'm pretty sure she'll see the season out, okay.'

'Going to cramp your style a bit though, I would have thought.'

'How so?'

'Having a woman – a very attractive woman – sharing house when you're wife hunting. It might give someone the wrong idea.'

'Yeah, well, not that it's related, but I've been thinking about that too, Han. I've dated three women from that site so far and –'

'Three?'

'You sound surprised.'

'I am, you sly dog. You told us about numbers one and two. What was wrong with number three?'

'She suffers from motion sickness,' he said, reeling out the excuse he'd come up with to explain Carly away because he could hardly tell them the real reason. 'Can't travel in the hills without feeling nauseous.'

Pop grunted. 'Bit of a dead loss as an orchardist's wife.'

'That's what I thought. Anyway, given it's getting to the pointy end of the season, I might wait until the cherries are in and I can focus on finding someone a bit more suitable.'

Hannah took another cherry. 'Interesting,' she said, rolling the cherry around her cheeks. 'We practically had to drag you kicking and screaming to the concept, and now you almost sound keen.'

'I am, Han,' he said, injecting as much sincerity into his words as he could. 'If I'd known how many women were out there waiting for a partner, I would have looked into this online dating gig a lot earlier. It's just cranking up at bit in the orchard right now. And like you say, it could get tricky with Lucy sharing the house.'

'Very interesting,' said Han.

'That was Sophie,' Nan said, emerging from the house. 'Nobody's actually bought tickets yet and she wants to get a table together for this quiz night at the school coming up. '

'We're all going,' said Han. 'It's a great cause. And Beth told me she's got the night off, so that's me, you two, Beth, Sophie and Dan – and Lucy said she'd come too.' She looked pointedly at her brother. 'You can give her a lift seeing as you won't be taking a date along. How convenient is that?'

Dan looked up at the single white cloud floating across the clear blue sky, at the roses flowering around the edge of the lawn and anywhere except Hannah's laser beam eyes. 'If I must,' he said, finding a place to scratch on his jaw that wasn't itching.

A little while later, he said goodbye to Nan and Pop out on the back verandah and Han saw him out. Siena was emptying out the last of the cherries and rinsing the bowl in the kitchen, and he saw his chance. He put his hand on Han's

arm and pulled her around. 'So what's up with Beth today?'
he asked. 'Do you know?'

She frowned. 'Apparently it's the anniversary of the first
time she and Joe made love.'

'Oh?'

'The tenth anniversary.'

'Ooh. Jeezus.' He ran a hand through his hair while that
sank in. 'She was only seventeen the first time?'

'Old enough.'

'God, some big brother I turned out to be, letting some
guy have his way with one of my kid sisters.'

'Don't say that. Everyone loved Joe, you included. And
you remember how happy she was when they were together.'

He nodded. 'But it's been more than eight years. Do you
think she'll ever get over him?'

'How can she, when she sees Joe's eyes every time she
looks at their daughter?'

Yeah, there was that. When Siena had been born, she'd
been a tiny black haired bundle with a snub nose and cupid
bow lips, and then she'd opened her eyes and Joe had looked
out of them and Beth had cried for two days solid.

Siena appeared with his bowl. 'Here you go Uncle Dan.'

'Thanks Siena,' he said, ruffling her hair and taking the
empty bowl, before kissing his sister on the cheek. 'Bye Han.'

'See you,'

'Say hi to Lucy for me,' said Siena.

'And me,' added his sister.

'Sure. If I bump into her, that is.'

Dan didn't look around when he heard Hannah snort. He
just kept right on walking. He wasn't sure how he was going
to avoid bumping into her, when they shared the same
house, but after what he'd said about not touching her again,
he could hardly go changing his mind, could he?

Even if he had ended it with Carly today.

He was no doubt doing her a grave disservice telling his family she suffered from motion sickness. Something told him she'd have the constitution of an ox. But when he'd been pacing the floors the other night because he couldn't sleep, when he'd lain awake all the nights since, when he'd thought about how Lucy had felt on his shoulder and in his arms and how she'd tasted in his mouth, all of a sudden he'd realised that if Carly had seriously meant anything to him, he could never have done what he'd done with Lucy. He could never have contemplated taking Lucy to bed if Carly was really the one – if she was meant to be.

But it was more than that. Because Lucy had taught him that he didn't want to settle. If he was going to get married, he didn't just want a sensible wife; he wanted one he was crazy about.

One that came with sizzle.

Lucy might not seem like marriage material, but she had sizzle.

Man oh man, she had sizzle.

All he had to do now was avoid her. He snorted. Piece of cake.

'LUCY! How lovely to hear from you. How are you?'

Lucy smiled. It was good to hear her mother's voice so clearly, even if she sounded slightly breathless over the thousands of kilometres that separated them. She'd been right to call. This was exactly what she needed to reawaken her travel bug. Then she heard what sounded like a slap and a deep rumble of laughter and her mother whispering something low.

And Lucy laughed. It was eight in the evening in Adelaide, which meant it would be ten thirty in the morning in San

Sebastian. But clearly her mother was still in bed. 'Not a good time to call?'

'How could you tell . . .?' her mother started before coming out with a husky laugh of her own. 'Okay. Silly question. His name is Mateo and he's lovely. And Lucy –'

'Yes?'

Her mother's voice dropped to a conspiratorial whisper. 'This time it's serious.'

'Uh huh.' Because weren't all her affairs serious? At least for the first ten minutes.

'Anyway,' her mother continued, 'where are you? What have you been up to.'

Lucy filled her mom in on everything that had happened since they'd last spoken in Melbourne. She talked of cherry picking and about the beauty of the Adelaide Hills and the orchard and then went on to describe the house and garden and the line of pencil pines along the hill, and how she had the strangest feeling she'd been somewhere like it before, somewhere there had been an old lady all dressed in black.

'You remember that? But you couldn't possibly, you were only a baby.'

A shiver went down Lucy's spine. 'Remember what?'

'My Nonna's house in Tuscany. Your great grand-mother's place.'

'In Tuscany?' Lucy repeated, doubtfully, her mind busy replaying her previous visits. She'd visited Florence and Pisa and the hill-towns of Siena and San Gimignano, and there'd been rows of pencil pines on every rolling hill wherever she looked, but never once had she experienced this strange feeling of being there before.

'Northern Tuscany. A little village called Agnino set high in the mountains. It's where her family came from. After Poppa died, she went back.' She gave a hollow laugh. 'She didn't get on with my father either.'

'And we visited?'

'We stayed there, oh, six months or more. She wasn't well and it was after I broke off with Sylvester, horrible man that he was - you wouldn't remember him - and I needed somewhere to put myself back together and she liked having someone to help. It suited us both.'

Warmth bloomed in Lucy's chest, like it had that first day. There was a reason she'd felt that way, she'd known it. 'Tell me about it.'

'Oh, there's not much to tell. She lived in an old stone farmhouse surrounded by wild garden filled with olive and fruit trees. You were barely a toddler but you loved running around in it.'

Lucy leaned forward. 'Really?'

Her mother laughed. 'Oh, and she adored you. Said having us there was like someone had switched on a light in her life - but I knew it was you she meant. You used to go to sleep in her arms every night. She was tiny by then, like a little bird, but she insisted on it. She'd rock you in her rocking chair and half the time she'd go to sleep with you still in her arms.'

There was a pause and Lucy heard her mother sniff and give a wistful sigh. 'And then one night she died in her sleep, and I remember you cried and cried and it broke your heart when we moved on. I can't believe you can remember.' Her mother gave a long sigh. 'Anyway Lucy, it's been so lovely to catch up, but I've got a pot on the boil here, if you know what I mean. Give me your phone number and I'll call you next time.'

Stunned and reeling, Lucy recited the number and hung up, feeling the snippets of her childhood memories falling into place. The white-haired woman dressed all in black that she remembered had been her mother's nonna – the distant memories buried in the churn of the years that followed.

When Lucy and her mom had moved back to the States and the two had resumed their shuffling, transitory existence, the memories of that happy time had begun to fade. No wonder those first few stirrings had seemed so dreamlike.

Lucy wandered into the kitchen. It made sense – why she felt such a sense of comfort, why she felt so at ease here, in this rambling bungalow amid the orchard. Maybe even why she had a hankering to stay a while for the changing seasons.

She opened the refrigerator and checked the vegetable crispers, selecting salad vegetables with a mind on autopilot as far as meal preparation was concerned. Since she'd moved into the house, she'd become the de facto cook for them both. She didn't mind. It sure beat the hell out of Dan's idea of cooking. On the weekend she'd used one of Dan's old frypans to make another batch of curry paste to replace what she'd lost in the van, but she was liking the barbecue for a change.

She was even making the odd vegetarian meal and surprising Dan when he found he actually liked them. She'd forgotten all about her Moosewood cookbooks in the drama of the fire, and she'd cried when Kate had returned them. It had felt like getting old friends back. She hadn't lost everything after all. She'd celebrated by making one of her favourite desserts from the books, a Ricotta Cherry Mousse, with honey and grand marnier but substituting cherries fresh from the orchard instead of canned, and Dan's eyes had all but rolled back in his head when he'd tasted it.

She'd looked at the expression on his face and wished that she could have put it there for an entirely different reason, but if this was the way he wanted it, she could cope.

She wasn't looking for a relationship after all.

HE HOPED he was doing the right thing.

Dan entered the shop like he was setting foot on another planet. This was so not his territory. He spent ten minutes wandering aimlessly around before a shop assistant wearing an apron and an overly cheerful smile appeared in the aisle in front of him.

'Can I help you?'

He sure hoped so. He told her what he was looking for and she was off like a rabbit with Molly hot in pursuit. He sighed. He missed that dog. Then he sighed again at the enormity of the task at hand.

There were so many reasons this wouldn't work. Too many. He reminded himself of each and every one of them as he ambled between display stands, testing those reasons one by one for soundness and finding them rock solid.

But of course they were. That was the way he operated. He never acted rashly. He thought everything out, dotting every i and crossing every t. He barely made a move without first undertaking a cost benefit analysis.

He caught up with the assistant who was standing next to a display waiting for him. In her hands, she explained at great and enthusiastic length, was the best money could buy, and so he bought it.

He waited while she gift-wrapped it, hoping he was doing the right thing.

Trouble was, he wasn't sure what the right thing was anymore.

LUCY WAS TOSSING the salad when Dan found her. The fact he was in the same room as her when it wasn't mealtime was unusual in itself – he'd been keeping his distance like he'd promised – but what was really weird was that he was holding something out to her, something gift-wrapped.

'What's this?'

'I bought you something.'

She looked at it warily. 'Why?'

'It's kind of a thank you. For doing all the cooking.' He held the box out to her, his dark eyes looked almost tortured.

So she took it, resting it on the table while she ripped off the wrapping. 'Oh wow,' she said, as the box beneath was revealed, 'You bought me a wok? Seriously?'

'I feel bad you lost your other one. Is it okay?'

'Okay?' she said, already pulling it from the box, 'It's perfect!' She hugged it to her chest. 'Thank you.'

He nodded, his lips pressed together. 'I'm glad. Um.' He looked at the floor and scuffed one foot on the timber.

'Lucy,' he started. 'There's something else I was wondering. This quiz night tomorrow night. Would you like to come with me?'

She clamped down on the flutter in her heart. Hadn't his sisters suggested this? 'You're offering me a lift?'

'No. I'm asking if you'll come with me. As my date.'

Whoa. The sizzle started at the top of her spine and worked all the way down till her toes curled. 'Just a date, then?'

'If that's all you want.'

Her mouth went dry. Probably because he was looking at it so hard and now his eyes weren't just tortured. They were burning up like coals. 'What happened to being not suited to each other, the fact that I'm leaving in a few weeks and there being no point starting something that has to end soon, especially given how I'm so much younger than you.'

He took a step closer. 'You remembered all those reasons?'

'You were pretty clear.' And she'd spent a fair bit of time

since then picking apart every one of them.

'Yeah, I thought so too.' Another step closer, so he was standing right in front of her and she had to lift her eyes to meet his. 'Until I came up with another one and it's bigger and more powerful than all the others.'

'Tell me.'

Without taking his eyes from hers, he tugged the wok from her hands and put it on the table beside them. 'There's chemistry between us, Lucy. No matter how much I've tried to pretend it's not there –' he touched a finger to her temple and traced a slow line down her cheek so breath hissed through her teeth as she swayed into his electric touch '– it doesn't go away. It won't go away.'

'I'd kind of noticed that.' She licked her lips. Saw his eyes target the dart of her tongue. 'But like you said, I'll be leaving soon. Are you quite sure you want to start something that has to end?'

'You're driving me crazy, Lucy. You've been driving me crazy ever since I first laid eyes on you. And if you are going to be leaving, I don't know why we're fighting it anymore.' His eyes searched her face, his features imploring her. 'I can't seem to help it. I want you.'

She gave a slow blink. 'What about that on line dating thing?,' she asked, because still she was afraid to believe him. 'I thought you were supposed to be looking for a wife.'

He shook his head. 'I was. For a moment there, I even thought I'd found her, but you know a funny thing?' He pulled her toward him, pushing a wayward tendril of hair from her eyes.

'What?' she whispered on a sigh.

'She was just too similar to me. She agreed with every-thing I said.'

'You didn't like someone agreeing with you?'

He rewarded her with a smile and her heart swelled.

'Maybe once I did. But there's something else,' he said, as he traced around the outline of her lips with the pads of his fingers. 'Something that happened when I kissed her?'

Lucy's breath stuck in her throat.

He'd kissed her? 'I don't really think I want to hear this.'

'Yes you do. Because I felt absolutely nothing.'

His hand left her lips, curved around her neck and pulled her closer to him.

'Whereas, when I kiss you . . .' His head dipped and his lips brushed hers. Once, twice, three times he teased her with a grazing pass before his lips settled on hers for a lingering kiss that left her breathless until, finally, on a sigh, he lifted his head. 'When I kiss you, all sorts of things happen.'

All sorts of things were happening now. Her body sizzled in his proximity. The air between them shimmered like a heat haze. This was more than mere spark crackling between them. This was a slow burn, building in intensity with every look, every touch, every heated kiss.

'So what do you say?' he asked before he kissed her again, his hands searing their fiery way over her shoulders and down her back, drinking in the curve of her waist and the round of her butt as he pulled her against his rising hardness. 'Do you agree we should do something about this inconvenient attraction?'

Her kiss – deep and hot – told him all he needed to know, their tongues tangling in a dance of promise. His grip tightened and she found herself lifted off the ground and swung onto the benchtop. He pushed between her knees so she was straddling him, and his thumbs stroked her thighs in lazy circles that sent wave after wave of pleasure rippling to her core.

His mouth dipped to her throat as his fingers lingered low, caressing her aching flesh.

'God, I want you,' she whispered, her voice hoarse with

need.

He replied with a guttural cry of his before he kissed her again. His kiss was soul deep and spoke of his hunger and his need and she matched it, giving him what he asked, promising more as the need spiralled and grew inside her, fuelled by the hungry hands that drank him in, every shifting muscle, every corded tendon. Each one a revelation, a delight.

His mouth dipped to her throat and Lucy threw back her head as she clung to his shoulders, overcome by sensation and the knowledge that this time they would make love. This time there would be no stopping. The house could explode into flames around them and there would be no stopping.

There was no stopping. She was in his arms and on his bed and he was kicking off his shoes and peeling off his clothes. And for one of the few times in her life, Lucy was rendered speechless. He was magnificent, this man; broad shouldered, narrow hipped, and built, and the look in his brown eyes – a combination of dark desire and wicked intent – sent a sizzle down her spine with the thrill of knowing what was to come.

SHE WAS like all his fantasies rolled into one, blonde and beautiful and smack bang in the middle of his bed. She was all wrong for him and he was wrong for her but right now he couldn't think of anything that he wanted more. How did that work?

Lucy reached out for him and he took her hand and joined her on the bed, and the whys and the wherefores ceased to matter.

All that mattered was that they were here, together.

He would have preferred to take it slow. He would have preferred to be all cool and controlled and not like some kid who had fifteen minutes before his folks arrived home and still had to get the dishes done before they did, but slow was the furthest thing from his mind. And then his mind went blank and all there was a rush of blood and a roaring in his ears because she was all around him and he was in heaven, but still it wasn't enough.

They clung to each other, moving as one while spark turned to flames fanned by a rhythm as old as time.

Until he felt her come apart in his arms and she dragged him with her, over the edge to spin and freefall all the long way back to earth.

Finally he slumped over her, spent and sweat slickened, and for a couple of minutes the only sounds were those made as they gasped for air, replacing the stores of oxygen they had consumed in the hear of their passion.

'I'm sorry,' he said, rolling off her shoulder. 'I couldn't wait any longer.'

She panted beside him. 'Do you hear me complaining?'

He looked at her. Her hair was a mess, her brow was damp with sweat, and she still had that stud in her nose, but there was a smile playing at her lips and her eyes were bright and somehow it didn't seem important right now.

'Maybe you're just being polite.'

'You got me. I'm always having orgasms just to be polite. You were rubbish really.' But she grinned with it and wrapped her arms around his neck and kissed him and he got a kick out of knowing she hadn't been pretending.

That wasn't the only thing that got a kick, and he smiled at the discovery.

Well, what do you know? Maybe he wasn't middle aged just yet. 'Let me know if you want to be polite again anytime soon.'

She pressed herself closer to him and ran the pads of her fingers over his lips. 'I thought you'd never ask.'

'Hi Dan, hi Lucy,' said Sophie, taking their tickets at the door of the big old Ashton Memorial Hall. 'It's so great you could come.'

'Wouldn't miss it,' smiled Lucy.'

'The others aren't here yet but you should both go inside and check out the displays. We're on Table four. Oh, and Dan, the good news is, mum and Dirk are joining us. I'll sit with you between categories. Otherwise it might look a bit dodge if I start answering the questions, being one of the organisers and all.'

Inside, the hall had been done up for the night with balloons and streamers and with bright posters painted by the kids from the local school lining the walls. On the stage up front was a display of photographs of the school kids in action, surrounding a picture of Jamie Hanson, the little boy whose fund the proceeds of the night would benefit.

'Oh, that cute little boy,' said Lucy, looking at the photos. 'What's wrong with him?'

'He's got a rare blood condition apparently,' Dan said,

'and the only place that specialises in treating it is in Germany and costs a bomb.'

'That's so unfair.'

'It is,' Dan said, pulling out a chair for Lucy at their table, 'Sophie's done an amazing job getting this all together at short notice.'

'All your sisters are pretty amazing, aren't they?'

'Yeah,' he said with a smile. 'They really are.'

The room began filling with couples and groups carrying baskets full of supper and they waited for the rest of Dan's family to arrive.

'So what exactly happens at a quiz night?' asked Lucy..

'The usual,' he said. 'Lots of questions and raffles and a prize for the team that comes first.'

'What's the prize?'

'I don't know, but I fully expect our table to win.'

'How come?'

'You haven't seen Han and Beth in full flight. Together with Nan and Pop, they make a formidable team.'

'What about you?'

'I'm just here to make up the numbers. Ah, speak of the devils.'

Hannah and Beth arrived first and greeted Lucy with big smiles, and hot on their heels came Clarry, or Pop as he'd told her to call him, and a woman she guessed must be Dan's grandmother.

'Ah,' he said pulling her into a big hug, 'And here's my favourite Yank.'

'Clarence Faraday, that's no way to greet anyone.' And then to Lucy, 'I'm sorry dear, he's got the manners of an old goat.

Lucy smiled. 'I don't mind. It's a pleasure to meet you - -'

'This is Nan,' Dan said.

'Joanie,' the older woman said, patting her hand. 'You can call me Joanie.'

Sophie sat down next to Lucy and fired questions at her about travel, the orchard and how much she was liking it here. And somehow through it all, baskets were filled with cheese and crackers, and snacks were unpacked and drinks organised from the wet bar.

'Where's Siena tonight?' Lucy asked Beth.

'The kids are all over at the school gym being entertained.'

'So they don't get bored,' said Han.

'So the parents can enjoy a wet bar, more like it,' said Beth with a wink.

'Hey, Dan, Clarry, everyone.'

'Nick, hi.' Dan stood and shook hands with a dark haired man who'd been heading for the table next to them when he'd spotted Dan. A good-looking man, thought Lucy as Dan introduced her. Nick had olive skin and dark eyes that smiled at everyone but zeroed in on Sophie sitting beside her.

'We're going to give you guys a run for your money this time,' he said.

'Don't get your hopes up,' warned Dan. 'It'll hurt all the more when you come second.'

'We're not planning on coming second.'

'Now there's a coincidence,' piped up Dan's Pop. 'But you Pasquales will never be a match for the Faradays, you should know that by now.'

'I better get back to my post,' said Sophie, sliding out of her chair. 'We'll be starting soon. I'll catch up with you guys at the first break.'

Sophie disappeared and Nick drifted back to his table and Lucy leaned closer to Dan and said, 'Did I see him at the cherry auction? Does he grow cherries too?'

'He's another orchardist, though he pulled out all his cherry trees a few years back to concentrate on apples and pears.'

'Would he be sorry about that now?'

'Probably not. Cherries can be a heartbreaking business. We might be ahead this year, but the past two have been shockers.' He shrugged. 'But that's how it is in this business. There's no right and wrong, it's all a gamble. You can only do what feels right and hope to hell you can pay the bills at the end of every season.'

'Are you two talking shop?' Hannah leaned over and reached for a tub of pumpkin dip. 'God, Lucy, don't let him bore you to tears.'

'I'm not bored.'

'Hmm,' said Han, 'and Dan doesn't seem half as grumpy as he normally does. Could these two things be related?'

'Is something going on?' asked Beth, her eyes narrowing. 'What have I missed?'

'Move along people,' he said. 'Nothing to see here.'

'I'm just glad to meet Lucy at last,' said Joanie. 'It's lovely to have someone new to talk to. It's a welcome change from seeing the same old faces all the time.'

'Are you having a go at my old face?' said Clarry. 'Because I wouldn't mind a change of scenery every now and then myself, I can tell you.'

She shot him a dark look. 'You can have a change of scenery any time you like, Clarence Faraday. You just say the word.'

'Oi! That's no way to talk to your dearly beloved.'

Nan huffed and crossed her arms over her navy twin-set. 'I'm just giving you a taste of your own medicine, for a change. You've been like a bear with a sore head lately. I can see where Dan gets it from.'

'Hey!' protested Dan, looking wounded.

'Settle down, you lot,' said Han and Beth together.

'We're supposed to be a team,' said Han.

'So can we try to look like it?' added Beth. 'And as for you, Pop, this is supposed to be my night off, so don't go having a coronary, okay?'

Clarry looked at the ceiling and Lucy watched on, smiling. Family was one very strange beast to her and this family was probably stranger than most, but they clearly adored each other under the ribbing.

'Phew, we made it,' a woman announced, dipping her head to kiss both Joanie and Clarry on the cheek. 'You're both looking good.'

Clarry puffed up like a balloon. 'Now that's more like it,' he said, as the woman kissed Hannah and Beth and Dan before sliding into the chair alongside. 'Thank you Wendy.'

Dan introduced Lucy to his step-mum and her fiance and Wendy reached out a hand across the table. 'Lovely to meet you at last. Sophie's told me a lot about you.'

'Uh-oh,' Lucy said with a grin. With her blonde bob and her wide smile, it was easy to see that Wendy wouldn't have looked so different to Hannah and Beth when she was younger.

'Oh, it's all good,' Wendy said, waving a hand and placing it on her partner's arm. 'Isn't that right Dirk?'

It wasn't hard to smile. Greying at the temples, and with warm, intelligent eyes and big hands, Dirk wouldn't have looked out of place as a trusted family doctor.

'All good,' he agreed. 'They tell me you're from the States.'

'Sure am, but then, I've kind of lived everywhere.'

'I've done my share of traveling. I wouldn't mind comparing notes sometime.'

She smiled. 'I'd like that.'

'Here we go,' said Dan beside her. 'It looks like we're about to start.'

Up on the stage, the MC took picked up the microphone, turned it on and tapped it a couple of times, waiting for the screech from the PA and then the winces from the audience to die down .

Lucy leaned closer to Dan. 'That's not the same MC they had at the cherry auction?'

'No,' Dan said, 'thank God.'

'Right,' the MC said, rubbing his hands together. 'Welcome one and all. Now you all know why we're here tonight – we want to raise a heap of money for this little tacker, Jamie Hanson –' he gestured toward the photo display '– whose family needs our help to pay for his medical treatment overseas. My job is to give you the time of your lives so you don't notice exactly how much cash I extract from you along the way.

'So let's get started. We'll have four rounds tonight, the categories selected by a poll of school parents, plus there'll be bonus questions in between rounds, so if none of the categories appeal, there'll be a chance to catch up.

'And sharpen your pencils, ladies and gentlemen, because the first category is British Comedy. Here we go with our first question – What are the surnames of the two comedians who starred in The Two Ronnies?

Team Faraday whispered in a tight huddle and Han said, 'Got it!'

Lucy sighed. 'Glad you're not relying on me, I'm not going to know any of this stuff.'

'It's okay,' said Dan, squeezing her leg under the table for good measure. 'I told you, this team is the bomb.'

And they were.

They made mincemeat of British Comedy and despite what Dan had inferred about just being along for the ride, he was no slouch in the trivia department. It seemed every one of these Faradays knew stuff about topics she'd never realised existed. Australian History they similarly took in their stride, so that Table four was five points up at half time, with the Pasquale table coming a close second, just two points behind.

Dan put a glass of white wine down in front of Lucy as the MC announced the bonus question, and a pixelated portrait of an actor appeared on the screen. 'I hate these,' said Dan. 'We hardly ever get these.'

'Who needs some points?' asked the MC, looking exceedingly happy with himself. 'Fifty dollars gets you a chance at this question and your very own jug of beer if you win. Fifty dollars to go in the kitty and help out little Jamie, but don't be too quick off the mark because this is a one shot deal. If you get it wrong, your team's out of the running.'

'Fifty bucks?' Dan shook his head. 'Bloody expensive jug of beer.'

'We have to,' said Han, when she saw Nick at the next table putting up a hand holding aloft his fifty dollar note.

'We're in,' Nick announced, throwing a smug look at his competition. Half a dozen other tables that were lagging in the count similarly put up their hands, and then Han shot up hers.

'Us too!' she said, tossing up her chin, and the game was on.

Piece by piece the picture was slowly revealed. A square of chin. A slice of nondescript hair. The corner of an eye. Team Faraday was baffled. A couple of teams made early guesses and were eliminated.

Lucy focused on the screen. Whoever it was looked kind of familiar. A bit like Dan. She sat forward in her chair. Very much like Dan. The next tile was revealed, showing the hint of a frown and she was pretty much sure. 'I think I know who it is.'

'Who?' they all demanded at once.

'Bradley Cooper.'

'Oh my god, you're right,' said Han and shot up her hand. 'Bradley Cooper!'

'Correct!' called the MC. 'Well done, five bonus points to Table four, and you can collect your jug of beer at the bar.'

'Woohoo!' they all shouted, except for Dan, who called, 'Raffle it!' The MC accepted and the free jug of beer raised another twenty dollars for the kitty.

'You're a genius, Lucy' said Han.

'I agree,' said Wendy, 'well done.'

'We never get those,' added Beth. 'How did you know?'

She shrugged. 'Because it looked like Dan.'

Everyone at the table looked at everyone else. Eyebrows lifted. 'Dan looks like Bradley Cooper?'

'You think Dan looks like a film star?'

'No way,' he said.

'Of course he does,' she said. 'Look at that frown.' And they all looked up at the screen where Bradley Cooper's un-pixelated face now loomed down at them.

'My God, you're right,' said Wendy, and they all laughed. All except for Dan, who was giving Bradley Cooper's giant scowl a run for its money.

'That was really nice of you,' said Lucy to Dan, in the lull before the next round was due to get underway. 'To let them raffle off the prize.'

Beth scoffed. 'He's just trying to get the opposition drunk, that's all.'

'Nick's table didn't bid, more's the pity,' said Clarry, who was looking a little weary but was hanging in there. 'Now, gird your loins, boys and girls, this quiz is getting serious.'

Australian Sports was the topic of round three. The girls groaned but Clarry rubbed his hands together and his eyes brightened.

'Which team,' the MC said, 'won the AFL grand final in 1997 against which other team?'

'Too easy,' said Clarry. 'Adelaide against North Melbourne. Write that down, Han.'

'Hang on,' said Dan. 'Wasn't it St Kilda they beat that year?'

'Of course not!' declared Clarry. 'Han, write down North Melbourne.'

Dan looked at Dirk. 'Do you know?'

The other man shook his head. 'It was Adelaide all right, but who they beat that year . . .'

'For God's sake put down North Melbourne,' barked Pop.

'How can you be so sure, Clarry?' asked Nan. 'Dan might be right.'

He leaned forward in his chair. 'Because I know, that's how!'

'It's okay, we're in the lead,' said Dan, putting up one hand in surrender in attempt to calm the old man down. 'The other teams are the ones under pressure.'

But the questions didn't get any easier after that, and when the round finished and the scores were totted up, they'd only scored seven out of a possible fifteen points, and all of a sudden they were one point behind Nick's team, which had scored a perfect round.

'I should have listened to you,' said Clarry, shaking his head. 'Bloody old fool, thinks he knows everything. It was North Melbourne Adelaide beat in '98 of course.'

'Don't worry, Pop, there's still the bonus round and then the final round.'

'Now for this bonus round,' said the MC. 'Name the television show that went with this theme music.'

The hall filled with the sound of wind instruments, trumpets and a clicky drum and even trombone in a very 1950s arrangement, and two hundred people looked at the person next to them, everybody twitching with a name on the tips of their tongues. Nan and Pop were no exception. 'That's . . .' said Nan. 'That's . . .'

'Spit it out woman!'

'Oh,' said Wendy, 'it's – '

'I Love Lucy!' yelled someone from the back.

'Correctomondo!' yelled the MC, as the screen filled with an iconic image of the show's title enclosed in a red heart. 'Give that joker a jug of beer.'

'You should have got that, Joanie,' growled Pop.

'Well, why didn't you get it yourself?'

'Hey, I should have got that,' said Lucy. 'Given my name.'

'And it wasn't Nick's team who won. We're still only one point behind. Come on!'

'The last category of the night, ladies and gentlemen,' the MC announced, 'is one for all you old James Bond film buffs. This round is sure to sort out the men from the boys.'

'Good grief,' said Dan.

'We're doomed,' Hannah added, dropping her head into her hands.

'Hmm,' said Clarry, not looking too confident.

'First question: Name the heroine in the 1964 movie, Goldfinger and the actress who played her.'

'Pussy Galore,' said Lucy, and seven heads around the table swivelled. 'Honor Blackman.'

'Question two: Name the hat-throwing henchman in Goldfinger.'

'Um,' Lucy thought for a moment. 'Oddjob.'

Dan was the first to recover. He blinked and then looked at Han. 'Write the answer down, quick!'

'Question three: What career did Australian, George Lazenby, have before he played James Bond in On Her Majesty's Secret Service?'

'He was in the army,' declared Pop.

'Model,' said Lucy.

The answers were so conflicting that Dan turned to his grandfather. 'Pop?'

'Don't ask me,' said Pop. 'He sure wasn't an actor.'

'Complete this quote,' the MC continued. 'M: When do you sleep 007?'

'Never on the firm's time, sir.'

The questions continued and Lucy spat out the answers and then the round was over and the answer card submitted and Sophie joined them. 'How did you go that round?'

'I think Lucy just saved the honour of the Faraday family,' said Dan, and Lucy screwed up her nose.

'We'll see.'

And then the MC turned from the scorers back to the microphone with the tally sheets in his hand. 'We have a result,' he said. 'In third place, on thirty-five points, Table number two!' There were whoops from a table near the front.

'In second place, with thirty-eight points, Table six.'

Nick's table. Dan sucked in a breath and they all exchanged glances. Under the table, Dan reached for Lucy's hand and squeezed it tight.

'And in first place after a crack round, and the winners of a night's accommodation and dinner with champagne for two in a spa suite kindly donated by the very posh Mt Lofty House and worth more than three hundred dollars –' he paused for dramatic effect '– Table four, on –'

They didn't wait to hear the score. They were already celebrating, whooping and hugging each other.'

'Congratulations,' said Nick, coming over to shake Clarry's hand. 'Looks like you were right, old fella.'

'When haven't I been?'

'Try North Melbourne,' Nan quipped, and Clarry shut up quick smart.

'You should have the prize,' said Han to Lucy.

'Yes,' agreed Beth. 'You won for that us.'

'But –' She looked at Dan, wondering how good would be a night in a posh hotel sipping champagne with Dan in a spa bath brimming with bubbles, but he shrugged, and she realised romance was no part of this deal. So when the MC asked who was coming to collect the prize, she smiled up at him and shouted, 'Auction it!'

The bidding was fiercely competitive and another four hundred and fifty dollars looked set to go into the kitty, when Sophie called out, 'Five hundred!'

Bam! The MC's gavel hit the lectern. 'Sold!' And Sophie jumped up to collect the voucher while everyone else at the table was left scratching their heads.

'What was that about?' Hannah asked her when she got back.

'What were you thinking?' Dan said.

Beth was more to the point. 'You don't even have a boyfriend.'

Sophie was unrepentant. 'It's for a good cause.' And nobody could argue with that.

Nick came over to congratulate Dan and the team. 'Good on you, Nick,' said Dan. 'Good to see there's no hard feelings.'

'We'll get you next time,' he said, 'So don't you Faradays go getting complacent.'

'Never,' said Dan, who was enjoying this cherry season than he'd ever thought possible.

'You were fabulous,' said Wendy to Lucy, as she packed up her basket. 'I hope Dan's bringing you to our wedding.'

Again she looked at Dan for help, sure her cheeks were burning. 'Um, I don't know. When is it?'

'January. After cherry season,' she said with a smile. 'I was married to Dan's father a long time, I know the drill.'

'I'd love to, but I doubt I'll still be here in January.'

'Oh, where are you going?'

'I'm not sure. I'm really only here for cherry season, and then I'll be moving on.'

Wendy looked at Dirk, who looked at Han and Beth, who both shrugged before they all looked at Dan. 'That's too bad,' she said, and went on packing up the table.

Only Nan seemed oblivious as she retrieved her cardigan from the back of the chair and stuffed it in her basket, and said to Clarry with a wistful sigh, 'I always liked that nice George Lazenby.'

DAN WAS HELPING bundle Nan and Pop into Hannah's car while he waited for Lucy to emerge from the bathroom where she'd rushed off while everyone was packing up. He'd just helped Pop find his seatbelt in the passenger seat in the dark when Beth came to say goodbye.

'So how's the wife hunting going, bro?' she said, pulling him to one side.

'A bit busy at the moment,' he said with a bit of a cough. 'Cherry season getting to the pointy end, y'know how it goes.'

'Yeah, Han mentioned you were taking a sabbatical. But even in the poorly lit car park, Dan could see something dangerous flaring in Beth's eyes that had nothing to do with agreeing with him. 'So what about Lucy, then?'

Ah, so that was it.

'What about Lucy?' he said, shifting his foot, pretending he had a bit of gravel stuck in the sole of his shoe.

'You two seem to be getting on all right.'

'So?'

'Well?' she pressed, as if he was missing the point.

He blinked, because suddenly he knew exactly what point

she was trying to make. 'What? You mean like, marry Lucy? Seriously?'

'Why not? She's funny. Hardworking. Everybody loves her and need I mention that she's drop-dead gorgeous?'

'Maybe so,' said Dan, thinking about his list – the list of all his requirements in a wife. He was pretty sure it didn't include funny or drop-dead gorgeous, and hardworking was only one out of three that really counted. 'But that hardly equates to marriage material. Besides, she's the same age as Sophie, give or take.'

'Sophie's our little sister, Dan. It's not like she's your daughter!'

'No.' He shook his head. It was ridiculous. 'Look, it doesn't matter anyway, because she's not the marrying kind, Beth.. You heard her yourself. She's not planning on staying around after cherry season.'

'No? Well maybe you should try changing her mind. She doesn't look like she's in a desperate rush to get away.'

'Coming?' said Han from the driver's seat.

'Sure,' she said, but not before she'd given her brother a pointed nod. 'Sleep on it, Bradley,' she said, before jumping into the back seat alongside Nan.

'Who?' he said, before groaning as the car drove off.

Marry Lucy? That was a joke. Lucy would get a big kick out of that idea. Not that he was about to share it with her.

He turned in time to see her coming out of the hall, and saw Sophie catch up with her to give her a hug before she left. Well, so yeah, she was huggable. All right, he couldn't argue with that. Sophie waved to him across the car park before turning back to do whatever she had to do, and he watched Lucy head down to where he was waiting.

He ended up walking back and meeting her halfway. It didn't mean anything. He just had plans for Lucy tonight that didn't include waiting.

'SO HOW DO you know all that stuff about James Bond?'

They'd made love once already and were taking a breather, both of them lying on their backs, watching the slow revolve of the ceiling fan.

Lucy shrugged. 'How does anyone know stuff? How did you know all that stuff about football and cricket and history?'

'I grew up with it.'

'There you go, then.'

'Yeah, but people don't grow up learning about James Bond.' He turned his face towards hers. 'Do they?'

She looked at him. 'Sure, if you've got a mom like mine.'

'She had a thing for James Bond?'

'More than a thing. Mom was crazy about Sean Connery. She always wanted to be one of those old time Bond girls. She had a couple of screen tests one time I remember, but she was way too late for Sean anyway, and I don't know how many times she took me to see the movies. She had her Bond girl name all picked out.'

'What was it?'

'Libby Godown.'

He snorted. 'What?'

And Lucy raised herself up on her elbow and said, checking names off her fingers. 'There was already a Pussy Galore, Honey Ryder, Xenia Onatopp, Plenty O'Toole and Holly Goodhead. What else was left?

Dan nodded his head as he casually stroked her arm. 'Yeah, I take your point. So what's your Bond girl name?'

She shrugged. 'I never had one.'

'Never?'

She made lazy figure eights through his chest hair with her nails. 'Oh, don't get me wrong, I'm a big fan of Sean

Connery's Bond, but being a Bond girl was never my dream.'

'But if it were?'

She gave a little feminine mewl. 'Are you going to go all 007 on me Dan?'

He gave a very masculine growl in return, and rolled her over, targeting first one nipple with his lips, and then the other. 'I might, if you make it worth my while.'

'Promises, promises,' she said, between gasps as his hot mouth and hand drifted lower over her belly. Much lower.

'Promises Promises is a lousy name,' he said. 'I'm thinking that given the season, something to do with cherries would be more apt.'

'Um, I hate to point this out, but isn't it a bit late for talking cherries?'

'Nope. This is the cherry that keeps on giving.'

'Cherry Pie?' she ventured, her head deep in her pillow and her voice squeaking as his mouth and his clever fingers ventured perilously closer to her sex. And so what if it sounded lame, how was she supposed to think with that clever tongue severing the connections in her brain and flicking closer to the only place in the world that seemed to matter right now?

'Cherry Pop,' he said, lifting his head, and then she was almost sure she felt his smile against her quivering thighs. 'No, Cherry Poppins.'

'I'm not sure Walt Disney would approve.'

'I'm betting 007 would.'

Oh wow. Her back arched, her head pushing deeper into the pillow. She approved too, of his hot knowing tongue and his clever fingers.

'Maybe,' she whispered, the storm within her building, 'I should have an umbrella, like Mary.'

'You won't need one,' he promised her, but he was wrong,

because a few moments later an umbrella would have been really handy as her world spun out of control and it was impossible to tell which way was up.

LUCY CRACKED OPEN AN EYELID, winced at the light flooding into the room through the gaps in the curtains, and gave thanks that it was Sunday, because there'd been no way they were ever going to beat sunrise today – cherry season or not. They'd made love long into the night, the pull of each other's bodies too much to resist and so they'd dozed briefly only to awaken and begin all over again. The tempo had slowed in those later sessions, allowing more time to explore and discover, to taste and wonder at each other's bodies.

And what a body. Dan's was amazing, a smorgasbord of delights – a washboard stomach, a sculpted chest with its whorls of hair and the hard nubs of his nipples, the corded tendons of his limbs pulling skin into dips and scooped hollows between muscles – there was so much to explore, so much to delight in. And the way he'd made her feel – how was it possible that two people who seemed so radically different could have bodies so in tune?

Amazing what spark could do.

He stirred beside her and she settled into her pillow to drink in the details of the face turned towards hers. He wasn't smiling in his sleep, but neither was he scowling. He looked deliciously at peace, his chest rising and falling with each slow breath. She could watch him sleep forever. She could wait forever for him to open his eyes and smile and reach for her when he saw her.

And something caught and held tight in her chest.

Because forever sounded suspiciously like love. She didn't

do love. She'd tried love and forever and settling down and look at the disaster that had turned out.

So she'd gone back to living for the moment and then moving on.

She wouldn't risk losing everything again. She couldn't.

She stared at his face, the whiskers on his cheeks and jaw, the dark lashes interwoven in sleep over his closed eyes, and wondered what it was about this man that had caused that F word to pop into her head.

Spark, she insisted to herself. It was just spark. Nothing more. It would fizzle into nothing, or it would crash and burn, just like it always did. Just like she wanted it to.

Liar.

More like she needed it to before something stupid happened and she did fall in love with him. She couldn't let it happen.

Alongside her Dan stirred and reached for her. 'Lucy,' he said with a growl. But she was already halfway out of bed and pulling on his shirt.

'I'll just . . . get us some coffee.'

SHE CHEWED her lip as the kettle boiled, her skin unnaturally cold and clammy as she circled the table with restless strides, the thoughts in her head spinning in useless circles.

Spark.

Dan.

Love?

No!

She knew what love was. Something that started with a spark but soon grew into a forest fire under your skin. A need to have and to hold. A yearning for forever.

But the forest fire soon burned out.

She knew that. She'd been burnt before. She couldn't let it happen again.

She couldn't fall in love again.

'God, you look sexy in my shirt.'

Her heart did a little lurch as she swivelled and saw him there, leaning against the wall, jeans zipped but unbuttoned, his arms crossed over his bare chest. She swallowed. And he was calling her sexy.

'Hi,' she said. 'I was just getting coffee.'

'I think the kettle's boiled.'

She turned and saw the steam rising from the spout and realised the kettle had clicked off and she hadn't even noticed. 'Oh, right.'

She moved to the counter and was spooning coffee into cups when he came up behind her and slid his arms around her waist. He kissed her throat and she jumped, feeling a sizzle all the way down to her toes.

'Are you okay?'

'Sure. Why?'

'You seem a bit – skittish.'

'Put it down to lack of sleep,' she said, as he pushed the collar of his shirt aside so he could nuzzle at her neck. She felt him draw the shirt back, felt his fingers trace over the outline of her tattoo. 'Why a bird?' he said, his breath fanning her skin. 'Is this you? Always moving on? Beautiful? Fragile?'

'No,' she told him, her voice choking a little as she slid the shirt up over her shoulders and turned in his arms. 'It's not me.' But she couldn't bring herself to tell him what it was. Not now. Not here when she was feeling so vulnerable.

She looked up at him, with his serious brown eyes and morning stubble and a dimple in his cheek that had taken her weeks to discover, and cursed herself to hell and back that she couldn't be stronger.

'Come back to bed,' he said, pushing down her arms and taking her hands in his as he kissed her lightly on the lips.

Somehow she managed to smile up at him. She couldn't let herself fall in love with him.

She couldn't.

DAN HAD NEVER SLEPT in so late. Not that they'd been doing a whole lot of sleeping. But after a night of the best sex of his life, he felt invincible. Unstoppable. Nothing was going to rain on his parade today.

So when the phone rang, not even that bugged him. Because he had a beautiful naked woman beside him and he was still basking in a post-coital glow he had no intention of shaking off anytime soon - a post coital glow that he knew would be turning into a pre-coital glow any minute from now.

And if it was a cherry order, they'd leave a message.

So he thought nothing as he let the phone ring and whoever was calling hang up three times, because he was otherwise occupied, until he heard a voice squawking into his answer phone for him to pick up.

A voice so tightly wound he barely recognised it. Beth?

He stumbled out of bed and picked up the receiver. 'What is it?'

'Dan, you have to come quick. Pop's had a heart attack!'

CHAPTER 19

'So that's what he was hiding all this time,' said Dan. He was sitting in the sterile visitors' lounge outside the ICU, while Nan and Hannah took their turn to sit inside with Pop for a few minutes. Sophie was on her way with Wendy. 'That's why the doctor had told him to slow down - and yet the old bugger still came to work every day like nothing was wrong.'

'He was in denial,' Beth said, her head in her hands. 'Pretending there was nothing wrong. Making out it was indigestion.'

'Silly old coot.'

'I told him not to have a coronary at the quiz last night,' Beth went on, 'I should have known. I should have been able to tell something.'

Dan put his arm around his sister. 'Hey, it is not your fault. I should have known something was up. He hasn't been himself for weeks. But he wouldn't say.'

'He didn't even tell Nan.'

'Is Pop going to die,' asked Siena, curled up against her mother's side.

'No,' they both said together. Thanks to the ambos and a crack team of cardiac specialists at the hospital, Pop was expected to pull through. He'd have a zipper line down his chest to show for his troubles, and the rest of them would be sporting a few grey hairs after he scared the hell out of them all like that, but the prognosis was positive.

At least now the old man would have to slow down. He'd been mad to keep working like a man half his age when he was supposed to be retired. And Dan had been mad to let him. Not that there was any telling the old man, but still, he should have made more of an effort to look after him.

He was pushing eighty for God's sake.

Eighty years old.

'Nobody lives forever,'

That's what Pop had said the night of Dan's birthday party. Had he known something was wrong even then? Sensed it was something more serious than indigestion, and then stuck his head in the sand once he'd seen the doctor and got a diagnosis?

Hannah and Nan joined them, Nan looking like the bottom had dropped out of her world. She looked like she'd aged twenty years overnight. 'How's he going?' they asked as Han herded her to a seat.

'As well as can be expected at this stage, they're saying,' said Han. 'So that's good. The specialist is coming to talk to us in a minute.'

Nan blinked and shook her head. 'Went down like a pack of cards, he did. I thought he was a goner,' she said before she pressed bunched up tissues to her eyes. 'Stubborn old fool, not telling anyone.'

'Hey,' said Han, her arm around Nan's back. 'He'll be okay.'

The specialist confirmed it when he appeared a few minutes later. 'The fact that Clarence is fitter than your average eighty-year-old has definitely helped his body cope with the trauma of a heart attack,' he told them. 'A couple of days in ICU and he'll be out in the ward. If he behaves himself, he should be home in a week or so.'

'A week?' said Han. 'Will he be ready to go home so soon?'

Nan sniffed. 'He's never behaved himself once, that one. You better do some stern talking to him, Doctor, because he sure as eggs won't listen to me.'

The specialist smiled. 'The hard work will start at home, I'm afraid. Sometimes cardiac patients lose confidence in themselves and their bodies after an attack. What we've found is that the patients who make the best recoveries are those who have something to look forward to. Some big family event down the track to focus on so there's motivation to keep up with the exercise and the physio. What we want is to keep Clarence feeling positive, so there's no chance of him falling despondent because he's had this setback.' He looked around the room. 'Is there something he might have to look forward to? Any babies expected in the next few months? Any weddings?'

And every single member of his family looked squarely at Dan.

'You've got something coming up?' the specialist said looking hopeful.

Dan cleared his throat. 'Um, well, Nan and Pop's daughter-in-law is getting married in January.'

'But we're hoping Dan might be tying the knot sometime soon too,' said Hannah pointedly.

And Dan thought about the arrangement with Lucy. Cherry season didn't have that long to run and soon he'd be back in the hunt. 'I'm, uh, working on it,' he said.

IT WAS dark by the time he got home, but Lucy came running

from the house as he drove up the driveway. 'Dan,' she said, wrapping her arms around him the moment he climbed wearily out of the car. 'How is he?'

'They think he's going to be okay.'

She wrapped her arms around him on a sigh. 'Oh thank God,' she said, and he let her hold him there, feeling her strength seep into him, and never had he been more grateful to see another human being in his life.

HE LAY in bed that night, Lucy curled against his body, her breathing slow and steady. Soothing. Hypnotic.

He thought about his Pop lying in ICU ward with an entire network of wires and tubes coming in and going out of him and with machines beeping to make sure he was alive. Because Pop could have been dead. He could have died right there in the middle of their lounge room before the ambulance even got there.

'Nobody lives forever.'

And never before, not even when his own father was killed, was Dan so struck by his own mortality. He'd been twenty-seven then, and life had stretched out endlessly before him. Miles and miles of it with endless possibilities and seemingly no end in sight.

Pushing forty, he no longer saw it that way. Not anymore. Not now he'd stared in the mirror. In another thirty-seven years he'd be almost Pop's age. What would he be doing? Would he have found a wife and made a family? Or would he have been forced to sell the orchard, because he'd thought he'd live forever and that he could just keep putting it off?

And when he collapsed on the lounge room floor, would there be anyone to call the ambulance?

Or would he die alone?

He put his hand to his head. God. Where had that come from?

He leaned his head over and kissed Lucy's hair. She stirred a little and snuggled closer, settling back into sleep on a sigh.

It could wait, he told himself. Surely few weeks wouldn't hurt. He could open that damned program and start looking after she'd gone. Because right now he didn't want a wife.

He wanted Lucy.

THE FAMILY all took turns visiting the hospital over the next few days, the twins and Sophie taking Nan down the hill to the city hospital, and Wendy and Dirk dropping by when they could, while Dan redoubled his efforts to make this the best cherry season ever, whatever the weather threw at him. He would make the orchard a success and make his Pop proud.

By the time Dan visited him a couple of nights later, Pop had been moved into a room of his own. He left Lucy in the waiting room with Siena while he went in to visit.

The room was an improvement on the ward he'd been in before, although the décor was still public hospital bland and still smelt of disinfectant and other things he didn't want to put a name to. And there were still a bunch of machines attached to him. It didn't look like the kind of place you'd go to have a rest.

He bent down and kissed Nan's cheek, and was pleased to see her looking a little less brittle. 'How's he going?'

'I'm not dead yet,' said his Pop from the bed before Nan could respond, his voice a husky shadow of its usual self but still with as much attitude. 'You could have asked me.'

'I thought you were asleep,' said Dan as he gave his Pop's

fingers a squeeze, careful not to bump the cannula in the back of his hand.

'Can't sleep in this place. It's like bloody Rundle Street. In-out-in-out. Might as well put a revolving door on the room.'

'Settle down, Clarry,' said Nan, rubbing his shoulder. 'You know you're supposed to be resting.'

'Sophie told me he was feeling better.'

'Don't talk about me like I'm not here.'

'Okay, good to see you're feeling better.'

'I'm not. I feel like a ten tonne truck ran into me.' He harrumphed, his hand clutching the sheet covering his chest.

'How's things in the orchard?'

'Good. Couldn't be better.'

'Good boy. Keep it ticking over and I'll be back on my feet before you know it.'

'Clarence Faraday, you can forget all about working this cherry season.'

'Says who?'

'Says the doctors.'

'And says me,' added Dan. 'You gave us all a hell of a shock the other night. If you don't mind, I'd prefer to go grey in my own time. We'll manage, Pop.'

His Pop sagged into the pillows. 'So I'm useless now, am I? One little heart problem and I'm thrown out onto the scrap heap.'

Dan and his Nan exchanged glances. This was exactly what the doctors had warned them about.

'You'll be a heck of a lot more useful to us alive, thank you very much.'

Hannah arrived with coffee from the cafeteria. 'Damn, if I'd known you were coming I would have got you one too, Dan.'

'What about me?' said Pop from the bed. 'Nobody asked me.'

Han squeezed his arm. 'You can have one when the doctors say so.'

A nurse came to check his vitals and looked around at them all disapprovingly. 'Quite the party you've got going in here. How are we feeling, Mr Faraday?' she asked as she scooped up his paperwork from the end of the bed and started checking numbers and drips and blood pressure. 'They're not tiring you out, are they?'

'It's all right,' Dan said. 'I'm just leaving. But can Siena come in for a moment, Pop? She's been worried about you.'

'Of course I want to see my great granddaughter,' he said. 'Not even Florence Nightingale here could deny me that.'

The nurse raised an eyebrow. 'She can come in. For a minute. And then the party's over folks.'

SIENA SWUNG her feet under the chair as she sat in the waiting room. 'What do you want for Christmas, Lucy?'

Lucy shrugged. 'I don't know. How about you?'

'I told mum I wanted a nose piercing for Christmas.'

'Oh?' Lucy guessed where this was going. She closed the magazine she'd been half-heartedly flicking through.

'She said no. She said I had to wait until I was fifteen. That's even longer than to get my ears pierced!'

'She didn't say no outright though. That's promising. And fifteen's not forever.'

'It is forever! It's like twice my age nearly.'

'I think I was fifteen when I got my nose piercing. Or sixteen.' She shrugged. 'I forget now.'

'You were that old?'

She smiled. 'Sure. Real old.'

'So how old are you now?'

'Twenty-five.'

'How old were you when you got your tattoo?'

'Old enough.'

Siena screwed up her nose. 'You sound like Mum.'

'I'm probably about the same age as her. That's why.'

'She's twenty seven, her and Hannah – though Han's ten minutes older.'

'There you go.'

The girl looped her calves around the legs of the chair and crossed her arms. 'I don't want to wait until I'm that old.'

'It's not so bad. It seems like a long time now, but it'll go quickly. Don't forget, a tattoo lasts a long time. You want make sure you choose a design that you're going to like forever.'

'How did you decide on yours?'

She smiled. 'Mine was easy. I lost something once, and I wanted a way to remember it. It makes me smile when I see it in a mirror, even when sometimes it makes me a little sad.'

'What did you lose? A bird?'

She shook her head. 'No. Just something I don't want to forget. Something special. Hey, where's your mom tonight? Working?'

Siena screwed up her nose. 'She's creating.'

'Creating what?'

'She does mosaics. Out in the shed, though she calls it her studio.'

'That sounds like fun.'

'It kinda is. Sometimes she lets me help. But every now and then she gets all serious about it and it's not a good idea to disturb her.'

'I get that.'

'Do you?'

'Sure. Everyone needs a bit of space every now and then. That's how we make sense of things.'

'But do you need space to make sense of things?'

Oh, hell yes. All the time.' Especially now.

'I want to be like you when I grow up.'

'Me?'

'Yeah, you're cool. Cooler than Mum anyway.'

'Hey, isn't your mum a paramedic? And she does mosaics too – that sounds cool. Being your mum must be pretty cool too, I reckon.'

'But Mum hasn't got any tattoos. She even let her pierced ears grow over.'

'I still think she's cool.'

Siena said nothing for a while, just started swinging her legs again, until she sniffed. 'The only thing I want for Christmas is a nose piercing.'

Dan reappeared then, and Lucy's heart did a little lurch at the sight of him. Oh, boy. She had it bad.

'Can I see Pop now?' asked Siena.

'Yeah, just for a minute though,' he said. He led her into his room, and when he came back, Lucy could see he wasn't exactly smiling.

'How's Clarry?'

'Doing okay. What was Siena talking about?'

'Oh, you know,' she said, putting the magazine back on the table and standing up, locking her hands and stretching them out in front of her. 'Just girl talk.'

'She's a good kid.'

Lucy smiled. 'I know. She's cute.'

He grunted as he looped an arm around her waist, taking her by surprise. 'So are you.' And he leaned down to kiss her, this man with the electric touch, a man who could blow her world into tiny pieces that sparkled in the summer night and still be waiting for her when all the pieces were back together again.

Moments later, Siena burst back out into the room. 'Can we get an ice cream from the cafeteria on the way home?'

And Dan sprang away like a guilty teenager, the spell broken.

Siena took in the scene with the knowing eye of an eight-year-old who'd watched too much TV and knew something was going on, even if she didn't understand exactly what or why. 'What?'

'What's your favourite kind?' Dan asked.

'Drumstick,' the girl said, still suspicious.

'Then a Drumstick it will be,' said Dan. 'Let's go.'

'Do you miss your dad?' Lucy asked that night after their latest session of love-making, their bodies were still humming their way down.

He turned his sweat slicked face to hers. 'Whoa. Where did that come from?'

'I dunno,' she said, her fingernails tracing the lines of the ribs in his chest as his breathing came down to normal. 'But it must be hard doing what you do. Hard enough with your dad gone. Harder still with Pop out of action.'

'That's true enough,' he said, his fingers stroking her shoulder. 'I never thought I'd be doing it on my own. You always think your folks will live forever and then one day you work out your mum is really your step-mum and that people die and it comes as a rude shock.' He shook his head. 'I never thought Dad would go so early though. He was so strong. He'd be so pissed off he'd rolled the four wheeler on a rabbit hole, of all things.'

He didn't say anything for a few seconds and all she could

hear was a cricket chirping outside the open window, and then, 'What about you? Do you miss your dad?'

'Ha. That's an easy one. How can you miss someone you never knew?'

'You never knew him - at all?'

She flopped back against her pillow. 'Nope. From what Mom's told me, it was a quick beach fling with consequences. When she did track him down to let him know the happy news, he was on the sand holding his surfboard on the way out to catch a wave. He told her congratulations and headed out to catch it.'

He laced his fingers in hers and squeezed tight. 'God, that's awful.'

'No. It's kind of cool. Because Mom did the right thing and told him he was going to be a father. It was up to him if he wanted to be involved. He didn't and to his credit, he was honest about it.' She swallowed back on a familiar stab of pain. And at least he'd never demanded that she get rid of it. *Rid of her.* 'Anyhow,' she said, forcing that bitter memory back down where it belonged, 'given my Mom has never settled for just one man for long, he probably did the right thing. So no, I never missed him.'

Dan lifted her hand to his mouth and pressed his lips to it.

'I kind of hope it's like that for Siena - if she's never known her dad - I mean.'

He turned to her. 'What do you know about Joe?'

'Only what someone told me, that he died before Siena was born. Before he and Beth had the chance to get married.'

'Yeah. It was the middle of winter and it had been hailing hard. His motorbike hit a patch of ice on a bend.'

'God. Poor Beth.'

'Yeah, and it was hardest on her because we'd lost Dad a couple of years before, so she had the double whammy to deal with, plus having a new baby and suddenly finding herself a single mum.'

'That's real tough.'

'Didn't stop her though. She went back to uni after Siena was born and switched from teaching to become a paramedic instead.'

'Because of what had happened?'

'Yeah. Because she felt helpless and because she doesn't want other people to suffer like they did – and like she did.'

'She's amazing. But she can't save everyone, surely.'

'Try telling Beth that.'

Lucy smiled. 'Siena's so lucky.'

'How do figure that?'

'Well, I mean, she's got such a great Mom and a supportive family around her, not to mention an uncle who adores her. She might have lost her dad, but she's never going to go short on love.'

The silence stretched on too long and she wondered if he'd fallen asleep. 'Dan?'

'Sorry, I was just thinking. I always feel so bad for Siena for all the things she missed out on. It never occurred to me, you know, that it could have been worse for Siena. It never occurred to me to look at what she had.' He leaned over and kissed her brow. 'When did you get be so wise?'

She laughed at that as she rolled towards him, snuggling closer. '

And when did you stop noticing what's right under your nose? Your family is amazing. Beth saves people and Hannah saves four-legged animals.'

'They make more sense,' Han reckons. 'Animals don't lie to you.'

'Ain't that the truth.' She looked up at him, suddenly curious. 'Did she ever have a significant other who let her down?'

'No. Not that we know about anyway. Not that she brought home.'

'So what about Sophie? What does she get up to when she's not working at the school?'

'I don't know. I don't think there's anyone special then, she bought that fancy accommodation voucher for something. I've got a feeling she might be looking for a boyfriend.'

'Because of the voucher?'

'Because of something she said when the girls gave me my subscription to that dating agency. I think Sophie might have tried it out.'

'Does that bother you?'

'A bit, I guess. There are some strange types out there. So long as she doesn't end up with someone who steals her cake. Did I ever tell you about Marie? Couldn't keep her fork out of my cake.'

She turned towards him. 'Ha, I stole your cake – that first night I was here, remember?'

How could he have forgotten that finger in his icing, that couldn't-fit-another-thing-in girl who managed to dispense with half his leftover birthday cake?

'You won't do it again,' he warned, but there was laughter in his eyes and his lips were curved upwards. 'Not now you're on notice.'

She traced the line of his lips with her fingertips. 'I like it when you smile. I didn't think you could smile for a long time.'

'Why?'

'You were always scowling whenever you saw me. Well, all the time, really.'

He sighed and leaned back against the pillow, one hand

going behind his head. 'Sorry. Sometimes, when you work on the land, there's not a whole lot to smile about.'

'And now?'

He collected her into his arms. 'So maybe I found something to smile about.'

Her heart did that tripping thing in her chest, and as he drew her closer and she was convinced she could taste forever on his lips and in his hot mouth and she knew that it was far too late to stop it. There was no denying it any longer.

She was a goner.

She'd fallen in love with Dan Faraday.

She gave herself up to his kiss, confessing her discovery in the dance of their tongues and the press of her breasts against his chest. Admitting her love for him in her worship of his body and feeling her love returned in his.

And afterwards, he let her go and rolled onto his back with a sigh. 'Wow,' he said, 'it's a bloody shame cherry season is nearly over. I'm going to miss you.'

Thud.

Her heart turned to a brick, heavy and laden with sorrow.

Her foolish, foolish heart. Because she knew why she was here in this bed. Not because Dan loved her, but because of that damn spark. Chemistry. Lust.

A single tear squeezed from her eye and she brushed it away before he could notice, sweeping away the very idea. Foolish heart and foolish woman, to fall in love.

She'd gone into this relationship with her eyes wide open. It was clear they were poles apart from the start. She'd come into this job as a casual employee for the duration of the cherry season and nothing had changed.

At the end of the season she'd leave.

She hauled in a deep breath, telling herself that she'd feel differently once she was somewhere else. She'd feel better. Free. She tried her damndest to believe it.

'So,' she said, aiming to keep it light and keep the desolation she was feeling from her voice, 'you think the season will be finished by Christmas then?'

'It's looking like it the way everything's ripening up so well and what with the team doing such a great job. No storms, no rain; it's been the best season for years.'

'Right. Well, that's good news then.'

He gave her a friendly slap on the behind and rolled her onto her back.

'Isn't it. So we'd better not waste any more time,' he said, burning a purposeful trail of kisses down her throat.

CHAPTER 20

*C*hristmas was bearing down on her like a runaway express train, and much as she wanted to ignore its rapid approach, there were constant reminders everywhere. It seemed every one of the pickers had made special plans for the holiday that they felt they had to share at smoko.

Kate happily admitted that she couldn't wait for the cherry picking to be over so she could go camping down at Normanville where her family went every January. Her enthusiasm may have had something to do with the fact Rod had been invited to join them. Kate and Rod had become quite the item. Others were simply looking forward to a break after the physically demanding orchard work before they went back to uni or waited for the apples and pears to ripen so they could do it all over again.

'Something will turn up,' Lucy would say, whenever she was asked where she was spending Christmas. Kate had already invited her to spend it with her family, but Lucy wasn't keen on the thought of playing gooseberry to the new lovers. . Besides, she figured it might be better to make a clean break and get right away once cherry season was over.

But where? The entire world lay waiting for her. She was able to travel wherever she liked, except now there was nowhere she hankered to go. Never before had she felt unenthusiastic at the prospect of moving on. She looked through an old atlas she had found in the living room shelves and scoured its maps for inspiration but found nothing more than meaningless coloured shapes on a page.

Her mom would welcome her in San Sebastian, she knew, but she was loathe to ring and ask if she could visit. She told herself it was because she'd then be playing gooseberry with her mom and Mateo too, but she knew she was really scared that if she asked, her mom would say yes. And then she'd have to book flights and make arrangements and it would be too final.

So instead Lucy drifted along, trying to avoid the question of the holiday unless directly asked, losing herself instead in the routine of physical work of picking by day, and Dan's wondrous love-making by night.

When she was in his arms it was easy to forget she would soon be gone. Then nothing mattered but being with Dan.

She was happy, she told herself, and she was, blissfully happy.

But each morning, as the first needles of sunshine speared through the gap in the curtains, she would hear that runaway train getting closer and she knew that very soon she would have to make a decision.

DAN COULDN'T PUT his finger on what was wrong, only that something was gnawing away at his gut like he had a rodent trapped inside, and it sure wasn't that the fuel lines were giving him grief again or that the gears on the bike were starting to play up.

It made no sense of course. The cherries were doing all the right things. There'd been no thunderclouds filled with lashing rain or icy hail to wreak havoc on the fruit, the birds weren't causing too many hassles and the team he had in place was working well. To top it all off, the cherry crop was just about in and it wasn't even Christmas. Faraday Orchard's best crop ever.

Even Pop was home and behaving himself and on the road to recovery.

And still . . .

He stopped halfway between the packing shed and the house, pulled off his hat and beat it against his leg, running his hand through his sweat slickened hair as he looked up at the westering sun throwing red light across the hillside.

Something wasn't right.

And then he smelt it, the unmistakable scent of one of Lucy's curries squeezing around the edges of the door and hooking into his senses, and he remembered. She'd be leaving soon. Cherry season was almost done and Lucy would be moving on.

Damn.

He gave his hat another belt on his thigh for good measure before jamming it back on his head, cursing the dumb luck that had the cherries ripening when they should for once, and not lingering into January.

She smiled when he went inside, and when he couldn't summon up a smile in return, he turned and found a peg for his hat instead.

'Hungry?' she asked. 'I'm almost done.'

'Yeah,' he said, because whatever was chewing a hole in his gut was leaving a yawning chasm behind. 'I reckon I might trade up the four-wheeler after cherry season and get something more reliable. It'll come in handy for the apples and pears too, I figure.'

'Sure,' she said, and he couldn't tell if he was imagining the tightness around her eyes as he took himself off to the bathroom to wash up. The phone chirped halfway there and he picked up, rubbed the back of his neck while he listened.

'So I figure,' the green grocer on the other end of the line said, 'the only way is for you to put my order in a cab and send the cherries down that way.'

'Are you sure? That's going to cost you an arm and a leg.'

'What choice do I have? What else can I do? My truck won't be fixed this side of Christmas and there's isn't a carrier that isn't already booked up. I need those cherries for my customers. Can you do it?'

Dan sighed. Of course he could do it. But surely there was another way. A better way.

And suddenly there was.

Oh yeah, that might work.

Lucy was dishing up when he got back to the table, a bunch of coriander on the chopping board. Funny, he thought. He couldn't remember ever enjoying coriander before Lucy came along. Dinners just weren't going to be the same after she'd gone.

And that rodent took another mighty mouthful of his gut.

'Can you show me how to make that?' he asked, changing the topic before he started to

analyse things too deeply.

She looked at him and he'd been right, there was definitely tightness around her eyes, but she smiled. 'Make curry? Sure. Grab a knife and you can start now with the coriander. I'll explain how it works. It's dead easy.'

So Dan found himself chopping herbs for the first time in his life, another first in the summer of Lucy.

'Got any plans for Sunday?' he said as Lucy dished up and he sprinkled the coriander over their meals.'

'No, not that I know of. Why do you ask?'

'Just wondering. The cherries will be about done and one of my clients down the coast has had his truck break down and is panicking about how he's going to get his Christmas order. Apparently all the carriers are booked up and the only alternative's a taxi that would cost a bomb. I thought I might go for a run and drop it off, seeing things are winding down here.'

'The coast?'

'Yeah, about an hour south of here. Nice beaches. Interested?'

And for the first time her smile touched her eyes. 'Sure, that'd be great.'

To Lucy's surprise, it was the Spitfire that Dan loaded with the boxes of cherries. 'We're going in Spitty?'

He smiled at her use of the car's nickname. 'Why not? It's a gorgeous day to have the top down.'

That it was. And she'd always intended to see the beaches while she was here. She tossed her bag into the storage area behind the seat.

'Got your bathers?'

'Oh, I don't have any. I didn't think to replace them yet.'

'You can get some down there. It's too good a day not to go for a swim.'

He took her what he called 'the back way' through the hills, through tiny towns with pretty stone cottages and wide verandahed pubs along the main road, and all strung together on a highway lined with huge gum trees. The little car clung to the curves and powered down the straights and the wind was in her hair and the mottled sunlight shone through the trees kissed her skin and Dan was beside her. She turned to look at his strong profile and his big hands on the wheel, the sleeves of his shirt rolled up, and felt the tug in her heart and thought, it wasn't so bad.

She'd always lived in the moment – that had been her strength all her life, her joy – and this was a moment to remember. A whole day of moments for the taking and she'd take each and every one and store them away.

He turned and caught her watching him. 'What?' he said, before looking back at the road.

She grinned and threw her head back and put her arms in the air over the windshield to catch the wind and said, 'I love it!'

He smiled and grabbed her right hand and pulled it to his mouth, kissing it before he dropped it to his thigh and her heart swelled and she thought, if this thing wasn't love, she didn't know what what was.

Live in the moment, she reminded herself. Just enjoy the day.

'Do you fancy fish and chips for lunch after we drop this lot off?'

'Sure.'

'Excellent,' he said, letting her hand go to change down gears and overtake a slow moving horse float. 'Not far now.'

A few kilometres later they crested a rise and started a long descent downhill and there was a sapphire blue sea and the town of Victor Harbor spread out along the coast. 'It's so pretty,' she said, 'the town sitting between the coast and the rolling hills.'

'You think this is good? Just wait.'

The main streets of Victor were bustling with holiday-makers and retirees who'd come to the coast for a sea change. The Spitfire burbled its way into a shopping centre car park's delivery bay. 'Be right back,' he told her, and true to his word, he was, with one very excited greengrocer bearing a hand trolley. So excited that once the boot was empty, he not only shook Dan's hand but then kissed him on both cheeks, and then Lucy's too.

'You have saved my life,' he said, talking with his hands as much as his words. 'The cherries, they are already sold out. I did not want to disappoint my customers, and now, thanks to you both, I will not.'

'You're a nice man,' she said to Dan as they drove away.

'I've never been accused of that before.'

'It's true. First of all I thought you were a bit uptight –'

He looked across at her, his eyebrows raised.

'Okay, so a lot uptight. But that was really sweet of you to come all the way down here and deliver them.'

'Maybe I had an ulterior motive.'

'Yeah?'

'Maybe I just wanted fish and chips for lunch.'

She screwed up her nose. 'Well, that's damning. Clearly in that case, you're not a nice person at all.'

'I thought that was supposed to be a good thing. Aren't girls supposed to fall for the bad boys?'

'Some girls, sure.'

'But not you.'

'Oh, I'm much more discerning than that. I don't conform to stereotypes.'

And he grinned. 'I had noticed that.'

'I'll take that as a compliment,' she said, smiling as she leaned back in her seat, enjoying this trip even more than she'd expected. Dan seemed different today, more boyish, like a holiday version of himself. She wondered if he'd once been more like today's Dan, before circumstances and obligations had bent him out of shape.

They were heading out of town, she noticed. 'Where are we going now?' she asked, her toes itching to hit the beach.

'Just down the coast. This place is a bit too crowded for me.'

He stopped in the small town of Port Elliot, pulling up on the main road outside a surf shop and opposite a fish and chippery. 'I'll grab us something to eat and drink if you want to find some togs.'

'Sure,' she said, thinking this had better be the fastest bathers hunting expedition ever. And it was. There were no other customers in the store and the first pair she pulled from the rack were perfect. She was back at the car before he was.

'Fast worker,' he said.

'So I'm hungry.'

'Then hop in,' he said, handing her the bags. 'Your five-star dining experience awaits.'

He took a right towards the beach and then another, parking on a headland overlooking the water. The roar of the ocean greeted them as an enormous wave slammed into the jumble of huge granite rocks jutting into the sea, sending spray high into the air. Just beyond, the cliffs fell away and the waves rolled onto a white sand beach which curved in a gentle arc, ending in the distance with a solitary mount.

They found a seat overlooking the crashing waves and he pointed out Knight's Beach before them and then the town of Victor Harbor along the coast where they'd come from, and The Bluff on the point with Granite Island in the fore-ground, joined to the mainland by a long wooden bridge.

The view was stunning. Lucy drank it in, watching the body-boarders seemingly risk life and limb in the mix-master of wave action between the massive rocks and the shore, while the sea breeze tugged at her hair and the smell of the clean salt air filled her lungs and the spray from the latest clash of water on rock fell over them like mist.

'You can sometimes see southern right whales migrating along the coast from here,' he said, as he handed her a paper bag containing an enormous piece of battered fish and a wedge of lemon. 'Mothers with their calves.'

'Wow,' she said, squeezing her lemon over the fish. 'Have you seen them?'

'Only once. We came down here one year for Nan and Pop's anniversary. You have to be here around August–September when they migrate around the coast. You wouldn't believe how big they are. It's pretty special.'

Something else she wouldn't see then, like the changing seasons in the Adelaide Hills and the cherry blossoms. She sighed, and concentrated instead on her fish. Outside was golden crisp while inside was flaky perfection, the flesh plump and white. 'Oh, my God, this is so good,' she said.

'Wait till you try the chips.' He pushed the bag between them closer and she couldn't resist and they were so good it was hard to stop. The first beady-eyed seagull circled about then, cruising in for a free feed, and it wasn't long before he was joined by all his winged mates and there was a battle going on between them for chip rights.

The waves kept right on crashing into the rocks, the black wetsuited body-boarders kept spinning and getting dumped and Lucy sat back and wiped her hands on a napkin and sipped on a soda. 'I thought you were kidding about the five-star lunch, you know.'

'I was. I'm not sure what you thought you were eating, but it was just fish and chips.'

'Definitely five stars. One each for the fish and the chips. One for a seat overlooking an amazing view and one for the music of the crashing waves.'

He looked at her, thinking about that a while. 'That's only four.'

She smiled. 'The other one is for the company.'

'You're giving one whole star to the seagulls?' He looked so aggrieved she couldn't help but laugh.

'No, one whole star for you.'

He nodded, looking better pleased. 'You're not bad company yourself.'

She took a deep breath and looked out at the ever-shifting sea, a single white cloud in the sky sending a blotch of dark scudding over its surface.

Yeah, she was good company. Good temporary company. A stopgap until she left and he could take up the serious job of wife hunting again.

'Come on,' he said, taking her hand and tugging her up. 'Let's go walk off lunch before that swim.' He scattered the last of the chips to the air and started an aerial world war three that had her laughing again. She would not feel sorry for herself. She had a great life and this had been a great day.

They took the slate paved coastal walk around the granite boulder clad shore, and around tiny bays and hidden coves where the waves shooshed in and out and it was impossible not to linger and take in the sheer poetry of it. Further on there were islands and a rocky breakwater where a glossy black seal was fishing and frolicking in the tumbling wash, and a bay named after its horseshoe shape where the water lapped gently at the shore and families played along its edge.

And Lucy, who had been to Paris and Rome and seen some of the most famous and beautiful sights in the world, was struck by how the simple elements of boulder, blue sea and white sand could be arranged in such a way as to take your breath away. 'It's gorgeous,' she said, as they stopped at a spot overlooking the bay and the beaches beyond, curving away until the sandhills disappeared in the far distance. 'You're lucky, you know.' she said.

'How so?'

'Because you have the hills and that's one type of gorgeous, and you have this just a way down the road.'

'Yeah, it can get a bit boring living one's whole life here.'

'Oh God,' she said, looking at him. 'I actually said that, didn't I?'

'Yup, you surely did.'

'You must have thought me unbearable.'

He tilted his head, and sighed. 'Well, I guess the feeling back then was kind of mutual. Come on, let's go for that swim.'

They hit the surf beach, where only a few hardy souls braved the waves, squirming into bathers beneath their towels.

'Cute,' said Dan, when he got his first look at her new floral bikini with the little ruffle at the top.

She smiled. There was nothing cute about Dan in his board shorts. He was damn near delectable. There was something about a man who had pecs and abs without looking overblown, like he'd spent the whole day pumping iron in the gym because he had nothing better to do.

'Watch out for the undertow,' he warned as he ran with her into the sea. She gasped as the cold water hit her heated skin, gasped again as he caught her unexpectedly and pulled her into his kiss. He tasted like the sea itself, salty and fresh, his body warm against the chill of the water, their kiss lasting until the sea sucked at their legs and pulled them off balance and they tumbled together, half laughing, half shocked, into the next incoming foaming wave.

THEY PLAYED in the waves and the foam until they'd been tumbled and dumped one too many times and finally they collapsed together, panting on the sand. Dan lay on his back, one arm around Lucy, the other shielding his eyes from the sun.

He was knackered. Totally exhausted, with sand in places

that didn't bear thinking about. And never had he felt so happy or so good in his life.

'How come you never got married?' Lucy was fiddling with his phone. She held it up above their heads and snapped a photo.

'Huh?'

She rolled over to check it out before putting it back in his shirt pocket. 'Why's it taken you so long?'

'Where did that come from?'

'I'm just curious. You don't seem the type not to be married at your age.'

Dan shook his head. He didn't know there was a type not to be married at his age.

'So I scowled too much and frightened all the girls away.'

'Be serious.'

'Ask a serious question then.'

'It is serious! You must have had girlfriends.'

He sighed. 'Sure I did. There was this cute girl on the school bus called Coralie.' He sighed.

'What happened to her?'

'Her parents were lawyers and they weren't that keen on her going out with a lowly primary producer's son.'

'And they stopped her from seeing you?'

'Yeah, pretty much. They moved to Sydney in the end. That sure put a stop to it.'

'Oh. Any others?'

'Is there a point to this?'

'Hey, just answer the question.'

'Okay, so I had dates of course, every now and then.'

'Did you ever think you'd found the one?'

He hesitated. 'Yeah. One time.'

'How old were you?'

'About twenty-four or twenty-five. Her name was Margot and I met her at a wedding and I thought I was in love.'

She snugged closer. 'Were you?'

He shrugged. 'At the time? Well, who knows? I thought so. Anyway, I thought she loved me back, and everything seemed to be going okay and it was fine when we went out, but then I'd bring her home to the orchard and she'd see Dad and Pop still working and Wendy and Nan picking raspberries or grading cherries and one day she asked how old you had to be to retire in the orchard business. I joked that you didn't retire, you died on the job.' He paused. 'Kind of ironic really, given how Dad died a bit later and now Pop can't stay away, but by then she'd already got cold feet and walked away. And once Dad was gone, there was nothing else for it but to take over and plough myself one hundred per cent into the orchard. I guess I haven't been paying as much attention to wife hunting as I might otherwise have done.'

'No wonder you never seemed to smile much.'

Maybe. Probably. Was it any wonder, come to think of it?

'Weren't you lonely?'

'No, I was busy and besides, I had Molly to keep me company.'

'Who's Molly?'

He raised an eyebrow. 'Now I've got your interest. Are you jealous?'

'I don't know. Should I be?'

He smiled and shook his head. 'Molly was my dog. A kelpie. Best working dog that ever lived.'

'What happened to her?'

'She was poisoned. She didn't turn up for dinner one night and I went looking.' He sighed, remembering her anguished yelping and finding her writhing in agony, her legs spasming, her mouth foaming. 'I found her all right. She was a mess. She died in the car on the way to the vet.'

'Who would poison a dog? You don't think it was Des?'

'No. He's a buffoon but I doubt even he could do something that nasty. She might have taken a fox bait, I don't know. Guess I'll never know.'

He watched the waves roll in for a while, felt the sun and breeze turn his salted skin tight.

'Anyway, enough about me. What about you?' he asked, because he wasn't that fussed with raking over the coals of his non-existent love life. It felt a bit sad to be as good as admitting that the love of his life had four legs and a tail.

'Ever been serious about anyone?'

She rolled away from him onto her back. 'No. Not really.'

'What?' He urged, 'No-one, ever?'

'I move around too much,' she said, suddenly sitting up and wrapping her arms around her knees. 'There's never much time to get close to anyone.'

He looked at the bird on her shoulder, now partially covered with sand, and just like Lucy, flitting from one place to another. 'But you've had relationships along the way, right? You've had boyfriends.'

'Oh, sure. Heaps.'

'But you've never been in love with any of them?'

'Hey, listen,' she said, jumping to her feet and swiping sand off her butt cheeks under the line of her bikini. 'I'm hot. How about another dip?'

'Okay,' he said, following her because he was hot too and it would be good to cool down before they drove home.

Real good if he was going to start stewing about those boyfriends – about how many and how meaningful. Where had that come from?

'Just for the record,' he said as they loaded their gear in the car, 'What type of men do you reckon aren't married by my age?'

She blinked. 'Oh, you know. Guys who are socially inept. Misfits. Losers. Gay men of course, although for entirely different reasons. Sleazeballs. Oh, and priests, of course.'

He nodded. 'Great. Good to know you don't think I fit into that any of those categories.' Maybe there was hope for him yet.

'You can see why I wondered. I mean, obviously you're not gay.'

'Bless you, my child,' he said, and she punched him on the arm, and he forgot all about stewing over her previous lovers

.

'I didn't know there was another reason for anyone staying unmarried so long,' she said, as she lowered herself into the car.

'You mean working too hard?'

'I mean waiting for your sisters to buy you a subscription to a dating agency.'

And he laughed.

As he pointed the little car out of town and along the highway, he realised that this had been his happiest, most carefree day for a long time. Very possibly his best day ever.

It was more than just that he was escaping to the beach at the near end of a successful cherry season. It was because of Lucy, and how he felt when he was with her.

It was because of Lucy, and the things she'd said today.

He'd been cursing a cherry season that wrapped up too early for his liking, wanting to make the most of the time left, and then she'd started giving the impression she wouldn't mind hanging around a little longer, that she wasn't in such a goddamned rush to get away. She'd sometimes sounded almost sorry she'd be leaving.

Dan took a left off the highway and used the turn as an excuse to steal a glance at his passenger.

Would she stay longer if he asked her?

Did he want her to?

God, that was a no brainer. Of course he did, and the only way he'd find out if she'd stay was to ask her.

He sucked in a breath.

But not now. Not in the car. He couldn't bear it if she said no.

Tonight, he thought. He'd ask her tonight after they'd made love and she was all warm and sleepy and receptive in his arms.

He'd ask her then.

CHAPTER 21

*H*e stopped at the post office on the way home to collect the post, leaving Lucy in the burbling Spitfire behind him as he pulled the bundle of mail from the box. He sighed. As usual, there were plenty of window envelopes in this lot, just as he'd expected. Something slipped from the middle of the bundle and fell to the ground. A postcard.

He frowned as he picked it up, recognising the Melbourne skyline in the photograph on the front. Who'd be sending him a postcard from Melbourne? He flipped it over to read the signature. Dylan? He didn't know anyone called Dylan. Someone had put the card in the wrong box.

But no, he realised when he checked the address. It was the right post box number. It just wasn't addressed to him. It started, "Dear Lucy".

'There's mail for you,' he said, climbing back into the car, stashing the bundle behind his seat before passing her the card. Damn. He hadn't meant to sound so gruff.

'For me?' She took it and looked at the photograph,

flipped it over and started reading. She was smiling, he couldn't help but notice, as he reversed the car and headed down around the corner towards home. And then when she'd finished, she put it away in her bag, still smiling.

So she had friends, Dan thought, hands tight on the wheel, trying to tamp down on the green monster growing inside him. Big surprise, of course she had friends.

Male friends.

Which should come as no surprise when she'd said she'd had boyfriends before. Heaps, apparently.

Deep breath, Dan.

Because whoever Dylan was, he wasn't the one here with her now. He was back in Melbourne and part of her her past. It was Dan who was going to make love to her tonight. Dan who would ask her to stay. Have Christmas here. Stay for New Year's. Longer.

By the time they got home, he was feeling better. More controlled. Yup, cool, calm and nonchalant, that was him.

Tonight he'd ask her.

Tonight she'd say yes.

THE PHONE WAS RINGING when they pulled up outside the house to unload their things. Dan threw his stack of mail on the table, made a grab for the phone, listened for a moment and then passed it to Lucy with a frown. 'It's a bad line, but it's for you.'

'You're what?' Lucy said a few seconds later, because the line was very bad, and she must have heard wrong.

'I'm getting married,' her mom yelled back, 'and Mateo doesn't want to wait so we're going to do it in Vegas.'

Mom getting married? Whatever had happened to

marriage is a door slamming shut? 'Um, congratulations,' Lucy shouted down the line. 'So when's the big day?'

'The day after Christmas. Can you make it? I want you to be my attendant.'

The day after Christmas! 'But –'

'I know, I know, it's short notice and flights might be tricky so book whatever you can. Don't worry if it's business or first class, I'll wire you the funds. Here's where we're staying . . .'

Lucy noted down the information, still shell-shocked.

'Uh, Mom, if you don't mind me saying, it's kind of out of the blue. I thought you were never getting married.'

'Why would you say that?'

'Well, because you always said there were plenty of men you could love, so why settle for just one?'

There was laughter down the line. 'That's true. Never settle for just anyone. Marry the man you can't live without. I found him, Lucy. It's taken me a lot of years, but I found him.'

'Oh,' she said, as her world shifted on its axis. 'That's great. Congratulations, I guess. I'll email my flight details as soon as I book. See you both in Las Vegas.'

She hung up the phone in a daze. Well, that was both Christmas and her next destination taken care of in one fell swoop. She should be excited. A trip back to the States to attend her mother's wedding, and in first class if that's what it took.

She should be very excited.

Instead she felt numb.

Dan walked back inside then, after putting the Spitfire away in the shed.

'Everything okay?' he asked with a frown, when he saw her standing statue like by the phone.

She blinked. 'Mom's getting married. She wants me to be there.'

He nodded, and maybe he didn't know her mom at all, but he didn't look too excited about it. 'That's nice. When?'

'The day after Christmas.'

'This Christmas?'

'Yeah. I'll have to leave by Christmas Eve at the latest to make sure I get there in time. They're getting married in Vegas.' She tried to find a bright side. To find a smile. 'I guess it's lucky cherry season is just about finished, huh?'

He blinked. 'Yeah. Real lucky. Let me know when you're planning on leaving. I'll run you to the airport.'

And then he turned and went back outside and her heart sank like a stone.

RELIEVED OF THEIR LOAD, the cherry trees stood tall in the orchard, as if their boughs were stretching high after being weighted down with the cherries. He wandered between the trees, the dark green leaves barely shifting in the listless sigh of a summer breeze, only a passing blowfly sounding energetic. It had been a good season. The perfect length too, being wrapped up right before Christmas.

None of that made him any happier.

Lucy had always been going to leave. He'd known that from the start. At one time, he'd eagerly anticipated it. In a way he was lucky she'd hung around this long.

But God, he was going to miss her now. He'd become used to seeing her around and, more particularly, very used to having her in his bed.

She made him laugh. She disagreed with him and then made him laugh some more.

She was not at all like he'd first assumed. She was much more complex than that. She was exciting and beautiful and spontaneous, acting from the heart with an innate belief she was right. And a lot of the time she was.

For a guy who didn't like to tackle anything without a cost–benefit analysis and a checklist, the way she embraced life was a mystery. But just because he didn't understand it, didn't mean it was wrong. He could see that now. She made her life a success by her optimism and her head-on belief in herself. In doing so she would never be a failure.

But in her heart she was like a gypsy. She was a drifter. From the start it was clear she wouldn't stay around long and he'd been kidding himself to think she'd want to. She would have said no, if he'd asked her. She wasn't the type to hang around. She'd just been waiting for an opportunity to turn up and now it had. And when it all came down to it, it was probably for the best that she was leaving now, before things got too awkward for either of them. Lord knows, he'd have a hard time asking her to leave if she didn't already have plans to go.

But God, he was going to miss her.

He took a deep breath, sucking in the dry summer air, the skin on his face so tight from the salty sea that it was a wonder it didn't snap. He rubbed his jaw with one hand. Things could get back to normal once she'd gone. He could get his life back on track and log in to that website and check all those emails he'd been ignoring that were cluttering up his inbox. He'd have a reason to read them again, only this time, he was going to take his time. Do it properly and find someone.

But first he had more important things to do. He grimaced, as the lining of his swimmers rubbed sand on skin. First of all he needed a bloody shower.

THAT NIGHT there was a new edge to their love-making, a degree of desperation urging them to even greater heights of passion and ecstasy. Lucy recognised his increased passion for what it was – stocking up for the lean times when he wouldn't have her in his bed. But there was never a thought of pulling back herself.

Not when she was stocking up too.

CHAPTER 22

*I*t was two days before Christmas and the last of the cherries had been picked, the last orders filled and delivered. Cherry season for another year had been well and truly put to bed.

Which meant Dan was free to take Lucy to the city to find a dress to wear to her mother's wedding. He told her it would give him a chance to do some Christmas shopping too, a rare treat in his line of work. But the real reason was that he wanted to spend as much time in Lucy's company as he could before she left.

He left her checking out some dresses while he headed across the Mall to a stationery store to look for a present for Siena. Mission accomplished, he returned five minutes later to find Lucy examining her reflection in front of a mirror. She was wearing a long maxi dress with a bright pattern that made her look like she had stepped right out of the seventies. It was okay he guessed, only it looked like it belonged on someone else – anyone else.

Her beautiful eyes caught his reflection in the mirror and

instantly lit up, turning his insides to mush, and then she spun around to face him.

'What do you think?'

It was time to be diplomatic. 'So it's a "come dressed as your grandmother" party?'

'No! It's a wedding and I'm supposed to be the attendant and it's in Las Vegas so I'm trying to find a dress that looks a bit – well . . . '

'Attentive?'

She groaned. 'Wait there,' she instructed, disappearing behind the flapping change room curtain. In less than a minute he was bored and started wandering around the boutique, convinced he could find something he'd rather see her in.

Only apart from today when she tried it on, he wouldn't be seeing her in it, would he?

He swallowed. Something pulled tight in his gut and he sucked in a great gulp of air to try to unwind it as his brain attempted to reason with him.

Life after Lucy was going to be different, but it would be just like it was before she arrived. He'd been happy enough then, hadn't he?

The trouble with that argument, though, was that when he thought about it, he hadn't been happy before. He'd never been happy. Not really. Even Nan had called him the grumpiest orchardist in the district.

So Lucy was going.

So what if he'd always known this day would come?

It didn't mean he had to like it.

His stomach was tying itself up in knots again when he saw it: In a small alcove framed by long silk curtains, there was a gown made entirely of lace with long sleeves and a modest neckline and tiny buttons down the front, and a little mini dress arrangement underneath it. It was demure and sexy at the same time, and instinctively he knew Lucy would look sensational in it. She probably couldn't get away with a bra, of course, because the straps would show under the lace and it had a really low back, but then, she didn't need a bra. She had such great breasts – such responsive breasts.

He sucked in a breath and looked around, trying to spot an air-conditioning duct. It sure was getting warm in here.

He held up a few hangers until he was sure he had the right size, put the rest back and wandered over to the change rooms. He was just in time.

Lucy emerged wearing a strapless red satin dress, already screwing up her nose in indecision. 'No?'

'Okay if you were going to a disco,' he suggested.

'Nobody goes to discos these days.'

He nodded decisively. 'That's why no-one's bought it.' He held up the hanger. 'How about this one?'

'It's beautiful,' she acknowledged with a nod, 'only I don't think it's really appropriate.'

'Why not?' he protested, baffled that she couldn't see it was perfect. 'It's gorgeous. Check it out.' He held out the skirt. 'See, you can see right through the lace. Your legs will look fabulous under that. Try it on.'

She looked from the dress to his face. 'I can't wear that, Dan.'

'Why not?' He looked at the dress. 'It looks all right to me.'

She shook her head. 'It's a wedding dress, Dan.'

He opened his mouth to say something along the lines of 'but aren't you going to a wedding?' when it hit him. Sweet Jeezus, what was he thinking? 'Oh, well,' he said. 'You won't be needing one of those.'

He turned and fled, the lace gown fluttering in his wake.

LUCY CLUCKED as she watched him go and then re-entered the change room. She'd been surprised when he'd offered to come shopping with her today. Sure, he'd had the pretext of wanting to do his own Christmas shopping, but she didn't know of too many men who enjoyed spending their spare time waiting outside change rooms in women's clothing stores, and she'd warned him she needed shoes and a new pack and wanted to find a small gift for Siena, who was coming up with Beth tonight to say goodbye.

But then Dan had been in a weird mood the last couple of days, ever since that afternoon they'd spent at the beach. No. Ever since her mom had called and Lucy had told him she was leaving.

She slipped the red dress back on its hanger. She knew it had come as a shock to him. Hell, she'd been knocked sideways herself. But Dan had seemed different that day at the beach and she'd felt that maybe she meant more to him than just a passing bed warmer.

But when she'd told him she was leaving it was like a wall had gone up between them. Dan was still there, but there was something missing, like she'd already gone, like he'd already assigned her to history. Like he didn't care.

He hadn't asked her what she was doing or where she might go after the wedding. He hadn't expressed one iota of interest in ever seeing her again. He was cutting her free.

And it hurt.

She sighed. There was one dress left to try. As she slipped it over her head she knew she'd found what she'd been looking for. The simple jade coloured silk shift fitted her perfectly, the colour of the fabric changing from shadow to light with her every movement. She stepped out of the change room and saw Dan standing there, arms crossed and staring into space. He looked . . . lost . . . and her heart went out to him.

'Dan?' she said, and he looked up at her and blinked, his frown receding as he gave a half smile that failed to connect with his eyes.

'Yeah,' he said, nodding as he looked her up and down. 'That one.'

Dan insisted on paying for the dress despite Lucy's protests.

'Consider it a . . . Christmas present,' he told her. He'd very nearly said going away present, only for some reason he couldn't quite bring himself to say the words.

IT WAS ALWAYS nice to see his sisters and his niece, it really was. Dan welcomed them anytime, they knew that. But tonight, he opened the chips and the dips while Lucy showered with no real enthusiasm. Why had they insisted on coming up tonight, Lucy's last night? His and Lucy's last night, for that matter.

Why did everyone have to make out like they were losing someone special?

It wasn't just the fact his sisters and Kate and even Wendy had hijacked his last night with Lucy, it was that the closer it got to her going, the crankier he felt himself getting. It wasn't just that Lucy was wearing this cheesecloth dress with skinny strap dress he wasn't going to be able to slip off till much later on, it was this horrible feeling that after tomorrow, he'd never get to slip off any dress.

So bugger this idea that things would get back to normal.

Bugger normal.

Beth and Siena arrived while Lucy was getting changed, and his niece immediately started demanding answers.

'Why is Lucy going?'

'Her mum's getting married.'

'So why isn't she coming back?'

'I guess you have to ask Lucy that.'

'She has to come back,' declared Siena. 'Have you asked her to come back, Uncle Dan?'

'Well, uh.' Not exactly. 'Go help your mum,' he said, and Siena sulked off to help Beth do whatever she was doing in the kitchen.

Ask Lucy to come back? What would be the point? He'd given up on the idea of asking her anything after she'd said she was leaving. She might have hinted that she liked it here, and told him he was lucky to live in the hills and not far from the coast, but that was hardly a declaration that she never wanted to leave. This was a woman who made a career out of moving on. And she'd said nothing about wanting to come back.

Not one word.

And while he wouldn't have minded if she'd stayed longer, that was hardly the same thing as asking her to come back. A question like that came layered with a whole lot of expectation. A whole lot of commitment. And meanwhile he was supposed to be finding himself a wife. Or had everyone conveniently forgotten that tiny detail?

No dammit, what he needed more than anything was for Lucy to be out the way so he could get back to the task at hand. He ran his hands through his hair with the sheer futility of it all, with the contradictions of it all; that he wanted her gone, that he wanted her to stay.

That he wanted her forever.

Fuck!

Where had that come from?

He was still reeling from the revelation when Sophie, who had just arrived with her own basket of goodies, said, 'Are you okay?'

'Never better,' he lied, feeling sicker by the minute as his gut churned and roiled. He'd been raised to believe he could do anything. That the going might be tough but it would be worth it in the end, that he would prevail and win out.

But now Lucy was leaving and he had not one clue where he was supposed to be heading or how to get there.

THE PARTY WAS in full swing, Kate arriving next and even Hannah turning up with a bottle of pink bubbles like it was a celebration or something. Then Wendy arrived and they all started talking weddings like it was the only topic of conversation worth discussing. What Wendy was wearing on her big day. What Lucy was wearing for her mum's. Shoes. Flowers. Music.

Dan knew when he was beaten, so he decided he needed to check on Spitty, and left the women to it.

LUCY WAS SO TOUCHED they'd all come, she had to take a moment outside by herself. She leant against a pergola post and breathed in warm night air scented with jasmine flowers, and waited for this little wave of emotion to pass. She'd never had family and the fact this one - and the community that went around it - had accepted her so readily made her almost wish things had been different. They were warm and inclusive and she hadn't even gone yet but already she was missing them.

The screen door squeaked behind her. 'Lucy?' she heard Beth say, 'Oh, there you are. We were wondering if we'd overstayed our welcome and you'd snuck away with Dan.'

She swiped the moisture from her cheeks as she turned. 'Sorry, Beth,' she said, finding a smile at the thought. Dan had looked more and more uncomfortable the longer they'd talked about weddings until finally he'd fled. 'Of course not. I just needed a moment.'

Beth peered at her suspiciously. 'Are you okay?'

Lucy nodded. 'Yeah. Just a little - overwhelmed, I guess.'

There was a burst of laughter from inside the house and Beth raised her eyebrows. 'Sorry. We can be like that.'

'No, you're great. All of you. It's just that I'm used to being alone. I'm not used to people throwing me a going away party or making me feel part of a family. It's -- nice.'

'You are part of our family! Or you could be, if that moronic brother of mine would only see straight.' She looked around. 'Where is Dan, anyway?'

'I don't know. I think all that wedding talk scared him off.'

'Ha. That'd be right. He's as bad as Pop, I reckon. In denial. Otherwise I don't understand how he could let you out of his sight without a return ticket all booked.'

Lucy shrugged. 'I guess he's not all that bothered.'

'He's a twit. Anyone can see he's nuts about you.'

'Yeah, well . . .'

'And you're nuts about him, aren't you? I mean, I don't know why you'd want to waste your gorgeous self on my grumpy brother, but--'

'He's not always grumpy.'

The woman looked at her levelly. 'You do care for him, don't you?'

Lucy sighed. 'Does it matter, when clearly he doesn't feel the same way?'

'He's a moron!'

Lucy smiled. 'I think right now he's looking forward to being free of a woman who's pierced and tattooed and going back to his quiet life.'

Beth went still. 'Lucy, feel free to tell me to mind my own business if you want, but can I ask you a personal question?'

'Sure.'

'It's about your tattoo. I saw one like it on a patient I was transporting yesterday. It was a bit different - it had two birds with a ribbon in between.' She bit her lip. 'You'll tell me to shut up if this is not okay, right.'

Lucy sucked in air as she felt a familiar stab of pain. She knew where this was going. 'No, it's okay. It's a miscarriage tattoo. I lost a baby a couple of years back. A little girl. I didn't want ever to forget her.'

'That's awful. How far along were you?'

'Nineteen weeks.' She gave a weak smile, remembering holding her in her hands. 'She was so tiny but she was perfect. I could see her heart beating under her skin . . .'

'Oh my God, I'm so sorry. Tell me you weren't alone through all of that.'

Lucy felt her lip curl. 'I'm glad he wasn't there. He wanted me to get rid of it. Turns out he got his wish.'

'I'm so sorry,' Beth said, pulling Lucy into a hug. 'Now I've gone and made you cry again.'

'It's okay.' She smiled through her tears and she clung to Beth, and Lucy knew she'd be leaving a part of herself here in the Adelaide Hills. A big part. 'It's good to remember, even when it makes me sad. That poor woman you were transporting yesterday though, she must have lost two.' She sniffed. 'Sometimes life just sucks.'

DAN UNLOCKED THE SHED DOOR, saw the Spitfire was right where he'd left it, and immediately felt the knot in his gut start to loosen up a tad. Yep, he was right to come out here. Right to come and get some fresh air and a fresh perspective.

He didn't want Lucy.

He didn't need her. He had everything he needed in the world right here and he didn't need anyone messing with it.

He checked that he'd locked the car and then found a pen gauge to check the pressure in the tyres, before flicking a bit of fluff from the roof. Then he mooched around a bit, looking with a critical eye at the arrangement of tools on the board behind the workbench, wondering if there was a more efficient way to organise the space. It was probably high time he put a bit of thought into that, given it'd been years since anyone had looked at it. Now that cherry season was done, he had a few days where he could put his mind to such pressing stuff.

He found a pad of paper and started sketching out a plan.

'UNCLE DAN! UNCLE DAN!'

He looked up.

'Uncle Dan. We're leaving!'

Already? He glanced at his watch and realised he'd been here for more than an hour. 'I'm in here!' he called, and folded the piece of paper into his back pocket as Siena came running around the door.

'We're going now, Uncle Dan. Everyone's wondering where you got to.'

'Sorry,' he said, looking up at her. 'I got caught up.' He went to turn off the lights but then he noticed something and left them on to check.

'Come here, Siena,' he said, taking her arm. 'What the bloody hell is that?'

Siena squealed. 'Ow! That hurts!'

He released his grip but his eyes remained glued to the abomination on her arm. 'Where the hell did you get that?'

'It was a present,' the girl said, her eyes wide.

'And who gave it to you?'

But he already knew the answer. He had that one well and truly covered.

. . .

'WHAT WERE YOU THINKING?'

'Calm down, Dan,' said Lucy. 'You've already scared everyone away.' His glowering visage and snarly attitude had been on show all night, though he'd saved the worst of the storm for after their guests had left.

'I knew this would happen,' he said, pacing the big family room. 'I bloody well knew it!'

'Relax! You'll be next in line for a coronary if you keep on like this.'

'Don't tell me to relax! She's just a kid – an impressionable kid. She'll have a stud in her nose and some kind of tractor tyre in her earlobe before you know it.'

'Dan, listen to yourself! It was a transfer. That's all. A transfer of a tiny little Korean symbol that means friendship.'

He shook his head, swiping his hand through the air. 'It doesn't matter what it means. It's what it is.'

'What, you mean temporary?'

'She told you she wanted a tattoo for Christmas. I heard her with my own ears.'

'No! You heard wrong. Siena said she wanted a nose-piercing. Is that what I got her? Is it?'

'Tattoo. Piercing. It amounts to the same thing.'

'Does it? And didn't you also hear me tell her it was okay to wait, that it was okay not to rush into it?'

'Sure, you say that now.'

'Fine. Don't believe me. Jeezus, Dan. I just thought something like a temporary tattoo might be a good way of keeping her happy in the meantime.'

'You thought.'

'And Beth said it was okay when I asked her, so what are you getting yourself so upset about? It's not like she's your daughter.'

'She's my niece, and who else is going to look out for her?'
He put his hands to his head and raked his fingers through
his hair, scraping his scalp with his nails. 'I knew this was
going to be a disaster from the moment I set eyes on you. I
knew you'd be a lousy example to an impressionable kid.'

'Lovely. A bad influence and a lousy example. Any other
insults you want to hurl my way while you're in full swing?
Might as well get it off your chest now while you've got the
chance.'

'Well, what would you call yourself? You shag your way
around the bloody world –'

'What?'

'Don't like the truth, Lucy?'

She was shell-shocked. 'How do you figure that?'

'Don't you? That postcard you got. Did you live with him?
Did you live with Dylan?'

'You read my mail?'

'I saw his name. That was enough. One of your "heaps" of
boyfriends, I take it?'

And shell shock turned to incandescent rage. 'How. Dare.
You!'

'Did you sleep with him?'

'I shared a flat with him while his flatmate was overseas.
Big deal.'

' Did you have sex with him?'

She waved her hand through the air and turned to leave.
'Oh, go away, Dan. I'm tired. I've had enough of this. I'll sleep
in the spare room tonight, thanks all the same.'

He grabbed her elbow and turned her back. 'It's a simple
question, Lucy. Did you have sex with him? Yes or no?'

She shook herself free. 'Is it really any business of yours if
I did?'

He ground his teeth together. 'I'll take that as a yes then.'

She turned to look at him over her shoulder. Took in his aggressive stance and his rigid jaw and the damning scowl that was back with a vengeance, and her heart wanted to break into tiny pieces. 'Why are you doing this? What does it matter?'

'It matters. Of course it bloody matters. It's about who you are. Because that's what you do, isn't it, you shag your way around the world, and I'm just one more dumb fuck before you move on to the next stop.'

'Is that what you really think of me? Is that all you think I think of you – after what we've shared?' She shook her head, feeling battered, defeated. 'You know, I'm sick of this. All you've ever done, ever since the first day we met, is judge me. You think I'm trash because I'm tattooed, I'm pierced, and I don't spend my life depressed and miserable and stuck in a rut. And, worst of all apparently, not only am I not a virgin, but more shockingly, I actually enjoy sex. Isn't that how you see it?'

'You're the one telling the story.'

'Okay, so let me tell you another story. I did sleep with Dylan. And I'm not sorry and I will not apologise for it, to you or to anybody else.'

'Why would you? You're probably proud of yourself. One more notch in the belt.'

'Listen to yourself, Dan! You sound like somebody's mother. Look, if it's such a big deal to you, Dylan and I had sex once and only once.'

'You expect me to believe that, after the shag-fest we've had here?'

'Nope, I don't expect anything, not with the jackass way you're behaving, but like it or not, it's true. We had sex, the night Dylan learned he'd lost both his mother and his sister in a car crash and he was stuck in Melbourne overnight before the first flight out.

It was grief sex, Dan. It was sweet and it was comforting and there was nothing more to it than that.'

'Grief sex.' He snorted. 'And what excuse are you going to come up with to explain me away to the next guy? What kind of sex was I?'

She laughed, if you could call it a laugh. 'Too easy, Dan. I felt sorry for you and your sad little life. You were only ever charity sex.'

CHARITY SEX.

He stood there long after she'd gone, after she'd fled and slammed the bathroom door as her words reverberated their way around his mind until his brain was set to explode.

Charity sex.

Like she was doing him a favour or something. Because why else would someone like her waste time with the boring likes of him?

Charity sex.

And the worst of it was that she was right.

CHAPTER 23

Christmas Eve dawned clear and beautiful in the Adelaide Hills. There was a wedding veil of mist in the valley when Lucy woke numb and empty and alone in the guest bed and looked out the window. It was a mist that would burn off, she knew by now, the moment the sun rose over the hills.

The numbness would burn off too, she knew, and she'd feel pain, but that would take longer and she'd be far away by then. For now it was good to feel nothing.

She made a call and finished packing then went to make coffee. Dan was at the table staring bleakly into his own cup and it was some compensation that he looked as bad as she felt. Good.

'I'll take a taxi to the airport,' she said, as she made herself a cup, and he simply nodded. They were beyond words now, there was no more they could say to each other, so she took her coffee outside and had a final stroll around the orchard, breathing in the clear air, listening to the call of the birds and the hum of machinery somewhere the other side of the valley.

Cherry season was over and so was her time here.

She looked back at the house and how it nestled into the overgrown garden, knowing that for the second time in her life she was leaving a place that had offered both security and warmth – even love.

There had been love between them. Even though it had come to this, with her leaving, she believed in a tiny corner of her heart that he had loved her – just a little, at least.

Soon enough the taxi arrived and it was time to gather her things. Dan watched as the driver loaded her pack into the car, and she noticed the firm set of his jaw, like he was clenching his teeth. He'd donned sunglasses so his eyes were unreadable. Hers, she knew from her lack of sleep and her overwhelming gloom, resembled road maps.

'So this is it,' he said, and she nodded, trying for a smile. But her mouth wasn't working properly.

She went to climb into the back seat but he stopped her with a hand to his arm.

'Lucy,' he said, sounding pained, hesitant, his gaze somewhere over her shoulder.

'Yes?'

'I was wondering . . .'

Whatever it was, it was killing him.

'What?'

And he sighed a deep sigh and for the first time his eyes flicked up somewhere near hers. 'Where will you go? What are your plans?'

And Lucy's emotions tumbled into one hysterical package. Did he have to use that word? The tears that had been stinging her eyes ever since she'd woken up squeezed their way out.

'I tried, Dan,' she started, straining to keep her voice calm. 'I really tried to get the hang of this planning thing.

But it didn't work.' She swallowed back a sob. 'And the

only thing I learned is what I've always known – that things can still happen without plans, and sometimes they're bad things, sure. But other times they're the most unexpected, magical, painful things of all.'

She waited, but he said nothing - maybe because there was nothing left to say - and in the end she took a deep breath and pulled the door closed. 'Goodbye, Dan.'

The taxi pulled down the driveway and Lucy swallowed hard as she watched the procession of trees pass her window. Then they were on the road and heading away from the orchard.

Don't cry, she told herself, knowing that if she started she'd never stop.

The taxi driver didn't say a word, for which she was grateful. She was in no mood for small talk as she mentally said goodbye to the passing parade of local landmarks she'd come to know so well.

Was it only six weeks since she'd arrived? It hardly seemed possible. So much had happened – and yet so much more that might have hadn't.

She blinked her eyes. She would not cry.

The taxi drove in stop-start fashion through the city, slowed by peak hour traffic lights. There was no chance they would miss the flight – they'd left in plenty of time – but now all Lucy wanted was to get to the airport and get on that plane and leave cherry season behind her.

She felt detached and removed, with nowhere to belong, nowhere to call home. All she had with her was a pack and a ticket to her next destination.

Once it had been enough.

Not anymore.

CHAPTER 24

*D*an cursed the four-wheeler and gave it a swift kick to one of the rear tyres and cursed again when his toes hurt like buggery. Bastard machine! This time it really was going.

He limped inside and pulled open the freezer door to find something for dinner but all there was inside were two stacks of matchbox-sixed containers holding Lucy's curry pastes – one tower of green, the other of red.

He slammed the door shut. He'd had a shitful day. A shitful week for that matter. Not even seeing a For Sale sign go up on Des's property had cheered him for long. But was it too much to expect that there'd be something to eat in the freezer? Something that didn't remind him of her?

He was over being reminded of her. The entire conversation at the Christmas dinner table had revolved around Lucy. Where would she be now? When was the wedding, Australian time? Would she be asleep now? And why hadn't Dan asked her to come back?

Siena was still sporting that ridiculous tattoo transfer thing and nobody was mad at Lucy for giving it to her.

It was like a little Lucy-fest with the guest of honour nowhere to be seen and yet dominating the conversation, regardless.

And it wasn't like he needed to hear about her. He was reminded of her every time he went to bed. Her scent was still on his sheets and on her pillow. It was driving him crazy but he'd be damned if he was washing them anytime soon.

He checked the fridge on the off chance there was any of the turkey leftovers Nan had sent him home with after Christmas lunch, but no, he'd polished that off last night together with what was left of the potato salad. Typical.

The fridge door didn't shut any softer than the freezer's.

Fine. He snatched up his keys. Chicken and chips for dinner then. It didn't have to be the end of the world.

He was about to hop in the ute when he noticed the lean at the front. He growled and went for a closer look and sure enough, the tyre was flat as a tack. Only it wasn't a tack he'd run over, it was a dirty great nail.

Bloody hell!

He kicked the tyre and cursed again when his sore toes smashed into the wheel. This time the pain was excruciating.

'Fuck!' He hobbled back into the kitchen and pulled open the freezer door. After all, she'd said it was dead easy, and while she'd always been there when he helped her out in the kitchen over their last days, he must have got the hang of it by now.

He pulled out a serve of red curry and then found coconut milk, potatoes and rice in the pantry before digging out some sliced steak buried in the freezer.

He could do this.

LUCY HAD NEVER BEEN a big fan of Vegas, but she had to hand

it to her mom and Mateo, it made for one hell of a wedding venue. It wasn't everywhere that Elvis Presley was on hand to walk the bride down the aisle and sing 'Love Me Tender' to the happy couple.

It was fun. It was insane. It was just what she needed to lose herself a while.

But a couple of days in fantasyland surrounded by fake Eiffel Towers, pyramids and more slot machines than you could count was more than enough. Where to from here? The newlyweds were off to Hawaii for their honeymoon and they'd told her she was welcome to join them, but three was a crowd and Hawaii was halfway back to Australia – and she was so not going that way.

Besides, it was warm in Hawaii. She wanted somewhere cold. Somewhere bleak and windswept and a long way from anywhere. Somewhere that didn't have cherry trees or sunshine or any chance of running into anyone who might remind her of Dan.

She was already having enough trouble avoiding him in her dreams.

So she sat on her ridiculously big bed in the ridiculously opulent deluxe fountain view room in the Bellagio Las Vegas and googled up a map of the world. Winter, she wanted, which eliminated the southern hemisphere right off the mark. Bleak and windswept? Yes, but she wasn't hankering for the Arctic – she wasn't a masochist – which ruled out a sizeable chunk of the northern.

Somewhere a long way from anywhere.

Her eyes narrowed in on the Mediterranean region and the tiny islands dotted across the sea. A long way from everywhere and no cherry trees that she could recall, and in winter the winds would be blowing a gale and whipping up the sea and the streets would be empty of tourists who might remind her of Dan.

And her mind was almost made up, until the moment her eyes shifted left on the map and landed on Italy and a shiver went down her spine and all the way to her toes.

Northern Italy and a town called Agnino where her mom's nonna had lived. A place she'd felt safe and happy for a while. A place that had offered sanctuary.

Perfect.

❀

'YOU'RE LIMPING,' Beth said to Dan, when she dropped off some freshly laid eggs Nan had sent. 'What did you do?'

'Broke my toe.'

'How did you do that.'

'Doesn't matter.'

'Oh, is that right?' she said, with the tactical sense of a cruise missile. 'I think it does.'

'Okay, so I kicked the quad bike and knocked something out of shape and ten minutes later I kicked the wheel on the ute and broke it good and proper.'

'Oh brother dearest, you are one sad puppy.'

'No I'm not.'

She nodded. 'You haven't shaved for days, your hair's flopping in your eyes and you look like you need a damned good feed.'

'It's summer,' he said. 'I'm on holidays.'

No, you're not. You're pining for Lucy.'

'Bullshit.'

'Is it? So tell me, how many times have you checked out that HEA.com website since Lucy left? By the look of the forest growing on your face, I'll hazard a guess and say exactly zero.'

'I've been busy.'

'You're pining,' she said. 'Face it, Dan. You blew it. You

had the perfect woman right under your nose and you couldn't even see it.'

'She wasn't perfect. She was all wrong for me.'

'You were crazy about her.'

'No, I was not.'

'And she, foolish woman that she must be, was crazy about you. Everyone knew it. Everyone but you.'

'You're talking rubbish, Beth.'

'Am I? Then why have we had the return of Mr Grumpy ever since she's gone? Only now it seems Mr Grumpy is intent in turning into the human Yeti. Lucy loves you, Dan, and you love her and we love her, and why the hell you let her go, none of us will ever understand.'

'Because I'm supposed to be looking for a wife, remember! A proper wife. Someone who'll be an asset to the orchard and a good mother. Look at that bullshit stunt Lucy pulled on Siena and you tell me, what kind of role model would she be, you reckon? What kind of mother do you think she'd make?'

Beth's mouth fell open. 'I sincerely hope you didn't say that to Lucy.'

He shook his head. 'What? Why? What would it matter if I did? It's the truth isn't it?'

The look she threw him would skewer a lesser man. 'You're my brother, Dan, and you know I love you, but sometimes you can be one dumb fuck.'

'What?'

'How long did you spend with Lucy, Dan?'

'I don't know. Five weeks. Six? What is this?'

'And in all that time, did you ever wonder what that tattoo meant? Did you ever ask? Or was it easier just to condemn her from the start because you don't like ink?'

'What are getting at, Beth? What's your point?'

'Lucy lost a baby. She miscarried. She got that tattoo so the child she lost would never be forgotten.'

The words clattered and banged their way around his mind and refused to make sense. 'Lucy did what?'

His sister shook her head, her eyes filled with pity. 'Yeah, think on that, Bradley.' She nodded towards the eggs. 'Save the cartons, won't you. Nan said she's running low.'

And with a slam of the screen door, she was gone.

LUNIGIANA, the land of the moon, stretched out before her, its tiny hill-towns in the distance barely visible as they poked through the fog that shrouded the lower reaches, and with snow covering the jagged mountain peaks beyond so they resembled sharp white teeth. A wild wind hammered into her as she stood on the edge of the broken terrace of a broken down house, the tiled roof collapsed, the walls cracked and falling apart and already being claimed back into the steep hill side by the creepers and shrubs, a garden long overgrown.

She was here, in Agnino, at her mother's nonna's house. The place where her mother had sought refuge, and the place where Lucy had built her earliest memories of security and warmth. The house she'd imagined was still standing and might provide those same feelings now, when she needed them so much.

She closed her eyes and tried to see herself as a toddler running through wild through the tangled garden as her mom had told her. Tried to remember and reclaim that feeling now.

Instead the icy wind buffeted her. It had snowed this morning, and drifts of snow still clung to the roadsides and under the trees. A glance at the clouds told her more snow was on the way. She zipped her jacket higher against the weather, wishing the wind could blow away the hurt and the pain of a love that was returned. A love that should never have been.

When would it stop hurting? When would the pain go away?

She turned full circle, trying to remember, trying to forget, and her eyes fell on that single line of pencil pines marching up the ridge and all she could think about was an orchard half a world away in the Adelaide Hills, and a man who didn't want her enough to ask her to stay.

Clouds darkened the sky above, blotting out whatever grainy sunlight had managed to squeeze through before, and sleet started falling, the icy droplets stinging her face.

Lucy abandoned the old house and made for the small apartment she'd rented nearby. She could never afford a room like this come summer, but in wintertime, when tourists were thin on the ground, it was a different matter.

She sat on her bed and pulled out some postcards she'd bought. There was one with a picture of a donkey with big eyes and wearing a saddle and with the mountainous view in the background, and there was no question who she'd send this one to. She flipped it over and started:

Hi Siena!

She fished out the little book where she'd got Siena to write in her address that night before she'd left. There was space on the page for eight names and addresses but Siena's eight-year-old script had taken up half a page.

It made her smile and that felt good. It was worth it for that alone.

HE WASN'T PINING for anyone, and he'd bloody well show his

smart-arse sister. Dan sat down at his computer and switched it on, cracking his knuckles as he waited for it to crank up. Oh yeah. He'd soon show Beth.

There were so many emails waiting for him, with subject headers like:

WE'VE MISSED YOU DAN.
   Twelve matches ready made for you!
   Your perfect match is waiting. Celebrate the New Year in style! Log in now!

HE CLICKED on the first email and logged in and there was another screen full of faces. He scanned the first page, turned to the second and then to the next, going 'No, no, no,' all the time. Until he struck a blonde with long hair and he wavered over the picture and realised what he was doing.

He was looking for Lucy.

Bloody hell.

He logged off and pushed his chair back.

Looking for Lucy. Not that that meant anything, exactly. He just liked blondes, that was all. It didn't mean that he was in love with her or anything. No way. That was crazy. That was mad. He was nothing more than charity sex to her. She'd said it herself.

She was all wrong for him and those words had proved it.

If he'd meant anything to her, why had she left?

He got up and headed for the door. Dammit, he needed to go check on the quad bike. He didn't have time for this.

And then he caught his breath as he replayed the words Beth had told him. She'd had a miscarriage. She'd lost a baby.

He raked his hands through his hair. Jeezus, why had he had to learn that from his sister? Why hadn't Lucy told him?

He stopped, his hand on the door handle.

Maybe if you hadn't judged her from the start, she might have.

God, he was an idiot. He wanted to wrap her in his arms and tell him he was sorry. He wanted to hold her and kiss away her pain

But it was too late.

Asking why she'd left was the wrong question.

Why hadn't he asked her to stay?

That night he smelt her scent on his sheets again. That night he felt her next to him, felt her body open to his, felt her smile and saw her eyes filled with desire, filled with love, and all he wanted to do was love her in return, but when he opened his eyes, it was her pillow he was hugging and he rolled away, disgusted with himself, burying his wet face in his hands.

He was such a fool!

HE'D BLOWN IT. He'd blown it sky high. He lay in bed with the hot hard light of nine am streaming through the window. He'd hardly ever stayed in bed so late, but he needed to be there now to work this out. To mourn.

Because he'd well and truly stuffed it. He'd had a woman who he'd loved, and who'd loved him, but he'd been blind. He'd been looking elsewhere, and like Beth had said, she'd been right there under his nose the whole time.

And he hated that he'd been such a coward that night she'd got the call from her mum. He hated that he'd assumed she was happy to go away and that he should just let her.

But what he hated most of all was that now he had no clue where to find her.

She'd been in Las Vegas what? A week ago?

She could be anywhere now. How would he ever find her?

And if he did find her, would she want to see him?

He dragged himself from the bed, pausing at the bathroom mirror when he didn't recognise himself. Well, he didn't want to. He didn't like the person he'd discovered he was.

A loser.

He dropped in later to visit Nan and Pop to see how Pop was going and return the egg cartons. 'Hi Nan,' he said, leaning down to plant a kiss on her cheek. 'Pop.'

'You look terrible,' said Pop.

'Don't say that, Clarry,' said Nan.

'Who'll tell him if I won't? What the hell's wrong with you, boy? Still pining for that Lucy gal?'

Jeezus. 'I just thought I'd drop these egg cartons back. Beth said you needed more.'

'Thanks Dan,' Nan said, opening a cupboard and putting them on top of a stash of what had to be at least two hundred egg cartons. 'Did you get a postcard?'

'What?' He shook his head. He was still thinking about the egg cartons. Talk of postcards brought the name Dylan skating across his brain and he remembered the accusations he'd thrown at Lucy that night and sent his despondency plummeting to new levels. 'Who from?'

'From Lucy of course. Siena got one today. Isn't that nice?'

His heart rate spiked, his blood fizzed. 'From where, did she say?' he said, trying to sound offhand and already itching to log onto one of those travel sites and see how long it would take to get there . . .

'Now, where was it again, Clarry?'

'Las Vegas?' Dan prompted.

'No, she'd left there, though she said the wedding was lovely, didn't she Clarry?'

'She did. Said they had Elvis Presley in attendance.' Pop chuckled. 'Jeepers, he must be getting on by now.'

'And she sent it from where?'

'Let me think. Somewhere in Europe.'

Bloody hell. That narrowed it down. 'England? France?'

Pop shook his head. 'Somewhere with a funny name. Somewhere in . . .'

Dan couldn't stand it, desperate to put the pieces together. 'Greece? Germany? Italy?'

'Ooh,' said Nan. 'Italy sounds right.'

'Northern Italy.' Clarry said. 'Little village up a mountain somewhere.'

'That'd do for starters. Dan was already saying goodbye and feeling for his keys. He'd drop around to Beth's and see for himself if there was a name for this place up a mountain in northern Italy and then he had to get home.

Had to book a flight.

Had to get to Lucy.

She might not want to see him. But he had to tell her he loved her. That he was sorry. He just needed a chance to tell her.

It was dark by the time the taxi dropped Lucy back in Agnino. She'd spent the day exploring the walled city of Fivizzano at the foot of the mountain. She'd located and paid her respects at the grave of her great nonna in the cemetery before visiting the market in the Piazza Medici where she'd eaten pizza and taken out her sketch book to draw the magnificent sixteenth century fountain with its fat spouting fish, while the medieval church tower bells rang out the hour. She'd pored over the displays at the museum and sat down for coffee in the square again to admire the quaint architecture when her feet had rebelled.

She'd been enchanted by it all.

But she'd felt like a tourist.

She let herself into her apartment with a heavy heart. There was no doubt Agnino was a picturesque village set amongst other picturesque villages in a beautiful unspoilt part of the world.

But she hadn't found what she'd come here for. Security. A sense of belonging.

Because she didn't belong.

It wasn't home.

There was no point staying any longer. Tomorrow she'd pack her things and move on. She went through the motions of making supper. Pulled the last of her crusty Agnino bread from the crock, cut some farmhouse cheese and filled a glass of water from the tap, staring out the kitchen window as she waited. There, on the ridge high above, she could just make out the line of pencil pines, and she felt her heart squeeze as she thought of the orchard and Dan. What would he be doing right now? Was he glad she was gone or had he forgotten her already, so busy looking for a wife that he hadn't spared her a thought?

She sat down listlessly at the table, and put her head in her hands. Why hadn't she been brave enough to tell him the truth?

Why had she hurt him when he was the last person in the world she wanted to hurt?

And why was she torturing herself rehashing all of this when it was clear they'd been doomed from the very start?

Her bread and cheese sat untouched before her, because she wasn't hungry any more. She didn't really have an appetite for anything. Ever since she'd realised that security didn't come with a place, it came from who you were with.

THE TRAIN from Rome was tossed around by the wind like a cork on the sea, and if he didn't know better, he'd almost think he was suffering from motion sickness. But this was a different kind of sickness. The sickness you felt when you were scared – scared the person you so desperately wanted to see had already moved on and you wouldn't find her – and then scared of what might happen if you did and she told you to get stuffed.

His ankle itched, and he itched to scratch it, but he knew he shouldn't, and then finally they were on the ground in Pisa and being crammed into buses to take them to the terminal. While everyone else headed into the city to check out the famous leaning tower, he headed straight for the car rental agency queue. He had more important things on his mind than sight-seeing.

EQUIPPED with a Fiat and a trusty Satnav, Dan was off and racing. The autostrada was batshit crazy, but Dan was on a mission and wasn't about to be cowed by driving on the wrong side of a car on the wrong side of the road in traffic traveling at one hundred and thirty k's an hour - not if it got him to Lucy faster. He took an exit off to the right just past the stark white of the marble quarries of Carrara, and headed along a valley that threaded its way between towering mountains, the highest topped with snow, until he took a switchback turn that headed right up the side of one of them on a road that looked more like a goat track. He cursed as a little blue bus almost collected him on one blind corner and he had to almost scrape the side of his car along the mountain wall to dodge it. Bloody hell, he thought, heart in mouth, that was close. If anyone tried to whinge about the windy roads in the Adelaide hills after this, he'd soon set them straight.

His heart was pumping when he reached the town sign but not just because of the dodgy road, but because he was close. Less than thirty seconds later he was at the other end of the town. Whoa. A tiny town. Not much more than a main street, and a few stone buildings, a bar and a bread shop as far as he could tell. Population less than two hundred according to Google.

He parked and climbed out of the car to get his bearings, flicking up the collar of his Drizabone against the icy wind. Below the road the land fell away steeply to the wide undulating valley that stretched for miles to the mountains far to the east.

Before him hunkered the pretty stone village built on the side of the mountain.

Less than two hundred people. He liked the odds.

He sucked in a breath of the cold mountain air.

He'd start with the bar, get some lunch, ask around.

If Lucy was anywhere nearby, he was going to find her.

He hit pay dirt the moment he showed the barman a picture of Lucy at the beach that she'd taken that day.

'Si,' the barman said, nodding. 'She's been here.'

Dan's blood was spinning. 'Do you know where she's staying?'

Two minutes later he was knocking on her door, busy rehearsing opening lines.

I was a fool.

I'm sorry, please forgive me.

I love you.

But he needed to say all of them and he wasn't sure where to start.

Except he didn't get a chance to test any of his opening lines, because there was no answer.

THE BEST THING about not having firm plans was it didn't matter if they changed. When Lucy discovered there were no buses running from Fivizzano on Sundays, it was no big deal. Instead she rugged up against the icy wind and headed out armed with her sketchbook. She stopped by the ruins of the old house and drew the stone walls with the jagged line of broken tiles where the roof had once been, and the windows that now looked in on shrubs as nature reclaimed it for its own. She drew the dark snow filled clouds and the majestic sweep of valley and the jagged peaks of the mountains all around. A falcon circled in the sky, lazily surfing the wind currents in its quest for a meal, and she captured that in pencil too.

And she drew a line of trees that had brought her back here in search of what she'd left behind, a line of trees that now made her yearn for another place, and she wished things could have beem different.

Snow started falling, white flakes that stuck to the fur around her hood and felt like needles when the wind pushed them into her face. Time to head back.

SNOW WAS FALLING thick and fast by the time Lucy made it back to the village. She stopped at the bakery for fresh bread and scurried back to her apartment to get warm.

Except there was someone sitting on her doorstep. Someone with his head in his hands. She frowned. Someone who looked a bit like --

No way.

It wasn't possible. He was in Australia, in the Adelaide Hills, half a world away. He couldn't be here.

She blinked but he was still there.

Her knees felt weak, her stomach was doing flip-flops and her heart was beating so fast, it sent her blood spinning.

He must have heard her crazy heartbeat, because he glanced up then, and turned stock still, in his brown eyes a tangle of hope and fear. She knew exactly how he felt. Oh God, she knew how that felt.

Without taking his eyes from hers, he pushed himself to his feet and he was there, in front of her, in glorious widescreen technicolour. His hair was longer and he had a stubbled jaw and his eyes looked wild and lost. But it was him.

Dan Faraday, in the flesh.

'Hello, Lucy.'

Her lips were dry, her throat tight, and all she could manage was a whispered, 'What are you doing here?'

He gave a half smile. 'I came to find you.'

And she felt hope blossom in her hurting heart.

CHAPTER 25

'J was an idiot,' he told her, when she'd let them both inside while the wind rattled at the door and tugged at the windows. 'I had to find you - to say sorry. Sorry for all those things I said to you that night, all the things I accused you of. Sorry for that last day and the way I made you leave. I'm sorry for all the grief I've caused you.'

They were both still standing. Both too tense to sit. Too wary to relax.

Lucy waited for him to go on. It was a nice speech and it was nice to have an apology, but she'd been half expecting something more. The silence yawned between them. 'You came all this way just to say sorry?'

He shook his head. 'No. That's just the start of it. There's more, but I didn't know if you'd want to listen.'

'I'm listening,' she said, as she perched her butt on the arm rest of the nearby sofa. Better to force her knees to bend than have them collapse under her.

He turned and ran a hand through his hair and turned around again, tension underlining his every movement. 'After you'd gone, I realised what a fool I'd been. I was a fool to let you go, but more of a fool to not see what was right in front of me.'

She sucked in air and wrapped her arms around herself, glad she was sitting down, the tiny room suddenly seeming too small for a conversation like this.

'And what was right in front of you?'

'You, Lucy. I've fallen in love with you. '

Bam!

She closed her eyes, her mind and senses reeling. Once upon a time, they were words she'd longed to hear, words she'd dreamed he'd say to her. But now the first wave of shock at his appearance had passed, and her mind was less of a tangle of emotion, she knew in her heart that i. It couldn't be that easy as saying a few words.

'I thought you hated everything I stand for. I'm a bad influence, you said. I shag my way around the world, you said.'

'Oh God, Lucy. You don't have to remind me. You don't know how many times I've wished I could take those words back. I was wrong, so very wrong. I was angry because you were leaving and I was going to lose you and I had to find any reason I could to feel better about you going.

'But nothing could make me feel good when you were gone. Nothing. And it didn't matter how much I tried to deny it, the truth was there. I love you, Lucy. And I had to tell you. And I know that what I did was unforgiveable and that I'm not worthy of loving you, but I had to tell you. If nothing else, I couldn't go on without you knowing.'

The silence stretched out between them, Lucy's heart thudding beneath her folded arms. 'Thank you,' she said at last. 'Thank you for finding me to tell me that.'

'That's it?' he said, holding up his hands. 'Thank you? Lucy, I love you." He looked crushed.

She shook her head. 'What do you expect me to say, Dan?

You think you can sorry all those words away and tell me you love me and it all be all right? Because it wasn't like it was just you anyway. We both said some pretty hurtful things that night. We were both aiming for the jugular.'

He swallowed and she followed the movement in his Adam's apple. 'I want you to come home with me.'

She covered her mouth with a hand. He was making this so hard. 'But how will it work? Even if I loved you too, sooner or later I'll do something crazy or act without thinking about consequences and you'll remember all the reasons we shouldn't be together, and get angry all over again.'

'No. I love you, Lucy. I know I was wrong, but I love you, just the way you are.'

Her hand shifted to her forehead. One of them had to be sensible. 'Don't you see, Dan? People don't change that much – at least, not as much as we'd both need to if we were going to be together.' Her heart was breaking but she knew this was for the best.

'You believe that?'

'Of course I do.'

He turned away.

'We're just not right for each other.' She shook her head. 'We're too different. You're conventional and straitlaced and I can't do that. I'm too spontaneous. I don't always think about consequences. I don't work that way. We'd drive each other crazy.'

Dan turned back to her, his eyes brimming with tears. 'I knew it.. I knew it would be impossible to convince you with just words. So let me show you something.'

Oh God, please let it not be a ring. Don't make it that hard. 'What's the point, Dan? Nothing you can show me is going to change my mind.'

'Maybe not. But at least take a look?'

'Dan . . .' She shook her head.

But already he had propped his leg up on a chair and was lifting his trouser leg.

'What are you doing?'

And then she saw the tape on his ankle and her eyes opened wide as he pulled it back. She blinked and looked again. 'Oh my God, is that for real?'

On his ankle was a red heart and inside it were the words 'I love Lucy'.

'Of course, it's real. It bloody hurt.'

'You got a tattoo?'

'Does it look like a transfer?'

'But I know what you think of tattoos.'

'How else was I supposed to prove that I loved you?'

Lucy's heart was set to explode. 'You really mean it, don't you? You love me?'

He held out his arms in supplication. 'How many times do I have to say it? Yes, Lucy. I really love you. And I can change. Maybe not as much as what you'd like, and maybe I won't get any piercings. Well, none. But I'm not made of stone.'

'I don't know,' she said, though she was already moving towards his outstretched arms. 'I'm not sure I should risk my heart on someone who does something so reckless and impulsive. Think of the consequences.'

'Bugger the consequences,' he said, as his lips came down to meet hers. 'All I can think about is you.

THEY MADE love in the double bed in her little apartment while the wind gusted rattled against the door and the soft snow splattered against the windows, their passion and their need for each other blotting out the world.

. . .

'Des is selling up,' he said, much later, while their bodies hummed down from the heights. 'The For Sale signs went up a few days back.'

'Good,' she said, lying on her stomach and sighing into her pillow. 'I'm glad. Are you going to buy it?'

'Not me. Not after last time. But Nick's expressed interest. Seems he's missing the cherries after all.'

'So no more shooting, huh?'

'Nope. And no more birds in the cool room.'

She chuckled softly. 'Life will be terribly dull.'

'Life with you could never be dull.'

He propped himself up on one elbow and softly traced the outline of the bird on her shoulder. 'Beth told me you lost a baby,' he said, placing his lips to her skin. 'I feel so bad. I had no idea what this meant to you.'

She shivered as his warm breath kissed her skin. 'It's not really something you want to have to explain.'

'Especially not to a boof-head who's got a thing against ink. I'm sorry you had to go through that.'

'I thought he was the one,' she said, hugging her pillow. 'He was my boss at a sports store where I worked and he was funny and smart and I thought he loved me. He told me he loved me.' She sighed, her skin tingling where Dan's fingers trailed a path down her spine and over her butt and back up again. 'And then I learned I was pregnant and he changed overnight into someone I didn't know anymore, someone angry. He told me to get rid of it.'

She squeezed her eyes shut as she remembered his ugly face and his uglier words. 'I wouldn't do it. I left him, and still the pain came and took her away.' She pressed her face into the pillow as the hot tears flowed.

He collected her against his chest, kissing her fevered brow, stroking her hair while he rocked her gently. 'I'm sorry. I know I can't promise you anything, but if I had my way, I'd never let you be hurt, ever again.'

He lifted her chin and kissed her, and they made slow, sweet, life affirming love, purging the pain of the past and starting anew.

'I love you,' she whispered afterwards as she lay nestled against his chest, and his arm hugged her tighter to him. She turned her eyes up to his. 'You were never charity sex, you know.'

He kissed her forehead. 'I knew that.'

'You were the best ever, actually.'

He smiled. 'I knew that too,' he said, before he got all serious again. '

Will you be happy living on the orchard, do you think? You won't get bored living in one place for a change?'

'Will you be there?'

'Of course, I'll be there.'

'Then I'll never get bored.'

He squeezed her tight, pressing his lips to her hair, and she sighed. 'I can't believe you got a tattoo.'

His lips pulled tight. 'I can't believe it either.'

'What were you going to do if I said no?'

'What do you mean?'

'If I wouldn't come back, and you had to find someone else to love. Someone not called

Lucy.'

'Oh, I thought of that. I had a plan.'

She rolled her eyes. 'Of course, you had a plan. What was it?'

He rolled up on his elbow, smiled down at her and kissed the tip of her nose. 'I was going to leave my socks on.'

EPILOGUE

*W*endy and Dirk were married at Mt Lofty House on the tiered lawn overlooking the beautiful Piccadilly Valley, a tinkling fountain providing the musical accompaniment while the adjacent rose garden provided the colour. Summer came to the party with a perfect thirty-degree day, a gentle breeze playing with the silks and soft cottons worn by the guests.

Siena was their one attendant, looking less like her usual tomboy self and very grown up in a sapphire blue dress with her hair twisted up behind her head. She led the way across the lawn, Wendy's elderly father arm in arm with the bride following behind. In a fitted skirt suit of champagne coloured silk, Wendy looked radiant.

'They both look beautiful,' Lucy whispered to Dan.

'You do,' he said with a grin, and squeezed her hand. Lucy was wearing the dress she'd worn to her mother's wedding in Vegas, the jade coloured shift getting its second outing in as many months.

'You don't look so bad yourself,' she said, and that was the truth. When he'd turned up on her doorstep in Agnino, he'd looked wild and lost. His hair and whiskers had been long, his eyes tormented, and even the way he'd carried himself had looked like a man who was beaten. Two weeks later there was no trace of that man. Today Dan stood straight and tall beside her, and handsome in a dark suit and snowy white shirt, and there was a mischievous twinkle in his eye she hadn't seen before.

They listened while the celebrant said his words and Wendy and Dirk exchanged vows and rings and were pronounced man and wife. Everyone applauded as they kissed, champagne corks were popped, and then the party really got underway.

'Congratulations,' Lucy said, as finally the well-wishers thinned enough for them to get close to the bride and groom. 'I'm so happy for you both.'

Wendy returned her kiss. 'And I am so happy you're back. We both are.' She turned to Dan and gave him a peck on the cheek. 'Good work, Dan, there's hope for you yet,' but she was smiling and Dan was smiling back.

'Not as happy as I am,' he said, turning his brown eyes onto her, and Lucy felt her heart soar.

Then Wendy and Dirk were mobbed by other guests and the Faraday family absorbed Dan and Lucy into their group. Joanie was looking very colourful in a floral dress with pearls and pink lipstick. A matching pink pill box hat sat on top of the hair she'd had set into waves. Clarry looked great in his grey suit, looking hale and hearty again and like he was almost ready for anything, and Dan's three sisters all looked beautiful in their wedding finery.

'A beautiful wedding,' sighed Joanie. 'Doesn't Wendy look a picture? And Siena all grown up and looking so ladylike.'

'It won't last,' said Beth with a snort, as Siena chose that moment to run past, her hair already uncoiling and flopping behind her head.

'I dunno,' said Clarry, 'I can't help thinking something's wrong with this wedding.'

Everyone looked at him. 'What on earth could be wrong?' said Hannah.

'It's perfect,' said Beth.

'Couldn't ask for a better day,' said Sophie.

'No, I reckon it's about high time it was one of my grand-kids getting hitched. You know what the doctor said, I need something to look forward to. I mean, Joanie and me, we're not going to be around forever, you know.'

'Speak for yourself!' Nan said. 'I'm not planning on going anywhere just yet.'

'Don't look at me,' said Hannah. 'I'm married to my work.'

'And me,' said Beth.

Sophie pouted. 'And nobody's snapping me up, so I guess that leaves Dan.'

They all looked at Dan, and Lucy laughed as they once again ganged up on their brother and grandson. But Dan didn't look uncomfortable or tug at his collar like she'd expected. Instead he was looking at her, a strange expression on his face as he reached into his jacket pocket.

'I was actually planning on doing this a bit later, after you caught the bouquet or something, and we had a quiet moment . . .'

She blinked as knelt down onto one knee before her, cradling the little box in his palm.

'- but now's probably as good a time as any.' He flipped the box open. 'I love you, Lucy. Will you marry me? Will you be my wife?'

Her mouth dropped open. Inside the box was a stunning ring, an oval shaped emerald surrounded by diamonds. 'It was my mother's ring. Will you wear it, Lucy?'

Siena screeched to a halt in the midst of their circle. She took in the stunned faces all around and at Dan kneeling on the lawn and said, 'What's going on?'

Beth put her hands on the girl's shoulders to steer her back towards her as she softly said, 'Dan's just asked Lucy to marry him.'

And Siena looked at Lucy, her big brown eyes wide with excitement, and cried, 'Say yes, Lucy! Please say yes! Please say you'll marry Uncle Dan!'

Dan looked from Siena to Lucy. 'Well,' he said, 'what do you say?'

What could she say other than what was in her heart? 'Yes,' she said. 'I'll marry you. I love you, Dan, so much.' And beaming with joy, he rose and swept her into his arms, spinning her around as his family cheered on.

'Yay!' yelled Siena. 'Everyone, Uncle Dan's getting married!'

And there were more cheers and more champagne as a new round of congratulations got underway.

'I'm sorry for stealing your thunder,' said Dan, when the newlyweds rushed over to congratulate them. 'It wasn't meant to happen quite like that.'

'Don't be ridiculous,' said Wendy, kissing them both. 'We wouldn't have missed this for the world. I'm so thrilled for you two. I only wish your mother was here to see you today, Dan, to see what a fine man you've become and what a beautiful wife you've found. She'd be so proud.'

There were tears in Wendy's eyes, Lucy saw, and tears in Dan's too as he hugged the woman who'd done so much herself to make him the man he'd become. 'Thank you,' he said, before Dirk drew her towards the small dance floor for their bridal waltz.

Soon the dance floor was full, and Dan managed to get Lucy to himself for a moment. 'Lucy, I know I've gone about this all the wrong way, but there's something I want you to know.'

She touched the tip of a finger to the crease that had suddenly appeared between his brows, wondering what would make him frown today. 'What is it?

He took her hand in his and pressed the emerald and diamond ring she now wore and brought it to his lips. 'I don't want you to worry about having babies or anything. I don't want you to think that's what this marriage is all about. Because as far as I'm concerned, I'm doing this because I love you and I want to spend the rest of my life with you. If you don't want to try - or if you can't - or if I can't for that matter, well, it doesn't matter.'

She swallowed. The obstetrician had said there was no reason she couldn't have children in the future, but the thought of having another baby - of losing another baby - terrified her. 'What about the orchard? What happens to that if we don't have children?'

He shrugged. 'I reckon the Faradays have had a good run. If there's not another generation to follow on, then someone else can make a go of it, what's the big deal? What do you say?'

'Thank you,' she said, unbelievably touched by his kindness. 'How about we take it as it comes.'

He nodded. 'I reckon a man can't ask for more than that.'

He put his arm around her shoulders and they stood in silence for a while as they checked up on what everyone was up to.

Hannah was nearby talking horses with a client and Sophie was chatting up the guy behind the bar while both Beth and Nan were trying to talk Pop down from the dance floor. Meanwhile Siena was laughing hysterically and spinning like a top in her blue flower girl dress before collapsing drunkenly onto the lawn, only to get up and do it all over again.

Dan shook his head. 'We're a weird mob, all right, us Faradays. Are you really sure you want to get tangled up with us?'

Lucy looked over at his sisters and Siena laughing as she fell over again, and at his Nan and Pop before turning her eyes to the man she loved. 'I can't imagine anything that would make me happier. I love you, Dan Faraday. I love you and your crazy family.'

'That's lucky,' he said, as he drew her towards his kiss. 'Because I happen to know we're crazy in love with you too.'

THAT NIGHT, as Lucy lay wrapped securely in the arms of the man she loved, listening to his even breathing, she marvelled at the turn her life had taken a few short months ago.

She'd wandered the world for all those years, travelled to so many different places, never knowing until she'd come to this place just what she'd been looking for all along.

Here, in this valley, she'd found a new life amongst the orchards. She'd found Dan, and together with him, they'd found love. He'd given her the focus she'd yearned for, giving her life purpose and a deeper meaning. And now, to top it all off, he'd asked her to marry him.

She smiled even as she yawned, drifting into sleep as she nestled into the slumbering body of the man she loved with all her heart, the man who loved her back.

She was home.

Thank yous have to go to Keri Arthur, Fiona McArthur and Jaye Ford, amongst many awesome authors, who finally gave me the push to do this.

It is so lovely to have a favourite story out there to share with people, and Cherry Season has always been a favourite of mine, so it's lovely to dust it off, give it a gussy up, and send it back out into the big wide world.

And to you, dear reader, thanks for picking up Cherry Season. If you enjoyed it, and you'd like to check out Dan's sisters' stories, The Trouble with Choices is once again set in the glorious Adelaide Hills, and features all the characters you've come to love in Cherry Season, plus a sexy Irishman called Declan who's caring for an adorable baby joey kangaroo, a big bear of a man called Harry, and a Vacola bottling outfit. What more could you ask?

Or maybe you'd like to explore South Australia's Yorke Peninsula? In which case, check out the excerpt of *Always on My Mind* in the following pages.

Thanks again and happy reading!

Trish
x

ABOUT THE AUTHOR

Trish always fancied herself a writer, so she dutifully picked gherkins and washed dishes in a Chinese restaurant on her way to earning herself an economics degree and a qualification as a Chartered Accountant instead. Work took her to Canberra, where she promptly fell in love with a tall, dark and handsome hero who cut computer code, and marriage and four daughters followed, which gave Trish time to step back from her career and think about what she'd really like to do.

Writing fiction was at the top of the list. Since then, Trish has sold more than 38 books, to Harlequin Mira/Harper Collins and Tule Publishing, with sales in excess of seven million globally, her books printed in more than thirty languages in forty countries worldwide.

Four times nominated and two times winner of Romance Writers of Australia's Ruby Award (the Romantic Book of the Year) Trish is also a 2012 RITA finalist in the US.

You can find out more about Trish and upcoming books at her website at www. trishmorey.com, and you can email her at trish@trishmorey.com.

Trish loves to hear from her readers.

facebook.com/TrishMoreyAuthor
twitter.com/MoreyTrish
instagram.com/moreytrish

The Ruthless Greek's Virgin Princess

The Italian Billionaire's Bride

Forced Wife, Royal Love Child

Back in the Spaniard's Bed - in The Latin Lover

The Italian Boss's Mistress of Revenge

The Sheikh's Convenient Virgin

The Boss's Christmas Baby

The Spaniard's Blackmailed Bride

The Greek's Virgin

A Virgin for the Taking

For Revenge…Or Pleasure?

The Mancini Marriage Bargain - The Arranged Brides

Bk 2

Stolen by the Sheikh - The Arranged Brides Bk 1

The Italian Boss's Secret Child

The Italian's Virgin Bride

The Greek Boss's Demand

TRISH MOREY

always on my mind

*She turned her back on her past -
so why won't her past let her go?*

Preface

Pip Martin saw her life as being made up of two distinct parts.

There was the before, when summers were long and hot and the days filled with girlfriends and the cute guy next door or chasing after her irritating little brother, with her mum and her gran whipping up cupcakes or a roast in the old wood stove. Days when her dad would come home tired and cranky after another long session in the paddocks bringing in the harvest on their Yorke Peninsula farm.

Then there was the *after*, where there was only Pip, and her ailing gran, and a bone deep sense of betrayal, for everyone it seemed had known or suspected the truth.

Everyone but Pip.

But by then it was too late to find out who she really was. All she knew was that she didn't belong and that she needed to be as far away from her lying past as possible.

Chapter One

Adelaide Airport had grown up while Pip was away. There was a shiny new terminal with air bridges now, and disembarking the plane had the same generic feel it had worldwide, so she could almost have been anywhere – if not for the unmistakeable line of hills to the east, with the three towers marking the highest point in the Mount Lofty Ranges.

That, and the twisting of her gut that told her she was nearly home.

Home.

After almost a decade and a half living and working in Sydney and then New York, she wasn't even sure what that meant any more.

Her recently turned on phone burped up the messages that had come in since last checking her phone during her connection in Auckland, and Pip held her breath as she scanned them. She smiled at the 'Missing you' message from her friend, Carmen, and frowned at the three from Chad but didn't bother with those now. She was relieved to see there was nothing from her gran's nursing home. No news was good news, although it didn't stop her calling as soon as she was inside the terminal.

'How is she?' she asked, to be told there was no change. She checked the wristwatch she'd already adjusted to Adelaide time and did a mental calculation – one hour at most for the formalities of immigration and customs and to collect the keys to her rental car, and another two for the drive to the town of Kadina – and told them she'd be there by lunch.

Too easy.

Her business class ticket meant a short queue at immigration, so she beat her luggage to baggage collection, the carousel still stationery. It wouldn't be long once it did kick into action, she knew, courtesy of the priority tag her suitcase was wearing. But still she felt impatient to keep moving, her stomach wringing itself tighter and tighter the longer the wait continued. Feeling conflicted. Needing desperately to see her gran, but knowing that visiting her home town for the first time in almost a decade was going to shake things up, things she'd sooner leave right where they were.

Like questions from the past she didn't know the answer to.

Like other stuff.

Like . . . *Luke.*

God, she didn't want to think about any of that, least of all Luke. That was history. So ancient, it shouldn't even figure. And then a siren sounded and a light flashed and the carousel kicked slowly into motion. A few bags in, her suitcase appeared through the rubber strips. She almost sighed as she hauled it from the carousel. She'd still be out of here within the hour. Thank god she had nothing to declare. Another ten minutes or so and finally she'd be free.

It was when she turned that she noticed the sniffer dog, trotting its way between legs and luggage. It was a beagle and cute as a button and for the first time in hours she managed a smile. Until it took one sniff in her direction and plonked itself down in front of her, and cute as a button turned into the incoming passenger's worst nightmare.

'I don't understand,' she pleaded, as the dog's handler asked to see an incoming passenger card that clearly stated she was carrying nothing that should be of any interest to a sniffer dog or its handler.

'Are you sure there's not something in your bag?' he asked, as curious heads craned around her. 'Some food from the plane, perhaps?'

She shook her head, the cold sick fear of what-if curdling the aeroplane breakfast in her stomach. What if someone had stashed something in her luggage en route? What if any one of a thousand other scenarios had happened? But she had done nothing wrong. She knew she had packed nothing that was contraband. She tried to smile. Tried to look confident. Tried, and failed. 'Nothing. Absolutely nothing.'

Of course, there was nothing else for it but to search her bags. As her hopes of a quick getaway faded, her sigh of exasperation didn't win her any friends.

'This won't take long,' said the stony faced official.

'I'm sorry,' she said, trying not to aggravate the man any further. Not that anyone seemed fussed about not aggravating her. 'It's just, I'm kind of in a hurry.' She licked her dry lips and wondered if she'd they'd give her a break if she explained why she needed to get through customs and immigration as quickly as possible. 'You see, my grandmother's dying and I promised to be at her bedside by lunch.'

The official paused, latex sheathed hands poised over her suitcase, and for one moment Pip thought that maybe he might actually let her go. 'That's too bad, miss,' he said, deadpan but with a glimmer in his eye that told Pip she'd probably made the biggest mistake of her life by playing the dying grandmother card. He looked convinced she was trying to hide something now. 'And now, if you'll kindly unzip your bag?'

After twenty minutes of rifling through her things, twenty minutes of excruciating embarrassment as his big hands sorted through her knickers and her bras and the stuff she hid in her toiletries bag specifically so it wouldn't spill out if her suitcase came undone en route, twenty minutes of questions during which the official found nothing before finally conceding that the beagle had likely smelled the banana she admitted taking most days to work, she was free to cram her belongings back in and go hunt down her rental car.

She sighed with relief at the agency as she gave her name

and the attendant pulled out the paperwork. Finally something was going right. Soon she'd be on her way.

Or not . . .

'Hang on,' she said to the car rental agency attendant, who seemed to be having a lot of trouble with her booking. 'I don't want a sports car!'

The man rolled his eyes and glanced meaningfully over her shoulder at the queue of mums and dads and kids and luggage already building up behind her. 'But you booked a cabriolet. It says so right here on the form.'

She shook her head, knowing that the last thing she wanted was a sports car. Her plan was to get in and out of Kadina making as few waves as possible. There was no way on earth she'd have asked for a damned sports car – or for that matter, any car that might draw attention to herself. 'I want an ordinary car. Something nondescript and plain. Haven't you got something boring? A Toyota or something?'

The attendant smiled. If you could call it a smile. More a baring of his teeth. 'That's actually a little awkward right now. We're fully booked with the Christmas holidays starting. And after all, you did book the cabriolet.'

Pip sighed. Clearly someone had stuffed up. 'Martin,' she said again for good measure. 'M-A-R-T-I-N. Can you check again please? There must be some mix up.'

'There is no mix up.' He didn't even pretend to smile this time, all attempts at the pleasantries over. 'This is your name on the rental document, yes?'

She glanced at the papers. 'Well yes,' she conceded, 'but for the last time, I didn't book –'

And with a cold shiver of realisation, it hit her. She hadn't booked it at all. While she'd been in a panic about packing, Chad had offered to do it for her, using his firm's corporate code because it offered a better discount than hers. 'Just a car,' she'd told him when he asked what kind she wanted. 'Any old car.'

Shit . . .

'Hang on,' she said, reaching for her phone, scrolling through the messages she'd ignored earlier, clicking on the first.

Figured you would have landed by now.

She deleted that and moved onto the next.

Thought you might be missing me.

Weird. She frowned and sent that one to the trash as well. It was the third message where she hit paydirt.

So surprise! Enjoy the wheels. Think of me every time you put your foot down.

What the hell? She'd think of him, all right. She'd imagine pushing him under her pedal and pressing her foot down hard. Dammit, why the hell had she ever trusted him with her booking?

She sucked in air and looked back at the attendant and gave a weak smile. He had no trouble lobbing a wide one right back, and she knew that whatever expression had been on her face when she'd read those messages might as well have been ringed with neon lights. He was loving every minute of this. 'All sorted then?' he asked smugly, and without waiting for the answer pushed the rental agreement closer to her. 'So maybe we can finish off the paperwork. If you just sign here . . . and here.'

Pip sighed. 'Okay,' she conceded, holding up one hand. 'Apparently someone did book that car in my name. But it was actually a misunderstanding. Are you sure there's nothing else available? Nothing at all?'

He blew air through his teeth and gestured to the queue behind her that was growing longer by the minute, full of fractious kids and their exhausted looking parents. 'Not a sausage. I'm sorry, these people have booked all our *boring* cars.'

Ouch! She glanced over to the other agency desks, wondering if she should threaten to take her business elsewhere, but those desks looked just as crowded.

'So there's really no alternative?'

'There's always an alternative,' he told her, and when she looked back at him, halfway interested, he continued. 'There's always public transport.'

All the way to the Yorke Peninsula? In what – a bus? And meanwhile she was supposed to be halfway there already, at her gran's bedside. Oh god, Gran! Two hours after landing she was still stuck here at the airport. 'Okay,' she said, scrawling her signature on the paperwork. So much for trying not to be noticed. 'I'll take the damned convertible. Please just tell me it's not red.'

The attendant looked studiously at the papers and didn't say a word, but still she caught the curve of his lips. She could only hope it was because he was happy to be finally seeing the back of her.

Five minutes later she knew it wasn't the only reason.

She surveyed the car. Her nondescript rental designed to fly under the radar and go unnoticed in her home town.

It was all kinds of red.

Look-at-me red.

Trouble-on-wheels red.

Sex-on-wheels red.

Enough!

Whatever the colour, she would have to deal with it. She would just have to cope. She wrestled her bag into the trunk – boot, she reminded herself – and opened her door, staring blankly for a moment at the missing steering wheel before she realised.

'Damn!'

She slammed the door, disgusted with herself as she rounded the car and found the driver's seat.

She was in Australia now. Driving on the other side of the car, and the road. She'd better not forget that again.

Like to read on? You can find *Always on my Mind* at your favourite bookstore. Here's the blurb…

From the golden wheat fields of Yorke Peninsula, to the financial hub of New York City…

Ten years ago, Pip Martin traded the tragedy and secrets of her past on South Australia's Yorke Peninsula, for a financial career half a world away in New York City. But now Pip's Alzheimers-ridden gran is dying and it's time for one last goodbye.

… and home again

Except the past Pip was so happy to flee is still there, including Luke Trenorden, the man she loved before betrayal and old secrets tore them apart. Pip Martin is the last person Luke Trenorden wants to see. If only her haunting vulnerability didn't remind him of what they'd lost.

And that's when it gets really tough.

Together Luke and Pip solve the mystery of her past, and between them the spark still smoulders brightly. But Pip's about to return to NYC and the life she says she wants, and Luke's about to lose her all over again. But after all they've shared, can either of them ever be really happy apart?

www.ingramcontent.com/pod-product-compliance
Lightning Source LLC
Chambersburg PA
CBHW030241120726
47903CB00005B/1572